ALOUZON [...]
DRAGONSWORD FREE—

She began to run as she heard the clump of heavy paws and the deep-throated howl. Ahead, figures were moving. One was that of a man. Three others, though, were four-footed, the size of lions. They glowed, their eyes like lamps, and their mouths dripped with phosphor.

Alouzon closed on the hounds. The Dragonsword sent one of the beasts writhing to the pavement, cut nearly in two. Phosphor spilled and smoked, boiling like molten sodium where it touched the water. Alouzon pulled her blade free of the carcass with another hound already coming at her. She skipped to the side and vaulted one of the park benches. The hound followed, giving her a clear opening. But before she could swing, she was struck from behind. She fell, narrowly missing the pool of corrosives that was already gathering. The two hounds rushed at her. . . .

Dragonsword #3

Dragon Death

Gael Baudino

A Byron Preiss Book

A ROC BOOK

ROC
Published by the Penguin Group
Penguin Books USA Inc., 375 Hudson Street,
New York, New York 10014, U.S.A.
Penguin Books Ltd, 27 Wrights Lane,
London W8, 5TZ, England
Penguin Books Australia Ltd, Ringwood,
Victoria, Australia
Penguin Books Canada Ltd, 10 Alcorn Avenue,
Toronto, Ontario, Canada M4V 3B2
Penguin Books (N.Z.) Ltd, 182-190 Wairau Road,
Auckland 10, New Zealand

Penguin Books Ltd, Registered Offices:
Harmondsworth, Middlesex, England

First published by Roc, an imprint of New American Library, a division of
Penguin Books USA Inc.

First Printing, April, 1992
10 9 8 7 6 5 4 3 2 1

To those who died.
To those who survived.
To those who are still lost
somewhere in Vietnam.

The author would like to express her deepest thanks to Jan Bender and Gary Echternacht of the Gryylthan Embassy, Los Angeles branch, without whose generous assistance this book would not have been possible.

Humility is enough.
                              —J.R.R. Tolkien

```
SO  188.01.01.10  06/16/91  14.15 7684
B.DALTON BOOKSELLER          DURHAM, NC

BOOK$AVER FEE        N              5.00
PREVIOUS    1320925974 06/91
RENEWAL     1295146441 12/92
0343570538                          4.95
12 PCT. MARKDOWN                   0.59-
0671720546                          4.50
12 PCT. MARKDOWN                   0.54-
0451450841                          4.50
12 PCT. MARKDOWN                   0.54-
SUBTOTAL                          17.28
SALES TAX                          0.61
TOTAL                             17.89
4352190059197 VISA                17.89
TOTAL SAVINGS     $1.67

------------------THANK YOU------------------
```

❖ CHAPTER 1 ❖

A mild sea . . . and a mild breeze that brought the little fishing boat across the cold gray water of the inlet that led to Quay. Skimming the waves like a seabird, it approached the charred pilings of the docks, hesitated, sails luffing, as though uncertain of its reception, then took the wind once again and came on.

Sheltered by the earthworks that ringed the town, Hahle watched it, frowned doubtfully, readied his bow. "Myylen."

Myylen was thickset, with muscles that were used to heaving on ropes and gathering sails: a seaman, like his comrades, dragged out of his boat and into battle. "Here, councilman."

"Your eyes are younger than mine. What do you see in that boat?"

Myylen crept carefully to the edge of the rough parapet. The breeze freshened. Spray wetted his long, dark hair. "Two men," he said after some time.

A boat. From Vaylle. But why so small a boat . . . and so few passengers?

"Alive, Myylen?"

Myylen squinted. The boat drew nearer. Hahle felt a chill that had nothing to do with his bare scalp or his years, that sprang rather from the intuitions of an old warrior: it was going to be a hard march, and a worse bivouac. And comrades would die. In fact,

Hahle was afraid that comrades had already died, and that among them was one of his students.

"Such a fine young lad," he murmured to himself. But no; the lad was gone. His place had been taken by a woman. And now she . . .

Myylen shook his head. "They do not move."

Driven haphazardly by the wind, the boat turned and ran broadside onto the gently sloping shore a stone's throw from the parapet. It rocked in the lap of waves for a moment, then, as though suddenly sure of its footing, it heeled over and was still.

Not a sound from the boat. Not a movement.

"Who comes?" shouted Hahle. He had fitted an arrow to the bow string, and his strong right hand was covering the nock: three fingers taking the string on the pads, the shaft gripped lightly between the index and middle. "Who comes to Quay?"

The wind died, then came up again. The sails rattled as though petrified. Behind Hahle and Myylen, crouching in the shelter of the earthworks, men drew swords and readied pikes with a set to their faces that told of frantic battles against weapons for which they did not even have names. Ten days before, Quay had been struck by a thing from the sky. The lady Kyria had labored mightily, but though she had healed the wounded, the dead were nonetheless dead, the houses were burned, the streets were choked with rubble and filled with the sweet odor of decay.

And now this boat.

"Sir," said Myylen, "we can—"

His words were interrupted by a faint, choking sound that grew abruptly into a forsaken wail. Hahle flinched and started to draw his bow, but he realized then that what he heard came not from any hound, nor from a thing in the sky, but rather from the throat of a man. Compelling as the voice was, though, he resisted the urge to run to the boat. "Myylen, Stahn," he said. "Follow me. With caution."

The three climbed over the parapet as the others

kept a lookout, and in a minute, they stood on the damp sand. The wailing continued, and now it took on the shape of words:

"For the love of the Gods, help me!"

Again, the urge to run. Hahle fought it in himself and quelled it in his men with a sharp glance. "But I know that voice," said Myylen. "The one called Helwych."

"That waterfly? But—"

The voice: urgent, compelling, almost commanding. "Help me!"

Myylen and Stahn stumbled forward as Hahle, his cautions sticking in his throat, ran to catch up. When they reached the boat, they found that Myylen was right: there were two men there. One, a stranger, obviously Vayllen, was dead. Helwych, though, was alive.

The lad seemed cut in a hundred places, burned over what little skin was not cut, and so bruised and battered that it was hard to recognize him for the swelling and discoloration. He was bleeding furiously from a gash in his forehead, and his eyes peered frantically from out of a blood-drenched face.

"The Vayllens," he gasped. "All smiles and favors until we reached their city, and then—" He broke off, coughing.

Hahle and his men vaulted into the boat. Myylen and Stahn bent over the sorcerer. Helwych shook, choked, vomited a mixture of blood and bile.

"—and then they turned on us, and . . ."

Helwych seemed in danger of bleeding to death as he spoke. Myylen and Stahn cut strips from the sail and attempted to bind up the worst of his wounds, working quickly as he choked and retched; but Hahle felt the cold again. "We need more than sailcloth here," he said, his throat as tight as the grip of his hand on the bow. "Stahn, run to the town and fetch what physicians we have."

Stahn nodded and, shouting for the physicians,

vaulted over the gunwale. But his weight caused the boat to shift and roll, and it pitched Hahle backwards and onto the corpse of the Vayllen.

Myylen looked up, startled. Hahle stared at the dead man. The skin of the body was lined and tan, and its blond hair was bleached nearly white by the sun. *Such as you betrayed my people. Such as you will pay dearly.*

Helwych was gasping through a froth of spittle and blood. "And they . . . and they . . ."

Frowning at his clumsiness, Hahle climbed to his feet and made his way to the young sorcerer. "And the others?"

"Dead." Helwych choked, winced at Myylen's rough ministry.

"All of them? No survivors at all?"

Helwych blinked, his mouth working. "All dead." There was an odd tone to his voice, and his eyes shifted a little in their bloody sockets. "I alone escaped to tell you."

As the days had slipped by into mid-February, the weather about Kingsbury had grown milder. The storm three weeks ago had spent the last of the winter's strength, and the winds had shifted to the southwest, bringing a warmth that presaged the coming of spring.

In the house of the king, Seena nursed her infant son, the tender expression of a young mother warm on her face. Her heart was full. She had her children and her husband, and Gryylth was changing in wonderful ways. Nearby, Relys watched as Ayya played with a toy broom, wielding it with childish carelessness; and though the girl might sweep some day in earnest, she would, Seena knew, never learn the bow of subservience, and Vill would never know a time when his sister was not his equal, save perhaps in strength.

But the sun was setting, and with nightfall would come things less of wonder and more of horror. Bandon had been destroyed in the night, and though that slaughter had not been repeated in Gryylth, still darkness brought with it the distant baying of spectral and murderous hounds and a curious, eager snuffling that visited many a door both within the town and without.

The light faded. Seena shuddered and held Vill closer. The infant mumbled, his soft hands padding at his mother's breast.

What would happen, she wondered, if the hounds and the things from the sky came to Kingsbury in earnest? Ayya might never learn the bow . . . but she might well never learn it because—

Seena jerked herself away from her thoughts. No. Alouzon had gone off to Vaylle, and if there were anyone capable of bringing that renegade land to heel, it was the Dragonmaster. The younger men might mock her behind her back because she was a woman, but those who had fought with her regarded her almost as though she were a God who had deigned to come to Gryylth to help Her children, face-to-face, hand-in-hand.

A heavy step at the door. Relys looked up from Ayya, and her hand went to her sword; but the guards outside murmured greetings, and Cvinthil's soft tenor carried into the house. In a moment, Seena's husband had entered. He shut the door behind him, took off his cloak, and hung it on a peg.

Seena smiled fondly. Another man might have decided that a king should have servants to attend to his garments. Not so Cvinthil. He had been a warrior. He still was. He would hang up his own clothes.

Now he bowed to her. "Wife."

"Husband." Seena nodded in return. She and Cvinthil had separate duties, perhaps, and different strengths, but they were equals nonetheless. It was a good thought.

Cvinthil greeted Relys, who had risen, and motioned her back onto her stool. Ayya ran to him, and he swept her up in his arms and made faces at her until she laughed.

"How is it in the wide world, husband?" said
Seena.

He bent, Ayya still in his arms, and kissed her.
"Well . . ." He looked toward the door almost uneasily, as though at any moment the matters he had
left at Hall Kingsbury might suddenly burst in.
"Well . . ." He shrugged. "The farmers are saying it
will be a good year, and the shepherds—thanks to Karthin's advice—have more lambs than they know what
to do with . . ." He offered a careworn smile. ". . .
though I am sure they will think of something. Karthin
has done much good for Gryylth. Tireas, he said, once
called him a hayseed. If so, then let there be more
hayseeds in this land, for they seem to be a good lot."

"And . . . Alouzon. . . ?"

Cvinthil's smile faded. Silence grew about him. He
sat down on a stool next to Relys and put Ayya on her
lap. For a moment, Relys looked almost terrified, and
Ayya added to her confusion by kissing her on the
cheek. Relys set her on the floor nervously, and the
girl laughed and resumed her sweeping.

He spoke at last. "No word has come. Indeed, I
fear that no word will ever come."

"Surely you do not—"

He shook his head quickly. "The hounds have made
travel dangerous. The messenger that came from Quay
ten days ago with word of Alouzon's departure was
attacked on the road by a pack. He barely escaped. I
imagine it is worse now."

He stared into the fire for a time, all the care that
had come to him since he had assumed the kingship
plain on his face. "O wife," he said softly. "I was
never meant for the duties of king. Marrget, I think,
would have been the better choice."

"Marrget is a woman, husband," said Seena.

"Aye, that she is. And a brave one. And a wise one.
Gryylth could do much worse."

Relys lifted her head. "My king," she said softly,
"if I may speak, I believe the captains made a good

choice. And Marrget would have refused the title. You know that.''

"Aye. Aye.''

"And, much as I am unwilling to say it, this land is not ready for a woman's rule, and will not be ready for a long time.'' Relys spoke dispassionately, but her words obviously pained her.

"Speak, Relys,'' said the king. "You seem to know more of the results of my reforms than do I. Captains and councilors sometimes tell a king no more than he desires to hear. What can you tell me?''

"The reforms?'' Relys shrugged. "I can tell you what I see, and what my women see. I can tell you that Wykla was almost raped. I can tell you that the young men from the country, new to their soldier's livery and their station, laugh and snigger at the First Wartroop. I can say that women are threatened daily in the marketplace by men who care little for decrees and laws, but only for old custom. There are many among your own Guard who would wish to see me bow to them, or at least . . .'' She smiled thinly. ". . . have me provided with a good husband who would make a proper wife of me.''

Cvinthil sighed. "You tell a grievous tale, lieutenant.''

Relys was impassive. "I am sorry to bear ill tidings, my king. But I would be so bold as to remind you that custom is hard to change. But it is changing.''

The king shook his head. "I wonder if it is perhaps changing on the surface only.''

Vill finished nursing, and Seena laid him on her shoulder and patted his back. "Time, my husband.''

Cvinthil looked as though he wondered how much time would be given him, but after a moment, Seena realized that he was listening to the horns of the guard posts along the road up Kingsbury Hill. Closer and closer they sounded: a messenger was climbing the switchback trail up to the town.

Relys went to the door, opened it, and slipped out

into the fading light, her hand on her sword. Another
horn, a different note: the messenger had reached the
gate to the city. Seena rose and sent Ayya up the stairs
to the loft, then took the seat beside her husband. She
was queen. Timid she was, and sometimes she even
longed for the old ways, but now her place was here,
with Cvinthil.

Horse hoofs clattered on the hard-packed earth of
the street, splashed in puddles. Exclamations from the
guards outside. Relys cried out: "By the Gods, man!
Your arm!"

"My arm is but a little thing, and it will heal," said
a voice with a coastal accent. "I would see King Cvinthil."

The sound of a clumsy dismounting, and then Relys
flung the door open to admit a tall man. His face was
dark with sun, and his hair was dark too, and long.
He wore a heavy cloak against the cold, and as he
crossed the threshold, he pulled it closely about his
left arm as though to hide it. Phosphor smoked on the
thick wool, and more smoke came from his hidden
arm.

He bowed deeply to Cvinthil and, after a moment's
thought, to Seena. "My lord . . . and lady," he said,
"I am Myylen. I am from Quay. Hahle sent me with
tidings of Alouzon Dragonmaster and her companions."

Cvinthil nodded. "Speak. Quickly."

Myylen's face had already told the story. "They are
dead, my king. All of them save Helwych. The Vayllens pretended friendship until our company was defenseless, and then they attacked with magic and
weapons. Even the lady Kyria was helpless."

Cvinthil had turned very pale. Seena clutched Vill
as though by doing so she could keep away hounds
and flying death and fire. "And . . . and Helwych?"
said the king.

"Badly injured, my king," said Myylen. "He killed

a Vayllen boatman and made for Gryylth so as to warn us of our danger."

Cvinthil rose and bowed stiffly. "Our thanks to you, sir." But he stood wavering. "Relys," he called uncertainly. "Relys, are you there?"

"Here, my king," came her clear, cold voice.

"Call my advisors and captains to the Hall," he said, his voice distant. "And you come also, and bring Timbrin with you. You are now captain of the First Wartroop, and Timbrin is your lieutenant, and your king is in desperate need of counsel."

"It shall be done, my king." Relys's icy calm did not thaw in the slightest. Marrget had been not only her captain, but her friend. Relys was, Seena knew, planning revenge and war even now. Terrible war. War without conscience or quarter.

And so was the king.

Darham sat on the simple stool that formed as much of a throne as he would allow in the king's lodge, listening to the messenger who had come from Cvinthil. The man's tale was one of deception, murder, and a single lucky escape, but beneath the surface considerations that would lead—inevitably, Darham knew— to war with Vaylle, there were other matters. A much-loved member of the King's Guard of Corrin was dead, as was a trusted captain who had proved himself both in battle and in council, and also the young woman that he himself had adopted.

The messenger finished. Darham hung his head. He had counseled for caution, and this was the result. "I cannot believe that they would have been so careless," he murmured, though he knew that the blame lay upon his own shoulders. "What madness made them walk, open-eyed, into a trap?"

Tylha, the commander of the women's phalanxes, was frowning. "The Vayllens seem to control potencies that even Tireas would have envied," she said. "Perhaps our people did the best they could."

The Gryylthan messenger, a young man, stared at Tylha as though surprised that a woman would raise her voice in council. Or perhaps he was irritated that she did. Darham marked his expression, recalled what Wykla had said of Gryylth's continuing difficulties with its women. *And more than likely such as this tormented my brave daughter.* "And what of Helwych, sir?"

The Gryylthan composed himself quickly. "Helwych is near death and far too weak to travel, lord. But the physicians of Quay have hopes that he will recover."

"He stole a Vayllen fishing boat, you say."

"Aye, lord. And to do so he killed the fisher who owned it."

Calrach, who commanded what few men Corrin still maintained, fought to suppress a smile. "It seems the lad had some teeth after all."

His sentiment was echoed in the faces of the guards and attendants who stood about the lodge. Beneath it, though, ran a deep anger. Helwych had always been irritating and annoying by turns, and his unexpected valor was heartening. But Manda had been a friend to many, and Karthin's abilities were legendary. Corrin had lost two heroes.

Wykla's sweet face swam in Darham's memory—blue-eyed, amber-haired, frightened and brave both—and his arm still ached with the wound that she had given him. She had a family, but they had rejected her, and Darham had offered himself in their place. Though the lass had said neither yes nor no, Darham had thought of her as kin from that hour.

Dead? So quickly? His new daughter taken from him a fortnight since he had found her? Anger surged up in his heart, and he was about to stand and give the orders that would gather men and women and send them off to war, but he recalled Tarwach's hasty temper . . . and what had come as a result of it. He remained in his seat.

Something felt wrong. Tylha had trained Manda, and she had not trained her to be a dupe or a fool. Wykla had a steady way about her. Karthin was cautious. And Alouzon Dragonmaster, and Marrget, and Santhe—Gryylth's best . . . Darham knew how they fought. He had, in fact, fought against them.

Helwych alone had escaped?

Composing himself, Darham stood up at last. "Our thanks to you, sir," he said to the messenger. "You have brought us grievous news, but we are thankful that you brought it. I fear, though, that we show ourselves poor hosts by making our guest stand and recite instead of sit and eat." He turned to a member of his Guard. "Sandyhl, see that this man is given lodging and food."

The messenger cleared his throat. "Does Corrin have a reply that I may take back to Gryylth?"

Anger. Wykla's sweet face. Manda's hot temper and her old sorrow. It would be so easy to lift a hand, to give the word.

But Darham steeled himself. "Not at present. I am sure that Cvinthil will agree that matters decided in haste lead to misfortune. I will consider this."

Tylha's eyebrows lifted. "My king! Manda . . . Karthin . . ."

Darham eyed her. "Helwych, too . . . almost." He allowed the last word to hang meaningfully. "Sandyhl."

The guard came forward, bowed to the messenger. "Come, sir," he said. He turned on his heel brusquely and led the Gryylthan out of the hall, his manner polite, but cold: he too had noticed the messenger's attitude towards Tylha.

When the Gryylthan was gone, Darham turned his attention to other matters: petitions, judgments, decrees—the daily business of a king. But he knew well that his captains and attendants were wondering at his caution. Raised eyebrows, murmurs, shaking of heads both in sorrow and in anger—all these and more told him that those about him favored a quick and deadly invasion of the land across the sea.

Darham kept to the business at hand, kept his voice even and his mind clear. But when the business was done, when evening had fallen thickly over Benardis, when the attendants were leaving, he motioned for Tylha and Calrach to remain behind. Together, the captains stood before Darham in the empty hall and saluted.

Darham shook his head. "I will have no formalities now, friends. The day's work is done, and we farmers can take off our boots and warm ourselves at the fire all together."

He gestured for them to bring stools and sit with him, and he himself threw another log onto the fire that burned at the side of the lodge. He called for wine, passed out full cups, and then sent the attendant away. "Well, friends," he said, "what do you think? Cvinthil has been of a mind for invasion and revenge since the turning of the year, and only my advice made him reconsider. Now he sends a messenger who all but says to my face: *Are you satisfied?* Doubtless the king of Gryylth wishes to sail with the first sign of fair weather. He asks for aid."

Calrach and Tylha exchanged glances. The woman spoke first. "I cannot blame Cvinthil. We ourselves have good reasons for invading Vaylle."

Calrach shook his head. "Reasons, maybe. But there is the matter of wisdom." His hair was thin and blond, and his scalp showed through, gleaming in the firelight. "I was with Tireas in the Heath, and I lost Flebas there. And I saw what magic could do in the last days of the war with Gryylth. We can help Gryylth, certainly, but would that do any good?"

"Hmmm." Tylha was nodding, her round face thoughtful. "It might provide us with an honorable death, perhaps."

Darham propped his feet on the warm hearthstones and stroked his big gold beard. Tarwach would have acted already, would probably even now be personally seeing to the gathering of phalanxes and equipment, making lists, making plans . . .

Tarwach, maybe. Darham, no. "Calrach," he said, "you know Helwych, do you not?"

Calrach's eyebrows lifted. "I know him. I suppose I know him as well as any, which is not saying much."

"Does he carry a knife? Or a sword?"

Calrach looked puzzled. "He carried an eating knife with which to cut up chickens at table. Nothing more. Poor care he takes of it, too."

Darham nodded. "Sorcerers doubtless have other concerns than the keeping of their cutlery," he said. "But does he know the use of a knife—I mean, for matters other than cutting up chickens?"

"Fighting? Nay, the lad is frightened to death of such things."

"Ummm, just so." Darham set his cup aside, picked up a stick, and poked it into the heart of the fire. The tip began to blacken. "I wonder, my friends. I ask you to wonder with me. Think of Helwych as you remember him, and then place that lad in the midst of a surprise attack that combines both magical and mundane weapons, an attack that kills Karthin, Manda, and even Alouzon Dragonmaster herself. A powerful sorceress, too, was there, and she did not survive. What would happen to Helwych under such circumstances?"

"He would . . ." Tylha pursed her lips for a moment. "He would drop like a slaughtered pig. If weapons did not kill him, fear would."

"Aye," said Darham slowly. "Yet now we hear that under just such circumstances did Helwych defend himself valiantly, escape, and with a weapon of which he did not know the use—and half dead from his wounds at that—kill a strong fisher and sail—"

His brows knit together of a sudden.

"When did Helwych ever learn to sail a boat? He is not from the coast."

And when Darham looked up, comprehension and suspicion were gleaming in the eyes of Tylha and Calrach.

Darham drained all but a mouthful of his wine, threw the remainder into the fire as an offering to the Gods, and stood up as the burning wood flared and hissed. "We cannot dismiss the possibility that Helwych's story is true, but I intend to delay my decision as long as I may, in hope that further knowledge might answer some of these questions. We might indeed send troops to Vaylle eventually, and we may indeed look for revenge, but my heart tells me that Vaylle may not be the target of our vengeance."

"Do you suspect Gryylth?" said Calrach. "Or . . ." He fell silent, chagrined.

"Or Helwych, you mean?" Darham shrugged. "As of yet, we may not even know the name that might someday be mated with our suspicions." He bowed to the warriors. "Friends, I bid you a good night. Let us all consider well what we have been told and what we think, but let us also keep silent for now."

❖ CHAPTER 2 ❖

Fever took Helwych shortly after he reached Quay, and he fell into delirium. But though his conscious mind had thrown down its burden and fled into the darkness, his voice—hoarse, stricken—gasped out a lengthening tale of the Vayllens' deceit and treachery in a frenzied babble that horrified his listeners far more than even the most lucid of chronicles.

By the time his senses returned, February was almost gone. Cvinthil had sent a group of the King's Guard to escort him to Kingsbury, but Helwych's condition was such that the trip was a long one, with frequent rests in spite of the increasing danger of attack from the roving packs of hounds.

Even the battle-hardened veterans of the Guard were shaken by the damage that had been inflicted upon the sorcerer's body; and they often murmured among themselves that it was some kind of miracle that the lad had not been killed outright. Hahle, who accompanied the party, said nothing, apparently regarding the sorcerer with a mixture of worry and sadness.

It was not until the beginning of March that Helwych came before Cvinthil in Hall Kingsbury. The boy leaned heavily on a stick, the reddened welts and thick scabs of Vayllen hospitality plainly evident on his pale face.

Cvinthil ordered a chair for him, and Relys herself brought it. Helwych showed no embarrassment at being seated in the presence of the king; rather, he accepted the favor with a kind of grave dignity that bordered almost upon the complacent. True, he smiled his gratitude at Relys as the woman's strong arms lowered him into the chair, but to Relys's mind, the smile had a taint of mockery in it, though she could not have said exactly how.

She shrugged and stepped back just behind and to the side of the chair. Cvinthil and Seena had taken seats on the dais next to one another, and their hands were clasped. The captains that had been chosen for the new wartroops stood nearby, and the members of the King's Guard had assembled also.

Up on the dais, Cvinthil was brooding; and if today there was a viciousness to his black mood, Relys shared it willingly. Marrget had been her captain and her friend. Alouzon had been a support and an example. Wykla—even Wykla—had grown to be as dear to her as a daughter—

Relys flushed at the thought. A daughter. As if her womb—thrust upon her by an angry sorcerer—would ever bear anything save a monthly flow.

How far from then forethought of, little Wykla, when on the road to the Heath I ridiculed you for what I called your effeminate ways.

Did her eyes suddenly smart? Relys thrust the tears from her as though they might suddenly strip her of her title and chain her to a man's bed. But the thought stayed with her: Wykla, too, was gone, and Vaylle would pay.

Cvinthil lifted his head. "Speak, lad," he said to Helwych. "I wish to hear from your own lips what occurred in Vaylle."

Helwych squirmed in his seat, and his voice was hardly more than a whisper as he began. The weather, he said, had been calm during the crossing, and when the barge had approached Vaylle, Alouzon had ordered it beached at the first opportunity, so as not to give the inhabitants a chance to raise any forces. Nonetheless, the Vayllens had appeared shortly after the party had disembarked: a delegation from Lachrae, the capital.

"They seemed friendly, my lord," said Helwych, "though beneath their gracious exterior, I detected a certain ambivalence, as though their words, actions, and thoughts were not in accord."

"Duplicity," said Cvinthil. The blackness deepened about him.

"Aye . . ." Helwych coughed. "Though the Vayllens appear to possess a few potent sorcerers, they could not cloak their lies against me."

Relys's brow furrowed, and she spoke without thinking. "And what of Kyria?"

A flash of annoyance crossed Helwych's face. "The Vayllens are not all-powerful, my maid," he said smoothly, "and neither was Kyria. Her foul temper and arrogance betrayed her into a false security."

"Continue," said Cvinthil. He glanced at Relys, puzzled. Relys shrugged and folded her arms, trying to ignore the condescension in Helwych's *my maid.*

Across the room, though, Hahle, who had been stroking his beard thoughtfully, now lifted his head. His expression, though, was noncommittal, and he did not speak.

Alouzon's party, Helwych continued, had been escorted to Lachrae with great courtesy. The attacks, the Vayllens had explained, came from yet another land, one called Broceliande. The Vayllens themselves— according to the Vayllens—were innocent, even pacifistic.

Helwych paused meaningfully. A fit of coughing suddenly shook him and he collapsed to the side. Only the arm of the chair kept him from sliding to the floor.

Relys stepped forward and offered a hand. Helwych hesitated, then, with a nod, grasped it and allowed himself to be hoisted upright once again. "I am weak," he said.

"No doubt," said Cvinthil. "If you wish to rest—"

"Nay, nay," said Helwych. "I must speak. If Gryylth and Corrin are to have vengeance, I must speak." For an instant, he glanced sidelong, almost slyly, at Relys, and she was once again struck by the discrepancy between his words and his manner.

All had been peaceful, Helwych went on in a hoarse voice, and after three days the party had been lulled into unguarded acceptance of the Vayllens' customs. And therefore, when Pellam, the king, had requested that they give up their weapons as a gesture of peace, they had assented.

Cvinthil blinked. "Marrget and Alouzon gave up their swords? I find it difficult to believe that they would do such a thing."

Helwych shrugged. "Women are frequently ruled by more gullible hearts than their male kindred."

Relys sensed that those present in the room had become suddenly divided into two camps. The veterans were shocked and insulted by Helwych's casual and bigoted generality. The untried soldiers from the distant villages and the frontiers, however, were nodding. Relys herself did her best to conceal her rage; but Timbrin was dark with anger, and the lieutenant's brown eyes said that, given a chance, she would have gladly knocked the sorcerer to the floor.

Cvinthil, though, seemed more interested in facts about Vaylle than in opinions about women. "They gave up their weapons, then," he said. "What happened?"

"I myself," said Helwych, "was suspicious. And therefore I made sure that I kept a large dagger with me that night." He attempted a triumphant grin and sat up straight. "And it is well that I did, for it was that night that the Vayllens broke into our rooms and slaughtered the members of the expedition."

"All but you," said Hahle in a deep, thoughtful voice.

Helwych stared at him as though to memorize his

face. "All but me," he said at last, and there was defiance in his tone.

Helwych's words said one thing, but Relys's intuition said another. Let the boy go on about a woman's heart, she thought. He knows nothing. A woman's heart can tell a great deal, it is something holy . . . is—

She brought herself up short. She had been guarding Seena too long, and the quiet femininity of the queen was infectious.

In detail, Helwych described how he had escaped through an unguarded window, fled through the gardens and the streets, and eluded the guards at the city gate. He had then set off across country until he had reached the coast, and had followed the shore southward until he had come upon a fisher readying his nets at dawn.

"I was weak," said Helwych. "But I fought him. And I killed him. Gryylth and—" He fought for a moment with a rebellious tongue. "—Corrin were in danger, and so I set off that very hour, without even tending to my wounds. The winds were bad—"

Hahle started noticeably, his eyebrows rising towards his bare scalp.

"—and it took me three days to cross the White Sea. I was near death when Hahle and his men found me."

Hahle spoke up. "Three days, you say."

"Aye. Three days with only a cold, stiff corpse to keep me company," said Helwych.

A long silence. Finally: "I see," said Hahle.

Timbrin spoke. She had a quick temper, and Helwych's remark had stung, but she kept her voice even. "Three days in Vaylle, Helwych? And three days to return? But it was the middle of February when you reached Quay. Where did the time go?"

Helwych's mouth worked. "Well, perhaps it was a little more than three days in Vaylle."

"You said *three days*."

Helwych glared at the lieutenant. "Well, girl, I must have made a mistake."

Timbrin's brown eyes did not falter. "You were wounded, of course."

"I was indeed." Helwych coughed weakly, and as though to confirm his words, he shuddered and slumped in his chair, gasping for breath.

"Enough, lieutenant," said Cvinthil. "I daresay I also would be hard pressed to tell one day from another were I in Helwych's condition." His words were soft, but they carried the weight of a reprimand.

Timbrin was silent, but Relys shared her thought: *He was not in that condition when he was in Lachrae.*

Cvinthil had heard enough, though. "The people of Vaylle have shown themselves cowards and traitors. We have done them no ill, and yet they destroy one of our cities and damage another. Their hounds prowl through our countryside in growing numbers, slaughtering cattle and breaking into steadings and manors to attack our people." He turned to the captain of his Guard. "Parrlen, did you sight hounds during your journey to Quay?"

Parrlen had a jaundiced eye but a steady hand. 'Aye," he said slowly. "A number of times. We drove them off with burning sticks, but . . ." His eyes narrowed. ". . . but I do not recall that we were troubled with them on the return journey."

Cvinthil nodded. "But now we have sent an embassy to Vaylle, and our people have been killed in their beds. Their deaths will not go unavenged."

The company in the hall, divided for a minute over the question of women's hearts, united once again. A murmur, a nodding of heads, and the question was settled.

Hahle, though, remained aloof from the general sentiment. Folding his arms, he appeared to sink into his own thoughts, his chin dropping towards his breast as though dragged down by a heavy heart. He opened his mouth once as though to speak, but he shut it again, then turned and started for the door of the Hall.

Cvinthil's voice brought him to a halt. "Councilman."

"My king."

"I will need to speak to you regarding the matter of ships. We will need many."

"My king, all shall be done according to your command."

"Come and see me this evening."

Hahle nodded slowly. "I will do that, my king."

But his expression told Relys that, though he would speak to the king of ships and of ship building, he would voice other concerns, too.

Carrying the bowl of gruel in both hands as much from a sense of responsibility as from the awkwardness that had pursued him from childhood into late adolescence, Lytham made his way across the open space between the buttery and the King's Hall and approached the side door closest to the guest chambers.

The lads who kept watch this evening were friends: young men who—like Lytham, like many in the King's Guard and the wartroops—had been farmboys and herdboys only a year before. They and their fellows had put on leather armor and the king's emblems, and they had quickly learned the use of implements more warlike than dung forks and shovels, but still they shared a common origin, common memories, common beliefs, and the swaggering irritation of young men slowly discovering that the affairs of the wide world take little notice of them.

Dryyim peered into Lytham's bowl. "Are you going to eat that? I am not sure we should allow someone with such tastes into the hall."

"We have responsibilities," said his fellow, a tall, gangling youth named Haryn.

Lytham held the bowl carefully. "This is not for

me. This is for the sorcerer. He is still weak, and must eat gruel.''

Dryyim snorted. ''We may all be eating gruel after Vaylle is done with us.''

''You heard the tale?''

''Of course I heard! I was standing at the side of the dais this afternoon. The sorcerer looked like a trampled puppy.''

Having never fought in a war, Lytham assumed that fighting was fighting, just as he assumed that conflicts between nations were conducted in a fashion similar to the arguments between village bullies: with shouting, and catcalls, and pummeling with fists, and rolling about in the dust of a shabby little street while a crowd of excited admirers looked on. ''Cvinthil would not lead us into Vaylle if certain death waited there,'' he said. ''And he has wise councilors.''

''*Had* wise councilors, you mean,'' said Dryyim. ''Santhe and Karthin went off to Vaylle.'' He glanced over his shoulder as though expecting to see hounds materializing at his back. ''And they did not return.''

''Marrget and Alouzon, too,'' said Lytham.

A sniff. ''What good are they?''

''Well . . . they were councilors . . .''

''Far better they should have gotten themselves husbands and left the fighting to men.'' Dryyim scowled, shook his head. ''Marrget was the worst: she gave herself such airs that I am surprised Cvinthil did not put her on the block.''

Lytham shrugged. ''She is dead now.''

''I would have given a great deal to see her in my village. My father never tolerated insolence in women. He beat my mother regularly.''

Haryn stifled a grin. ''And was beaten back upon occasion.''

Dryyim glared at him, then turned back to Lytham. ''She should have been taught her place from the beginning. And Alouzon . . .'' Dryyim's mouth tightened. "Kerlsen was a friend. She killed him in cold blood."

Lytham frowned. "I thought the hound killed Kerlsen. He was drunk, and—"

"Alouzon killed him," Dryyim insisted. "She stood aside and let the hound tear out his throat while he was helpless. It is better that she is dead. She brought nothing but grief to this land, and then Cvinthil began his reign with his decrees." He spat. "Women!"

The gruel was growing cold. Lytham bettered his grip on the bowl and shrugged. "I like it no more than you, but we can do nothing."

Haryn straightened. "Here comes Relys. Look out: she is playing the man again."

Dryyim snickered. "It would be interesting to bed her—if one could knock some sense into her first."

Lytham glanced over his shoulder as the new captain of the First Wartroop passed by, head bowed as though in thought. When she looked up, though, the young men felt the immediate scrutiny of her dark eyes, and they hid their laughter and looked attentive.

Lytham stepped quickly through the door and made his way hastily down the corridor to the guest chambers. There he found the sorcerer sitting propped up in a chair, furs and blankets piled up about him in spite of the large fire that roared on the hearth a few feet away. Helwych's eyes, half closed as though in meditation, flicked fully open as Lytham entered. "Ah, my brave guard," said Helwych, "come with my supper. My thanks."

Lytham put the bowl into Helwych's hands and shuddered at the sight of the lacerated flesh. Even Helwych's hair was shredded and patchy.

Moving as though in pain, Helwych set the bowl on his lap and stirred its contents. The skin that had formed on the surface of the gruel clung to the spoon in a damp clot as pale as the sorcerer's face. Lytham took a step back. Helwych's eyes flicked back to him, dark blue, almost black. "Do I frighten you, lad?"

Lad? Lytham was struck for a moment. Helwych was scarcely older than he himself. But sorcerers, he recalled, were a strange lot. Mernyl, it was said, had often been called womanish by Dythragor; and so perhaps where one man foolishly assumed the concerns of women, another might do better and take on the privileges of age. It was not the business of a soldier to question any of it.

Helwych's question hung, waiting. Lytham felt acutely embarrassed. "I . . . ah . . . that is to say . . ."

The sorcerer shrugged. "Vaylle is a terrible place," he said, dipping up a spoonful of gruel. "I am glad that Gryylth has such men as you to oppose it."

Helwych's tone was warm and fervid, and it carried with it a deep sense of pride. And feeling suddenly as though praise from a sorcerer was of infinitely more worth than that of even the king himself, Lytham blushed. "I . . . am glad that you think so, master sorcerer."

Helwych bent over his gruel. "Call me Helwych. And your name is . . . Lytham, is it not?"

"Yes, sir."

"Helwych." The sorcerer grinned out of a pale face crisscrossed with welts and patched with scabs.

Lytham swallowed. "Helwych."

"Good."

The sorcerer sucked and mumbled the gruel, the fire roared, and Lytham felt the sweat begin to pool beneath his armor. "Is there anything else I can do for you . . . Helwych?"

The blue-black eyes examined Lytham, and the soldier was suddenly afraid that the praise Helwych had so unexpectedly bestowed was going to be abruptly withdrawn. But the sorcerer only smiled—a little sadly, Lytham thought with a pang of sympathy—and shrugged. "If you could spare a few minutes, Lytham," he said, "I should be glad of your company."

"Ah . . ."

"Fetch up a chair, now. There is a good fellow."

Without knowing really why, save that he did not wish to give Helwych reason to regret his compliments, Lytham pulled up a stool and sat down as far away from the fire as he could.

Helwych did not speak for some minutes. Finally: "People have so little time for a wounded man. Cvinthil had me in to tell my tale, and now I do believe he has forgotten me entirely."

"I am sure, sir, that he thinks of you a great deal."

Helwych smiled tiredly. "Helwych."

"Ah . . . Helwych."

"Just so." Helwych nodded in the manner of an aging grandfather. "I am more than likely wrong. It is so easy to be wrong . . ." He stirred his gruel. "You are afraid, maybe, of Vaylle?"

"I am . . ." Sorcerers could read the truth, it was said, in one's eyes, but Lytham was unwilling to admit weakness. "I am . . . cautious," he said, trying to sound like an experienced captain of the Guard.

"Ah . . . caution. That is a good thing, caution." Helwych seemed to savor the word. "And is Cvinthil also cautious?"

"He is a good king."

"But is he cautious?"

"I . . ." Helwych was asking him to pronounce judgment upon his king. Relys, if she ever heard of such audacity, would make him wish that his tongue had been cut out. But Relys was a woman—she merely played the man by the king's good will—and so Lytham held himself up straight. "I believe he is."

"Indeed? Has he made no mistakes?"

It occurred to Lytham that that had not been the question, but he answered bravely. "Oh, I am sure he makes mistakes."

"Everybody makes mistakes," said Helwych. The blue-black eyes were fixed on Lytham, and the guard was suddenly conscious of nothing save the sorcerer's gaze. "Corrin has made mistakes."

"Oh . . . well . . . that . . ."

"I am not speaking of the war, lad." Helwych leaned toward Lytham with an air of confidentiality. "I am speaking of the women."

The sweat ran down Lytham's cheek. Helwych might have overheard the conversation at the door of the Hall a few minutes before.

"Now you and your friends," the sorcerer went on, "are wise beyond your years, and . . ."

There it was: pride, respect. Lytham gulped it down and wanted more.

". . . and you know better. Gryylth has been here for a long time, and so have Gryylth's customs. Now you tell me: is it a wise thing to change them?"

"But, ah, Corrin?"

"Corrin is an unhappy place these days," said Helwych, and Lytham could not but believe him completely. "It is unfortunate that Gryylth cannot learn from the mistakes of its neighbor. Now Cvinthil has to take what weapons he has and go across the sea to Vaylle, leaving an unhappy land and an unhappy people behind him."

It seemed to Lytham then that Helwych was no longer sitting down. It seemed, rather, that the sorcerer had risen, that his wounds had vanished, that his scars had disappeared. He was suddenly taller, stronger, as arrogant and as swaggering as the most flamboyant bully boy of Lytham's old village; and the guard found himself nodding in agreement and admiration, wondering not at all about the change in the mousy little sorcerer.

"But he himself sails into danger," said Helwych, and he was back in his chair, sunken among a heap of furs and blankets.

Lytham blinked. "Can you not dissuade him, sorcerer?"

"Helwych."

"Ah . . . yes, Helwych."

"I cannot. But, as I said in the hall, Vaylle is not

all-powerful. It has its weaknesses. And I am sure that Cvinthil will find them. And I am sure that, with such men as you under his command, he will conquer.''

Lytham sighed with relief.

''But, you know, Lytham,'' said Helwych as his eyes bored once again into the lad's face, ''matters other than Vaylle threaten Gryylth, too. Matters that Cvinthil has brought upon himself.''

''Cvinthil is a good king,'' declared Lytham.

The dark eyes grew wide. ''Oh, I am sure that he is,'' Helwych said sincerely. ''But would you not agree that, should Cvinthil return from an arduous campaign to find a prosperous and happy land, he would be lavish with praise and rewards for the men who made possible that prosperity and happiness?''

The blue-black eyes, as dark as void, rooted Lytham to his chair, and he saw Helwych's point as clearly as if it had been etched into the sky with liquid fire. It all made sense, perfect sense, and though he swallowed with a dry throat, the words came quickly to his lips. ''Yes. Yes, I would.''

Helwych nodded. ''You are very wise, Lytham. I think I shall sleep now. If you would, please bring your friends with you tomorrow evening at this same time. I would like to meet them.''

Lytham rose. The world seemed open and easy of a sudden, and the heedlessness he had previously found in its workings had been peeled away to reveal a willingness to serve and to be controlled. ''I shall do that,'' he said. ''Good night, sir.''

Helwych smiled patiently. ''Helwych, lad.''

❖ CHAPTER 3 ❖

Darham's wish for further knowledge was granted, but not as he had hoped. When a month had passed, another messenger from Cvinthil arrived bearing not only a detailed account of Helwych's report, but also a description of the lad's wounds and an impatient request from Cvinthil that Darham declare whether or not Corrin would aid Gryylth in the invasion planned for the beginning of June.

To be sure, Cvinthil's message was respectfully and formally worded, and Darham found nothing amiss in its content, but there was no mistaking its tone. The king of Gryylth was angry, and, given the circumstances, he had a right to be. So, for that matter, did everyone in Corrin.

Tylha and Calrach conferred softly as Dryyim, the messenger, finished up with the standard formalities. When he was through, Tylha raised her hand to request leave to speak, and at Darham's nod, she addressed Dryyim. "The recent war left both Corrin and Gryylth with few . . . men . . . able to bear arms," she said, and though the Corrinians in the lodge understood her meaning, Dryyim did not: the women's phalanxes had been kept back during the war with Gryylth. "We of Corrin would like to know what kind of forces Cvinthil expects to raise, that we may better respond in kind."

Dryyim heard her out with a kind of mixed astonishment and irritation. "We estimate a body of twelve wartroops," he said. "That is twelve score men, maiden."

Tylha smiled. "I know well the number of men in a wartroop. And it has been years since I have been a maiden." She glanced at the Corrinians in the lodge. They were smiling, too.

Dryyim stared at her, annoyance plain on his face.

Darham cleared his throat. "Commander Tylha leads fully half our army, Gryylthan."

Dryyim folded his arms. "Indeed."

Tylha's smile turned brittle, an indication that she was seething. But she remained polite. The Gryylthan was, after all, a guest. The Vayllens might kill their visitors: not so Corrin.

The thought brought Darham straight back to the question of arms and war. He looked at Calrach and Tylha. They nodded. Despite the inconsistencies and the problems inherent in Helwych's story, Vaylle's treachery was clear. Darham had to respond. And he could only respond in one way.

Feeling the hollowness, feeling the loss, he stood and lifted his hand. "Let it be done, then," he said. "We will gather what phalanxes we have and send them to Vaylle. I myself shall lead them. And if Cvinthil wishes to depart come June, then we shall leave the shearing and the haying and depart with him."

Dryyim bowed. "I shall tell my king what you have said." He glanced at Tylha and the female members of the Guard and shook his head with an almost audible sigh.

Darham sent him off with a male attendant, ostensibly for rest and refreshment, but more because Dryyim's arrogance was driving a number of his more prideful warriors—men and women both—close to violence. Even his scribe looked angry.

But Darham could not but feel that anger—even justified anger—had no place here today; and though, years ago, he had with Tarwach formulated battles and campaigns against Gryylth with seriousness and gravity, still he had never approached those conferences with such grim emptiness as now characterized his preparations for the assault on Vaylle. As Darham spoke with his commanders and advisors, in fact, he felt as though he were moving through events at an arm's length, as though it were not really Darham of Corrin who spoke of men, transport and invasion, but rather a dancing puppet of a king who was being led through his antics by strings and tethers that willynilly jerked him about like a hapless doll.

It was late when he finished. Below the lodge, Benardis lay deeply shadowed. He dismissed his people and sat down before the fire, weary, his head in his hands.

Wykla. Dead. Such a lovely, noble child. But then, all the children he had ever seen had partaken of a sense of nobility. Even when, dirt-streaked, screaming with temper in the marketplace or the town square and plunging their mothers and fathers into the depths of red-faced humiliation, still they were only themselves, as unselfconscious and immanent as a strong stallion that pranced across a spring meadow, rejoicing in his strength.

And at times—fortunate, fortunate times—a few of those children carried with them even into young adulthood some of that immediacy and that presence. Wykla had it. Manda, in spite of her sorrow, had it also. Karthin, too. And so how was it that such as these could be slaughtered in their beds in a far land, leaving a rank weed like Helwych to come home bearing the news of their deaths? It did not make sense.

Some time had passed before he noticed that Tylha had stayed behind. She had been waiting in the silent lodge, standing at attention, not wishing to interrupt yet unwilling to depart.

Darham nodded to her tiredly. "Commander."

"I do not wish to grieve you, my king. If this time be inopportune for a question . . ."

Darham leaned back in his chair and propped his feet on the hearth. He might have called for wine, but his stomach was already sour with frustration. "You do not grieve me, Tylha. Vaylle grieves me. Gryylth grieves me. But not you."

Tylha nodded. Her leather armor creaked. "My king," she said, "I noticed this evening that you chose your words carefully regarding the forces that would depart for Vaylle. You consistently referred to men, but not to women. Was this an oversight? Or maybe an attempt to be polite to the Gryylthan?"

"I had sent the Gryylthan off some time before, Tylha."

"Aye. Indeed."

Darham sighed. Any appetite for battle he might have once possessed had been thoroughly spoiled by the final drive into Gryylth and the fighting at the Circle, and he looked towards this new conflict with a sense of leaden inertia.

"I dislike all of this greatly," he said. "I have no other reason for war with Vaylle than the fact that there is now no reason *not* to. If we plowed our fields with no greater excuse, we should be assured of some hard harvests."

"Manda and Karthin, my lord, are sufficient reason, I think. And then there is also Wykla. You called her daughter."

Darham was silent for a time. He had called Wykla daughter, but she had never called him father. Now, according to Helwych, she would never have the chance. "Your question, commander: aye, I spoke of men."

Stocky, matronly, Tylha might have been chiseled out of a block of granite. "Do you forget that my phalanxes, kept back from the war with Gryylth, can still be raised almost to full strength? Peace has sent most of the women home, and some have taken husbands and are raising children, but many are free to come and go and would be quite willing to pick up their swords and pikes, particularly in reprisal for Karthin and Manda, who were much loved.''

The fire crackled as Darham considered his reply. Tylha had noticed. Of course she had noticed. Her women had chafed at their inactivity during the war with Gryylth. Now here again was an opportunity for battle, and . . .

"What," he said finally, "did you think of our messenger, Dryyim?''

Tylha's eyes narrowed. "He is as arrogant as a tup in October.''

"Aye. Even more than the first Cvinthil sent. And though Wykla did not speak openly to me about her status in Gryylth, her manner told me much. Women are not esteemed in that land.''

Tylha obviously did not like the trend of Darham's thoughts. "I should think that no one, man or woman, is esteemed in Vaylle.''

"True.''

"A month ago, we spoke of our suspicions, but with this sending from Gryylth, I think we must put our suspicions aside.''

Darham bent his head, studied his thumbs. "I think so. Indeed.''

Again a silence. Tylha's mouth worked. "Will you be sending the women, lord?''

"No.''

Jaw clenched, Tylha bowed and prepared to depart, but Darham called her back.

"Hear me," he said.

"The king has given his order. He need make no explanation.''

Darham snorted. "We are farmers and the sons and daughters of farmers. We do not stand on formality as do the Gryylthans. Your king, therefore, wishes to make his explanation nonetheless. I respect Cvinthil and his motives, but Gryylth still maintains many of its curious attitudes regarding women, and I am therefore unsure of its warriors' conduct towards your phalanxes. Good women, wounded, might well be left to die on the battlefield because they are seen as being of lesser worth than their male comrades.''

Tylha nodded unwillingly. ''I see your point, lord. But—''

''I have another.'' Darham counted for a moment on his fingers. ''Cvinthil is committing twelve score warriors and soldiers, but given the attack on Bandon and the presence of the hounds—thank the Gods they have not yet entered Corrin!—I am sure that he is reluctant to leave his land bereft of all defense.''

Realization dawned on Tylha. ''He is keeping back some wartroops then.''

''Aye. Some three or four, I would estimate. And with the demonstration of cheek provided by our friend Dryyim, I am afraid to consider what mischief they might do while Cvinthil is across the sea.''

Tylha had the look of a mother suddenly confronted by a pack of misbehaving boys. ''I . . . understand. I do not like it, lord, but I understand.''

''I do not like it either, commander. I am sorry.''

But after Tylha left, Darham stayed by the fire, peering into the flames, pondering. He had not spoken all his thoughts because he did not know all of them as of yet, but he was afraid of where they might lead, given time.

March, and then April, and then May. The weather warmed. In the fields the green crops pushed their way out of the brown earth, and in the pastures the lambs grew up, the foals frisked, and the calves turned sturdy.

In Quay, the shipwrights labored, and the ships that would carry the men of Gryylth and Corrin slowly took shape, first as skeletal carcasses of ribs and keels that lay on the shore like so many clean-picked whales, then as fleshed-out barges and boats with oak planking that gleamed in the morning light. And in a hundred towns and villages across Gryylth, men who had only

a year before known the heedlessness of childhood
were taking up pikes and swords, were hacking and
stabbing at straw men and inch-thick saplings under
the critical eyes of their future commanders, were
marching away from their homes and converging on
Quay.

The absence of men and older boys had brought a
quiet to the streets of Kingsbury, and Relys noticed it
keenly as she made her way across the market square,
for there were no deep voices booming and shouting,
no shrill yelps of mock battle and fistfights. With the
failing of the light, in fact, only a few women from
outlying villages remained, packing up an unsold
chicken or two, or a remaining bolt of cloth. In soft
sopranos and altos they chatted with one another, their
gestures and movements small and graceful; but if they
stared at Relys for a moment because she wore a
sword, they made no comment.

Relys passed by, and in a minute, came in sight of
the large house that had been given over to Hahle for
his use during his frequent visits to the capital. As
head of the council of Quay, Hahle was in charge of
the ship building, and he had grown to be a powerful
man these days. Relys, therefore, could not help but
wonder what would cause the councilman to request—
politely—that the captain of the First Wartroop come
and have dinner with him.

But as Relys turned a corner, shadows—tall, mannish—suddenly blocked her path, and she stiffened.
She was a warrior, but she was also a woman alone in
a darkened street. Despite Cvinthil's decrees, this was
still Gryylth.

She caught herself, gritted her teeth, attempted to
ignore the men. She had almost convinced herself that
they were also ignoring her when one of them stopped
and pointed at her. "And what are you about tonight,
woman?"

"She has a sword, Dryyim."

"And so she does. Most strange! Come here, woman, and explain yourself."

Even had Relys been the lowliest dairy maid of the frontier, Cvinthil's decrees had given her the same respect as was due a man. But, as she was reminded constantly—subtly or overtly—what Cvinthil had decreed was considerably different at times from what actually happened. Nonetheless, she was no dairymaid, but rather the captain of the First Wartroop, and so she planted herself before the men and folded her arms. "Gods bless," she said. "Have you anything to report, Dryyim? And you, Lytham?"

But the three men examined her ironically. "Do I know you, woman?" said Dryyim.

Relys knew that they recognized her, but their insolence and disrespect had been growing over the past several weeks, and where before they and their comrades had only sniggered at the women of the wartroop, they now laughed openly. This evening they had an opportunity to harass Relys herself with comparative impunity, for if questioned about their actions, they could easily plead ignorance. The light was bad, and they had not expected to meet her. How were they to know who she was?

Relys steeled herself. She stood a head shorter than Dryyim and his companions, and though she knew herself and her sword, three opponents could make a fight unpleasant, no matter what their skill. "I am Relys of Bandon. You know me. Do not pretend that you do not."

Lytham scoffed openly. "Does your husband know that you are out alone?"

"Or that you make a practice of lying to the King's Guards?" put in the third young man.

"Or going about in man's garb?" added Dryyim.

"I tell you—" began Relys, but she caught herself and stood back a pace. How was it that she deigned to argue with such as these? Inwardly, though, she felt sick, for here was a woman's lot staring her in the face. She had said it herself, to Alouzon, on that terrible first night: *A pretty piece I would make on the block in Bandon, eh?* Now she wished that she had never uttered those words.

Dryyim turned to Lytham with a swagger, saying: "I think we should teach—"

Frightened, and angry because of her fright, Relys drew her sword, lifted a foot, and planted it in the small of Dryyim's back. The kick sent him into his companion, and as they fell in a tangle of livery and leather, Relys turned to face her third antagonist.

The sound of swords starting out of their sheaths. "Hold," she said quietly, and there was a hiss in her voice that kept the swords where they were. "You are so untried that Cvinthil himself has given orders that you and your wartroops be kept at home for further seasoning—like squabs—when the rest depart for Vaylle. And if even one of you survives my sword, do you know the penalties for attacking a captain of Gryylth?"

"Ah . . . I see . . ." Dryyim flailed out and managed to sit up. "I see that you are indeed Relys of Bandon."

Relys's voice was as cold as the ball of ice that had formed in her stomach. *A pretty piece* . . . "You knew that from the start, you insolent whelp. Think twice in the future before you even think to give me offense." Shuddering at the thought of ever being at the mercy of the newer men of the King's Guard, she turned on her heel and, sheathing her sword, continued up the street.

She did not realize how deeply she had been affected by the encounter until she lifted a hand to knock at Hahle's door. She was shaking violently, and for a moment she struggled to compose herself and wished that she had some of Marrget's strength.

Womanhood? Marrget had met it as an adversary, and had conquered without yielding an inch. And yet here was Relys, trembling like a girl because of three men barely out of boyhood.

When she finally knocked, the door was opened by a serving girl who bowed to her in the old manner and gestured her in with a gentle wave of her hand. "My master is waiting for you," she said. Her voice was high and sweet, and Relys, thanking her, could not help but notice that her own voice was just as high, and—had she allowed the defiant edge to slip even for a moment—just as sweet.

She followed the girl down a short hall, clutching her sword as though it were a dry stick in a rushing torrent.

Hahle was waiting at the table, his head bowed in thought and his right hand covering his face. His bare scalp glistened in the firelight. He was a large man, and his arms, though old, still showed the muscles left by years of sword work. Once, he had been Marrget's teacher, though he freely admitted that the student had far surpassed the master.

Relys's throat tightened. Marrget was gone, killed in her bed. Had she had a chance to awaken? To draw her sword?

But Hahle had risen and was coming forward. After a moment's hesitation, he bowed to Relys as to an equal, but when he seemed baffled as to whether or not to offer his hand, Relys saved him the decision and offered hers. "Greetings, Hahle. Gods bless."

He took her hand in a firm grip, as relieved as his guest. "Gods bless, Relys. Welcome to my house. Please: come sit and eat. And . . ." He shrugged. "I pray you, forgive my discourtesy. We of Quay are still rustics."

Dinner was simple: soup and meat, bread, wine. Unadorned country fare. The serving girl passed to and fro quietly, with hardly a footstep to indicate her passage. She herself was from Quay, Relys thought, and had maintained, even in liberal Kingsbury, the customs that dictated that women's comings and goings should be unobtrusive.

And the mocking faces of the three young guards leered at Relys from out of the liquid reflection in her wine cup. But for her sword, but for her title, she might have been beaten or even raped.

A pretty piece . . .

Hahle gave no indication of the reason for his invitation. He chatted amiably with Relys about the gathering of the new wartroops, about the ship building and the readying of the invasion fleet; and he grew nostalgic as he told some tales of Marrget's training, though at times he seemed uncertain whether to refer to the captain as man or as woman.

"It was the first time Marrget had bested me," he was saying as his girl cleared the table and refilled their cups. "He tumbled me right into the dirt and laughed . . ." He shook his head. "He was usually so serious. But when he . . . ah . . . when she laughed . . . it was like . . ." He fell silent suddenly.

Relys nodded. "She is gone."

"Aye. And cursed be them that slew her." Hahle's jaw tightened. "Killed in her bed. Not even a warrior's death. The death of a commoner, or of a . . . a . . ."

Relys's eyes flickered to the councilman. Hahle had turned crimson. "Or of a woman?" she offered quietly. There was no rancor or anger in her voice. Slips these days were common. Had she avenged every one of them, she would have killed a hundred men since January.

"Forgive me, lady. As I said, I am a rustic."

"Errors are greatly preferable to insult," said Relys. "No pardon is necessary."

Hahle seemed to be sorting out his feelings about dining alone with a woman who was neither his wife nor a potential mistress. To cover his uncertainty, he drank from his cup. "Do you . . . receive much insult?" he asked after a time.

Relys allowed himself a thin smile. "Some of the

younger men of the Guard think themselves entitled to the privileges of their fathers. They are angry that times have changed.''

"They have changed for all of us.'' Hahle sighed. "Marrget came to Quay's gate with her companions. I had heard . . . I mean, I knew of her transformation, but I . . . I did not recognize her at all.''

Relys heard confusion and sorrow in his voice. "We are all very different,'' she said simply.

"I was . . .'' Hahle passed a hand over his face. "I did not make it easy for Marrget while she was in Quay,'' he said. "I was thoughtless. She was so different. And . . .'' He bent his head suddenly. "And that was her last memory of me.''

"Councilman,'' said Relys, "a warrior knows that any parting might be his or her last. Marrget knew that better than anyone.'' She noticed, chagrined, that her voice had turned light and soft, even comforting, but she went on. "She always spoke well of you, and I am sure that any memories she took with her into death were tempered by all your previous words and deeds.''

Hahle did not speak for a time. Then: "My thanks, lady.''

"No thanks are needed, sir.''

"She will be revenged.''

Relys glanced across the room. Her sword leaned against the wall, ready. "She will be well revenged. They will all be well revenged.''

"Indeed,'' Hahle nodded. "The ships are all but ready—I could die tonight knowing that the invasion will proceed as planned.'' After a moment's pause, he continued, but his voice had lost some of its heart. "The Gods cannot help but favor us, I think, for our actions are just.'' He paused again. Hesitated. "I think.''

Relys set down her cup. "You think?''

"Aye, I . . .'' Hahle dropped his eyes and spoke quickly, as though he were confessing a shameful act.

"That is why I asked you to have dinner with me, captain. I spoke with Cvinthil this afternoon about some concerns that I have had for some time. Lately they have been growing."

"What concerns?"

"Helwych."

The sorcerer had been mending slowly. Pale, scarred, he still had to lean on a stick when he walked or stood for any length of time; but though his advice to Cvinthil had been invaluable, Relys had never quite trusted him. Mernyl had been an odd man, too circuitous and too veiled for her taste, but he had been a good man nonetheless, and in the end had given his life for Gryylth and Corrin both. Helwych, even in health, was a feeble little thing, and he seemed to hide more smirks than smiles, more prejudice than power. He appeared to be always within earshot of anything that was said about him, and he constantly gave the impression of knowing more than he ought.

Hahle had leaned forward, waiting for her reaction. But she only shrugged. "I do not like him, either."

"It is not that I do not like him," Hahle insisted. "Though in truth I do not. You have a clear head, captain. You are rightfully outraged by Marrget's death, but you can think as a warrior, also."

Relys laughed in spite of herself. "No talk here of women's gullible hearts?"

"Will you hear me out?"

"Tell me. Please."

Hahle spoke softly. "Helwych's story about the conduct of the Vayllens is reasonable, considering all that has happened. Now, over the weeks, I have noticed small inconsistencies and contradictions in his tale—the matter of the missing days, for example—but they have all been explainable. More or less. But there is one that is not, and it gnaws at me."

Relys waited.

"Helwych," said Hahle, "told us that he killed the Vayllen fisher in order to steal his boat, and that the crossing to Quay took three days. Now, I will not question the fact that the Vayllen was still in the boat when he docked, because I myself would have had a difficult time hoisting a body out of a boat were I wounded as badly as Helwych. Nor will I question his comment about the weather being bad: Helwych is no sailor, and cannot be expected to know bad weather from good. But the Vayllen . . .'' He fell silent, musing, as though he wished to be sure of his words.

The serving girl appeared, refilled their cups, and departed, her steps silent, her hair long and dark, her eyes downcast.

Hahle still had not spoken. ''Master?'' said Relys.

''Aye.'' Hahle straightened up, resolved. ''I felt the body just after Helwych's boat beached.''

Relys's brow furrowed. ''And?''

''It was warm. Quite warm. It takes at best a day and a half to cross the White Sea, and Helwych insisted that the voyage took twice that; but the man in the boat could not have been dead for above an hour.''

Relys turned the fact over in her mind. ''It does not make sense,'' she said. ''If Helwych killed the man to steal the boat, the corpse would have been cold. But the only other possibility is that the Vayllen fisher brought him to Quay willingly, and then was killed by Helwych when just offshore.''

Hahle was nodding. ''Exactly.''

''What did the king say?''

Hahle shook his head. ''He is angry at the Vayllens. When I spoke to him of this matter, he shouted at me and asked whether the loss of Bandon and Quay and the lives of my friends were not enough. In truth, I wonder at my own thoughts, but Helwych . . .'' He shook his head. ''It should make sense. But it does not.''

''What do you want to do?''

''I am not sure that there is anything we can do. I have only a suspicion that something is amiss. And the king will not hear it.''

"Are we being betrayed, do you think?"

Hahle spread his hands. "Helwych's wounds are genuine enough. He nearly died of them. What but a monster would do such a thing to a lad?"

"Does Helwych know of your suspicions?"

"I think not. Nor does anyone else. Cvinthil, you have noticed, is surrounded mostly by youngsters these days. And the veterans are all angry and spoiling for a fight. I have no one to talk to save you."

Relys deliberated. "Without the will of the king," she said slowly, "we can do nothing. But if Helwych has erred once—he might well err again. My lieutenant, Timbrin, knows how not to be seen. I will have her watch him closely and report any further anomalies. That, I am afraid, is all we can do for now."

The night was very dark when they finished their talk, and as Relys prepared to depart, she noticed that Hahle took up a cloak and a stout stick as though to accompany her. "I have no need of an escort, though I thank you," she said. But she recalled the three young men, and her mouth tightened.

Hahle donned the cloak and fastened the brooch at his throat. "Neither women nor warriors should travel alone through hostile territory, captain," he said. Relys colored. "Nay, I have heard what the young men say. I do not trust them."

He offered his arm, and, after hesitating, Relys took it, hovering somewhere between shame and gratitude.

Hahle strode gallantly, as though he found nothing unusual in accompanying a capable and attractive warrior. The guards at the town gate—novice and veteran alike—murmured greetings, but Relys felt their eyes on her as, with her hand on Hahle's arm, she took the road down the hill.

For a moment before he left her at the edge of the isolated cluster of huts belonging to the women of the wartroop, Hahle clasped her hands: the gesture of warriors, young and old, united by weapons and experience. Then he turned and set off into the darkness that would lead him home.

He had not quite vanished into the shadows when Relys called out: "Master."

"Eh?"

"Warriors and women do not travel alone, you said."

"Aye," he replied slowly, and Relys could hear the smile in his voice. "But I am an old man now, the hounds have dried up for the time, and no one else wishes to bother one so harmless." With a wave, he disappeared into the night.

Relys strained her eyes after him. "He is wise," she murmured. "Marrget had a good teacher."

But she had hardly turned for her door when the night was suddenly split by the deep-voiced howl of a hound. She saw a distant flash of glowing eyes and heard Hahle cry out, but she was already running to his aid.

❖ CHAPTER 4 ❖

Alouzon stared up at a lurid sky that seemed the color of blood. Out of the distance came sounds: roars, shrieks, a clattering as of iron locusts. Nearby, papery rustlings and the lap of thick, oily waves were interspersed with the inexplicable chirp of crickets. A siren arose and sent a lance of sound through her ears. She rolled over and saw the Specter moving like a pillar of night across the desert wastes of Broceliande, through the once fertile pastures of Vaylle, over the waters of the White Sea, into Gryylth. It stood over her, and it lifted a sword that still dripping with the blood of innocents.

With a cry too faint to be a scream, Alouzon twitched her numb limbs into a semblance of action and grabbed for the Dragonsword. But her arms were too weak to lift the blade, and the Specter's weapon descended like a scythe and ripped through her belly. Her flesh parted to reveal the dripping form of a blind fetus that writhed out of a tangle of smoking viscera.

No . . . no . . .

Holding herself together with her bare hands as blood and bile oozed between her fingers, she staggered to her feet. "I know . . . I know what you are," she gasped at the Specter. "And I'm gonna—"

Pain drove her to her knees, and when she lifted her head again, Solomon Braithwaite's corpse was staring her in the face, its breath fetid with months of decay, its eyes glazed. "Going to what, girl?"

"I'm gonna . . ."

"Say it. *Say it!*"

The Grail. The Grail was the only way out. But where was it? Signs hung in the air about her—*Westlake, Olympic*—their letters traced as though in flame, but she could not comprehend them.

"I'm gonna do it . . . somehow . . ."

Specter, fetus, corpse: all were suddenly gone then, swept away by something that roared by and shattered the air with rock and roll. The sound was a fist that put Alouzon on the ground again, but her eyes were open now, and the delusions of her horror-filled dreams had scattered like shadows before a mercury-vapor light.

She stared at the sky, at the moving lights of a jet-liner that crossed from north to south, at the faint stars. She understood.

She was in Los Angeles. And she was Alouzon.

Hahle survived the hound's attack, but only because Relys and the wartroop arrived within seconds. Several of the women were burned and bitten, but they drove the beast off with no serious casualties save for Hahle.

Now, badly wounded and unaware of himself or his surroundings, the councilman lay in bed, attended by the king's own physicians. Cvinthil ordered that prep-arations for the invasion be hastened, for, as Helwych had quickly pointed out, the attack of a hound after such a long hiatus indicated that Vaylle was growing stronger with each passing day. It might even be pre-paring an invasion of its own.

Relys admitted that Helwych's logic was good, but Hahle's words had taken root in her heart; and as May flowed towards June like a swift river, as the last of the men and supplies departed for Quay, as Cvinthil himself, angry and eager for revenge, prepared to join his men, she found herself increasingly disquieted.

She had always thought of herself as a lieutenant, not as a commander, and she had been comfortable in the role of adding to, rather than formulating, plans and strategies. As a result, when confronted with the responsibilities of a captain, Relys had grown cautious; and now, with Hahle's words ringing in her mind's ear, a vague reluctance had enveloped her.

Cvinthil and the last of the troops would soon be leaving. Four new, untried wartroops would remain behind, along with their young commanders. Helwych—too weak as a sorcerer to fight, too feeble of body to travel—would also stay, acting as councilor to Seena, who would reign in Cvinthil's place.

Relys did not like it. The king could decree equality, but experience was another matter. Seena, though queen, was a properly socialized woman of Gryylth, and she could easily become overwhelmed by the running of a country. She would then turn to Helwych, and the sorcerer would eventually command the queen.

No, Relys did not like it at all. Nor did she like the single course of action that was left open to her, for on the surface it smacked of cowardice, and in its depths it reeked of a danger that she had not yet learned to confront. Nonetheless, a few days before Cvinthil planned to depart, she stood with Timbrin before the king and queen and asked that she be allowed to remain in Gryylth. Timbrin made the same request.

Cvinthil was surprised. "You two have never been laggards in war, Relys."

She stood tall. "Nor are we now, my king. It is not out of fear that we ask this. Consider: all the experienced men of Gryylth are crossing the White Sea. There is always a chance that Vaylle might attack Gryylth while its defenders are absent."

"But Helwych said . . ." Cvinthil looked to the sorcerer. Helwych was slumped and crumpled into a chair, the scars still plain on his face. Timbrin had been spying on him for the last few weeks; but though she had nothing to report save that at night he locked himself in his house, Relys was becoming all the more certain that Helwych had plans for Gryylth, plans she could not prove, plans so subtle that she could not even make a formal accusation.

"May I ask, lord, what Helwych said?"

Helwych tottered to his feet. "I will answer myself. I believe that the Vayllens will eventually try to strike Gryylth again, but only after a delay of another several months. Our strength is to strike first."

Timbrin spoke up. "Still, you cannot be sure. You are no warrior: you might have made a mistake."

"By the Gods, woman!" exclaimed Helwych. "The hounds are only a foretaste of what might come. Look at what happened to Hahle!"

"We know well what happened to Hahle," said Relys. "If you recall, we were there to defend him. We have not the faintest idea, though, where you were."

Her slip of temper had exposed her suspicions. Helwych seemed to waver. He sat down, slumping back into a pile of flesh and rags.

Cvinthil was angry. "What would you have the lad do, captain? Pick up a sword? He is still weak from his wounds."

"Aye," said Relys. Cvinthil had, fortunately, misinterpreted her words, and she did not correct him. She tried to think of what Marrget would do. "I was hasty, lord," she said. "I beg pardon. But as for my request: Timbrin and Helwych are perhaps both right." She snorted inwardly at her subtle turning of the sorcerer's words. "Helwych could indeed have erred in his estimation of Vaylle's preparations, and the hounds are indeed returning. I am a captain and an advisor, and therefore my counsel is that there should be some warriors with experience left in Gryylth when you leave."

Helwych was motionless. Cvinthil was still angry.

Seena finished nursing Vill and wrapped him in a fold of her cloak. "Husband," she said softly.

Cvinthil swallowed his temper and turned to her. "Wife?"

Seena spoke hesitantly. "I think Gryylth would benefit from the presence of Relys and Timbrin. I would . . ." She dropped her eyes.

"Nay, wife," said Cvinthil. "It is not unseemly. You are my queen. Speak."

"I would also feel safer myself, were my friend with me."

Relys felt Helwych's eyes on her. Black. Blue-black. Eyes of void. Helwych wanted her out of the country, she was sure, and therefore was she all the more determined to stay. She kept her gaze on the queen and tried to ignore the hate that she sensed was pent within the frail, wounded body of the sorcerer.

Cvinthil pondered. Finally: "Are you sure of your request, my ladies?"

The women exchanged glances. Relys lifted an eyebrow: she would not ask any woman of her wartroop to place herself in such peril save of her own free will. But Timbrin squared her small shoulders and nodded.

"We are," said Relys.

"Granted then." Cvinthil said the words reluctantly. "Make whatever arrangements you must."

Relys and Timbrin bowed and left the hall; but as they passed through the door, Relys noticed that Dryyim was on guard that day. The young man examined the two women critically—since being disciplined for harassing Relys, his resentment had doubled and redoubled—and Relys wondered suddenly whether she had sufficient courage to face the task she had set for herself.

Four wartroops of young men who had little respect for women. The king out of the country. A strange sorcerer advising the queen.

And two women standing alone.

Relys spoke softly as they stepped out into the street. "I hope a woman's heart is a strong thing, Timbrin."

Alouzon got to her feet in the wash of blue-white incandescence that rained from the lamps bordering a small lake. Ornamental date palms rose up spectrally from the parched grass of a Los Angeles heat wave, and, off on an island across the water, ducks and sea gulls stirred uneasily at the pre-dawn intrusion.

Staggering, almost blind with thirst and the stifling heat, she groped her way to the shore. But though she had drunk many times from the clear streams of Gryylth and Vaylle, the water here was fetid and polluted, and she could not even bring herself to splash her face.

She was Alouzon, but she recognized this place: MacArthur Park. It was miles away from Helen's house and UCLA, but Silbakor had doubtless been making whatever interdimensional approach characterized its entries into the mundane world of Los Angeles, and the White Worm had attacked before the Dragon could bring her safely down. And so she had fallen.

Fallen. Fallen forever. And yet, impossibly, she had struck ground in Los Angeles with no more damage than a bump on her head.

"It must be the Grail," she murmured, her throat parched and aching. "It made me see that booby trap in the mountains. It got me down here. I suppose it's a good thing Silbakor didn't drop me in the middle of a freeway."

But she looked up. Where was Silbakor? The Specter? The White Worm? Aside from the lights of jetliners and the far-off strobe of a police helicopter, the sky was empty.

And then she recalled Kyria. The sorceress—or was it Helen, or something else?—had been lying at the base of a wall, crumpled in a heap of broken bones and shredded robes. And Santhe, and Wykla and Manda, and Dindrane, and Marrget and Karthin: they were still there in the temple. The Grayfaces had been killed, and the jets had been banished, but Alouzon's friends, as far as she knew, were in Broceliande, at the mercy of whatever horrors that land could create.

And she was in Los Angeles.

She lifted her arms as a scream forced its way up out of the mire of fear and frustration within her. Silbakor was doubtless holding the White Worm and the Specter away from her. It would protect her with all the potencies that a reification of physical law could command. But it would defend no one else. Gryylth could be a wasteland as far as the Dragon was concerned: all that mattered was its existence.

Hopelessness bore down on her like a weight. *Some God.*

She turned away from the lake. Where did displaced Gods go when in Los Angeles? For that matter, where did fifth-century warriors go? The Salvation Army? The shelters down on San Pedro Street?

Up on Wilshire Boulevard, a car drove by, its headlights splitting the darkness. Somebody heading for an early morning job or coming home from a night shift. About Alouzon, the city was slowly struggling out of slumber, preparing to shake off the night and resume the commonplace business of the day.

Where, indeed, did warriors and Gods go? This was Suzanne Helling's world. It had no place for warriors and deities. Its own God had, in fact, been declared dead.

Alouzon felt dizzy, but the safety of her world and her people depended on her, and therefore as Suzanne Helling—newly arrived in a strange world and a strange body—had once shoved aside all thoughts and goals save those of survival, so now Alouzon Dragonmaster did the same.

Slowly, she stripped off her armor and bundled it around the Dragonsword, leaving herself clad only in a relatively unobtrusive knee-length tunic and boots. Recalling the existence of such things as public rest rooms, she found one, and though derelicts and junkies stared at the tall, well-muscled woman who strode up to the dirty sink, they said nothing to her, for Alouzon cleaned the cut on her throat and rinsed off the slime and blood that coated her arms and face with the manner of someone who would tolerate no questions or interference.

The water cleared her head. Her scrapes burned, and her throat stung, but that helped too, for it kept her focused on the task at hand. Slinging her armor and sword over her shoulder, she climbed the slope to Wilshire Boulevard, crossed to the westbound side, and stuck out her thumb to flag down a ride.

She was going to save her world and her people. But first she had to survive.

Early June. The sun had not yet appeared above the Camrann Mountains, but the invasion fleet bobbed in the quiet inlet, waiting for the word to sail.

Darham met Cvinthil on the dock. The morning air was fresh, with only a hint of the night's chill remaining, and a coracle waited at the base of the steps down to the water. "Well met," said Cvinthil, extending his hand. "I am sorry that our visits must stem from war and not from neighborliness."

"Ah, well. We must take our calves as they are born." Darham clasped hands and reminded himself to smile. But he glanced at the men who were with Cvinthil: one or two veteran members of the King's Guard, a scribe, a scattering of officials from Quay. "Is Helwych not here?"

Cvinthil shook his head as though puzzled by the question. "He has stayed behind in Kingsbury. He is still weak from his wounds."

"Ah . . . yes . . ." Darham glanced to the side. Calrach's lips were pursed, and the commander shook his head slightly. "I had hoped to talk with him."

An older man, one of the representatives from Quay, spoke up. "It is indeed strange, lord, that he would not come to meet his king.'' His voice was weak, and he leaned on the arm of a woman.

Cvinthil pressed his lips together, bent his head. ''Are you still suspicious, Hahle?''

The man nodded slowly. ''I am, lord. I will not lie.''

Darham met Hahle's eyes and there read that not all of Gryylth had been wholly convinced by Helwych's tale. Some who had seen and talked with the young sorcerer obviously felt that something was not right.

The coracle bobbed like a cork. Sea gulls wheeled in the blue sky, crying mournfully. The sun suddenly flared in an arc of gold above the mountains.

Darham took Cvinthil's arm. ''A word with you in private, brother king,'' he said softly. He pulled Cvinthil out of earshot of the others.

''Well?'' said Cvinthil. ''If I guess rightly, you seem not to trust your own sorcerer.''

''He was a good lad, Cvinthil. If there was anything wrong with him, it was but the product of frustrated ambition and too many hours spent over books. A nature like that of a colt kept too long penned. But this Helwych that comes back bearing tales of slaughter . . .'' Darham shook his head, his beard glistening in the new sunlight. ''Something is wrong.''

Cvinthil's eyes had hardened with kingship. ''Can you tell me, friend Darham, what that might be?''

Darham shook his head. ''He does not seem the same, somehow.''

''And this you can say without meeting him face-to-face.''

Darham heard the flatness in Cvinthil's tone. *Hasty. Too hasty. Tarwach was like this, but he listened to me . . . until that last meeting.* But aloud he said: ''I could not help but mark the words of the man you called Hahle.''

''He could give me no more reason than you,'' said Cvinthil, impatience plain in his voice. ''By your advice I sent a scouting party to Vaylle. Among them were two of your people. Well, they are now dead.''

Darham did not respond. Out across the water, the boats were waiting.

''Do you not care?'' Cvinthil pressed. ''Are you willing to leave a member of your own guard unavenged? And what about Karthin? He was your friend.''

The accusation stung, and Darham glared Cvinthil in the eye. ''My friend, and my guard, and one other,'' he said. ''Wykla was too modest to tell you that I called her daughter while she was in Corrin. So I have lost a child, and Corrin has lost a princess. And if there is vengeance to be had, then by the Gods I will have it.''

Turning abruptly, he strode back across the dock, the planking echoing hollowly beneath his boots. With a gesture for Calrach to follow, he descended the steps to the waiting coracle.

Alouzon did not have to wait long for a ride. The sky had barely begun to lighten when an old Mercury pulled up, radio blaring. Alouzon winced at the music. A little over a week ago, in Quay, she would have given anything to hear rock and roll. Now the music was merely a reminder of the foreignness of this place.

''Where ya goin'?'' said the man behind the wheel. He was in his twenties, his thin face pocked with old acne scars, and he reeked of cigarette smoke.

Alouzon shrugged inwardly. She had survived Bandon and Broceliande. She could deal with a little nicotine. ''Out towards UCLA,'' she said. ''Bel Air would be even better.''

''Gotcha. Hop in.''

He gestured, and she pulled the passenger door open, tossed her armor and sword in the back seat, and settled in on the worn upholstery.

Despite the Mercury's faded exterior, its engine was

in excellent shape. Acceleration shoved Alouzon back in her seat as the car roared out into the left lane.

"Jia would be jealous," she murmured to herself.

The driver blinked at her with dark eyes. "Jia?"

Lights were passing: street lights, traffic signals, the neon glow of bars and storefronts. Alouzon regarded them with a clenched throat. "Uh . . . a friend of mine."

"Don't I know you?"

She nearly laughed, but she stifled it: she was afraid she would start crying. "No. You don't."

The big Mercury cruised out towards Western. "Sure I do. Lessee. Uh . . . waitaminute. I remember: you're a waitress. I seen you up at the . . . uh . . . Tropicana. Yeah, that's it. I go there all the time. You do that mud wrestling. You girls got some muscles, I'll tell you. And you're built like goddesses." He grinned at her. "I got me a celebrity."

Despite her efforts in the park rest room, Alouzon decided that she probably made the mud wrestling girls look clean by comparison. "Sorry. You're out of luck."

The driver was unfazed. "You comin' back from a party?"

She snorted softly. "I wish."

The city went by. Western Avenue and the green porcelain of the Wiltern Theater, then Wilton Place. Early morning, pre-dawn: traffic was light, and the Mercury purred and grumbled along Wilshire as though it were a jungle cat marking its kingdom.

"What'cha do for a living?"

Trainee God came to mind. Alouzon shrugged. "I get by."

"You interested in earning a little extra cash?"

She read his meaning. It would have been easy to become angry, but she had other things on her mind. "Sorry. Not interested."

"Come on, I'm not a cop. Fifty?"

"No. Give it up." *Just get me to Bel Air, dick-head. I've got things to do.*

He frowned petulantly. Face set, he glowered over the wheel, took the turning onto Highland, and cruised up the street at ten miles an hour over the speed limit.

"This isn't going to get us to Bel Air any time soon," said Alouzon.

"I know what I'm doing."

"Suit yourself." She settled back, tried to decide what she should do after she had picked up her car. Go home? What was home? "By the way: what day is it?"

He grinned. "You don't know? It's Saturday. Musta' been some party."

"Yeah," she said. "Quite a party." 3.5-inch rockets, and Skyhawks, and hounds whose blood melted flesh like hot lye. And then the Specter.

The Mercury passed beneath the Hollywood Freeway, but, caught up in her thoughts, Alouzon did not notice for a minute. When she did, she chewed it over in her mind for a moment, then: "All right, dude. Where are you taking me?"

He did not look at her. "I got some friends that want to meet you, girl."

"Not interested."

He pulled up at a stop sign. "Sorry, dude," said Alouzon. She reached for the door handle. It had been removed. The Mercury pulled out again, tires screeching. "Say, guy, what the fuck is going—"

She broke off. He had drawn a knife and was holding it a few inches from her linen tunic. "Just sit still, babe, and you won't get hurt," he said. "You got a cute body and you had your chance to make a few bucks with it. But you turned it down. Now it's all gonna be for free."

The Mercury picked up speed. Alouzon examined the knife. Sharp, but thin and cheap, it was, she decided, suitable only for abducting properly socialized females. "Cute," she said, biting back her anger. "Does it come in an adult size?"

He drove on. The car was traveling too fast for her to make a move. As Gryylth, Corrin, and Vaylle hung balanced in precarious existence, she bided her time.

The man turned into the maze of streets that wound through the hills east of Hollywood Lake. Houses here were dark and set back behind overgrown gardens and unkempt lawns. Trees that had not seen a pruning in twenty years straggled and drooped over roofs and power lines.

The Mercury slowed because of the twists in the road. The shoulders of the road were unpaved, and a vacant lot appeared ahead, overgrown with grass and weeds.

The lot was on the right now, passing swiftly. Alouzon moved. Grabbing the hand that held the knife, she bent it back until she heard the wrist snap. The sound was as gratifying as the harsh, sucking intake of breath that came from the man's lips.

The Mercury wavered. Backhanding the driver with a fist, Alouzon grabbed the wheel and ran the car over the unpaved shoulder and into the tall grass of the vacant lot. With a free hand, she grabbed the ignition key and pulled it out, but when the car continued running she cursed aloud and pushed down on the brake pedal with her hand until the engine lugged and stalled.

Wary of another knife, she shoved herself away from the man, but he was looking at a right hand bent back at a crazy angle. Pieces of bone stuck out of his wrist, and blood was oozing from the rents they had left.

Pain finally cut through his shock, and he started to scream. "You . . . you . . ."

Cities had been razed. Dindrane's people had been decimated. And Cvinthil and an army bent on revenge were making for Vaylle. There was too much death in the past and future for Alouzon to be bothered by the whining of one bully.

She reached to her boot and extracted her own dagger. It was small, but its leaf-shaped blade was broad, sharp, and built for fighting. It made the man's stiletto seem a child's toy. "You're playing with the big girls now, shit-for-brains," she whispered, laying the point against his throat.

His screams cut off. He started to whine frantically, and he made a lunge for the door handle, but she caught him by the shirt.

"You're not going anywhere," she said. "And shut the fuck up. I've seen men with wounds a lot worse than yours holding their own against three." Alouzon gave him a shake. "You goddam wimp."

She kicked out the passenger side window, opened the door from the outside, and sprinted around the car. Jerking open the driver's door before he had time to move, she shoved him to the far side of the car and slid in behind the wheel. "Don't even think about trying anything," she said.

Terrified, holding the ruin of his wrist, he stared at her as she restarted the car, backed out of the lot, and drove down to Highland. Taking the turning onto Sunset, she made her way westward, faintly astonished that she could operate anything more technologically complex than a horse. But the Mercury purred along under her guidance as her would-be abductor cowered in the corner.

She glanced at him. His eyes were glazed with pain, his wrist was bloody, swollen, and discoloring with massive bruises. But her pity evaporated when she thought of what he had intended to do to her—what he would have done to another woman with less experience in fighting.

The man groaned and shut his eyes, obviously expecting no more mercy than he himself had been prepared to give. But Alouzon shook her head and turned onto Helen's street, still wondering at the anomaly of her strong brown hands on a welded chain-link steering wheel. Just around a bend from the house, she made a U-turn, stopped, and pulled on the parking brake. "OK, buddy. It's your turn again."

He stared, unbelieving, but after dumping her armor and sword onto the asphalt, Alouzon got out, grabbed him by the shirt, and dragged him over behind the wheel. Her knife was in her hand again.

"Now," she said, holding the blade to his throat, "you drive. And you drive real good. The UCLA Medical Center is at Le Conte and Tiverton, right by the campus. They've got an emergency room there: they can fix your wrist." She started to close the door, but a thought struck her and she stopped and leaned towards him. "And don't ever think you're gonna use a knife to grab a little piece of ass again, 'cause I'll fix you good if you do."

She slammed the door and picked up her armor. The man dithered at the wheel, groped for the parking brake and the shift with his good hand.

She kicked the side of the car. *"Move."*

Shakily, weaving back and forth, he drove off down the street. The sound of the Mercury's engine faded into the distance.

But its rumble was replaced by another, and when Alouzon turned towards the bend in the road, she saw the trees and shrubs lit by the reflection of flashing lights: red, blue, yellow, white. A helicopter was circling above, its searchlight stabbing down into the darkness, the roar of its engine blending with the distinctive sound of idling fire and rescue trucks.

She suddenly remembered the attack on Helen's house. Weeks had passed in Gryylth. Los Angeles had known only a few hours.

Lugging her armor and sword, she turned the corner and found that the house was a ruin of glass, brick, steel, and wood. As though a great weight had fallen upon it, it had been demolished so thoroughly that the two-story structure now rose no higher than the head of a tall man. Police cars were parked in the street and on the lawn, and officers and firefighters were examining the wreckage cautiously.

Radios crackled with unintelligible orders. The odor of smoke and diesel exhaust hung in the damp air beneath the trees. Alouzon hesitated, then forced herself forward, trying to walk casually. She was just here to pick up her car. Clenching her teeth at the alien sights and sounds, she took the spare key from beneath the VW's bumper, unlocked the door, and put her armor and sword inside.

But for a moment before she got in and drove away, she turned around to the lights and the wreckage. Helen's house was as ruined as Bandon. All that was missing was the stench of napalm and the charred bodies of the dead.

And then she saw that the paramedics were wheeling two gurneys out to the waiting ambulance. A still form occupied each cart, and white cotton blankets were pulled up over the faces.

❖ CHAPTER 5 ❖

At times now, Helwych wondered if he could see everything, for the world at times had come to resemble a great, open map, like one of those in Tireas's old texts that depicted other worlds and distant countries spread out before his curious eyes.

He was indoors, and the shutters were closed. Physically, he could see no further than the walls, floor, and ceiling; but, in his mind's eye, Gryylth was a particolored daubing of life and activity, its people minute, antic dancers. He saw Cvinthil aboard ship with Darham. He saw the months-old ruins of Bandon sprouting with grass and weeds. He saw Seena caring for her children with the same obsessive single-mindedness that had driven her husband from her side. He saw Relys pacing nervously in her house. He saw Timbrin standing on the other side of his shuttered window.

Toys, all of them. Little toys that would soon be his.

Deep within his mind, blue-black eyes suddenly blinked curiously, and he hastened to re-direct his thoughts. *Ours,* he thought. *They will soon be ours.*

But in the few corners of his mind that remained his own, he had formulated other plans. There, the possessive remained *mine.*

The Specter had given him much: wizardry that made the potencies of Tireas and Mernyl seem mere dabblings, a will that could wrap itself about the thoughts and feelings of others and manipulate them as a child might play with a doll, a sense of subtlety.

But for the Specter, all those gifts were as spears that wounded the hand, for in sending him to Gryylth and turning its attention to whatever end it had planned for Alouzon and her company, it had given Helwych a certain freedom, a certain breadth of thought; and, empowered as he was with borrowed magics and skills, he had surreptitiously turned along his own road, one that would lead first to Gryylth, and then to Corrin itself.

Daydreaming, savoring the success of his plans, he had allowed his eyes to close, but now he opened them. He was sitting in his working chair to the east of the circle he had inscribed on the floor of the house Cvinthil had given him. Triangles, squares, and multi-pointed stars—mnemonic emblems of the powers he commanded—filled the floor within the circle, and at the very center, floating a hand's breadth from the ground like a lifted scepter, was his staff. To others it had seemed a crutch, but that was as much the stuff of illusion as the injuries he had been feigning for the last three and a half months.

That the staff was floating was a good sign: it meant that the potencies he had summoned the evening before were building towards their climax. Even as he watched, the outlines of the circle were taking on a nimbus of red and violet, and when he reached a hand towards the edge of the working space, he felt his flesh tingle.

Good. Very good indeed. The Specter had wanted only a curtain wall that would bar the return of the flotilla, but it was about to receive much more than that.

He paused and looked beyond the walls of his house. Timbrin was still at the window, keeping watch. The flotilla had sailed halfway across the White Sea. The potencies he had summoned were at their peak. It was time.

He rose from his chair, not with a tottering lurch, but with the spring of a young man, and he removed his shabby outer robe to reveal an inner garment of white samite. A wave of his hand opened a door in the circle through which he entered. Another wave closed it behind him. Here, in the heart of the raised potencies, magic crackled across his skin in hot waves that lifted his lank hair away from his scalp and sent coruscations of crimson fire through the expanding field of his inner vision.

Now he could see Timbrin as though he stood behind her. Silly, meddling woman. She would learn her place. As would Relys.

Helwych took up his staff with a quiet smile. He had a wall to create, but there would be a sizable backlash of energy. It would be a simple matter to direct a handful of it at Timbrin. She might die; she might not. In any case, Helwych was not worried. Gryylth and its queen would be his, and his four wartroops would be without opposition in the land.

He was not shielding his intentions. He had no need to. In minutes, not only would Cvinthil, Darham, and all their warriors be barred from Gryylth, but also the Specter itself.

But as he began the working, a thought came to him unbidden: Corrin was his homeland. Darham had always treated him decently, and had, as though to make up for Tireas's neglect, even encouraged his studies. And Alouzon and her friends might have smirked at him, but on the road to Bandon they had fought against the hounds in order to save his life.

Why did he want to bring destruction and pain to such as these?

He steeled himself, recentered his thoughts, and went on. The energy mounted. Physical reality seemed to part before him, revealing the intricate workings of the universe—wheels within wheels, living light, planes of reified causality—and he stretched out his staff and stirred the matrix of existence as though it

were one of the courtless bowls of gruel he had eaten
and despised since he had arrived in Gryylth.

With a roar as of an angry ocean, worlds shifted,
blurred, flowed. In another minute, he would lift his
arms and send the result of his workings into the physical and non-physical world. It would become not
magic, not desire, but reality.

The blue-black eyes within him suddenly opened
wide. Too busy to gloat, Helwych only marked their
astonishment. But he noticed that the eyes were, for a
moment, not fixed on him at all. They were turned elsewhere, towards something that—incredibly—terrified
them.

He had little time to wonder. The energies were
building fast. Seconds now. Heartbeats. Then all
would be done.

A blinding scream slashed through his mind, loos-
ening his hold on the spell, and only the energies that
had solidified about him kept him from staggering to
the side. Reeling nonetheless in the suddenly chaotic
flow of power, he saw that the eyes were gone, banished by . . .

Banished by what? Nothing could drive those eyes
away. And yet . . .

But now even the scream was eclipsed by the thunder of energies in Helwych's ears. Released from his
careful manipulation, the spell was now out of control,
the energies whipping into raging turbulence as Helwych struggled desperately for balance. Gripping his
staff with sweat-slick hands, he grabbed for the strands
of the working and stuffed them back into their
carefully-wrought channels.

Shakily, the barrier formed, and a blackness rose up
in the White Sea, gusting mightily and wrapping itself
around the coastline of Gryylth and Corrin like a sable
curtain. But the world was quivering. All the Worlds,
in fact, were quivering. Rents were forming. Fissures.
Unintended gaps . . .

A flash of daylight. Timbrin, aroused by the tumult

within the house, had battered through the shuttered windows. She stared at Helwych for a moment.

Now the backlash was coming, falling like mountains. The entire spell was lashing out at Helwych; and with a last, panicked effort, he swung his staff over his head and managed to deflect the brunt of the catastrophe onto Timbrin. Caught full in the face by the energies, the small warrior was smashed away from the window.

But the tail end of the magics, sharp as a scorpion's sting, drove into Helwych: he fell heavily onto the flagstone floor, dimly aware not only of the wall he had formed, but also of eyes. Blue-black eyes. Eyes of void and darkness. *Stupid little Dremord fool,* they said. *But it really didn't make any difference now, did it?*

Alouzon drove home to the apartment of a stranger.

Her armor and sword rattled incongruously on the passenger seat of the VW, and her hands looked distant and tentative on the black plastic steering wheel. As the morning grew over Los Angeles, the sun glinting alike on high rise windows and her steel wrist cuffs, she peered out through the front window of the automobile like a child grappling with a fearful dream: wondering and yet afraid, defiant and yet impotent.

Suzanne Helling was dead.

The police had not identified the body yet, nor would they soon, for Suzanne's purse and its contents had been charred and smeared with corrosives beyond all recognition or retrieval. But Alouzon knew whose bodies were now traveling to the coroner's office, and she admitted that it made a kind of warped sense. In bringing down the Circle, Dythragor had died, crushed by his impact and incinerated in the resultant blast of energy. And yet Solomon Braithwaite's body had been waiting for Suzanne when she returned to the archaeology offices at UCLA.

Alouzon maneuvered the VW into the streets to the west of the campus. Suzanne had been dead since the attack on Helen's house. But where did that leave Alouzon Dragonmaster? And what about Kyria?

Shaking, she parked and shut off the engine. For a moment she was almost afraid to get out of the car for fear that whatever life and existence she possessed would suddenly prove to be illusion. But she pulled herself away from the thought, held her hands up before her face, and stared at them as though she would burn their images into her retinas. No: she was alive, and she was Alouzon. And this was Los Angeles.

Her boots made hollow sounds on the asphalt as, carrying the tackle and weapons of a warrior, she got out of the car and walked across the street to the apartment building. In spite of the heat and morning glare, the sunlight had an ephemeral, watery look to it; but it was not the sunlight that was wrong, it was Alouzon. She did not belong here. This was Suzanne's world.

And Suzanne was—

For a moment, she stood in the courtyard, staring up at the second-floor apartment that held as much of home as Suzanne Helling had known for the last three years. There she had lived, studied, made oatmeal and granola cookies, raged at the childish actions of her lover and the imperious methods of her professor. She had huddled in its bed, terrified of her past, and then— as Guardian of Gryylth—of her present and her future. She had dreamed of M1s, tear gas, and bullets . . . and of a campus slaughter that had pursued her throughout the years with a vicious memory that had eaten away at her life.

She was Alouzon now. It was all gone.

She found the spare key that Suzanne had hidden in the rock garden, and she climbed the stairs to the apartment and let herself in. She had never been here, and yet here were things she remembered: twenty pages of a first-draft dissertation hammered out on a

Smith Corona portable, a blow drier propped up on the shelf beside the bathroom sink, barrettes and clips that had held hair much longer and straighter than her own bronze mane, a notebook filled with scribbled memos and outlines in a hand that was perhaps not dissimilar to that which Alouzon herself would produce had she taken up a pen.

Alouzon set her bundle on the sofa, sat down on the floor where someone else had once done her morning yoga, and put her face in her hands. Her friends were in danger . . . or dead. She did not belong here. And she could do nothing about any of it.

"Please," she murmured to the Grail. "Don't do this to me. I can't take it. Just help me save my friends. That's all I want."

Fatigue fell on her then, and she nearly toppled: the adrenalin rush that had been sustaining her had exhausted itself. She realized fuzzily that she had not slept for several days.

But I can't sleep now. My friends . . .

There was a golden light in the room, though, a light that grew out of the corners and shadows and softened even the harsh glare of the Los Angeles sun that was pouring in through the windows. It lifted her as a mother might lift a weary child, put her on her feet, and guided her to the bedroom. It made her hands draw the blinds and turn on the air conditioning, and it laid her gently down.

Her eyes were closing. "I can't," she said softly. "I can't."

But the golden light was insistent, and she drifted off, clutching to herself like a beloved doll the memory of the words she had heard long ago: *Yeah, kid. It's gonna be all right.*

"Please," she whispered. "Please."

The sky was blue, the sea calm, the breeze from the east almost uncannily fresh. If Vaylle possessed sorcery, Cvinthil thought, then surely it was making a

poor showing of it by not opposing in the slightest the
progress of the men and weapons coming to attack it.

He wondered what Vorya would have thought of all
this. In the space of a little over three months, an army
had been raised, trained, and provisioned—and now it
was en route to battle. Cvinthil took no pride in the
achievement, for it seemed to him to be no more than
the proper response of any king of Gryylth. But he
still hoped that the old man, were he still alive, would
have nodded his white head gravely and uttered a soft
well done.

Though Vaylle was the enemy, it was Vorya, perhaps, with whom Cvinthil actually competed. For ten
years, the late king had guided his country through a
morass of war. To be sure, he, like everyone else, had
been wrong about the Corrinians, and there had been
breaks and cracks in the honor of both sides that eventually led to the transformation of the First Wartroop
and the slaughter of an entire generation of young men,
but Vorya had maintained through it all, and even in
his last days he had lost nothing of the stature of a
king.

And have I myself done the right thing?

Vaylle was appearing, rising up out of the water and
taking on detail as the flotilla approached. With any
luck at all, Gryylth's unexpected resolution and quick
reprisal would catch that evil land off guard. But
though most of the warriors and soldiers were looking
ahead, Darham, silent and thoughtful even after a day
and a half on the ocean, was staring back towards
Gryylth. He seemed to be pondering, examining the
distant fading land as though he hoped at this remove
to pierce the veils of distance and semblance and so
see, beneath the surface, something that would confirm or banish the suspicions that still gnawed at him.

Oh, we are but little kings, thought Cvinthil. *Tarwach and Vorya were giants, Darham and I but children in comparison.*

And what place had children in the business of war?

Cvinthil shrugged wearily. Child or not, he had to act, and he hoped that he acted rightly. Still, though, he wondered as he always wondered: What would Vorya have done? How would he have done it?

"Brother king," said Darham with his farmer's courtesy.

Cvinthil looked up dully. Vorya would have done just this, in just this way. He made himself believe that. "Aye?"

"Look behind."

At first Cvinthil saw nothing save blue water, blue sky, and a smear of green haze that indicated the distant coastline. But in another moment he had detected the obscurity that was shimmering into existence, dimming the sunlight about Gryylth.

"Clouds?"

"There are no clouds," said Darham. "The sky is clear."

Darkness grew in the distance. The wind died. The ocean turned glassy. Sails, deprived of the breeze, rattled uselessly, and the air turned leaden.

An attack from the Tree had numbed Vorya's arm, but the old king had dismissed the wound with disdain. Cvinthil's shoulder suddenly ached, and he wondered whether he could do the same. "Vaylle?" he said uneasily.

"Attacking Gryylth and Corrin in our absence?" Darham passed a hand over his beard. "Why would they wait so long? If they meant to attack, they might have killed us all while we lay at the docks of Quay."

Cvinthil shook his head. "They might not have been ready. And, in any case, Vaylle seems to thrive on cruelty. But we will give them a fight." Cupping his hands about his mouth, he shouted to the other boats. "Put about!"

The darkness turned to gray, then black. Darham shook his head. "A field half reaped is a field wasted. We are closer to Vaylle than to Gryylth, and if, as

Helwych says, each attack weakens the Vayllen sorcerers, then they are now open for conquest.''

Cvinthil was incredulous. ''You would leave your people to die?''

There was a touch of amusement in Darham's blue eyes. ''A day and a half ago you were all but accusing me of being faint-hearted,'' he said. ''Now you think me unfeeling.''

His voice fell flat in the sullen air, but then his words were swept away by a rising wind. A gale arose from the east, filling the sails to bursting; and though the steersmen fought with their oars and the pilots barked orders, their efforts were useless, for the wind drove the boats towards Vaylle like a child sweeping rushes with a broom.

Cvinthil lost his footing and would have toppled overboard but for Darham, who grabbed the Gryylthan and pulled him down below the level of the gunwale. ''Kings cannot command the winds,'' he shouted over the storm. ''Best to let the sailors do their tasks without our meddling.''

The ship bucked and tossed like a frightened horse. The wind continued to rage, and the very substance of the sea and the ships seemed to quiver in its blast. As though a curtain had fallen over it, Gryylth was now hidden in a shroud of darkness, and Cvinthil thought of Seena and his children, wondered what might be happening to them behind that veil. He wanted to scream, he wanted to weep, but he could not allow himself that luxury.

He held to Darham. What would Vorya have done? This very thing, he hoped. But Vorya, confronted with the loss of his homeland, would do something else, too. And so would his successor. ''I swear to you, brother Darham,'' he said, though his words were all but blown away, ''Vaylle may well bring us to its shores for sport, but it will find its pleasure turned to pain when we arrive.''

* * *

Solomon's office was much as Alouzon remembered it: severe and cluttered both, the battered mahogany desk shoved into the corner beside the packed bookshelves, and the old man's reading glasses perched atop a stack of papers. But one wall opened out onto a dark seashore, and that she did not remember. The water was gray, troubled, unlit by the overhead fluorescents; and breakers foamed up the shingle and crept almost all the way to the institutional linoleum that covered the floor. The sky was black, and no stars relieved its sable darkness.

Alouzon sat at the dead man's desk, leafing through old photo albums and indices of Anglo-Saxon and Welsh names. The names—Sandde, Cynwyl, Morgan—told her little more than she already knew, for Gryylth was, after all, a study in recreation, an old scholar's frantic fantasies touched with history and then brought to life in a tangle of wish-fulfillment, repressed hope, and unadmitted fear.

The photos—some faded and yellow with age, some sharp and clear with the exacting precision of quality Polaroids and expensive SLRs—were of her own life and origins: her grandfather marching with the Wobblies at the Lawrence textile strike, her parents taking their daughter to picnics and political rallies, prom dresses and tuxedos, high school graduation . . .

. . . and then—blurry with half-tone reproduction, endless handling, and tears—there were the pictures of Kent State.

Alouzon leafed through them all slowly, noting as she did that the pages vanished after she turned them, the images they carried dissolving into mist. And when she was done, even the album faded. She was left in an office lapped at by turbulent waters and filled with the sounds and smells of a dark, endless sea.

She waited. She was supposed to wait.

Finally, floating above the water with a steadiness that disdained the surging of the waves beneath it, came a shrouded, golden thing. It approached in a haze of light, passed soundlessly up the shore and into the office. It hung before Alouzon Dragonmaster, a beating, pulsing glory that seemed not so much precious metal as living flesh and blood, and beneath its veil she sensed an upwelling of eternal waters, waters that invisibly, cascaded to the floor and inundated the universe.

Take what you need.

She understood and reached out her hands to the flow. She could not lift this cup yet: it was too early. But the Grail nurtured those in need, and Alouzon washed her face in what seemed to be pure life, the endless fatigue falling from her, the breaks and splits and fissures that had marred her existence beginning to fill and heal.

Face dripping with something that was like immortality, she gazed at the wondrous thing before her. "Please," she said softly. "Can you help my friends?"

The glory wavered and then was gone. Alouzon understood: without doubt, the Grail would help her friends. It could, by its very nature, do nothing else. But by having to question it, Alouzon had shown her ignorance, and therefore her unworthiness to attain it as of yet.

When the questions are all done, then you will be ready.

"When they're done?" she murmured into the roar of the sea, "or when they all just don't matter anymore?"

But out on the ocean, tossing on the waves, there was more movement. Bobbing and rocking, a boat with sere, torn sails floated to the shore and ground to a halt on the gravel. For a moment, it lay as though untenanted, but then a pale hand gripped the gunwale, and a withered head rose into view.

Slimy with decay, his long-dead fingers stiff with rigor mortis, his bloodless face pale with embalming fluids and seamed with the slippage of mortician's wax and make-up, Solomon Braithwaite crawled out of the boat and dragged himself up through the lap of waves. He made his way almost blindly, as though drawn by the Grail, but he stopped at Alouzon's feet and lay down beside her boots.

"I'm here," he said.

Alouzon was shaking. "Why?"

The corpse lifted a dripping, mottled head. "I'm here to confess."

Solomon's eyes were glazed with rot, and Alouzon tried not to meet them; but the plea that thrust itself out of their yellow ruin was such that she could not turn away. "Confess?" she managed. "Confess what?"

And then Solomon started. Bit by bit, the accumulated horrors and atrocities of his life passed the lips of his corpse. His anger, his cruelty, his willingness to inflict both upon others dribbled out like a flow of impure blood, and the tale of Helen's forced abortions racked his decaying body as the stainless steel instruments ravaged her womb.

His hands fumbled and clutched at the linoleum as he supplied one damning detail after another, and his polished oxford shoes scuffed helplessly, doll-like. It was all, really, a kind of a war. A war upon the innocent. A war upon all the quiet, little people who had stayed at home while the battles raged through the falling snows of Korea. And overlaying it all, tinting it with the hues of blood and envy, was the frantic ambition of a soldier chained to a desk and a pile of reconnaissance photographs.

Alouzon listened, and she thought of Vaylle. How much of Solomon's feelings had she unconsciously shared? How much anger had been hidden by the wall of despair and guilt that she had erected in the days following the shootings at Kent State? And upon whom had she vented it?

Frightened by the correspondence, she recoiled from

the decaying thing at her feet. "Why . . . why do you have to tell me this?" she said.

Solomon fixed her once more with his rotting eyes. "I want to be clean," he said. "I have to be clean. I turned away from the Grail. I'll never find it now. But I'm not clean, and so I can't rest." His hands clutched at her boots and left a film of slime on their smooth brown leather.

Alouzon swallowed her fear. "How am I supposed to help you to be clean?"

"You're the Goddess."

The title smacked her in the face. "I'm just a dumb shit girl!"

The corpse almost smirked. "No. Maybe once. But not any more."

"I didn't want this."

"You got it anyway." Solomon rested his head on the linoleum, panting with the exertions of a dead thing that clings stubbornly to a semblance of life. "Once I thought that it was Silbakor that chose you to be Guardian. Now I know that it was much bigger than that. It was the Grail. It's always been the Grail."

"But Silbakor—"

"Don't listen to Silbakor," the corpse snapped. "Silbakor doesn't understand anything except Gryylth. Listen to me." He cackled: the dry sound of a file on metal. "I'm dead. I'm supposed to know a few things."

The darkness that bore down upon the ocean suddenly wavered, shifted. In the night, a deeper night appeared, flickered, subsided.

Solomon lifted his head as though sniffing the air. "Helwych."

My boy, Helwych, the Specter had called him in the temple of Broceliande. And Cvinthil and an army were bearing down on Vaylle. And her friends . . .

The deeper darkness gnawed at the edges of dream and distance. Alouzon stood, reached for her sword. "What's he done?"

The corpse shook his head. "Maybe ended the world. Maybe saved it. It's hard to tell sometimes, even when you're dead." He started back for the waves, but paused at the shore. "I didn't make it, but you might. You've got the stuff."

There was a roar, the night split, and darkness surged forward in a rushing wall, foaming towards the shore in a wave of nothingness.

The corpse turned to meet it. "I'll be there if you need me. Remember that."

❖ CHAPTER 6 ❖

Though they were burned by phosphor, cut by shrapnel and stone splinters, and had gone without sleep or even rest for several days, the surviving members of Alouzon's reconnaissance party pushed on through ravines and stagnant pools and stands of elephant grass that razored their already-lacerated skin. The peaks and cliffs of the Cordillera were high and jagged, the jungles fetid and hot, and the way down the slopes was no easier than the way up; but Cvinthil and an army were on their way to Vaylle.

Night came, then morning. The sun rose out of the shroud that hung over distant Gryylth, flickering with lightning and pulsing like a black heart. That it was a barrier of some kind was obvious, but Kyria—probing with her art while her body grunted and sweated down the mountainside—sensed something more about it, something that smacked of space, of distance, and of worlds.

What, she wondered, had the Specter done? What had Helwych done? Certainly not anything completely expected. By anyone. Including, possibly, the Specter itself.

The summer sun was at the zenith when they reached the slopes below the jungle, and the warm breeze from the flatlands smelled of crops and of the distant sea. Santhe took the point as the party wound down a narrow defile that followed the contours of the mountainside, but the way ended suddenly in a broad slope of bare stone. It was wide and even, but its angle and the debris that covered it would make any descent treacherous.

Santhe's arms and legs were cut and bleeding, and the leech bites that studded his skin still ran with trickles of blood. He stared blearily at the slab. "Did we really climb that?"

Marrha—Marrget no longer—forced a tired smile. "Did you fly, councilor?"

Her voice made him brighten, and a shred of humor forced its way through his exhaustion. "Indeed, dear friend, we often wished that we could at the time. But in looking at this I think we must have done so in truth."

Marrha nodded. "Then I must double and triple my thanks to all." She offered a hand to Manda, and the maid took it.

Santhe examined the slopes above and below. "I believe this is the way we came."

Dindrane was leaning heavily against the wall of the defile. She nodded. " 'Tis true."

Reluctantly, still puzzled by the barrier surrounding Gryylth, Kyria turned her powers to her immediate surroundings. "There was a landslide," she said after a moment. "Much has happened in the three months that has passed in the world."

Out on the horizon, the darkness roiled and billowed. Somewhere on the ocean were Cvinthil and a flotilla of ships. Three months. Indeed, much had happened.

Santhe shrugged. "We must descend somehow, and quickly. Is there another way, priestess?"

Dindrane shook her head. "Not for some distance." She sat down heavily and buried her face in grimy hands. Manda made her drink what was left of her ration of water.

Wykla looked up at Kyria. Her face was worn. "I dislike this place, lady Kyria. It makes me think of

more than landslides. And we have seen traps before.''

''Thank you, child. Haven't we, though . . .'' Kyria
frowned, pondering. Wykla was right. There was more
to the slab ahead than the fresh scars of abused rock,
and when she reached out with her mind, feeling it as
though with great, invisible hands, she discovered, just
beyond the far edge, a deep pit filled with upright,
pointed stakes and, yes, another trip wire.

With an inward nod, she returned to herself and told
the others to retreat back up the trail. When they had,
she sighed and shoved a large rock down the slope. It
slid across the smooth slab, teetered on the far edge,
and finally fell in a clatter of sand and gravel. Kyria
threw herself flat in a tangle of ragged robes and black
hair, and the air was suddenly filled with detonations
as concealed claymore mines sent waves of buckshot
across the surface of the slab in a crossfire sufficient
to disintegrate a human body.

The explosions died away. Kyria rose, shaking.
''You think your kind supreme in the world,'' she said
when she found her voice, ''but while I am here you
shall not triumph.''

She cast her arms to left and right. With Helen gone,
she was in full possession of her powers, and without
effort she lifted her thoughts to the bright sun and
called down a torrent of yellow flame that enveloped
her in a swirling maelstrom of incandescence.

It burned, but it cleansed, too; and for a moment
she allowed it to play on her body and sear away what
it could of Broceliande. After a minute, though, she
roused herself, cupped her hands, and by double handfuls scattered the solar fire out onto the stone slope.
The rock sizzled and ran like water.

And then the flame was gone. The slope had been
carved into steps that would provide a sure footing,
and the pit on the far side had been filled.

Kyria bowed, thanked the sun, then bent and

touched the first step. The fused rock was glassy, but cool. "I suppose, given time, I might become fairly good at this," she murmured. She turned to the others with an encouraging smile. "Come. To Lachrae."

But her companions stayed clustered protectively around Dindrane, who was sitting on the bare rock beside a twisted pillar of basalt. The priestess had been maintaining her composure admirably in the face of the losses and revelations she had encountered, but the shock of the explosion had finally pushed her endurance past its limits. Arms wrapped about herself, she wept softly, swaying back and forth like a lonely, frightened child.

" 'Tis all gone," she sobbed. "Everything is gone."

Her sorrow was genuine and bitter, and it wrenched at Kyria's heart. She sent the others on ahead, and when she was alone with Dindrane, she knelt beside her. "It is not all gone," she said gently.

Dindrane would not look at her. "I judged you all. I thought you murderers, and I hated you. I thought you barbarians, and I despised you." She finally lifted her head, and her eyes, as blue as the sea, held the desolation of arctic waters. "And you have more nobility in the fingers of your hands than I have in my entire being."

Karthin was helping Marrha over the edge of the slab, his expression tender and anxious, his hands strong and loving. He touched his wife as though she were a queen. Dindrane watched them for a moment, then bent her head and sobbed again.

Time was passing. Cvinthil was on the way. But Kyria's voice was soft and gentle. "Give yourself the grace you now extend to others, sister. Regardless of your judgments on them, those people are your friends, and they love you."

The phosphor burn was a dark blotch on Dindrane's pale cheek, and her long blond hair was matted with dirt. The golden torque about her neck seemed not so much a symbol of rank as a cynical incongruity. "Everything . . . everything is gone. My husband is dead. And my land, eighteen months old and the creation of a woman like myself, is being destroyed from within and without."

Gentleness was accomplishing nothing. Clenching her teeth at the brutality of her action, Kyria grabbed the priestess by the front of her tunic and pulled her up until they were nose-to-nose. "I cannot undo what has been done, sister of mine," she whispered. "Baares gave his life for another. And Vaylle is as it is. And Alouzon is its Goddess. If you think us noble, then be grateful that you also have such nobility in your deity and your land."

Dindrane's eyes turned bleaker. "Eighteen months."

Kyria nodded. "Yes, and a little over a decade for Gryylth."

"And we are so wrong. Wrong about everything." Dindrane looked down at her boy's clothes as though they told the entire story of the error.

Kyria jerked on Dindrane's tunic until she looked up. "I know where you came from," said the sorceress, "and I know why, and I can tell you that you and Vaylle are all the hopes and aspirations that Alouzon has ever had."

Dindrane blinked at the revelation.

Kyria shook her. "Do you think that Gods have it all made?" she cried. The idiom sounded strange on her tongue, but the words were appropriate. "They have their problems just like we have ours."

Dindrane's eyes seemed fixed on something a quarter mile away. "But we are being killed! And now your king . . ."

"Then do something about it!" Abruptly, Kyria let go of Dindrane's tunic and folded her in her arms. "You told us once that you were Vaylle," she said softly. "But now it is important to everyone that you

be Vaylle indeed. You have seen the Grail, and you
have spoken face-to-face with your Goddess. There is
strength there. Use it. Take it to your people. Help
them. If they must fight, teach them to fight. If they
have to die, show them how to die well. But for Alouzon's sake, bring them word of Cvinthil's approach.''

Marrha's voice carried to them suddenly, clear and
sweet: "Kyria! Dindrane! Do you need help?"

"In a moment," called Kyria. *Please, Dindrane.
You can do it.* The darkness roiled. The flotilla drew
closer. *You must.*

Staring, but thoughtful, Dindrane nodded slowly.
Her hand reached out and drew the ritual knife that
was stuck in her belt. After Baares had been killed,
she had performed the Great Rite herself, holding both
cup and knife in an act of spiritual union that had
reached out beyond the symbolic to encompass the
change in her very identity.

Male, female; active, receptive: she had both sides
of all qualities and attributes. She was Vaylle indeed:
as it had been, as it was, as it could be.

She shoved the blade back into its sheath. "Sister,"
she said, looking up, "will you help me down this
slope?"

Her eyes had cleared. There was steel in her voice.
Kyria offered her arm, and Dindrane took it.

Seena.
The queen of Gryylth struggled in the grip of nightmares that pinned her in sleep. She fought against the
dark shadows, but they pulled her farther down into
sights and sounds that she did not want to see.
Seena. Seena.
The voices called mockingly. What could she do for
Gryylth? She was a woman. She understood children
and households, cooking and spinning and weaving,
but not commerce, markets, and decrees. Cvinthil
could declare equality with a lifted hand and a few

words, but he could not so easily make it real; and so Seena stared at the dream landscape that surrounded her, a realm populated by pleading eyes, outstretched hands, empty bellies. Homeless child-wraiths wandered the countryside in search of food and shelter, were dragged down by ravening hounds, were killed by strange beings with gray faces and incomprehensible weapons.

Seena.

Houses burned, people died, and children with empty eyes and amputated limbs were driven into rain and storm. It was the antithesis of everything she desired as a woman and a mother.

And where are your own children, Seena?

They were, by the grace of the nameless Gods, safe in the most secure fortress in Gryylth. Helwych had thought it best to move the queen and her children to Hall Kingsbury, and Seena had bowed to his caution. There were awful things abroad in the night—Hahle himself had been attacked just outside the town, and now Timbrin had been missing for several days—and only four wartroops were left to defend the land.

Your children, Seena?

She saw them then: naked and bound, stretched out before the implacable hounds. Eyes like lamps burned down on their faces, and glowing mouths opened to drip phosphor on their soft throats.

Seena was suddenly screaming, battling her way through rank vines and fetid hands, struggling towards her son and daughter. "Take anything you want," she cried. "Take me, take my life, take my land, but spare them!"

Anything?

Hedges of thorn and pools of slime now. She tore the thorns asunder, leaped across the pools. A sword was suddenly in her hand, and though all her womanly conditioning and instincts rebelled at the touch of the weapon, she lashed out at the beasts that threatened her children.

The hounds fell, and their blood ran in a putrid stream away into the far distance where a black wall had suddenly arisen to bring a deeper darkness to the endless night. But when Seena fell to her knees beside Ayya and Vill, they were unmoving. Bound and gagged, their eyes closed, they did not even struggle.

Where are your children, Seena?

With a shriek, she pulled herself out of the dream and opened her eyes. Lit only by a low fire, the walls seemed to shift and flicker, and she was not at all sure that she was not still asleep. But not even when she rose and stumbled across the room did the sense of nightmare dissipate. She felt as though she waded through water, or forced herself through thick hedges; but she knelt beside the sleeping forms of her children—Ayya in her white gown, Vill still in swaddling—and shook them gently. "Ayya. Vill."

But they did not stir.

It was just at dawn that the soldiers came to the house of Kallye the midwife, pounding on the door and shouting in the loud voices of young men who are feeling self-important. Kallye—used to being roused at all hours—was throwing on a robe and padding barefoot across the floor even before she realized that she was awake, and Gelyya, her apprentice, was already gathering up pouches and pots and stuffing them into Kallye's scrip.

"The instincts of a midwife," Kallye mumbled fuzzily, and she swung the door open and blinked at the tall soldier clad in the livery of the King's Guard.

"I am Dryyim," he said. "The queen commands your presence."

"Seena?" Kallye shook off the last shreds of sleep. "Is something wrong with Ayya and Vill?"

"My orders are to take you to the queen," said Dryyim flatly; and, behind him, his companions nodded.

Gelyya's red hair was a dusky blaze in the halflight. "What else shall I pack, mistress?"

Kallye considered. Dryyim was being uncooperative, but perhaps he knew nothing of the situation. Perhaps he did not want to. Many men were like that. Children meant little to them save as heirs and producers of heirs; and messy things like pregnancy and childbirth could easily send them running. "Just the usual, Gelyya."

Kallye threw a cloak over her robe, and Gelyya handed her the bundle. But when the apprentice made as if to follow her mistress, Dryyim scowled and shook his head. "Just the midwife," he said. "No more women present than needed."

His tone was ugly. Kallye flared. "Man," she said, "you came from woman."

He made as if to strike her, but seemed to think better of it. More than likely, Kallye considered, it would be difficult for him to explain the delivery of a damaged midwife.

But the possibility that Seena's children were ill quickened her steps as she followed the men up the street, and she kept pace with their long strides until they reached the palisade. Then she was shoved roughly up to the guardhouse at the gate, and a young man—they were all young men, these soldiers—examined her critically. "This is Kallye," he said at last. "Let her through."

Kallye had never been in Hall Kingsbury before, for she had—fittingly, she thought—attended Seena, her births, and her children in Cvinthil's house, a setting infinitely more domestic than this place of guards and questions. Kallye was concerned with homely things: mothers, mothers-to-be, children. She did not care about politics or policy.

But here, seemingly, the two had suddenly come together, for she was shown to a room within the hall where Seena was pacing frantically, wringing her hands. The queen's eyes were red with crying, and when she saw Kallye, she threw herself at the midwife. "There is something wrong with Ayya and Vill, Kallye. I cannot wake them. They just . . . they just lie there . . ."

Helwych, bent and in a ragged robe, stepped out of the shadows in the corner. "The physicians have examined them," he said dispassionately. "They can find nothing wrong. Actually . . ." He cleared his throat. "I suspect the worst."

Seena whirled on him. "Such blessings you call down on my children!"

Helwych's black eyes flickered. "The worst, my queen, is not death. I speak of sorcery."

Kallye set down her bundle. Midwife's instincts. There was something unhealthy in this room. Helwych's comments reeked of it, and the presence of so many young guards—jostling and glowering and hating every particle of these woman-matters—made her feel hemmed in and even frightened. Sorcery? Maybe. But whose? And what else?

Wondering at her thoughts, Kallye tried to soothe Seena, but the queen was hysterical and dragged her towards the unmoving forms of her children. The physicians had failed. Seena had called on her last hope.

Kallye was unwilling to leave Seena's side, but after a moment, she noticed that Relys was in the room. The warrior looked slender and almost fragile compared to the big men of the guard, and she stood as if she had decided that she was helpless in the face of Seena's distress. Kallye called her over and put the queen into her arms. Relys took her stiffly, unused to such womanly gestures, but her black eyes met the midwife's and then flickered earnestly to the children on the pallet by the fire.

Bending over Ayya and Vill, Kallye found that Seena had spoken accurately. The children lay as though asleep, but they did not stir when called or shaken.

Kallye lifted them one at a time, but she might have held sacks of flour for all their response.

She held her ear close to their faces, then called for something made of polished metal.

One of the soldiers scowled. "She can do no more than the physicians."

"And maybe even less," said another.

Kallye ignored them. Still holding the queen with one arm, Relys pulled a dagger from a belt sheath with her free hand. Kallye took it and held it up to the children's lips, but no mist appeared.

"No breathing?" she murmured.

And no heartbeat, either, she found. But every instinct she possessed told her that Ayya and Vill were not dead.

"I do not understand," she said at last. "They live . . . but . . ."

Helwych was a dark presence in the dark room. "Sorcery," he said. He folded his arms inside his sleeves. "A palpable attack."

Relys looked up. "Why would Vaylle strike in this manner? It has shown itself able to command magics that can raze a city."

Helwych smiled thinly. "Vaylle is subtle, captain. Very subtle." He allowed his words to hang meaningfully for a moment, then turned to the soldiers. "Take the midwife away. She is useless." He might have been ordering them to discard a piece of burnt wood.

Seena freed herself from Relys's arms and stood over her children, stricken, hands pressed to her mouth. Knowing her feelings, Kallye reached out to her, but Dryyim interposed himself. "Come on," he said, taking the midwife's arm. "You are going home."

"But—"

"Now. We have had enough of your interference."

"Interference!"

Relys eyed him coldly. "Captain Dryyim," she said, "I would suggest that you use our midwife with more respect. She has cared for the king's household for many months.''

"Then, Relys," said Helwych. "*I* would suggest that *you* take Kallye home yourself.''

Relys was unruffled. "My duty is to my queen," she said calmly.

Helwych's eyebrows lifted. "Seena?''

The queen was distraught. "Do what he says, Relys,'' she whispered, lifting and cradling the still body of her infant son. "Helwych knows best. Go. Go, both of you.''

Relys seemed shocked at Seena's acquiescence, and Kallye herself wanted to protest, but she had lived long enough in a male-dominated society to know both a woman's limits and the dangers inherent in exceeding them. In the room were over a dozen strong men. The odor of intimated threat was in the air. She caught Relys's eye, shook her head.

Relys turned, stared at the queen. "Seena, I—''

Seena was sobbing. "Do what Helwych says.''

"Yes, Relys,'' said Helwych. "Do what I say.''

Jaw clenched, Relys bowed to Seena, walked across the room, and held the door open for Kallye. "This way, my lady,'' she said. Reluctance and anger were thick in her voice.

But as they left the room, Helwych turned to Seena. "I think I can say with certainty, Seena,'' he said, "that if you wish to save your children, you will have to do exactly as I say.''

Relys was halfway through the door, but she paused at the words, and Kallye saw that she was on the verge of plunging back into the room. The midwife laid a hand on her arm. "Come, captain. You can do no more here.''

"Vipers and eels,'' muttered Relys. "Kingsbury is infested with them.''

Kallye was moved by the captain's loyalty, but heroics would accomplish little at present. She took Relys's arm. "Come, captain. You have your duty.'' Relys muttered. Kallye tightened her grip meaningfully. "Woman," she whispered seriously, "you are in peril."

Her tone finally penetrated Relys's anger. "Aye," said the captain after a long moment, and then she guided Kallye down the corridor and out of the Hall. "I picked my battlefield weeks ago," she said when they were away from the palisade. "And so I suppose I must be satisfied with it. But I wish Timbrin were here."

Relys's loyalty had touched Kallye deeply, and the fact that the captain was a woman—despite her mannish trappings—had gained her sympathy. "Your lieutenant?" said the midwife.

Relys spoke cautiously, but there was a weight of worry in her voice. "Aye. She has been missing now for days. No one knows anything of her. I . . ." Her voice caught. "I fear the worst."

The worst, Kallye thought, had already happened. If Helwych was correct about sorcery, then Gryylth had been struck at its very heart. Relys, perhaps, was too new to her womanhood to know the grief and helplessness that Seena was feeling, but then . . .

Kallye took the captain's hand as she might take the hand of a grieving mother and Relys did not appear to resent the gesture.

. . . but then again, maybe she knew exactly. The captain had no children, but she had a missing lieutenant and a country that she obviously felt was in danger.

"I am sorry, captain," Kallye said softly.

"I am helpless, midwife. Helwych rules the queen now, and I have no more power in the matter than a prostitute on the block in Bandon." Relys turned to her suddenly. "I have watched you with Seena, my lady. You are wise, and so I ask you: What power does a woman have? If there is any to be had in my sex, I need it now, for I am no longer a man, and therefore am I now mocked and disregarded by the very men I am supposed to command. Do I simply give up? Do I have nothing?''

They entered the market square. About them, women from neighboring towns, awake and on the road since before sunrise, were setting out their cottage-work and the early produce of a warm and clement summer. Kallye had caught the babies of many of them, and knew by name a great many more. She nodded greetings while she considered her answer.

''If you ask me what a woman's power is,'' she said at last, ''I would have to speak as a midwife, and I would have to say that, from what I have seen, a woman's power lies in change, and in patience, and in endurance.''

Relys frowned, her fists clenched. ''I would I could act.''

Kallye shrugged. ''Sometimes even a man cannot act.''

Relys turned her head away abruptly. Kallye realized that she might as well have slapped her. She squeezed Relys's hand. ''Forgive my stupid words, captain. Do you understand, though, what I am saying?''

''Aye . . . aye . . .'' Relys looked back up the street. Hall Kingsbury was silhouetted against the bright sky, its solid, peaceful exterior giving no clue that there was anguish contained within.

About them, dogs barked, chickens squawked, bolts of cloth shone with bright colors. The market—men or no men—was open, but a woman was approaching the midwife. ''Kallye,'' she said. ''May I speak with you?''

Kallye stopped and bobbed her head by way of a bow in the new fashion. ''Of course, Paia. Is something wrong?''

Paia looked worried, and Kallye began to fear that the affliction of Seena's children had been repeated elsewhere. But Paia—round and maternal—had her full compliment of toddlers clinging to her skirts. ''I am not certain,'' she said. ''The other day, my boys found a woman wondering in the forest near our steading. They thought her mad, and so they did not approach her, but they told me of her. What with Nedyyc off with the king and all, I was almost afraid to go and look; but we all seem to be playing the man these days, and so at last I went.'' She glanced at Relys, caught her breath, and paused uncertainly.

But Relys shook her head. ''Pray continue.''

''I found her as they told me,'' said Paia with an attempt at resolution. ''Truly, she is deranged, but she was hungry, and she had no home, so I took her in. My older girls are keeping watch over her today, but I do not know what to do with her.''

''Is she a country woman?'' said Kallye. ''What does she look like?''

''She is small and slight,'' said Paia, ''but dark as a fisher's daughter.''

Relys stiffened.

Paia paused, blinked at the captain, went on. ''Her hair is thick and curly—''

''What is her name?'' Relys demanded suddenly. ''How was she dressed?''

''I do not know her name,'' Paia stammered. ''Her . . . her clothes were so torn that they were no more than rags. Because of her boots I thought she might be of the First Wartroop, but she shrinks from the sight of even the smallest knife.'' She tore her eyes away from the captain's intense gaze, turned to the midwife. ''She needs help, Kallye. I have approached the men of the guard, but they will not listen to me. They call me a silly woman and tell me to run along. Can you help? Will you come see her?''

Kallye read Relys's unspoken thoughts. Timbrin. ''By the Gods,'' she said, ''let us go to her now.''

❖ CHAPTER 7 ❖

Head down, clad in a gown that was too big for her, Timbrin sat huddled by the fire in Paia's house. She was not a large woman—in the months following her transformation by Tireas, she had come to joke about her stature—but now she seemed almost pathetically tiny. Paia's daughters had made an effort to brush her hair and tend to her cuts and bruises, but she had the air of a child who had been beaten and abandoned.

Relys entered the house and stood by the door, stricken. Kallye, though, bobbed her head at Paia's daughters and went immediately to Timbrin. "Good morning, child," she said kindly, kneeling beside her. "Paia sent me to see to you."

Timbrin's brown eyes opened wide, and she scanned the midwife anxiously, but though Kallye was no stranger to the First Wartroop, she only huddled further into her gown and lowered her head.

Relys found her voice at last. "Lieutenant."

Timbrin's eyes turned feral, frightened, and she made a frantic motion as though to flee, but Kallye took her hands. "It is all right, child. No harm will come to you." She looked at Relys sternly. "Call her by name."

Swallowing the lump in her throat, Relys set aside her sword and approached. "Timbrin," she said softly. "Dear friend."

Timbrin's mouth trembled. "R-Relys?"

She barely whispered the name, and Relys's eyes were aching with suppressed tears as she went down on one knee. "How is it with you, Timbrin?"

But Timbrin's face turned pained, her brow furrowed. Mouth turned down in a grimace, she shook her head in small, rapid movements.

Kallye nodded understandingly. "Too many people?"

Timbrin nodded slowly.

"Are you afraid of us?"

Again the nod, but quicker.

"Do you know who you are?"

Timbrin only looked sad.

Kallye turned to Paia's girls. "Leave us alone with her," she said. They nodded and withdrew in a swish of skirts and aprons. Timbrin relaxed noticeably, but she had still the look of a beaten thing.

Relys's throat was dry. First Seena's children, and now this. And in both cases she was helpless. Slowly, she reached out a hand. Slowly, almost fearfully, Timbrin clasped it. "What happened, my friend?"

Timbrin fought with words. "I . . ." She looked anguished, as though speaking had become a physical pain for her.

Relys was close to tears. "Hounds?"

With a frantic whimper, Timbrin turned to Kallye and threw herself into the midwife's arms. Eyes clenched shut, mouth again set in an agonized grimace, she whined like a starving dog. But she shook her head.

"I . . . saw Helwych . . ." she managed.

Relys leaned forward. As she had feared. And she had sent Timbrin to spy on the sorcerer . . . alone. "What about Helwych?"

"He . . . walking . . ."

Relys exchanged glances with Kallye. "I do not understand."

"No . . . no crutch."

Stranger and stranger. Timbrin's wounds were hardly more than superficial cuts and bruises: nothing that would explain the mental damage that had been inflicted upon her. But her comments about Helwych were only growing more cryptic. "But he is ill."

Timbrin's face remained buried in Kallye's shoulder. It was obvious that speaking brought her close to screaming with pain, but she was forcing herself nonetheless. "Not ill . . ."

Gradually, with frequent hesitations and backtracking, Timbrin sketched out the story. She had been watching outside Helwych's house when noises, lights, and the presence of something indefinable had made her drop her caution and open the shutters. Immediately, she had been battered senseless by powers that she could only describe in terms of light that was heard, sounds that were felt, and vague swirlings that had struck to the heart of her psyche. But before she had been so savaged, she had seen Helwych standing in the middle of the conjured potencies, erect and healthy.

Relys's eyes hardened into obsidian darkness. If Helwych's wounds were a sham, then everything that he had told Cvinthil was a lie. The story of Vaylle was a lie. The men of Gryylth and Corrin had gone off to exact revenge for . . .

. . . for what? Quite possibly nothing.

By the time Timbrin was done, she was a crumpled doll. Her hands clutched at Kallye's gown, and she whimpered softly, constantly, like an infant. Relys's face was damp with tears, the first she had allowed herself since the First Wartroop had been struck, and her hands were clenched into fists that she would have liked to turn instantly upon the body of the Corrinian sorcerer.

"Dear friend," she said, reaching out to touch Timbrin's cheek. "Dear, dear friend. Our thanks. Fear not; we will protect you; and, given time, you will heal. For the time, I ask that you stay here. Do not be afraid of Paia or her children, for Kallye vouches for their trustworthiness. Rest. You will be provided for."

Timbrin—shaking, gasping—nodded without looking up. Kallye called Paia's daughters, and together they helped the broken lieutenant into bed.

Later, when Timbrin had fallen into an exhausted sleep, Relys stood outside the house with Kallye. The midwife finished giving instructions to one of the girls and handed her a pouch of herbs. "Boil this in a kettle of water, and give her a cup of the infusion as often as she will take it." The girl nodded and ran off to prepare the brew.

Kallye straightened, shaking her head. "I have never seen anything like it," she told Relys. "The herbs will soothe her, but I am afraid that the body of her affliction is beyond me." She shook her head again.

"Beyond anyone, I fear," said Relys. "Save perhaps the Gods. But this is not the first time that we of the First Wartroop have been deeply stricken. We survived then. Timbrin will survive now. I will see to it that Paia is given what she needs to tend her. In secrecy." She looked meaningfully at the midwife. "But I will do something else, too."

Her jaw clenched for a moment, and her hand fell to her sword.

When Alouzon's party reached Mullaen, they found it in ruins. But though the burned and blackened heap of stone and charred wood was beginning to soften with the encroachments of weeds, moss, and an occasional patch of wildflowers, summer seemed not to have come to the surrounding fields. Where crops had once grown, there was now only bare earth and the browned and dead remains of an aborted spring.

Desolation. The lake lapped at the shore, the wind sang in the ruins and among the dead grass. It was a place fit for ghosts.

Wykla shuddered. Manda looked equally uneasy, but

she gave Wykla's hand a squeeze. "Courage, princess."

Wykla colored. "Manda. Please."

"You showed no such modesty when you called yourself a king's daughter in Broceliande."

Wykla's blush deepened. "I spoke in the urgency of the moment, and to distract the Specter."

The maid of Corrin grinned. "As I spoke to distract you."

Karthin, who was scanning the area for signs of hounds or Grayfaces, chuckled at her words; but Kyria was examining the party critically. "We will fall over unless we rest," she said. "Magic can help, but flesh and blood needs real sleep, and we have gone too long without."

Santhe rubbed at the stubble on his chin. "And Cvinthil?"

The sorceress shrugged. "If we keep pushing ourselves and collapse halfway to Lachrae, what good have we done?"

The sun had slipped behind the Cordillera some time before, sending cold fingers of shadow reaching across the land, and now dusk was coming on. Santhe debated. "The full moon is just rising. Half a night? What say you, Marrha?"

Marrha was leaning against the remains of a stone wall. She passed a hand back through her hair, felt the frizzy remains of what had once been a precise braid. "A week, I think, would do us more good, but half a night it will have to be."

Wykla was still uncertain about the ruins. "Do we wish to camp here?" she said. "Perhaps the fields would be better."

Kyria shook her head abruptly. "Stay out of those fields." Her face was drawn, and she was staring at the dead farmland as though a nightmare had invaded her waking hours. After a moment, she dropped her eyes, shook her head. "Chemicals," she said softly. "Defoliants. Nothing will grow in those fields for years now. If you spend much time in them, you might well become ill. Or worse.''

Dindrane was outraged. "What kind of monster would do such a thing?'' But she broke off and sat down heavily. She knew. She had seen it, confronted it, fought it . . . and learned some of its secrets. ''Oh, my Goddess . . .''

"Go to sleep," said Kyria. Her tone was muted. "We have a few hours: let us make the best of them."

Karthin and Wykla claimed the first watch, and sleep took their comrades quickly. The wind swept the surface of the lake, and the moon, full and bright, splashed silver across the land. Karthin scanned the ruins at their backs, then turned and checked the fields. Nothing moved. Mullaen was gone. "They treated us well here, Wykla," he said softly. "Enite and Ceinen and all.''

The Mullaen that Wykla remembered was alive and full of faces that had not turned away from the sight of swords and armor. It was a place where the wounded had been healed, and, more important, where she had finally ceased her struggles against womanhood. In Mullaen, she had at last embraced her new life fully, with no regrets, and acceptance and optimism had filled her heart like water.

But now the square where she had worn a gown and plaited flowers with Manda was burned and blackened, its songbirds gone. The fountain was dry, and the circle of standing stones that was as much of a temple as the Vayllens needed had been overthrown.

"Tell me of Darham, Wykla," said Karthin. "Manda said a little, but matters . . .'' He shook his head as though he contemplated the failure of a crop. ''. . . matters have kept us from lengthy talk. How is my king?''

Wykla tore her eyes from the ruins, fought to keep clear her memories of the town. "He is well, Karthin," she said. "Good-hearted and strong, though he seems at times sad.''

He nodded. "As are we all at times." He leaned on his sword as he kept an eye on the fields. "He called you his daughter, I hear."

Wykla squirmed uncomfortably. "Aye, Karthin. He did. At first I thought it but a figure of speech, or courtesy, but Manda told me that his words were in earnest."

"They were indeed." Karthin's gaze rested for a moment on Marrha. "His wife died of illness years ago, and she had borne no children. Since then, Darham has looked upon all of Corrin as his child." He nodded to Wykla. "And now you also, my princess."

Acutely embarrassed by the title, Wykla fought with her tongue. "Why?" she managed.

Karthin shrugged. "He is a deep man, Darham is. The loss of his wife and then his brother have brought him wisdom." For a moment, he paused as though listening. Silence. "I would guess that he saw an honorable woman who lacked only one thing: a family that esteemed her."

Wykla looked away. Her eyes smarted. Months now, and the wound still bled freely.

"Aye, my friend." Karthin's voice was compassionate. "I heard what happened."

"They are nonetheless my family."

"That is so. But now so is Darham. And you may believe me when I say that should you ever bring yourself to call him father, he will answer gladly."

Wykla wiped her nose with a ragged sleeve and sniffed softly, irritated that she sounded like a simpering child. "I . . ." Whenever she thought of it, Darham's generous offer plunged her into a sea that seemed of equal parts happiness and grief. And so she tried not to think of it. "But I have a father already, and—"

A noise. Her head snapped up. Her tears choked off instantly.

Karthin lifted his sword. Together, they slipped towards a group of ruined buildings that stood off a little distance from the town, a straggling heap that lay like a decaying arm across a path of undefoliated land. Weeds and dust silenced their steps as they climbed through the tumbled wood and stone. Cautiously, they lifted their heads above the crest of the pile.

Even without the bright moon, Karthin and Wykla would have been able to see the three faintly glowing beasts that shambled amid the sterile fields, their eyes flickering like lamps and their teeth glinting. The hounds, though, seemed unaware that they were not alone. Rooting in the dead ground, pawing at one another, their playful jibes flaring now and again into snarling hostility, they milled and wheeled in the moonlight.

"I wonder what they ate last," said Wykla tonelessly.

"For now," said Karthin, "I care not about what. I am more concerned with when."

"I am not sure that it matters. Shall we wake Kyria?"

"It may not be necessary. Let her sleep."

Squatting down in the ruins, they resumed their watch. A good sprint would take them back to their friends long before the hounds could arrive, and their clear view in all directions precluded a surprise attack; but aside from the movement of the hounds, the fields were still.

Wykla was still nervous. "I am not sure that we two should stay together like this."

"Agreed. One of us should . . . ." Karthin squinted at the fields. "Wait. Look at that."

"What? The hounds?"

"No. To the right. Near the water."

Wykla followed his pointing finger, and in a moment she noticed something wrong with the moonlight near the lake. An odd patch had appeared, shimmering with faint light like a piece of dark cloth woven with silver threads. It flickered and pulsed in the air, and as they watched, it brightened and spread slowly until it reached the ground.

"I do not understand," she said.

"Nor do I."

"Sorcery."

"Well, yes . . ."

Dead ruins, strange apparitions. Wykla did not like it at all. "I will run and fetch Kyria," she said, but when she turned, her sleeve caught on a splintered beam and pulled it down in a clatter of gravel and dry thatch.

The hounds looked up, eyes glowing, mouths grinning.

"Curse me for a stupid girl," Wykla cried. She tugged at the sleeve, but the beam had ground down to the stone beneath it, wedging the cloth firmly between.

Grinning and yelping, the hounds were on their way. Karthin tugged at the snag, shrugged dourly, and cut it away with a knife. "Do not speak unkindly of yourself, dear lady," he said, and then he turned to the rubble and kicked a passage clear.

They ran for the camp, hair streaming, boots thudding on the hard packed ground. "Kyria!" shouted Wykla. "Hounds!"

The camp struggled into consciousness, but the sorceress was already on her feet. "Where?"

The cries of the hounds carried clearly through the night air. "Behind us," said Karthin, pointing.

Kyria nodded and lifted her hands. Moonlight suddenly wove about her in a bright nimbus, and when the hounds rounded the heaped ruins, they were met by a wave of silver fire. Yelping and whining frantically, they tumbled to the ground as though struck by a club. For a moment they scrambled among the weeds, claws furrowing the damp earth, and then they found their feet and fled.

Kyria's voice came out of the shimmering aura that surrounded her. "Enough for a start. But I do not want them running about loose. Let us go and make an end of this."

The sounds of the beasts' retreat was loud as Kyria and the others made for the ruins, but instead of fading gradually, the whines and frantic yipes cut off of a sudden. When the party reached the ruins, they found only empty fields beyond.

Wykla strained her eyes. "Killed?"

"No . . ." Kyria rubbed her eyes tiredly, and the nimbus of moonlight faded. "That was not a lethal blast. It was . . ." She dropped her hands, staring. Out by the lake, the shimmer hung from sky to earth like a doorway into a realm of mist and light. "What in heaven's name is that?"

"It appeared as we watched the hounds," said Wykla.

"And you did not call me?"

"Dear lady," said Karthin without apology, "you were asleep."

Kyria stood with folded arms. Lips pressed together, she watched the shimmer. "Did it do anything?"

"Nay."

"Did the hounds pay any attention to it?"

"Not that we noticed."

"Well, in that case . . ." The sorceress fell silent.

Shaking, Dindrane clutched her healer's staff and stumbled to Kyria's side. "What is it, sister?"

Kyria shook her head. "I cannot be sure. I wonder . . ." She fell silent, musing, then roused herself suddenly. "Go to bed, all of you. I will watch."

The others protested, but she shook her head and pointed them back to the camp with an air of authority that sent even Santhe to his blankets without another word. And when Wykla curled up next to Manda, the last thing she remembered before her eyes fell shut was the sorceress standing atop the ruins, her ragged robes gleaming with moonlight and silver and her arms folded as though in defiance of any power, no matter how great, that might threaten those whom she, like Darham, had claimed as her children.

* * *

Helwych's work had been long and taxing, but it was almost done now, and as he lounged back in the king's chair that evening, he allowed himself a brief moment of unalloyed satisfaction.

The backlash from the spell that had created the curtain wall had shaken him, but he had recovered quickly enough to immediately set about arranging the magic that had bespelled Seena's children and, to a certain extent, Seena herself. To merely suspend the children's lives without actually killing them was difficult and exacting work, but he had learned his lessons well, and the results were as he had expected: the queen had put the running of the country into his hands so that she could devote her full attention to the futile task of nursing Ayya and Vill.

Timbrin was gone. She had received the full brunt of the energy backlash, and though her body had not been found, Helwych did not doubt that she had been killed by the blast, if not disintegrated, her remains dragged off by roving hounds.

As a matter of form, he had announced the news of her disappearance, but he had seen no regret in the eyes of the young men in the hall, for they had disliked Timbrin no less than they despised Relys. Now the only four wartroops left in Gryylth were, beneath a veneer of devotion to their queen, loyal only to the young sorcerer they saw as a leader who would bring their country back from the brink of fatal error.

All was going according to plan. His plan. The Specter, on the other hand, was not faring quite so well, for with the erection of the curtain wall, it had been banished from Gryylth. No eyes of void and darkness inhabited Helwych's thoughts now, and what hounds prowled the land were firmly under his control, responding with puppetlike docility to his wishes and orders.

He allowed his mind to stretch out and touch the pack that roamed outside Kingsbury. For an instant, he saw with the hounds' eyes: moonlit fields, solitary steadings, stone walls and hedges that were nothing to long legs and preternatural muscles. He felt the roiling of empty bellies, the slavering of caustic mouths, the eager ache of needle-sharp fangs.

Not yet. Eat your fill in the forests and pastures. You will not have human flesh unless I say.

The hounds turned away from the steadings and houses, slipped into the shadows among the trees. But as Helwych brought his awareness back to himself, he felt a brief flash of hostility. Close. Very close. Just outside the very walls of Hall Kingsbury, in fact.

Relys.

"Hmmm." He opened his eyes. Dryyim stood before him. In the months since Lytham had first brought him to speak with Helwych, he—like his fellows, and with the help of a little magic—had grown from weedy youth to strong manhood. Now Dryyim and his friends swaggered through the market square and barked orders like seasoned veterans, and, more important, they followed Helwych's orders without question.

"What was I saying, captain?" said Helwych.

"The garrisons, lord."

"Ah, yes. The garrisons." Helwych considered for a moment. Relys was approaching, and she had murder on her mind, but he had time. Time enough to finish the business at hand and then make the necessary arrangements. "Tell me, captain," he said. "What do you want for Gryylth?"

"I want what is best. '

"And are you loyal to your king and queen?"

"Indeed."

Fine. Fine. "Seena has put me in charge of Gryylth," said Helwych smoothly. "It is a terrible responsibility, and my wounds still trouble me, but I will do my best for Gryylth. Have you any question about that?"

Dryyim answered promptly. "None, lord."

Helwych nodded. "Dryyim," he said, "you are my

first in command. In matters of war and battle, I listen to you.'' Dryyim drew himself up straight, and Helwych felt his pride. "Now, tell me: what garrisons do we have in the land?''

Dryyim enumerated them. With most of the men and arms of Gryylth in Vaylle—trapped now, as Helwych knew—there were only a few: essentially nothing more than aging men in administrative posts. Cvinthil had staked everything on a sudden, unexpected invasion.

"And we have . . .'' Helwych pretended to deliberate. "How many wartroops left?''

"Four, lord.''

"Ah, yes. Four. I am glad you are with me, Dryyim. I value your counsel.''

Dryyim preened. Helwych felt out towards Relys. The captain of the First Wartroop was approaching the palisade that surrounded the Hall. She greeted the guards at the gate familiarly, and though they did not like her, they allowed her to pass. They had no reason not to.

Helwych smiled. They were about to have a reason. And, he reflected, perhaps some recreation, too.

"Take a few of your men,'' he said, "the best, mind you, and send them off to take charge of the garrisons. If Gryylth is going to be put to rights, we need to start work.'' Helwych felt rather light-hearted. A palpable thorn was about to be removed from his side. "Bring them to me before they leave, and I will have instructions for them.''

"As you wish, lord.''

Helwych dismissed his guards with a gesture. Gryylth was now his. There remained only a few tasks ahead of him. Mere housekeeping. Nothing of any concern. And as for the question of whether he ruled in his own name or in Cvinthil's, that could be settled much later. For now it was enough that his orders were heeded and his wishes obeyed.

Alone in the dark hall, he rested his staff across his

knees and began to assemble a spell. Though a few months ago it would have been well beyond his abilities, the magic had become simple for him; and if he took his time with it this evening, it was because he enjoyed seeing it take shape under his hands.

Murmuring a soft chant under his breath, he cupped his fingers under the spell, cradling it like a bowl of water. It glowed with a life of its own to Helwych's eyes, and when it was done, he sat waiting patiently for Relys.

Stealthily, her steps silent among the rushes on the floor, she approached. The barest flicker of shadow at the doorway indicated that she had entered the Hall, and if Helwych had not possessed the sight of his mind as well as of his eyes, he would never have seen her as she slipped towards him.

He pretended to be dozing. Relys's sword was in her hands. Carefully, she eased into striking range.

But Helwych acted first. With a careless gesture, he flung the spell into her face. The effect was instantaneous: the captain stood as if struck, dropped her sword, and collapsed amid the rushes.

Helwych regarded her disdainfully for a moment. "Guards," he said, and then he recalled that, under the circumstances, he should appear more startled. "Guards!" he cried. "Help!"

Dryyim arrived on the run with a half dozen soldiers of the Guard. They stopped just inside the door, looked at Relys in shock, then turned to Helwych.

"She tried to kill me," said the sorcerer, making sure that he trembled.

Every man present knew that Relys was loyal to Gryylth, and Helwych watched as the guards hesitated between their reason and their resentments. He could have bespelled them, forced them to see matters his own way, but to so seize their loyalties and hold them fast would have meant a constant expenditure of power. He wanted his men's decision to be their own. Much better their allegiance take care of itself.

Dryyim looked to his men. A moment of unspoken communication, decision . . .

And then Dryyim bent and seized Relys by the arms, hauled her to her feet, and cuffed her roughly. "Come to your senses, woman," he said. "You are under arrest."

Helwych folded his arms inside his sleeves. "In the king's name," he prompted.

"In the king's name," said Dryyim.

Relys was still fighting her way out of the spell. She blinked stupidly at the men, at Helwych, at the Hall, then suddenly came to herself and made a lunge for her sword; but the men had already bound her hands behind her back.

She stumbled, was dragged back to her feet; and then the full realization of what had happened fell upon her. Helwych watched her face turn pale as she realized that she was bound and friendless.

He rose, feigning weakness. "You have threatened violence against the king's own representative, woman," he said. "You are guilty of treason."

"I . . ." Relys was fighting with her fear. She was strong. Too strong. "I am loyal to my king," she said. "And you are not he."

"Silence, girl."

"I—"

Dryyim cuffed Relys across the mouth. A trickle of blood found its way down her cheek.

She forced the words out. "He is lying, Dryyim."

He struck her again.

She was undeterred. "By the Gods, has he bespelled you all? Seena's plight is his responsibility!"

Dryyim was lifting his arm for another blow when Helwych spoke:

"Stop, captain. It would be a pity to damage such a pretty face." He smiled at Relys. "If a woman cannot be trusted to be a captain of Gryylth, I am sure that she can at least be counted upon to be a woman, and for that she will need her looks."

Relys's eyes narrowed. Her blood was dark against her white skin.

Helwych examined her for a moment. "I have heard that you are a native of Bandon. Is this true, Relys?"

Relys looked away. Dryyim shook her. "Answer him, girl!"

She licked a split lip. "You have said it."

"And what is the law of Bandon regarding such women as you?"

She met his eyes levelly. "The law of Bandon was suspended by the order of the king, Helwych. Its charter was revoked."

"The law and charter of Bandon," said Helwych, "have been reinstated. Effective immediately." He touched her cheek. She flinched away, and he smiled. "Now, Relys, you will have to become used to men touching you. You are, after all, an attractive girl, and in your future occupation you will be touched a great deal. By a great many men."

He turned to Dryyim. "Relys is stripped of her titles and status. In accordance with Bandon's charter, she should be put up for sale, but I think it might be well for her to learn her trade first. Therefore, captain . . ." He smiled again at Relys. A palpable thorn. ". . . take this prostitute away to your men and teach her what it means to be a woman."

He examined the faces of the guards. One was eager. One expectant. Another looked a trifle frightened. No matter: they would encourage each other, they would all use their new plaything well, and Relys would give him no further trouble. She might not even survive the night.

Relys struggled against her bonds. "Fools!" she cried. "You do not know what you are doing!"

Dryyim laughed. "We know well enough, Relys. And soon you will know also. Come on."

Helwych had only a glimpse of Relys's face—eyes clenched, mouth set—before she was jerked away and led out of the Hall. Silent, fully cognizant of what lay

ahead of her, she was dragged off towards the Guards'
quarters.

Stooping, Helwych reached down to the rushes and
picked up her sword. He examined it for a moment,
then flung it casually aside. It rang on the hard earth,
and then was silent.

❖ CHAPTER 8 ❖

The apparition at the lake shore had done nothing—had, in fact, not even moved—when Kyria and Santhe led the party away from Mullaen. Even at a distance, though, Dindrane could feel it: an inexplicable absence in the fabric of the world, a wound in the continuum of matter and time.

But then, as the sun rose, it vanished, dissolving with the morning like a strange frost. At a rise in the road, Dindrane looked back, and though Lake Innael shimmered like a mirror that lay cupped among rolling hills, the apparition on its shore was gone.

She questioned Kyria, but the sorceress shook her head: she had no answers. And so the day passed, and the party pressed on, fighting a bone-deep fatigue that turned the green land white and raw. Towards noon, they came in sight of a village, but where before Dindrane had carefully avoided any contact between Alouzon's people and her own, now she had no qualms: she led her friends straight to the town square.

The thick grass of summer was a relief to feet that had trodden on hard pavement and dirt for days, and the sound of a clear fountain was liquid music. The village showed signs of attack—broken walls, scorched and burned-out houses, ribbons of black that hung upon doors and door posts—but the signs seemed months old, the people were alive, and the streets were filled with faces and voices.

Dindrane nodded silent greetings to the shocked people of the town as she pushed past them without explanations. Determined and frightened both, she was quite prepared to batter down the door of the magistrate's house with her staff, but a tall man with a barrel chest had already flung it open. "Dindrane!" He stared, then found his tongue. "We heard that . . . I mean . . . you had disappeared and—" He broke off, stammering.

Dindrane could hardly blame him, for her friends, man and woman alike, looked like nothing so much as vagabonds, ruffians, and killers. She was almost surprised that he had recognized his own high priestess. But though she was dirty, phosphor scarred, and in boy's clothes, she drew herself up as though she stood in the King's House. " 'Tis horses we need, Caerl. Immediately."

He goggled, stared at the armor and weapons. "But—"

"Now." Dindrane's tone sent him back a step, but he recovered, nodded, and shouted to the townspeople. "Six horses for the magistrate of Lachrae. Instantly!"

Commotion. Shouting. Three young men set off at a run, and within fifteen minutes the party was riding out of the village on docile but sturdy Vayllen mounts.

Marrha cantered up to Dindrane's side. "How far to Lachrae?"

"Over thirteen leagues."

The captain smiled as though she faced an uncertain battle. Dindrane had seen the expression before, and though she still thought it out of place on the face of one who would bear a child by the next spring, she no longer found it uncomely.

"Then we had best ride quickly," said Marrha. "Are there other villages? Will they give us fresh mounts?"

"They will."

The captain laughed out loud, and her strength

seemed suddenly replenished. "Wykla!" she cried. "Let us show them how the First Wartroop travels!"

Wykla joined her at the head of the line, and they spurred their horses into a gallop. The others followed, keeping pace. Thirteen leagues lay ahead of them, and Cvinthil and his army were perhaps even now beginning to land, but Marrha—head low, eyes scanning the road ahead—rode as though in absolute confidence that she could prevent tragedy and slaughter.

Side by side with Kyria, Dindrane suspected that the sorceress was weaving some spell of strength and speed about the horses, but as the white mare that bore her seemed to exult in her pace, the priestess found herself exulting too, and by the time the horses wearied, the party had reached the next village.

Dindrane demanded and received new mounts. Once more they set off at a gallop.

Three leagues. Four leagues. Scattered hounds appeared, but the company simply outran them. They changed mounts, changed again. The miles fell beneath strong hoofs, and still Marrha led the way. Woman she was, and mother too, but she was captain of the First Wartroop, and her pride spurred the party on as much as Kyria's spells.

Raising clouds of dust, striking sparks from the stones in the road, foam flecking their bridles and scattering like snow in the wind of their passage, the horses pounded on; and just at sunset, when the Cordillera was backlit by a crimson tide that seemed compounded of blood and anger both, the company rode past the ruins of the manor houses, galloped down the street, and clattered into the main plaza of Lachrae.

Dindrane reined in, straightened up in the saddle. "People of Vaylle!" she cried, " 'tis I: Dindrane. In the name of the Goddess and the God, bring us horses and assemble the healers and harpers!"

Lights flared in the neighboring houses. Shutters that had been bolted in fear of attack were thrown open.

Faces—dark against bright windows—peered out, and a murmur of surprise arose and grew into a roar.

Dindrane was still shouting. "Send to Pellam! He has an army on his doorstep!"

Tangled among sweat-soaked sheets, Alouzon Dragonmaster awoke to the ringing of the telephone.

The sound jarred her into action. Days of living on the run and in peril had irrevocably wedded the strange with the dangerous, and she reached automatically for the Dragonsword, came up empty-handed, grabbed her boot knife instead, and found herself in the novel position of holding a razor-keen blade to a set of touch-tone buttons.

The phone, unruffled, continued to ring. Dry-mouthed, shaking with abruptly broken sleep, she picked up the handset. "Hello?"

"Suzanne?" Brian O'Hara.

She swallowed. She wanted to say yes. She felt that she must say yes or go instantly mad. But Suzanne was gone. Dead and gone. She was Alouzon now. Forever. "No."

"Who the hell is this?" demanded Brian.

"I'm . . ." Who, indeed, was she? Suzanne's alter-ego? A Goddess? "I'm Alouzon." She kept herself from adding *Dragonmaster* only with conscious effort.

Brian was in one of his moods. "What kind of a name is that?"

She clenched her jaw. Brian's comment seemed ex-cruciatingly rude after the exacting courtesy of Gryylth and Vaylle. "Call me Allison."

Allison. The name had come out before she had considered it. She felt suddenly warm in spite of the air conditioning.

"Are you her roommate?"

Well, she considered, she and Suzanne had slept in the same bed. She supposed that counted for something. "Kinda."

"Well look, Allie . . ."

Alouzon winced. Kyria's use of the diminutive had been bad enough.

". . . I need to talk to Suzanne . . ."

And, indeed, what about Kyria? Alive? Dead? Helen's body had been on one of those gurneys.

". . . about some tests she's got . . ."

And all her friends. What about them?

". . . you know, you can't just go running out on a teaching job. You have to be responsible about it."

She nearly laughed. Responsible? He did not know the meaning of the word. But she suddenly felt disoriented. What day was this? The dude in the Mercury had told her that it was Saturday morning, but Brian did not usually pester on weekends.

Holding the phone to her ear while he continued to whine about Suzanne's sudden absence, she opened the venetian blinds. The sunlight dazzled her for a moment, but when her eyes adjusted, she could see the San Diego Freeway grinding through morning rush hour.

How long did I sleep? Long enough, it appeared. The Grail had seen to that.

"Listen, Brian," she said. "What day is it?"

"Huh?"

She sighed with frustration, though she felt like screaming. She was probably sounding utterly deranged, and she knew without asking that she had slept through the weekend. "Never mind. Suzanne's . . . uh . . ."

Odd. Her old name sounded as foreign on her tongue as *Alouzon Dragonmaster* had when she had first arrived in Gryylth.

"Uh . . ." She groped for a plausible story. "Suzanne went out of town. Back to her . . . uh . . . folks."

"Why the hell did she do that?" said Brian. "She's got a teaching job."

Alouzon snorted. "She told me she'd quit."

Brian fell silent. "I wasn't aware," he said at last, "that we'd reached any final decision about that."

"Well, I think you'd probably better consider it final."*Why the hell am I talking with this simp when all hell is breaking loose in Gryylth?* "She's gone."

A long silence. Then: "Fuck. She left the university, too?"

"Probably."

Another silence. Brian, Alouzon knew, was stewing. Fine. Let him stew. In his own way he had caused Suzanne as much grief as Solomon.

"Listen, Allie," he said, "could you do me a favor?"

Do I have anything better to do? "Depends."

Brian did not hear the qualifier. "Suzi's got a bunch of papers and books that I gave her for research, and a bunch more that had to do with the classes she was teaching. Can you get them together and bring them to my office?"

She looked around the bedroom. The glare from the sun turned it into a dusty study in white walls and graduate student neglect. She found that she missed very much the pallets and furs of Gryylth. "Well . . ."

"I just can't figure out what got into her. She blew up at me and stomped out when I tried to give her some advice about her job. Now I've got to cover for her."

Alouzon sighed. She was committed to Gryylth and the Grail completely now, but she had once been Suzanne, and the least she could do for her old, shattered, tangled life was to leave it neat and tidy, with all its pieces ordered and put away. Gods knew, it had never been that way when she had lived it. "Yeah," she said at last. "I'll bring them. Give me a few. You in your office?"

"Kinsey Hall 288. You come out Bruin Walk past Powell Library and—"

"I know where it is, Brian. I'll be there."

She hung up without further comment or explanation, and for a moment, she stood, her hand still on the phone, wishing that she could call someone. Anyone. *Hello, Mom? Dad? This is . . . well, I mean, I used to be your daughter Suzanne. I've changed . . .*

"Yeah, right. Sure." She realized that she was still holding her knife, and Cvinthil's gold signet ring winked at her as she slid the weapon back into its sheath. For a moment she considered, then sat down on the bed and pulled off her boots and rubbed her feet. The trek across Vaylle and up the Cordillera had been hard and long, and though most of her thoughts were still pent up in a frustrated turmoil about the fate of her friends and her world, a small part of her was grateful to the agency—draconic or divine—that had brought her to Los Angeles, put her to bed, and given her a chance to clean up and think about what she was going to do next.

It was an enforced leisure, but it had its advantages. Her last weeks in Gryylth and Vaylle had been spent at a dead run, with no chance for planning or deliberation save over the immediate future. Now she had been given a chance to ponder the depth of what was being asked of her: no longer only a Guardian, she was to be a Goddess.

She passed a hand over her face. "Haven't got much choice, do I?"

Rising, she stripped off her soiled tunic and padded into the bathroom, rubbing sleep and dirt from her eyes. Her wounds, characteristically, had healed quickly, and now a shower and clean clothes sounded very good. But when she switched on the light, the sight of the utter stranger in the mirror—naked and brown and uncompromisingly real amid the prosaic familiarity of tile, sink, and toilet—made her cry out involuntarily.

Suzanne Helling had been rather average: a plump, round-faced earth mother who wore her dark hair straight and parted down the middle. Alouzon's body was muscled like that of an athlete, and her bronze

mane, dirty though it was, hung in thick ringlets and
framed features that would not have been out of place
on a fashion model save that they were stronger, more
serious, the brown eyes flashing and intent.

The face and body of a Goddess.

She hung her head. Real. Too real. Like the sword
waiting for her in the living room. Like the white-
shrouded bodies on the gurneys. "You're not gonna
let me forget, are you?"

And then, steeling herself, Alouzon Dragonmaster—Guardian of Gryylth and Goddess of a world—
bent over the sink, turned on the tap, and began to
brush her teeth.

The flotilla had been scattered by the sudden storm,
and Cvinthil fretted while it slowly regrouped: if there
had been any chance of taking Vaylle by surprise, it
was rapidly eroding out here on the White Sea. And
Gryylth was still hidden behind a curtain of absolute
night.

By the time the ships were once again gathered together, the wind—strong and raging during the storm—
had fallen to a faint breeze that was barely enough to
fill the sails. Any remaining hope of a speedy, unexpected crossing perished as slowly, very slowly, the
fleet made its way towards the Vayllen shore. Nearly
a week past the planned landing date, it finally came
within striking distance.

As the men of Quay who were piloting the ships
searched the shore for a safe landing, the warriors and
soldiers inspected weapons and prepared the horses
and supplies. Near sunset, the ships were beached a
short distance from what, from the water, had appeared to be a village. Close up, though, it turned out
to be a heap of ruins, broken and blasted, weedy and
overgrown, silent save for the squawks and cries of
nesting birds.

While the army made camp and posted sentries,
Cvinthil and Darham inspected the ruins. Cvinthil was

reminded strongly of Bandon: the same evidence of explosion and fire, the same riddled walls and leveled houses.

But this was a Vayllen town. What did it mean?

"My king." Alrri of the First Wartroop approached, her golden hair a ruddy flame in the afterglow of sunset. "We have found the barge used by Alouzon and her company."

Cvinthil straightened up from a fallen wall. Destroyed. Utterly destroyed. It did not make sense. "Is it damaged?"

"Apart from the effects of wind and water these past three months, lord, it is quite sound."

He swallowed with an effort, found his voice. "Was any message left in it?"

"None."

Darham frowned. "Did you not say, my brother, that the barge had been destroyed?"

Cvinthil felt uneasy. He had. Helwych had told him so.

Off in the distance, far off, the shroud that had cloaked Gryylth flickered with hidden lightning, blotting out the first stars like the carcass of an immense animal. Hidden behind that darkness were Seena and Vill and Ayya, and all his people. Vaylle was up to some evil sorcery, but what kind?

He prodded at the rubble with a booted foot. "It does not make sense," he said, and he flushed when he realized that he was echoing Hahle's words precisely.

Alrri was waiting for orders. Like the rest of the women of the wartroop, she stood with a warrior's ready ease, the set of her shoulders at once feminine and mannish. Darham did not seem to notice, but Cvinthil was acutely aware of it, and it reminded him of the potencies that sorcery could unleash.

He looked out at the shroud again. *No. Not that. But perhaps something even worse.*

Alrri folded her arms.

Fighting with a dry throat, Cvinthil spoke: "Prepare for a march at dawn," he said.

"My king, it shall be done." Alrri saluted and left, her hair rippling, her hips swaying gracefully.

Darham was nodding. "Brave women you have in your service, my brother."

Cvinthil thought of Marrget and Wykla, dead in their beds. And then he suddenly recalled Relys and Timbrin. The younger men of the Guard had never much liked the women of the wartroop, and he wondered now what had made those two elect to stay behind in spite of the difficulties they might face. Was it because of Helwych?

The thought choked him. "Very brave, indeed," he managed, and then he walked back to the camp.

Morning came up in a welter of red. The sun pierced the gloom on the horizon only with reluctance, and before it rose clear it was no more than an amber-colored disk. Cvinthil went over his plans with Darham. Any strike would have to be swift and ruthless, so as to give the Vayllens no time to counterattack. Any inhabitants would be slaughtered on sight to prevent an alarm from being raised, and the destruction of towns, villages, and cities would, by necessity, have to be complete.

"I dislike greatly the thought of firing the crops," he said to Darham. "But I am afraid that it will be necessary."

Darham's blue eyes grew sad for a moment. "I believe that there has been a precedent."

"Aye. A blow which much of Gryylth wishes had never been struck."

"Much?" Darham nodded understandingly. "Not all then . . . eh? Ten years of war is difficult to forget, I guess." He looked off towards the distant gloom, and Cvinthil knew that he was thinking of his people, of Corrin, of Manda and Karthin and—perhaps especially—Wykla.

Dead? Helwych had said so. But those ruins. And the barge . . .

"Mount and forward!" He called out the order quickly, so as to escape the doubts that were suddenly assailing him.

The road led north, and a haze that lay in that direction told of a large city. Cvinthil estimated that the army could reach it by nightfall, but before the wartroops and phalanxes had been on the march for an hour, a scout arrived with the report that a large group of people were approaching.

"Armed?" said Darham.

The scout shook his head. "We saw nothing but harps, scrolls, and staves in their hands," he said. "They were dressed richly, and an old man rode ahead of them all, robed and crowned as a king."

Cvinthil glanced at Darham. The Corrinian was nodding, keeping his gaze pointedly off in the distance. "I see . . ."

"Helwych told of such a welcome," said Cvinthil.

"Yes," said Darham. "You said that he did." But a crease had appeared between his blond eyebrows, and beneath his beard he was frowning.

"And . . . you heard what happened after."

They rode in silence for the better part of a minute. The crease in Darham's brow deepened. "I heard what Helwych said."

Cvinthil looked at him sharply. "Do you not believe your own countryman?" he demanded.

Darham considered before speaking. "My own countryman would have come to his king to make his report, wounds or no. He would not dissemble. And despite his pride, arrogance, and sullen demeanor, my own countryman would have been the first to explain the inconsistencies in his tale."

Cvinthil found himself shouting. "Are you saying that he was lying?"

Impassively, Darham stared him straight in the face. About them, the soldiers and warriors paused, con-

fused by the sudden argument. The scout fidgeted,
awaiting orders, hearing nothing but contradictions.

"I am saying that I believe our common enemy
might still lie across the White Sea," Darham said
softly.

Off on the horizon, the darkness pulsed and rolled.

"My king," said the scout.

Cvinthil turned to him abruptly. "How close is the
Vayllen army?"

Darham started to speak, but Cvinthil hissed him
into silence.

"An hour away, my lord," said the scout, clearly
bewildered.

"Then we shall prepare our attack," said Cvinthil.
"We shall entrap the Vayllens as they entrapped our
friends."

Darham spoke: "My brother—"

Cvinthil whirled on him. "Do not call me your
brother, Corrinian, until you begin to act like one."

Darham dropped his eyes. He turned away from
Cvinthil. Calrach cantered up and halted before his
king. "My lord?"

Passing a hand over his face, Darham deliberated.
Cvinthil waited. At last the king of Corrin said: "Prepare for attack, Calrach. But be cautious. I suspect
that there are adders among our corn."

"The Vayllens are indeed devious," said Cvinthil.

"Perhaps," said Darham bitterly. "But our crops
do not lie in Vaylle."

A short distance ahead, the road rose and passed
through a range of low, rolling hills, then once more
descended to the coastal plain. On the far side of the
hills was a village that should have been taken first,
but time did not allow for that; so Cvinthil sent his
troops into the hills, there to lie hidden until the Vayllens could be surrounded, and Darham's phalanxes
moved into position for a simultaneous assault on the
village.

By the time the Vayllens came into sight at the crest

of the low pass, there was not a trace of the Gryylthan and Corrinian forces. Even the baggage and supply wagons had been hidden. Sword in hand, Cvinthil waited behind the lip of a ditch with Darham, but doubts were still nagging at him, doubts that were increased by Darham's silent but obvious opposition. "You do not believe that they are our enemies, do you?" he said in an undertone.

"I would find another way than this."

The very words of Alouzon to Dythragor, once upon a time. Cvinthil was shaken, and he tried to shore up his crumbling convictions with his memories of what Vaylle had left of Bandon. To be sure, he had no great love for the town that had attacked him when he was in the company of the Dragonmaster, but the weapons that had been used against it were strange, inhuman: the mark of a people who were ruthless enough to slaughter sleeping men and women without remorse.

But was this not Cvinthil, king of Gryylth, who had carefully hidden his wartroops so as to better fall without warning upon an unwitting party of Vayllens? So as to better slaughter them without a fight? Was this what Vorya would have done? And what about Marrget?

He clenched his hand on his sword. Marrget was dead. They were all dead. Helwych had said so. Helwych had . . .

He looked at Darham. The Corrinian was waiting patiently. In the distance, his phalanxes were lying ready.

The Vayllens crested the pass and began to descend. There were no more than fifty of them, and they were traveling in a tight group as though in fear of an attack. Well, Cvinthil thought as the last Vayllen crossed into the killing zone, their caution would not save them.

The hills grew tense with imminent attack, and as though suddenly aware of the slaughter that was about to fall upon them, the Vayllens stopped. The white-haired man at the head of the party looked behind him. He called out, but his words were too faint to hear.

Cvinthil shouted for the charge.

The hills sprang alive with men and women. Swords slid out of scabbards with a shrill ring. Pikes rattled against one another. Shouts echoed Cvinthil's command. Within seconds, the wartroops were advancing on the Vayllens.

The old man looked up. He saw the men and women and weapons. His face turned sad.

But before the charge reached the Vayllens, before spears could be launched or warhorses could grind the apparently unarmed men and women beneath their hooves, a stirring went through the Vayllen party. From among the rich robes, gold jewelry, harps, and staves, a woman appeared. She looked worn and weary, and the braid in her ash-blond hair was dirty and frayed with days of inattention. But in her hand was a sword, she wore the leather armor of a Gryylthan warrior, and she carried herself as proudly as a queen.

Cvinthil was on his feet. He was running. He was screaming:

"For the love of the Gods, stay your weapons! That is Marrget of Crownhark!"

❖ CHAPTER 9 ❖

Relys drifted in a foggy haze of pain and violation. She had long ago lost any cognizance of day or night, was, in fact, no longer sure where she was, or even at times who. Such matters had been rendered meaningless by the utter reality of her circumstances: the hard pallet beneath her naked body, the faces—young faces of young men—bobbing above her with the rhythmic thrust of violent penetration and climax, the white hot pain of mass rape.

Afloat in a universe of bloody thighs and an inner pain that rose like a river in flood to engulf everything of what she had been, she gazed almost sightlessly at the ceiling above her, at the faces, at the floating phosphenes that swirled in her vision as she clenched her eyes with repeated torment; but she clung to the words that Kallye had spoken: *A woman's power lies in change, and in patience, and in endurance.*

Endurance.

Change had been forced upon her, patience was a thing unthought-of, but, fists clenched, jaw clamped shut against her screams, she endured. Her abdomen bucked and burned with each new entry, but she endured. Hours passed. Days passed, but she endured.

A woman's strength. Helwych had told the Guard in jest and irony to teach her what it meant to be a woman; and, in a way, Relys had indeed learned that. Entered, entered again, her vulva bleeding and raw as

a fresh wound, she held to the midwife's words, held
herself, held the tattered shreds of her mind and consciousness—and she gathered them all up and retreated at last to what small region of comparative
oblivion lay deep within her, beyond the reach of the
faces, the rapes, and the mocking laughter.

Thunder, suddenly.

She opened her eyes. The room was dark. Her wrists
were still chained to the top of the pallet, and the thin
mattress beneath her was soaked with semen and blood
and sweat; but she was alone, and she could hear,
faintly, the sound of rain pattering on thatch, splashing
on bare ground, running off roofs and eaves.

Endurance.

She forced herself to feel, to listen, to see. She
forced herself to become aware of her body once more.
She had been violated, invaded, forced repeatedly; but
she was a woman: she would endure. Her pride had
been battered and crushed, her very identity shredded;
but she was a warrior: she would fight.

The rain poured down on the thatch, drumming now
softly, now fiercely. Lightning flashed, and she saw
that the barracks was indeed empty. Her tormentors
were, for the time, gone.

Why? The question rose automatically, the product
of a lifetime of command and soldiery, but her body,
with a deeper wisdom, raised its own: *How long?*

For a minute she struggled with herself, for despair
was an open pit at her feet, one that beckoned invit-
ingly and pointed the way into madness and oblivion.
But her pride jerked her back like a strong arm, and
Kallye's wisdom had become a litany of hope for her.
Endurance.

She had nothing to lose by trying. Continued rape
would be no more than a simple prolongation of what
had gone before, and death would be a welcome release. Her thighs and belly were on fire with pain, her
legs so bruised and strained that movement was an
agony, but wincing, stifling her groans, she drew her

knees up, set her feet against the filthy pallet, and pushed herself up until there was slack in the chains that bound her hands.

By the light of the low-burning fire in the corner hearth, she examined the fetters. Designed to shackle a man, they had been bent rudely inward so as to grip a woman's narrower wrists, but the one fastened at the base of her left hand was loose.

Painfully, gasping through clenched teeth, she pulled against it. The iron ring slid part way along her hand and stopped, but her flesh was slick with the rank sweat of pain and fear, and once she consciously relaxed, she managed to slide it completely off.

Trembling, she felt her face as though to reassure herself that, in spite of the horror and the degradation, she was still herself. Her fingers examined the features of a woman, slid down over a small, finely boned chin, touched a slender throat that, inside, was raw with suppressed shrieks.

She wanted to weep. She wanted to cry out. She did neither. Although within her was an edge of fear that surpassed even the sharp brilliance of the lightning outside, it vied against the calm skills of an embattled warrior and her newfound knowledge of a woman's strength, and as Relys examined the shackle on her right wrist, she felt a calmness returning.

But this iron had been bent more tightly against her flesh, and her hand would slide only a little way through before it caught.

Ears straining for the sound of returning guards, she dragged herself up and examined the band more closely. It had been pounded shut—no key on earth would free her—and she had neither hammer nor file. There seemed to be no way out: she would remain here, bound to the bed of her violation, until the men of the Guard returned and resumed their sport.

No. The thought hammered at her. *No.*

She looked up at the door. It was shut. There might

be men waiting on the other side, but once again she had nothing to lose.

With an endurance born of the unendurable and a patience chipped out of walls of despair, she slid the fetter back, set her teeth to the base of her little finger, and began to gnaw.

Yyvas of Burnwood came as Senon of Bandon had come: exhausted, wounded, his body charred by what only Helwych knew to call napalm. When he staggered up the road to Kingsbury Hill the gate guards, frightened by his appearance, rushed him directly to the Hall, and the quick rumor of his coming and his wounds brought the other men from their barracks, their pleasures, and their duties to fill Hall Kingsbury and hear what he had to say.

Parts of his flesh had literally melted and fused under the deluge of liquid fire that had enveloped him, and Helwych was reminded strongly of Tireas's description of the man—Flebas was it?—who had accidentally touched the Tree. But his tale was even more alarming than his appearance.

"They came . . . out of the sky," he gasped. "Roaring and shrieking. And there were cracks and roars . . . like . . ."

Thunder shuddered along the roofs of Kingsbury. The rain poured down. Yyvas cowered. Several of his wounds still smoked in spite of the drenching he had received: the emblem of white phosphorus.

"Like that . . ." he managed. "And then there were hounds . . . like a flood . . ."

Helwych started. Hounds? He controlled the hounds, and he had been keeping them away from the towns. By what improbable autonomy had they—?

He felt cold, and he did not have to remind himself to waver with illusory wounds as he shifted in his chair. "These . . . things from the sky," he said slowly. "Did you see them?"

"Lights only, master."

Dryyim prodded Yvvas. "The title, hayseed, is *lord.*"

"Let him be," Helwych snapped. Jets. Hounds. A sudden and sadistic attack on a small village of Gryylth. Shaken, he cast about in his mind, searching, wondering whether the dark recesses of his consciousness still belonged to him alone. Was that a flash of blue-black off there in the distance? Did he detect a faint echo of mocking laughter that faded even as he strained to hear?

"And there were others," Yvvas rambled on. "They walked like men, but their faces were gray and glistening, and they bore weapons that killed at a distance."

And the words rang in Helwych's memory: *Stupid little Dremord fool . . .*

It had not mattered, then. The Specter had not been stopped by the curtain wall. It might even now be closing in on Kingsbury, looking for the petty little sorcerer who had betrayed it.

Helwych fought down the sudden flare of panic. He had controlled the hounds. He could control the planes and the Grayfaces, too. For now, he sent riders out into the storm to alert the garrisons and inform the towns that he was taking charge of the defense of the land. He did not bother with the formality of using Seena's name. The Guard knew who was running Gryylth, and the Guard would make sure that everyone else knew also.

Yvvas stared stupidly as the sorcerer parceled out tasks and orders. Eyes glassy, the man sat slumped in his chair like a tree struck by lightning.

"Go," said Helwych to his men. "Now. I will make other arrangements by myself, in private. If the Specter—"

He caught himself. Yvvas was staring. So were his men.

"If Vaylle wishes to attack," he faltered, "it will

find out what kind of reply it receives. We shall meet sorcery with sorcery.''

Even Dryyim was puzzled. ''My lord,'' he said. ''If you command such powers, why did you not go with our king?''

Helwych was tempted to slay Dryyim on the spot. ''If I had gone,'' he said, ''we would all be dead in our beds.'' He struck his staff on the ground, and the starburst of light made the men of the Guard stagger back a step. ''Go. *Now.*''

But as the men fled into the night, Helwych wondered whether what he was doing would prove to be of any use. The Specter had been unaffected by the curtain wall. It might be unfazed by his most potent spell. After all, it had taught him all that he knew. Perhaps it had only taught him what it wanted him to know.

Stupid little Dremord fool . . .

What did the Specter do to those who betrayed it?

Helwych looked down at Yvvas. ''Tell me,'' he said, ''were there any survivors of Burnwood?''

Yvvas did not reply. Helwych realized that he was looking at a corpse, that his question had been answered.

Stupid little . . .

He turned and ran from the room. He needed time. Time for plans. Time for magic.

Although exhaustion threatened to tumble them to the ground, the men and women of Alouzon's expedition insisted upon giving an immediate report to the three kings. Cvinthil listened attentively, and though he judged that Darham and Pellam were as distressed by the condition of the members of the party and unsettled by the tale that they told as he himself, still his own emotions were exacerbated and deepened by the stark knowledge of his own part in the workings of entrapment and betrayal.

A fool. An utter fool.

It was dark by the time that Marrha, who had shocked the men of Gryylth and the women of her own wartroop with her new name, her braided hair, and her attachment to Karthin, finished with a description of the ruins of Mullaen and the frenzied ride to Lachrae. The man she now freely called her husband stood by her, his thumbs hooked in his belt, nodding slowly as she spoke. Her hand had slipped into the crook of his elbow midway through her speech, and before she was done, Karthin had covered it tenderly with his own.

Dumb horror had, long before, rooted Cvinthil in his chair, but Darham stood and bowed deeply to Manda. "To attack six to save one comrade was a brave deed, and . . ."

Manda and Marrha exchanged glances that said that there was more to their tale than had been told. But the maid of Corrin only mustered a sad smile. Marrha nodded in return, then looked away, wiping her eyes with a dirty arm.

". . . and the odds and weapons you faced made it all the more valiant." Darham bowed again. "I am proud that you are my countrywoman, and proud also to call you a captain of my Guard, and my friend."

Several men of the Corrinian Guard cheered and whooped, and the Gryylthans murmured in approval, but the Vayllen harpers and healers looked bewildered. They had been obviously disturbed by the appearance and behavior of their own high priestess, and now, surrounded by these strangely polite and gentle warriors who had, a few hours before, been bent upon killing them, they were awash in confusion.

Manda blushed. "My thanks, my king. I . . ." Groping, she reached out and took Wykla's hand.

Smiling and extending his arm, Darham turned to Wykla, but she only bowed and withdrew slightly. Darham stood for a moment, nodded slowly, and resumed his seat.

"They are all valiant," said Cvinthil softly. Betrayed and betrayed again. And not just by Helwych, but by his own heart. Would Vorya have been so swayed by the wheedling voice of a boy sorcerer? "They fought against their own wounds and weakness to warn the people of Vaylle, so as to keep us from doing a great wrong."

Marrha had hung her head, and now she leaned close to Karthin and murmured to him. The big man bowed to the kings. "Lords," he said. "I would take my wife to bed. She is with child, and she needs rest."

Cvinthil blinked. Pregnant, too? At the front of the warriors who had gathered to listen, the women of the First Wartroop looked at one another in confusion, but Pellam nodded understandingly. "By all means," he said. "Rest has been delayed too long." He stood, regal and white-haired, the campfires flickering on the gold and silver embroidery of his robe and cloak. "To bed," he said. "All of you. Let those of us who have strength bear your burdens for a time."

The members of the party bowed and allowed themselves to be led away to the blankets and cushions prepared for them. Dindrane, though, remained at the edge of the firelight as though she had not heard. Indeed, she looked so worn that Cvinthil thought that quite possible.

Pellam regarded her for a time, then, limping, he went to her and took her gently in his arms. "As all my children are precious to me," he said softly, "so are you precious. 'Tis little I care for appearances, or for change. You are safe, and alive. I grieve for Baares, but I rejoice for you."

"I . . ." Dindrane shook her head, blinked at the harpers, could not meet the eyes of the healers. "I have seen too much, my king."

He rocked her like a child. "Peace."

Kyria appeared. Her eyes were dark with fatigue, but she smiled and offered a hand to Dindrane. "Come, sister. You saved my soul and my life both. Now let me help you to bed."

Cvinthil looked up. "Saved your soul, Lady Kyria? You said nothing of that."

Kyria straightened, met his gaze. "It would be ill to speak of it, lord," she said softly. Her courtesy was perfect.

Marrha had, freely and joyfully, embraced her womanhood, a husband, and a child. Wykla and Manda had fallen deeply into a love that any man and woman might envy. And Kyria had turned from a raging demon into the epitome of gentleness and power. "You have . . . changed, my lady," said Cvinthil.

Kyria smiled thinly. "I have indeed. We all have changed. Some found peace, others a horror that led to peace." She curtsied deeply. "My liege, my powers are at your command. Call me at need." Pellam put Dindrane into her arms, and she led the priestess away.

Cvinthil hung his head. "And do all who come to Vaylle grow in wisdom?" he murmured. "Then perhaps it is good for Gryylth that I have proven such a fool."

Darham had not uttered a word of accusation or shame, but it had not been necessary: Cvinthil was unstinting in his self-reproach. But now the Corrinian put a hand on Cvinthil's arm. "Brother," he said, "do not torment yourself."

Cvinthil lifted his head, eyes flashing. "Do not torment myself? Tell me, then: who shall be tormented? My wife and children? My people? My land? The captain and lieutenant I left at the mercy of a possessed sorcerer and a pack of bigoted soldiers? Who shall suffer in my stead?"

"Enough," said Pellam. "The question at hand is not what we have done, but what we shall do." He looked at Cvinthil, and the Gryylthan king suddenly felt himself the object of an examination as penetrating as any that Vorya had ever offered. "Are you satisfied, my friends . . ." Pellam paused meaningfully. ". . . that Vaylle is innocent?"

Darham nodded. "More than satisfied. But Broceliande, given Marrg—" he caught himself, smiled.
"Given Marrha's description, the spirit that dwells beyond the Cordillera cannot be fought with ordinary
bronze and steel. And even Alouzon Dragonmaster and
Kyria were daunted."

"Alouzon is gone," said Cvinthil. "And Kyria ad-
mits that she cannot do again what she did once." He
shrugged. Despair, horror, and shame fought against
his devotion to duty. He had to do something. But he
had no idea what.

Pellam spoke. "I am no warrior, good sirs. 'Tis a
priest and a ruler I am. But as much as your people
learned from us, so did we learn from Alouzon and
her companions. The lessons were painful, and not all
of us have accepted them, but . . ." His eyes were
wise and deep. ". . . the Goddess and God give us
abilities commensurate with our tasks."

Cvinthil shook his head. What good could five hundred warriors do against a Specter that could defeat a
Dragonmaster and a sorceress?

But Pellam continued. "That Kyria and Alouzon ac-
complished something is unquestionable, for since they
entered Broceliande, the random attacks on the people
of Vaylle have decreased. Hounds still prowl, but they
are fewer. Much fewer. And no Grayfaces or flying
things have been sighted for some time. Indeed, the
main conflict . . ." He paused at the word as though
examining an unpleasant taste. ". . . appears to be
behind you; in Gryylth. I would therefore counsel that
we learn something of the nature of the barrier that
has been erected about your lands, and from that perhaps we can judge how you might return home to deal
with the threat there."

Darham folded his hands, nodded. "I hear you and
agree."

"We have boats," said Pellam, "and quick and ag-
ile they are. If you are willing, I will send several out

to examine the curtain. 'Tis afraid I am that no more can be done at present.''

"No," said Darham. "There is more that can be done." He stood, his arms folded, and looked out over the young men he had brought from Corrin. "The beings you call Grayfaces are gone for now, but the hounds continue to roam. If Vaylle cannot fight, then Corrin will fight for Vaylle."

Cvinthil stirred. What would Vorya do? He was suddenly struck by the fact that it did not matter. It was what Cvinthil would do that mattered. He would not—could not—compete with a ghost. "Aye," he said, feeling stronger. "And Gryylth too. Kyria offered her service. I will ask that our blades be enchanted, and we will make this land as secure as possible before we must leave it." He stood up shakily and bowed to Pellam. "For your kind offer, friend Pellam, my deepest thanks. We came to do violence, and you have given us friendship in return. It will never be said that Gryylth does not protect its friends."

He looked up, out toward the east. There, far away, he could feel the shroud of darkness pulsing, roiling.

He dropped his eyes. His shame still cut deeply, but if Vaylle taught lessons, it would find him willing to learn.

The birth had been long and difficult—breech, the cord tangled, the mother frightened—but though all had gone well in the end, it was not until nearly dawn that Kallye, carrying her lamp and her bundle, left Anyyi's house and made her way through the rain and the muddy streets that led to her own bed.

This birth, though, could not but remind her of two others. Once, she had worked with Seena to bring a son and daughter into the world; and now Ayya and Vill lay motionless in Hall Kingsbury, seemingly neither alive nor dead. If what was called birth was, as she believed, only the first of the unfoldings and flowerings that made up the continuing birth called life, then those two births were in grave danger, and Kallye's midwife instincts made her worry and fret constantly both about them and about her inability to offer any aid or assistance.

In fact, she had not been allowed to see the children since the night she had first examined them. She had gone to Hall Kingsbury, had asked for permission to visit the queen, but her requests had been denied. Somewhere—behind the guards, within the palisade—Seena sorrowed and cared for her children, and all three were as far away from Kallye's help and support as they would have been had they been imprisoned.

Timbrin, though accessible, seemed equally beyond help. Kallye had stopped in on her frequently since that first morning, but the lieutenant had remained much the same: terrified, shocky, her speech confined to halting monosyllables. Paia and her daughters were taking good care of her, though, treating her like a member of the family, and Kallye hoped that such unstinting affection might eventually soothe whatever wounds she had sustained.

Ayya. Vill. Seena. Timbrin. Kallye no longer had any doubt that Helwych stood at the root of all four afflictions. And as the thunder dwindled to a far-off rumble and the lightning grew faint and intermittent, she could not help but wonder whether Helwych was behind even the workings of the weather, whether the sorcerer and his magic had twined—like the cord about the neck of Anyyi's child—throughout all of Gryylth.

She sloshed across the deserted market square, picking her way carefully. The worst of the storm had abated, but the rain was still falling, and the puddles were deep. Her cloak was sodden and cold, and it would be good to dry off and lie down for a few hours before—inevitably—she was called out to attend to another laboring woman. Maybe Gelyya could handle the next baby alone. Maybe—

Across the square, movement. Kallye stopped, peered through the falling rain, lifted her lamp a little higher. Faintly, very faintly, she made out the huddled shape of a figure crouched in the shelter of some rough lumber that had been left leaning against one of the houses. Curious and concerned both, she approached, made out pale skin and dark hair, realized that it was a naked woman.

And her stomach twisted when she saw that it was Relys.

She ran to the captain and dropped to her knees beside her. Relys was a mass of damage. Her groin ran with blood, and her right hand looked as though it had been chewed by wild beasts. Her face was bruised, likewise her belly and breasts, and her skin was frigid to the touch. She hardly seemed aware of Kallye's presence.

"Relys!" said the midwife. "Relys!"

In the distance, she heard the sound of footsteps. Two men, perhaps three. Relys's eyes flickered open and focused with an effort on Kallye's face. Her lips moved soundlessly: *Help me . . . please . . .*

"Oh, dear Gods." Kallye knew what had happened. She did not know why—but it did not matter why.

The footsteps drew nearer, approached the square.

"Child," said Kallye, "can you stand?"

Relys made futile movements with her arms and legs. Blood loss as well as emotional devastation had weakened her, but Kallye saw her straining against her injuries and pain, and gradually, with the soldiers drawing ever closer, she staggered to her feet.

"I must take you to my house," said Kallye. Relys stared with hollow eyes. "Immediately. But there are soldiers coming. Are they looking for you?"

Relys's eyes indicated that she did not know. Perhaps they said also that she did not care.

Kallye cast a glance over her shoulder. The soldiers had not entered the square yet. She put her midwife's bundle into Relys's good hand. "Hold it against your belly, child. Tight. It will help the pain, and it will help us both also."

While Relys struggled to do as she was told, Kallye cast her cloak about the captain's shoulders, made the clasp fast at her throat, and pulled the hood up. With the bulk of the bundle standing out from her belly, Relys looked vaguely pregnant—close enough to deceive those who knew nothing of womanly concerns, who cared little about them, who were, Kallye knew, a little afraid of such things.

She had barely finished when two men clumped into the market square. As she had expected, they were of the King's Guard.

King's Guard? More likely Helwych's Guard now.

Kallye leaned towards Relys's hood-shrouded face. "Say nothing," she whispered. "Just do as I say."

And as the soldiers approached, Kallye began to pull Relys across the square. "Rayyel!" she exclaimed. "Just look at you! Your child coming in the dead of night and you wandering about looking for me! You should have sent your husband to fetch me: you are in no condition to be out."

"Midwife?" boomed one of the men.

"Yes," said Kallye. "It is I."

"What are you doing out?"

Kallye did not flinch. "I was attending a birth, and on my way home, I find another lady in need of my skills."

The soldier strode up to the women. The rain ran down their faces, spattered and hissed in the torch they carried. "Who is this?" one said, pointing at Relys.

"This is Rayyel, wife of Carren," said the midwife promptly, grateful that these men from distant towns did not know the people of Kingsbury very well. "She is very near to giving birth and she—" She broke off. "Oh, Rayyel, you are bleeding! The baby cannot be far behind!"

And, true, blood was pooling in the mud at Relys's feet. It had nothing to do with impending delivery, but Kallye knew that the soldiers were ignorant of that. As she fussed over Relys, she stole a glance at the soldiers

and saw them looking at one another in obvious re-
vulsion.

She continued to fuss. Messy things, births. Not at
all to the taste of soldiers.

"I need to get you home quickly," she said. She
turned to the soldiers. "Can you help us? Please? We
do not have much time."

But the soldiers plainly wanted nothing to do with a
woman who was close to giving birth. They backed up
a pace, mumbled something about orders, escorted
Kallye and her charge to the other side of the square,
and then left.

Kallye wanted nothing more. She would, in fact,
have been satisfied with a good deal less. Talking
soothingly, cajoling, ordering and dragging when gen-
tler methods failed, she managed to get Relys as far
as the doorstep of her house; but there the captain's
knees buckled, and she collapsed in a wet and bloody
heap.

Kallye pounded on the door. "Gelyya! Open up!"
Relys's right hand had fallen out of the cloak. The
little finger and side of the palm were completely missing. Blood was running out, staining the puddles and
mud. "Quickly! Help!"

Gelyya flung the door open and cried out at the sight;
but in a moment she was helping Kallye to carry the
captain in. Relys's eyes were glassy, unseeing, and
though the room was clean and warm, as was the bed
in which they laid her, she had already slipped into
the merciful release of unconsciousness and knew
nothing of either.

❖ CHAPTER 10 ❖

Alouzon spent a long time luxuriating in the shower with soap and shampoo that seemed to her as much a miracle as the hot coffee and bagels she had for breakfast. By the time she gathered up the papers and books she had promised Brian, it was late enough in the morning that the traffic on Sunset Boulevard had settled into an order and predictability that allowed for contemplation; and as she skirted the northern border of the campus—just another Los Angeles driver on this hot October day—she recalled the dream that had come to her in the course of what she had discovered was forty-eight hours of unbroken sleep.

The Grail. The Grail had come. It had been shrouded, true, but that was to be expected. The important thing was that it had come, willingly, helpfully . . . even, she suspected, eagerly. As much as she needed its wholeness, the Grail wanted her to have it. She had suspected as much since the council in Kingsbury, but now she knew it for a fact: in the midst of her trials and difficulties, it had vouchsafed to her a partial vision of its glory so as to strengthen and nurture her.

And Solomon—no, not the Specter, Solomon—had once again returned from the dead. His sins were manifold, his hates and anger a plexed concatenation of emotions and failings that resonated too tellingly with her own. Perhaps for that very reason he had made her his confessor; but though he had not found final absolution at her hands, he had found enough peace so that he could turn his head at the very end and promise help.

Help? What kind of help could a corpse give?

She did not know, but as she pulled into a space in the teaching assistant section of the parking structure, she was deeply grateful for help in any form, from any hands. Goddess she might be, but in spite of the Grail's manifestation, the title sounded terribly hollow to her as she climbed out of the VW and removed the two boxes of paper and books.

Unable to figure out an excuse for transporting the Dragonsword across campus, she left it and her armor on the back seat. She kicked the door closed, and, balancing the heavy boxes one on top of the other, she descended the stairs and started across the warm lawn. The flip-flops she had dredged out of the back of the closet made limp noises on feet that were accustomed to boots, but though—tall, tanned, and attractive—she passed as a coed in the eyes of the students who crossed to and from class, her thoughts were of another world and another people, of past blood, and of memories of murder that were only exacerbated by the clothing that necessity had forced upon her.

Nothing she had found in Suzanne's closet had fit her, and Alouzon had been unwilling to don any of the oversized caftans that the plump little earth mother had been affecting for the last two years. But a decade ago, Suzanne Helling had been thinner, and in a cardboard box at the back of her closet were the clothes she had been wearing when blood had spilled across the R-58 parking lot. The elastic yoke of the peasant blouse now accommodated Alouzon's broad shoulders, and though the jeans had proved too short, a pair of scissors had turned them into respectable cut-offs.

But Alouzon felt as though she had cut up her past, and the faint blood stains on the blouse reproached her for her sacrilege. Suzanne had preserved these clothes as a reminder of the killings; and now, like everything else in her life, they had been sacrificed to Gryylth, to Vaylle, to all the urgent concerns that made up the workings of a world.

Alouzon scuffed up the steps to the north door of Kinsey Hall, having no idea what she would do in Los Angeles, or how she might ever return to Gryylth, or whether there might be anything for her to return to if she actually did. She wore these clothes, but her old life had been cast off like the chrysalis of a butterfly.

Butterflies don't live very long, though . . .

"Hey, mama, you lookin' good!"

She set her back against the heavy glass doors and mustered a smile at the black student who was crossing the rectangular lawn that lay between Kinsey and Haines Halls. His compliment, earthy and sincere, was a welcome tonic this morning. "Have a good one, guy."

"You need some help with those?"

"Nah. I'm OK." She pushed open the door and entered, murmuring: "Considering the circumstances, I guess."

She climbed the inner stairs into a world of fluorescent lights, beige walls, and institutional linoleum. Double doors stood open before her, and she passed through them and climbed the stairs to the second floor.

Suzanne Helling had felt alienated from the current generation of students and their ways, but Alouzon Dragonmaster had no business even setting foot on a modern campus. Her existence was, in fact, impossible, and she would not have been overly surprised had she faded into mist when, bracing the boxes against the wall outside the door marked 288, she touched something as concrete and prosaic as a door knob.

But she remained as she was: Alouzon. As she shouldered the door open, the secretary, not recognizing her, jumped up from her desk and held it wide, and Alouzon went down the inner corridor as though

Dragonmasters who were a combination of fifth century history and contemporary wish fulfillment were a common presence at UCLA.

Happens all the time. Sure. Like exchange students.

Brian's office lay at the end of the hall, but for a moment she stopped at another door. Beyond the thickly varnished wood lay the room in which Solomon Braithwaite had worked, tyrannized over his graduate students, and alternately dreamed and raged. There, Suzanne had resented him, argued with him, and finally departed for Gryylth with him.

If Alouzon Dragonmaster had a birthplace, it was here. Now, though, another professor occupied the office, the mahogany desk was gone, and the old man was as dead and buried as his status would allow.

"I suppose someone ought to put up a plaque or something," she said softly, and she was about to turn away when something held her. It was no more than a faint feeling, but it rooted her, for she had experienced it twice before—at Solomon's grave and at Helen's house—and it smacked both of unreality and absolute being, as though a door had opened into another world and a strange, impossible breeze were blowing through.

No howls this time, no wings, no glowing eyes; but Alouzon knew that there was something here. Supporting the boxes with a lifted knee, she knocked tentatively. No one was in. She tried the knob, and the door, unlocked, swung open to reveal a relatively ordinary office. Metal desk. File folders. Books. A picture of a man and woman embracing. An eighth generation Xerox of a crudely drawn cartoon with the caption: *"I think I'm a mushroom. Everybody keeps me in the dark and feeds me bullshit."*

"Yeah," said Alouzon. "I know exactly what you mean."

But though the sense of unreality persisted, she saw nothing unusual. Walls were solid, likewise floor and ceiling. No ocean lapped at the linoleum, and the windows gave a view only of Haines Hall.

"Miss?"

Alouzon jerked her head out of the office. "Uh . . . isn't this Brian's office?"

The secretary approached and shut the door. "Dr. O'Hara's office is at the end of the hall," she said helpfully. "On the right."

The woman obviously noticed nothing strange about the room. Alouzon feigned embarrassment and surprise. "Oh. Oh, yeah. Sorry."

But as she continued down the hall, the oddness glowed at her back like a hot furnace. Something. Something was going on.

Brian, thin and academic, looked up from his desk when she entered. "Hi," he said, rising. "I'm Dr. O'Hara. You must be Suzanne's friend."

She stared at him. He barely came up to her shoulders. "Uh . . . yeah." She plunked the boxes down on a vacant chair beside a cluttered desk covered with Suzanne's work: notes, papers, books. For a moment, she tried to imagine her own hands wielding a pen, or typing, or leafing through the binders. She could not.

Her steel wrist cuffs glinted in the light from the windows, and her hip felt painfully bare without the presence and weight of the Dragonsword. Unnerved by so much that was at once familiar and foreign, she nodded to Brian and turned to go.

But he wanted to talk. He sat down and propped his feet up on his desk. "So what happened with Suzanne?"

She stifled a sadistic urge to tell him. "She went home to her family."

Brian blinked behind his wire-rimmed glasses. "Just like that? I mean, she didn't even call."

Alouzon, trying not to look at him, found herself staring with horrified fascination at the poster of the A-4 Skyhawk cockpit controls. With a gasp, she tore her eyes away. "It was . . . uh . . . the weekend. I . . . I mean we . . . I mean she doesn't have your home number."

Brian sighed in frustration. "I'm really sorry to hear that, Allie."

Alouzon winced.

"I mean, she was quite a scholar. She was going to be one of the best. Damn near lived her work. I suppose I was a little too hard on her." He shrugged. "But, you know, there always seemed to be something that was bothering her. She never told me what it was, though."

The blouse and cut-offs suddenly felt ready to crawl off her body. "She was at Kent State."

"Kent? You mean in Ohio? I don't understand."

No one understood. Vietnam was something everyone tried to forget, something that the men would argue about during half-time, over cold beer and bowls of potato chips and pretzels: *I tell you, we coulda won. All we had to do was* . . . And the protests and the demonstrations were by now just a bad joke: idealism as silly as the fashions that had accompanied it.

She dropped her eyes. The faint blood stains on the blouse glared at her like a blazon of adultery. "She was there when the National Guard gunned down the students."

Brian was nodding, but he had suddenly averted his eyes. "Oh, yeah. I . . . uh . . . remember that. Weren't they just a bunch of hippies or something, though?"

Alouzon glared at him, recalling all the lives that she, once a pacifist and a war protester, had taken. The Dremord in the mountains. Bandon. The Circle . . .

Just a bunch of hippies. Just a bunch of Commies. Just a bunch of Dremords. Sure.

"They were people, Brian," she said. "Like you and me."

Brian still did not look at her, and his unease was such that she began to wonder if, maybe, he did indeed understand. Maybe he understood too well. Maybe he understood too much for him to be comfortable save with the false and vicarious experience of death given him by his research into the Vietnam War. In the 60s, some had gone off to battle, and some had taken to the streets, and others . . . others had hidden behind their books, denying their involvement, denying their concern.

And when the revolution comes, motherfucker . . . But the sentiment tasted stale and flat. Alouzon also understood too much now.

"Hey," said Brian after a moment, "I didn't mean to upset you. Were you there too or something?"

She was not sure what to say. "Kinda."

He turned back to his desk with studied casualness. "Well, look, if you happen to talk to Suzi sometime soon, tell her that I'll hold the position open for her until the end of the week. She'd better make up her mind by then, or we'll have to get someone else."

For a brief instant, the utter horror nearly overwhelmed Alouzon, and a part of her was suddenly screaming, clawing its way back towards a familiarity and a security that was now forever out of reach. A sob rose up in her throat, but she forced it down.

"I'll . . . I'll let her know," she said, and she groped her way out of the office and down the hall past the invisible strangeness that still burned at the edges of perception.

I've gotta get back . . .

But for now she was here in Los Angeles. The Dragon—her only link to Gryylth—was gone, and regardless of half-felt perceptions, she had to live, she had to survive.

Suzanne's purse had perished in the destruction of Helen's house, and the only money Alouzon possessed was a little over five dollars in bills and assorted change that she had scrounged out of the dresser drawers. Five dollars would not buy much food, but it would, along with a birth certificate that was mercifully vague about titles, godhood, and current appearances, allow her to procure a replacement driver's license. And with that she could withdraw funds from Suzanne's checking account.

An hour and a half later, sweating as much from the lie she was forced to live as she was from the heat, she was pulling out of the Department of Motor Vehicles lot with a license that blandly insisted that she was Suzanne Helling. Armed with a new book of checks from Suzanne's supply, she turned the VW towards the Erewhon Market on Beverly.

She had parked and was halfway out of the car when she realized that Suzanne was too well known at the market. Someone was going to notice that the name on the license did not match the remembered face. Shaking, she sat back down, closed the door, and rested her head on the steering wheel. She felt sick— fevered and cold at the same time.

"How the fuck am I supposed to live this way?" she said, hoping that a certain Holy Cup would hear. "I can't keep this up forever."

The temperature rose in the stationary VW, and to keep from stifling, she pulled back out onto Beverly and turned south on Fairfax, windows down and vents open. There were other health food stores in Los Angeles, places where Suzanne had not been known, where this counterfeit who had taken her place could buy brown rice, granola, and quarts of yogurt without notice or comment.

It was not until late in the day, when she was trying to find some clothes that would fit her, that she heard about the killings.

The May Company at the corner of Wilshire and La Cienega was a faded relic of art deco elegance, the gilt on its tall sign corroded with the constant attacks of smog and heat, the tiles of its facade cracked and unwashed. But inside it was cool, and the sales clerks were attentive and polite, and though Alouzon was struck again with the strangeness of this place, it was almost a relief to go through half-remembered commonplaces of her old, outworn life.

The stiffness of new Levi's. The clean drape of t-shirts fresh out of the plastic wrap. The whiteness of unworn sneakers. Outside, waiting for her in the VW, were a sword and armor and boots, but for now she was just another tall woman trying to find the right inseam length.

"Will that be all, then?" said the clerk, smiling, when Alouzon approached the counter.

Alouzon set down two pairs of jeans and four t-shirts. If she stayed in Los Angeles long enough to wear these out, she was sure that she would go mad. "Yeah. This is it."

"Cash or charge?"

What did one do in Gryylth? Cattle, she supposed. Or sometimes gold. Vorya and Cvinthil had always seen to her needs. But this was Los Angeles, and she was on her own. She pulled out her checks. "This OK?"

"With a major credit card."

"Uh . . ." She had forgotten about that. "Well . . . I guess I'm kind of stuck then."

The clerk paused, her hand hovering above the register keys.

"I suppose I could go get cash . . ." For a moment, Alouzon wanted to throw down the checks and walk away, raging at Silbakor for bringing her here, at the Grail for confronting her with incomprehensible situations, at herself for having gotten involved with Gryylth at all. But she had nowhere to go. "You see," she said apologetically, "my wallet got burned up. I just got a replacement license today."

The clerk looked genuinely concerned. "Was it a bad fire?"

"The whole house," Alouzon said truthfully.

"Oh, you poor thing." The clerk took Alouzon's license. "Let me see . . . is this all correct?"

"Yeah."

"All right then." She turned to ring up the items.

"You have an honest face, and I'm in charge of this department today. I'll just go ahead and approve it."

Alouzon swallowed. An honest face. What else would a Goddess have? "Hey, thanks a lot."

"Well . . ." The clerk's hand flew over the keys, punching in employee number, inventory codes, prices. "This has gotten to be such a terrible world these days. I think we all have to look out for one another. People are hurting themselves, girls are getting raped . . ." She was an older woman, perhaps fifty. Her face, pale and lined beneath its coat of makeup, was fragile—someone's grandmother, a widow perhaps, a woman who had grown up in a more secure world, who had found that society had changed out from under her, who now found herself burdened by concerns and problems of which the young girl she had been once (sweet and naive and looking forward to a man, marriage, and a blissful life) had never dreamed.

Alouzon nodded understandingly as she wrote out a check for the total. Her own life had once been peaceful, and after the horror had set in, she had made a final, desperate bid for security. But that was all gone now.

The clerk went on. "Like those murders out by MacArthur Park the other night. Awful. Just awful. To leave those poor men dissolved like that. I mean, they were hobos, of course, but what kind of monster would do that?"

Alouzon stared at her, heart suddenly pounding. It took her a moment to find her voice. "D-dissolved?"

"Oh, yes. Didn't you see it in the paper?"

The *Los Angeles Times* lay rolled up and unread on Suzanne's coffee table. Alouzon Dragonmaster had not thought to concern herself with current events. Gryylth was quite enough for her.

Alouzon forced herself to concentrate on the signature on the check. Painstakingly, she spelled out the name of the dead woman. "Uh . . . no."

"The police found them in the morning." The clerk shook her head. "They'd been . . . well, you know . . . eaten . . ."

Alouzon tried not to shake as she creased the check at the perforations, tore it from the book, and handed it over. "Eaten? I . . . thought you said they'd been dissolved."

"That too."

"Yeah . . . that's just . . . terrible . . ."

The clerk bagged the clothes and put them into Alouzon's hands. "Well, you be careful out there, young lady. And you have a nice day."

Alouzon blinked at the glare that shone in through the distant glass doors. MacArthur Park. Eaten. Dissolved.

Hounds.

"Yeah," she said. "You too."

Escorted by the harpers and healers of Lachrae, the forces of Gryylth and Corrin took the coastal road north to the capital. Though most of them had been prepared to slaughter the Vayllens without quarter a few days before, they accepted the alteration in objectives philosophically. They were warriors and soldiers, not butchers, and the sense of honor upon which their culture was based was such that they were revolted by the thought of killing innocents.

Hounds, though, were another matter.

Kyria, refreshed by a day and a half of sleep at the side of her beloved Santhe, had enchanted the blades and pikes of the army in a few hours. And when an ill-fated pack of hounds showed up near midday, it was immediately dismembered by an army eager to vent its frustrated anger on a definite enemy. No magic was used, none was necessary: within minutes, nothing but twitching limbs and rent carcasses remained of the beasts.

The Vayllens—ever polite and courteous—tried not to show fear or horror at the methodical violence, but

Dindrane noticed many of her people watching the battle with drawn faces. More than one turned to her looking for comfort and advice, but she had none to give them. This was war. This was fighting. And she had seen enough and felt enough that she could no longer disapprove of either.

And that, too, was a horror for the Vayllens. Pellam nodded sagely at the alteration in her manner, and the members of Alouzon's party embraced her as a sister, but Dindrane's own people were profoundly shaken.

Dindrane herself was shaken, but there was no going back. As irrevocably as the forces of Broceliande had killed Baares, as completely as they had destroyed Daelin and the manor houses, so had they changed the priestess of the land. Clad as a boy, her face scarred with phosphor, she rode towards Lachrae, at one with her comrades, separate from her people.

But though she entered the city with her friends, there was still a road that she had to take alone: the road home. Pellam and his attendants escorted the warriors to the King's House, but Dindrane dismounted without explanation and made her way along the street she had walked on a morning long ago, when Gryylth was but a name and a faint haze on the horizon.

She entered her house and shut the door. Untenanted for over three months, it was nonetheless clean and ready for her, for Pellam had so ordered. But her footsteps sounded terribly, terribly hollow and alone as she crossed the hall and climbed the stairs; and when she reached the second floor, Baares's big harp stood proudly in the corner like a loyal dog waiting to greet a master who would never return.

She sank down on her knees beside the instrument, put her arms about the wood and wire, rested her head against the forepillar. Baares had died in her arms, but only now had she come to the leisure and the solitude necessary to fully comprehend and mourn that death.

She cried for a long time, remembering all the nights

he had harped her to sleep, all the mornings he had
joined her on the terrace, conjoining cup and knife and
breakfasting on bread and wine as the sun rose in yellow splendor, the sea sparkled, and the city awoke.
Physical and spiritual both, their love had in its own
way sustained the land as much as the standing stones
of the temples, for as the Goddess and the God loved,
so had Dindrane and Baares, and the sight of the
priestess and the harper standing together hand in hand
had, she knew, heartened many who otherwise would
long before have fallen to the horror of Broceliande.

Gone. Baares was gone. And Dindrane had changed.
And what would sustain the land now? The Goddess?

Alouzon?

Daylight was fading into dusk when she lifted her
head, her eyes swollen almost shut. She realized that
a knock had come to the door a while before, and that
someone was now ascending the stairs.

Soft steps: the tread of a woman.

"Who comes?" she called, her voice faint in the
empty house.

Kyria answered her. "A friend."

In the dusk, the sorceress was a dark shadow against
the white marble of the walls and stairs, but Dindrane
saw that she had bathed, trimmed the phosphor-tatters
out of her hair, and donned a robe the color of the
evening sky. A cluster of silver stars gleamed at her
right shoulder, and her mantle was fastened with a
brooch bearing the crest of the king of Gryylth.

Kyria's voice was soft and sweet. "We missed you.
I came to look."

"I have been here."

"I knew."

Dindrane still clung to the harp, not desperately, as
one unwilling to release the dead from memory or desire, but sorrowfully, sadly, as a child about to marry
might embrace a loved parent. "He is gone," she
whispered. The bronze strings thrummed softly in res-
onance. "I have no husband."

Kyria knelt beside her. "It is so, my friend. He is gone."

Dindrane hung her head. The wood of the forepillar was smooth against her scarred cheek. " 'Tis no use even to ask why. 'Tis no use to regret or to sorrow."

Kyria nodded, her black hair rustling in the silence.

The priestess touched the soundbox. Her tears still flowed. "He died well, though. As valiantly as any man or woman of Vaylle could wish."

"Vaylle or Gryylth or Corrin."

" 'Tis true."

Kyria slipped an arm about Dindrane's waist. "Are you . . ." Her eyes, black as jet, were as compassionate, Dindrane thought, as if she too had seen loves lost, lives changed. "Are you concerned about his soul?"

"Because he died fighting?" Dindrane sobbed and laughed both. "Would Alouzon, my Goddess, reject such a one?"

Kyria smiled softly. "No. Never."

"He is well," said the priestess. "But I shall not see him again this side of the Far Lands."

Kyria was silent.

"But Alouzon . . ."

The sorceress's eyes flickered. "What of her?"

Dindrane lifted her head. "Where is she? Dead?"

"Do you think that is possible?"

Blue eyes met black. "I do not," said Dindrane. "Nor do you. But my husband is no more, my country lies burned and scarred, and my people live in fear. Alouzon is our Goddess and our hope. Therefore I ask: *Where is she?*"

Kyria shook her head.

Dindrane frowned. "You know more than you are telling."

Kyria was still shaking her head. "I am telling as much as I know. I think many things, I hope for many others, but I do not know them with certainty."

"Where is Alouzon?"

"I do not—"

"What do you *think* then, sorceress?" the priestess demanded. "Do not ridicule me, I pray you. I wish to know of the welfare of my Goddess."

The house was silent. Even the streets outside were devoid of sound or movement.

"I think," said Kyria, "that Silbakor took her."

"Where?"

"To . . ." Kyria looked away.

"Where?"

Kyria's words came reluctantly. "To the world from which she and I came."

"For what purpose? To what end? Why has she not returned?"

"I do not know, my friend." Kyria's voice was deeply sorrowful. "Upon my word I do not know. I wish I did."

Dindrane passed a hand over her face, felt the dampness of her tears. "Forgive my harsh manner, sister," she said. "So much has changed, so much has been taken from me. I had hoped to . . ." To what? Worship? Curse? Weep? Vent the anger of hopeless impotence upon one who, whether Dindrane liked it or not, had created her and all her people?

Kyria nodded slowly. "There is nothing to forgive. I understand."

Dindrane rested her head again on the forepillar. "I . . . do not think that I can sleep in this house," she said. "There would be . . . dreams."

Gently, Kyria tugged at her arm. "Come then. You have friends at the King's House who love you. There is water to wash in, and food, and rest. Come be with your friends. Come live with us."

Comrades, Kyria might have said. *Fellow warriors.*

Dindrane rested a hand on the harp, ran her fingers down the sound box. What she had become had no place in this house. Nor, really, any place in Vaylle. And so should she now bathe and rest and don the garb of the magistrate of Lachrae—mantle and torque, skirts and staff?

Clad as a boy, knife at her belt, she rose, stood silently for a time. "I will go with you," she said at last. "A moment, though."

She went through the door into her bedroom, opened a carved chest, took out a pair of shears. And as Kyria watched—solemnly, understandingly—Dindrane stepped to the mirror and, lock by golden lock, cut off her hair.

❖ CHAPTER 11 ❖

Weakened by blood loss, her soul as torn and bruised as her body, Relys writhed deliriously for a week. Kallye and Gelyya salved her wounds, bathed her, and held her good hand during her worst flashbacks, but as midwives they could do little more, and calling a physician would only have attracted attention. Fortunately, fever did not set in, but Relys's condition was nonetheless critical.

Her circumstances, too, were grim. Within a day, soldiers were searching for her, questioning townsfolk, knocking on doors, demanding entry. They came to Kallye's house once, but the women had already hidden the captain under a pile of laundry; and the men of the Guard, ill-at-ease in a midwife's house, gave the room only a cursory glance before they departed.

But out of the guarded and palisaded Hall eventually seeped the tale of the attack on Burnwood—a more pressing matter, really, than the disappearance of one broken toy from the barracks—and the search was given up, the men of the Guard turning instead to other tasks. Within days, the fortifications at the edge of the hill had been strengthened, young boys of the countryside who were skilled with the bow were being recruited as valuable members of the expanding garrisons, and the wartroops were drilling several times a day in the fields surrounding Kingsbury.

Explanations came quickly—though not from Hall Kingsbury—for a week later, when the sky was blue and cloudless, two things that flew like birds and shrieked like damaged souls blazed down out of the north, straight towards the town. Things like seed pods or eggs fell from them, and the hillside at the edge of the plateau suddenly exploded into flame.

At the same time, cracks and pops and ripping sounds came from the opposite side of the hill. Gray-clad figures were climbing the slope, and their weapons—like those reported by Yyvas of Burnwood—sprayed projectiles that spattered against the earthworks and the wooden barriers and turned them to clouds of dust and splinters.

There were many gray men on the hillside, all armed, all deadly, but the wartroops now sent several volleys of iron-tipped arrows down the hill, accompanied by a wave of rolling boulders. One or two gray figures fell, the rest retreated a short distance.

But as the flying things approached once again, Helwych arrived. The weedy youth had seemingly recovered from his wounds, for he and a number of personal guards sprinted out of the hall and down the street. The guards looked nervous, but Helwych, his lips drawn back and down in a grimace that could have been either of concentration or fear, lifted his staff and uttered a word of command. The sky was suddenly pocked by two billowing orange and yellow fireballs.

Amid an outbreak of relieved cheers from wartroops and civilians alike, the young sorcerer ran to the other side of the hill and confronted the figures on the hillside. Projectiles smacked for a moment into the logs at his feet, but Helwych's power flowed, he barked orders, and the figures abruptly stopped, saluted, and turned back down the hill.

More cheers, but as Helwych returned to Hall Kingsbury, he groped for a way through the press of people and soldiers almost as though he did not see what was before his open eyes, and he was curt and abrupt with his men when he bumped into them, like someone who, deeply frightened, sought to deny his fear.

Kallye and Gelyya spoke of it that night while, across the room, Relys tossed in fitful dreams. Thin to begin with, she had grown emaciated, for she had eaten nothing since Kallye had found her. It was all her nurses could do to get her to drink.

"We will have to get Relys out of Kingsbury," said Kallye. "We have only a few days."

"How? If the land is full of hounds and . . ." Gelyya shook her head. "What did the men call them? Grayfaces?"

"Aye."

"Then travel will be impossible. The soldiers are already telling people not to leave the town save by daylight."

Kallye snorted. "A fine plan that is. As if you and I will huddle indoors in our beds while our ladies deliver alone in the night."

Gelyya shrugged. "I have no intention of staying in if a woman needs me. But travel . . ." She glanced at Relys, shook her head.

"I think what Helwych did this afternoon gained the Grayfaces' allegiance," said Kallye. "The countryside about Kingsbury should be safe for a time, and we must take advantage of that fact. If Relys stays here, she is bound to be discovered eventually."

Gelyya looked doubtful. "Do you . . . do you think she will recover?"

Relys had stopped thrashing for the moment. Her wounds were grievous, both physically and emotionally, and Kallye had, to be sure, seen better. But she had seen and heard of worse, too. "She will live," she said.

Relys stirred. "I will . . . live."

Kallye and Gelyya exchanged startled glances and rushed to the bed. Relys's eyes were open. Her face was pale and drawn even against the white pillow, and her cheeks had grown hollow. Painfully, she lifted her right hand, examined the dressings that covered it. "How . . . long?" she said.

"A few days past a week, child," said Kallye.

"Where . . . am I?"

"In Kingsbury. In my house."

Relys nodded slowly. Her eyes, though they seemed to comprehend what was before them for the first time since Kallye had found her, still held the hollow, ravaged emptiness of the rape. "Timbrin . . ."

"With Paia still. She is well. The men do not know of her presence there, nor of yours here."

"We must send you both someplace safe," said Gelyya.

Relys closed her eyes slowly, and her face clenched for a moment. "Safe?" she said. "What is . . . safe . . . anymore?"

Helwych had been thorough; when Kyria and Dindrane, taking to the astral, attempted to penetrate the curtain wall that now surrounded Gryylth, they found that the spiritual Worlds had been riven apart with such force and efficiency that passage was impossible. And when the boats that Pellam had sent out returned, their captains reported that several of the crafts had, upon approaching the wall, been incinerated. The rest had kept a good distance after that, but their cautious explorations indicated that the impenetrable barrier encircled the entirety of Gryylth and Corrin.

Very thorough. Very thorough indeed.

That night, lamps burned in the great hall of the King's House as the rulers and advisors of three nations met in council. Pellam, by now used to the oddity—and the necessity—of arms and armies in his land, was as solemn and at times as strangely informal as ever; and Darham as usual seemed to be turning the facts over in his mind, avoiding both despair and impetuosity. Cvinthil, though, had changed, rising above his anger and setting aside his single-mindedness to be-

come thoughtful and deliberate in his questions and
ideas.

"Could you and Dindrane protect the flotilla from
the effects of the wall so that we might come to a safe
landing in Gryylth?" he asked Kyria. Kyria looked to
Dindrane. The priestess was leaning on her staff, eyes
downcast, her close-cropped head as bright as a gold
coin in the torchlight. Silently, she shook her head:
she and Kyria had already talked about that.

"I fear not, my king," said the sorceress. "Our
potencies are not trivial, but to protect an entire flotilla from an attack that might take many forms is
beyond us."

"What about a frontal assault?" said Manda. "Perhaps the answer lies in battling straight through the
wall rather than in defending against it."

The Gordian knot itself would have given no more
problem to Manda of Dubris than it had to Alexander
of Macedon. Because of her forthrightness, Wykla had
a lover, and Marrha was alive and well. Kyria wished
that everything could be so simple. "Under normal
circumstances," she said, "that would indeed be an
option. But this wall . . ." She looked for intelligible
explanations, but succeeded only in vexing herself. She
knew magic by instinct alone; when she attempted to
explain what she did, she was reduced to groping for
words. "Attacking it," she said at last, "would be
like trying to empty the sea with a bucket. From moment to moment it is renewed, and its sources of existence lie in the universe itself."

"Are you saying that Gryylth is lost?" Cvinthil's
tone was one of careful neutrality.

Kyria shook her head. "I am only saying that a direct attack on the wall would accomplish nothing."

"You said also that defense is impossible."

"So it is."

Cvinthil spread his hands. "Then what do we do?
Will it take an act of the Gods to restore us to our
lands?"

An act of the Gods was what Kyria prayed for nightly. But Alouzon, she suspected, was in Los Angeles, light years away from Gryylth or Vaylle.

Alouzon in Los Angeles? What could she be doing there? How could she live?

She groped into a past life for counsel. "In a place where I lived once," she said, "there were some women I knew who called themselves witches." How far away it all seemed now! Consciousness-raising groups and feminist religion had become as outlandish to her as dragons and swords had seemed to Helen Addams. "They had many things to say about life, some wise and some silly. One of the wise things, though, was that for every problem there is an infinity of solutions."

Darham was nodding. "Presented with two unsatisfactory choices," he said, "seek then a third."

Kyria smiled. "Exactly."

"You are counseling patience, then," said Cvinthil.

"Aye," said Kyria, trying to soften the response as much as she could. "I am afraid so."

The king of Gryylth nodded slowly. "Patience is a bitter medicine to swallow when your land is locked away and your wife and children and comrades are in the hands of an enemy. But I have been hasty . . ." He looked to Darham. ". . . as hasty as Tarwach, as hasty as Dythragor, and I have found no more joy than they. Therefore, lady Kyria, if you counsel patience, I will accept your counsel."

Kyria curtsied formally. "Thank you, my king. Dindrane and I will continue to search for another way."

Marrha, at Karthin's side as usual, was nodding agreement, but she said: "Alouzon spoke of other ways once, Kyria, and the need was speedily answered. But this time I fear that we may wait for a long time."

Kyria spread her hands. "That may well be. And I am afraid that when it comes, it may well come unlooked-for and unrecognized."

Wykla laughed suddenly. "Friend Kyria, you have obviously studied your arts well: you have become as enigmatic as Mernyl."

"Indeed?" Kyria discovered that she was blushing. "I had not intended to be so."

Pellam was nodding. "Fear not, child. It is seemly for a sorceress to be enigmatic."

But Santhe spoke, his manner uncharacteristically serious. "If we are to wait for a solution, lords, then I would suggest that we make ourselves useful to our hosts. There has been an increase in the attacks of the hounds, and the beasts are becoming bolder with each passing day. When first we arrived, we offered help to the Vayllens. I say it is now time to make good our offer."

Pellam turned his deep eyes on the councilor. "You have seen how violence affects my people, friend Santhe. What is it you propose?"

Santhe met Pellam's eyes with his own. He had lost men, had nearly lost his lover, and his expression was that of a man who knew what it was to be touched by violence. "The hounds are strong," he said, "and they rove freely, but with enchanted weapons, a well-armed troop of warriors can defeat easily all but the largest packs. If we split our forces into wartroops and phalanxes, each group could patrol a given section of the land. They would be able to engage the packs before any villages or steadings are attacked."

Kyria lifted an eyebrow. "Search and destroy patrols," she said.

Santhe's brow furrowed at her terminology, but he nodded. "If you will, my love."

Santhe's plan would relieve the Vayllens both of the fear of attack, and—if the hounds were destroyed far away from the villages and towns—the necessity of witnessing constant slaughter. Still, it made Kyria uneasy: these methods had not worked particularly well in Vietnam, and she could only hope that, in a more open land, and with the support and friendship of the inhabitants, it might succeed.

No Grayfaces had been reported, but there was always a possibility, as Marrha now pointed out, that they—or the jets—would return. "And, as we have seen," she said, "swords and leather are of little use against them."

"If there are Grayfaces or jets," said Dindrane, speaking so suddenly that she startled the assembly, "then do not engage them. Hide from the jets. And in the case of Grayfaces, send for Kyria . . ." She hefted her staff. It had, in Baares's hands, killed hounds. It could, both Kyria and the priestess knew, kill more. ". . . or for me."

Pellam blinked. He bowed his head for a moment. "Are you sure, priestess?"

Dindrane met his eyes. "I am. Do you wish to dismiss me from your service, my lord?"

Pellam was still and silent for a long time. Then, finally, he shook his white head. "I do not." He sighed. "Perhaps, in the end, you will prove wiser than I, Dindrane. I cannot foresee your future well, though I suspect it leads along some dark roads."

Dindrane nodded.

Pellam attempted a thin smile. "But no darker than those which you have already traveled," he said.

Santhe spoke up. "Brighter, lord. Much brighter, I hope."

Dindrane's friends echoed him, and the priestess straightened up proudly, smiling through her tears.

Relys seemed to go through the motions of life with a kind of numb acceptance. She ate when pressed, took medicine when told to, allowed the changing of the bandages on her hand without a murmur of protest.

Her pain, Kallye knew, was terrific. Herbs and salves had kept her mutilated hand from becoming infected, but the flesh along the edge had been gnawed away, as had the whole of her little finger. The tendons and

muscles that traversed her palm had been severely
damaged, and even if the terrible wound healed, she
would probably never lift a sword again.

As gently as she could, Kallye told Relys of that
possibility. The captain took the news without emotion. "Perhaps I will learn to draw a sword with my
left hand," she said tonelessly. She shrugged, looked
down at herself. She was wearing women's clothes,
the first she had ever donned. "It perhaps does not
matter any more."

Gelyya looked up from stirring supper. Her eyes
flashed. "It matters a great deal, Relys. I wish that I
could use a sword."

Relys nodded absently. "I will not say that it is unseemly for women to carry weapons, for that would
be what Helwych wishes. But . . ." She clenched her
eyes suddenly and turned towards the wall. "I fear I
no longer have the heart for it."

"Your heart will come back, child," said Kallye.

Relys bent her head.

She remained in pain, and though Kallye could supply bandages and poultices for her hand and the physical aftereffects of the rape, the greater pain—Relys's
day-to-day knowledge and memory of what had been
done to her—was beyond the skills of the midwife.

Over the next two weeks, the captain's body healed
enough so that she could walk without stumbling. But
while Relys was regaining her mobility, Gryylth as a
whole seemed increasingly restricted. Decrees and orders that confined the people to their villages flowed
from Hall Kingsbury, and there were rumors that the
sorcerer would soon order the inhabitants of the outlying steadings to leave their homes and relocate to
towns and easily defended camps.

Helwych was popular with the Kingsbury folk after
his defense of the town, but his popularity was rooted
more in fear and necessity than in love, and his orders
made everyone uneasy. Free steadings and farming
were the foundation of the Gryylthan way of life, one

that had remained unaffected both by ten years of war and Cvinthil's decrees on women's freedom. But now it was being directly threatened. That the king had taken the men away overseas was bad enough, but mass relocations would disrupt it thoroughly.

But there were reasons for Helwych's orders. Anyone who looked out from the edge of Kingsbury at night could see flashes of light and hear distant rumbles that had nothing to do with summer storms. Flecks of light raced up from the horizon, and starbursts pocked the dark sky like puffballs after a heavy rain. At night, too, there were hounds. The beasts did little more than snuffle at shuttered windows and barred doors, and now and then a chorus of howls would split the pre-dawn darkness, but their simple presence made the townsfolk very willing to heed the nightly curfews.

Nonetheless, Relys could not stay in Kingsbury forever, and now Timbrin also was in danger: if Paia and her daughters had to move into the town, Timbrin would be found out.

Kallye considered her options carefully, discussed them with Relys. The captain, confronted with a situation more of strategy than of helplessness, rallied momentarily. "Quay," she said after a minute's thought.

Kallye was puzzled. "So far?"

Relys spooned soup into her mouth. "With that serpent in Hall Kingsbury, better far than near. I know Hahle a little, too; and I doubt that he has given Helwych's orders a gracious reception. He is a good man . . ." Her eyes seemed to see nothing for a moment. ". . . and I think he would take in two broken women and . . ." Again the stare. ". . . and protect them."

"Courage, warrior," said the midwife.

"Courage? Nay." Relys shook her head. "It requires no courage, only a will to survive." She examined her bandaged right hand. "A fox will gnaw off its leg in order to escape a trap, will it not? Perhaps it is not surprising that I must leave my hand, my heart, and my maidenhood behind in order to gain my freedom.''

A few days later, Kallye and her apprentice passed through the gate of the town with no comment from the guards. Given the urgency and necessity of their trade, midwives were still allowed to come and go as they pleased, and if the men noticed that Gelyya wore her hood up in spite of the warmth of the afternoon, they said nothing.

Together, the two women made their way down the hill, but about halfway down, Kallye's companion staggered suddenly and sagged against her. ''A moment, please,'' said Relys from within the cloak. ''Forgive my weakness.''

''You are still ill, child,'' said Kallye. She caught Relys and sat her down at the base of two big rowan trees. ''And you have had no more exercise these last weeks than walking from bed to table.''

Relys pushed the hood back enough to better examine the road. It stretched off and down, switchbacking across the slope of the hill. ''I do not know if I have the strength for this,'' she whispered.

''You do.''

''Kallye—''

Kallye gave her a gentle shake. ''You do, woman.'' Relys flinched, but the midwife went on. ''I have had mothers screaming in fear in the first hour of their labor, but faced with a task they must do, both for themselves and their child, they conquer their fear. They endure. They endure because they are women, and because they *must*.''

Relys dropped her eyes. ''Endure.'' She spoke with bitterness.

''Aye, endure. You have yourself to save, woman, and you have your lieutenant, whom I know you care for as your own child. Do not deny it: I saw the look in your eye that morning at Paia's house.'' Kallye straightened, folded her arms. ''So.''

Face pale, sweating from the heat and effort, Relys seized a low branch and pulled herself to her feet. She swayed, but she stood. "Let us continue, then."

Relys drove herself on, but with the frequent rests that she needed, the afternoon was well along before she and Kallye reached the base of the hill. The women and boys who were tending the fields were already packing up and going home, and Kallye began to doubt that Relys could reach Paia's house before night fell and the hounds began to prowl.

But a girl in a light cart was waiting at a turning in the road. "Mother sent me to fetch you," she said. Her bright, unbraided hair shimmered in the westering sun. "She is with Timbrin and the babies, Father is off with the king, and my brothers and sisters are at work in the fields. So I came."

Kallye bowed to the girl. "Our deepest thanks, Vyyka."

"Well, after what you told Mother, she worried," said Vyyka, bobbing her head up and down. "And I rather liked the idea of taking the cart alone." She grinned. "If this is what men do every day, then I think they must have a fine time in the world!"

Relys pushed back her hood, smiling wanly. "The Gods bless you," she said. "But I wonder sometimes how fine a time they really have."

Together, Kallye and Vyyka helped Relys onto the cushions and blankets that padded the back of the cart, then climbed up onto the front seat. With the horse doing the work, they made good time, and dusk had not even begun to fall when Vyyka brought the cart through the gate in the embankment surrounding the steading and stopped before the house. Paia was waiting for them, and at her side was a slight figure in a blue gown. At first, Kallye thought it was one of Paia's daughters, but then she realized that it was Timbrin.

The lieutenant had mended slowly. Physically, she was almost well, but her mind still suffered from the blast of magic. She smiled and came forward to help

Relys out of the cart, but she did so uncertainly, tentatively, as though a sharp word might send her fleeing back into the house.

Relys's legs had stiffened, and she swayed when her feet touched the ground. Timbrin held her tightly. "Oh, Relys." Her dark eyes were troubled and sad. "They told me what happened. I am sorry. I would I had been there."

Relys let her cheek rest against Timbrin's curly hair. "Peace, my friend," she said. "Do not blame yourself. There was nothing that you could have done." Relys's eyes were clenched again with pain. She sucked in a slow breath, let it out. "What is left of the First Wartroop on this side of the sea is together again. Let us thank the Gods for that."

At the mention of the wartroop, a shadow crossed Timbrin's face. "Please, Relys." Shock had erased her defiance and temper, and in women's garb she looked soft and vulnerable: a girl, no more, recovering from an illness. "Not yet."

Relys examined her for a moment, searching. Timbrin dropped her eyes. "Aye," said Relys softly. "Not yet. There will be time enough for that later." She touched Timbrin's face tenderly, as a mother might caress a child. "Much later."

❖ CHAPTER 12 ❖

The autumn dusk fell early over Los Angeles, the sun setting in a haze of smog out to the west and turning the ocean the color of blood; but darkness brought no relief from the heat. The Santa Ana winds continued to blow, the city continued to parch and swelter, and the twilight sky held a sense of oppressive weight as Alouzon Dragonmaster drove out towards MacArthur Park through the tail end of rush hour traffic.

The story in the *Los Angeles Times* had been simple and blunt, the lack of evidence and the horror of the murders precluding any journalistic sensationalism. The two men who had been found by an early morning police patrol had been unrecognizable, their bodies scattered over a wide area; and what was left of them—where the flesh had not been gnawed from the bones—had been partially dissolved by corrosives that the forensic specialists were still trying to identify. The police had theories that ranged from a drug deal gone bad to Satanism, but Alouzon knew otherwise.

Wilshire Boulevard split MacArthur Park into two halves, the north grassy and open and dotted with picnic tables and playgrounds, the south occupied for the most part by a lake. Alouzon pulled into a parking space near Alvarado Street and climbed out, her new jeans stiff and sweaty both. The hot wind stirred her bronze hair as she shoved a coin into the meter, and she leaned on the wall and examined the park to the south.

She remembered the lake. She had fallen out of nothingness and onto the grass near the lake. But the men had been killed in the same area, and if there was any logic left in the universe, the two facts had to be connected.

She entered the park at the corner gate and made her way south. The fast-food stand was doing a brisk, last minute business in soft drinks and hot dogs. Over her left shoulder, the Westlake Theater sign came on in neon red, and she could see, just over the roof of the *Botica del Pueblo,* another sign hanging from a rickety scaffolding of criss-crossed girders and beams like an ancient god crucified upon the indifference of civilization: *Olympic.*

But here, on this broad swath of grass that extended from Alvarado to the lake, were tokens of the violence. Despite the efforts of the park service, patches were still greasy and brown from phosphor, and Alouzon's warrior eyes detected the trail of the men who had seen, and then had fled, and then had died without even vaguely comprehending the nature or purpose of the beasts that had slain them.

Night was coming on, but there were still a few sightseers about, come for the trees and grass or to examine the scene of the killings. Alouzon passed on, crossed Alvarado, and spent the next two hours in Langer's Delicatessen, lingering over a pastrami on rye and a soda while she watched the park clear and the artificial lights come on.

Light was not desirable, for she wanted to examine the park leisurely, without worrying about junkies or the police. But she had to put up with it, and when darkness had fallen as much as the city would allow, she sloshed her way north through the pools of mercury vapor light until she reached her VW. She fumbled in the back seat, withdrew the Dragonsword and wrapped it in a big beach towel, then climbed over the low wall into the park.

A fountain hissed in the distance. Waves lapped softly on the shore. Discarded hamburger wrappings rustled in the dry wind. Styrofoam cups rolled along the bare dirt and rattled to a stop at the base of date palms and flame trees.

For the next two hours, Alouzon prowled through the park, searching, feeling, her sword ready beneath its terrycloth wrappings. She had fallen into Los Angeles on Saturday morning. In the course of the day, crowds had visited the park—picnicking, plashing in the paddle boats, playing frisbee or volleyball—and no one had noticed anything amiss. But that night, one or more hounds had made their way into Los Angeles, and they had killed.

And then what? Evaporated?

Standing on the northwest shore, Alouzon shrugged. Maybe. Cut off from the source of their being and stranded in a strange world, the hounds might well have killed, eaten, and then simply vanished . . . as was appropriate for impossible beasts and, perhaps, Dragonmasters too.

Something flickered across the water.

Headlights? Her eyes narrowed. It was late, and traffic was intermittent on Alvarado. At present there were no cars to cast reflections on the water. But something had glimmered—was still glimmering—out on the lawn between the lake and the street: a hazy curtain of shifting light and mist.

Silently, undetected by the vagrants and the drug dealers, she slipped around the lake shore and skirted the edge of the white fence that surrounded the fast-food stand. The glimmering grew more distinct: a wavering door of light.

Door. The word came to her unbidden, but she knew it to be appropriate. She quickened her steps, feeling a sensation of otherworldliness growing about her, one that reminded her of Solomon's grave, Helen's house,

and the indefinable and invisible aura about the office
at UCLA.

A clump of heavy paws—and a deep-throated howl
suddenly rang through the night, echoing off the water
and the line of shops across Alvarado Street.

She ran. Ahead, figures were moving on the lawn.
One was that of a man, his clothes tattered, his skin
lined. Three others, though, were four-footed, the size
of lions. They glowed, their eyes like lamps, their
mouths dripping with phosphor.

Alouzon pulled the Dragonsword free of the towel
and approached at a run, her sneakers silent on the
grass. The beasts were intent on other prey, though,
prey that was defenseless, slow, weak . . . and much,
much closer.

Cut off from the street and the lights, the old man
stumbled out towards the lake, screaming at the sight
of the waking nightmares that pursued him. He
slammed into the benches that lined the walkway about
the lake, spun to the side, and nearly fell; but an eager
yelp from the beasts pulled him to his feet again, and
he staggered onto a small tongue of land that projected
into the water near the island reserved for the ducks
that nested in the park.

The hounds closed on him. Alouzon closed on the
hounds.

The Dragonsword slid out of its sheath and sent one
of the beasts writhing to the pavement, cut nearly in
two. Phosphor spilled and smoked, boiling like molten
sodium where it touched the water. The ducks erupted
into startled flight. Alouzon pulled her blade free of
the carcass, but one hound was already dragging down
the old man while the other came at her.

She skipped to the side, evading the needle teeth
that smacked together inches from her leg, and vaulted
one of the park benches. The hound followed, bounding over the obstacle with ease. It was a clear opening,
but before Alouzon could swing, she was struck from
behind. She fell, narrowly missing the pool of corro-

sives that was already gathering. The two hounds rushed at her.

"Not on your life, guy." She caught the nearest beneath the chin with the sheath of her sword and planted a kick between the eyes of the second. The hounds tumbled, but they rose again.

She was now between them, with only the Dragonsword and her instincts to defend her. Backing, she put herself at the end of the narrow tongue of land, confining the beasts to an approach only twenty feet wide. It was not much, but it was better than being directly in the middle.

They came at her simultaneously, mouths gaping, needle teeth dripping, eyes glowing like blue lamps. While she managed to open the side of the one on her right, she could not avoid the other, and it struck her in the stomach and pitched her into the lake.

She floundered, the hounds thrashed, phosphor steamed and frothed in the water. The wounded hound staggered to the side, still snapping; but its fellow, unhurt, waded towards her and sprang just as her feet, betrayed by the algae-slick lake-bed, went out from under her. The hound passed over her head, and she sat down in two feet of stinking water, arms flailing, expecting at any moment to feel iron jaws snap closed on her.

But, distantly, she heard a voice. An impossibly familiar voice:

"Gryylth!"

The morning after Relys arrived at Paia's house, word came down from Kingsbury that the villages and steadings were to be cleared, their inhabitants moved into Kingsbury and the other major towns. When pressed, the guards who brought the orders merely said that it had to do with adequate defensive measures, that the order applied to villages and steadings all across the country. Paia protested, but the men were big, gruff, and armed; and by way of a reply they

asked her whether she wanted to be left to the mercy
of the hounds and Grayfaces.

Paia looked at her steading—neat and trim, its veg-
etable garden showing the promise of a good harvest.
She wore the agonized expression of a woman about
to be sent away from everything familiar and secure,
but the toddlers clutching at her skirts could not but
make up her mind for her.

"I will go," she said at last.

The soldiers gestured towards Kingsbury Hall. "Immediately."

Paia flared. "I will go," she snapped. "That is all
I will say. Now take your evil news to the other farmers and leave me alone."

She turned on her heel and stalked back to the house,
her children following behind her. After slamming the
door, she sent the children up to the loft, sat down at
the table before the big fireplace, put her face in her
hands, and sobbed.

Relys, moving slowly, rose from her pallet. "It was
bound to happen," she said. "We heard the rumors a
week ago."

Paia was not comforted. "Why? It is the action of
a fool! Helwych takes the people off the land . . . and
who will feed the people then? Or can he make feasts
and banquets for us out of straw and weeds?"

"Nay, I do not think he can," Relys admitted.

The housewife was crying weakly, tears running
down her plump cheeks. "I would defy the orders,"
she said. "But my children . . ."

"Courage, my friend," said Relys, putting her good
arm about the midwife's shoulders. "The king will
return. And perhaps Alouzon too. All will be well."

Paia lifted her eyes. "Do you believe that, sister?"

Relys dropped her eyes. "I . . . know not what to
believe."

The housewife's eyes were sad. "You and Timbrin
will have to leave immediately. I am sorry."

"Peace," said Relys. "We would have left in a week

in any case. That we must leave early is of no concern.''

Paia only looked at Relys's hand. It was trembling from weakness.

Relys and Timbrin departed before dawn the next day, starting off when there was just enough light in the sky to find the road. It was a doubtful journey to be sure: neither woman could wield a weapon, and they would be skirting the edge of the night battles that lit the horizon to the north of Kingsbury. But Relys doubted that any sword or armor would be of use against weapons that illuminated half the sky, and therefore their strategy—if simple necessity could be dignified with that term—would be to travel to Quay quietly and unobtrusively.

They took back ways and farmer's roads northward, making the most of the cover of forests and foothills. Paia had given them the cart, supplies, and a dependable horse, so their way was slow, but not arduous.

Timbrin, still locked in hellish timidity, sat in the back of the cart, clutching a shawl about her thin shoulders, trying not to cower. She wore a gown given her by one of Paia's daughters, and, clad as she was like a child, she looked almost absurdly young. Her large brown eyes scanned the passing landscape with a mixture of fear and curiosity.

Relys drove, and though her hard black eyes watched the leagues unfold before her—the roads and tracks glowing white under the summer sun, the breeze whipping up dust devils and clouds from the abandoned fields—she saw also the barracks, and the faces of the men who had raped her, and her hand bared of flesh and muscle . . .

The wound throbbed, and she clutched her hand within its bandages, stifling the cry of pain that surged up in her throat. She would never wield a sword again. Never. What, then, was she? Just a woman?

The words stung like bile in her throat. Just a

woman. She had seen and felt what women were: she would never utter those words again.

Three days, and they were still traveling; but the land changed. Out on the broad plains east of the foothills, large expanses of once fertile fields were brown and dead, and even Relys and Timbrin, who had no skill or knowledge of farming, knew instinctively that the blight was not natural.

Further north, craters pocked the fields and forests in strings of house-sized depressions that stretched for the better part of a league. Full-sized oaks had been felled, their trunks splintered like sticks blown in a hurricane; and long black scars cut through hill, field, and abandoned village alike, as though the landscape had been furrowed by a titanic piece of charcoal.

"No wonder that Helwych is bringing the people into the garrisoned towns," Relys murmured.

Timbrin looked up.

Relys gestured with her mangled hand at devastation that appeared to cover hundreds of leagues. "Whatever he is fighting demands room in which to fight. Helwych is considerate enough to remove the innocent from the path of the destruction."

"But . . ." Timbrin peered over the side of the cart. "But what about the crops? We might starve this winter."

"Might?" Relys snorted. "Dear friend, we probably will."

That afternoon, they saw the Grayfaces.

Timbrin spotted them first, and her quick intake of breath alerted Relys. But even before her words confirmed the presence of intruders, the captain had already turned the cart off into a stand of trees. Together, the two women hid the vehicle behind thick bushes and crouched behind a screen of ferns to watch.

Five hundred yards away, a group of twenty Grayfaces was crossing a green field. In the hot son, the men labored through the crops as though wading through deep mud, and they repeatedly lifted their strange, glistening faces as though they saw enemies everywhere.

"Helwych turned some of these to his own use," Timbrin whispered. "Do you think they are ours . . . or theirs?"

Relys shook her head. "Ours? Theirs? What is ours or theirs anymore?"

Whatever their allegiance, the Grayfaces had enemies, for the women heard a sudden, dull thump from a low rise to the north, and a minute later, the field in front of the men erupted in a detonation that sent dirt and rock flying and left three of their company lying lifeless and shattered in the sunlit field.

A second detonation was not far behind, but the soldiers were already moving, scattering into the cover of a clump of tumbled boulders below the position occupied by the women. In a minute, voices crackled through the silence left by the explosions, strange voices speaking stranger words:

"Victor Six, we have you located. Roger your request for dustoff and air strike. Suggest you mark hostile position with smoke. Repeat, mark hostile position with smoke."

Relys glanced at Timbrin. The lieutenant looked terrified, and when two more detonations rocked the Grayface position, she clung to Relys, her eyes clenched against the incredible blasts. Relys stroked her hair, trying to remain calm herself.

Two thuds from below, dull, yet potent enough that Relys felt them in her chest as much as she heard them. She peered through the ferns in time to see one of the men drop something into a short, angled tube and turn away with his hands pressed to his ears. Another thud and concussion.

A minute went by. The rise to the north of the fields was suddenly cratered by the Grayface weapons, and seconds later three muffled booms drifted across the open ground.

Cracks, rippings, smoke. Now the Grayfaces had

turned their hand weapons on the ridge. Sparkles of light replied, and projectiles spattered off the rocks about the men, tore up the foliage, splintered the trees.

"We must flee," said Relys. "On foot."

Timbrin looked at her, owl-eyed. "How far can you walk, Relys?"

"As far as I must."

A screaming came across the sky. Three flying things streaked out of the north, lined up on the rise. They passed over and left in their wake a trail of blasts and craters, and it seemed for a moment that the Grayfaces' troubles were over, but just then three more came up out of the east. Traces of light streaked from beneath their wings, and one of the first group was suddenly falling in flames.

And then more came. And more. Ungainly things hovered in the air like spiders in their webs, bringing more Grayfaces and more weapons, but Relys and Timbrin had already turned away from the battle. Leaving the cart, setting free the cart, they climbed—slowly, painfully—up through the wooded slope. They found their way through heather and bracken and dense stands of oak and beech, moving ever toward deeper forest and higher ground.

Towards evening, they reached the crest of a ridge, and there they rested and ate a meager dinner of bread and smoked meat. A stream allowed them to drink and wash, and Timbrin helped Relys change the dressings on her hand.

Night fell, and still the battle raged in the fields east of the foothills. Unnatural thunders cracked across the miles, and the air screamed with things that flew like birds and killed like men. But come morning, silence had fallen, and from the song of lark and magpies and the buzz of honeybees and dragonflies, one might never have guessed that yet another piece of Gryylth had been transformed into a sterile waste.

The women started off again. Now their progress was slower, and another two days had passed before they sighted the ruins of Bandon, smeared out across the flood plain of the river like a child's sooty fingerprint.

"Not too much farther, Timbrin," said Relys. "Beyond Bandon is the pass across the mountains, and my guess is that we will find no Grayfaces there."

At this altitude, the breeze was cold. Timbrin clutched her shawl about her shoulders. "Why so, Relys?"

"Because Helwych is in Kingsbury," Relys replied softly, "and he is both the cause and the object of this war."

Within a week after Santhe's plan was implemented, the number of hound attacks on the Vayllen settlements and cities fell off sharply. No longer confronted by pacifist Vayllens who made no attempt to defend themselves, the roving packs were met instead by efficient warriors and thoroughly enchanted steel.

As quickly as they were killed, though, the ranks of the hounds were replenished. A seemingly endless supply of the preternatural beasts was trickling over the Cordillera, and so the job continued.

Wykla and Manda had been riding for many days now, leading a phalanx of Corrinian pikemen in a long, sweeping patrol that stretched from the Waelow Hills that lay to the south of Lachrae all the way out to the Cordillera. But as Wykla rode across the greening miles, her thoughts returned often to the look with which Marrha had bidden her farewell at the gates of Lachrae: the expression of one who was watching a portion of her life ride away amid a glitter of weapons.

A woman's life . . .

. . . yes, was one of changes, and as Marrget the captain had turned into Marrha the councilor, so her new duties kept her in Lachrae and forced her to watch wartroops and phalanxes depart into the west without her. But with much the same expression—tearful and prideful both—had Wykla once ridden away from

Burnwood, from a family that had rejected her; and
the sight of Marrha's face had freed that particular
memory from the thin bonds that held it, dragged it
up before her mind's eye like a tormented prisoner,
and forced her, in her thoughts, to live again the old
pain.

I will never call you daughter, her father had said
on that terrible day. *I have no daughter.* And her
mother, terrified, had stayed by the cooking fire,
hunched over, occupying herself with the preparation
of a dinner that would in all likelihood go uneaten.

I will never call you daughter.

Again Wykla saw her father, arms folded, glowering
like some dark god at the door of his house, his jaw
set with anger. *Begone. I have no daughter.*

But she saw also another man, this one tall and
proud, his beard as golden as a sunrise, his eyes blue
and kind. *Should you need someone to call* father, *call
me.*

She spoke of it upon occasion with Manda, blurting
out her feelings to the woman who had awakened her
emotions and her sexuality. Manda held her, made love
to her, comforted her as she could; but not even a lover
could fill the aching void left by the rejection of her
family, or settle the confusion into which Darham's
offer had plunged her.

"Darham is a good man, my love," Manda said as
they lay together one still night when the sentries had
been posted and the camp lay asleep.

Wykla gazed at the dark line of the Cordillera. They
were camped near Mullaen, having driven a large pack
of hounds before them for several leagues before darkness had intervened. "But my father lives," she said.
"How can I have two fathers?"

Manda touched her cheek. "Your father turned you
away. Why should you not accept Darham's offer?"

"It is not the same, Manda."

Manda nodded understandingly. "I know, beloved."

Across a mile of withered fields, Mullaen bulked like a heap of black rocks. Manda and Wykla had warned the men to stay out of the blasted areas, and so they had made camp on a patch of untouched greenery that bordered the lake shore.

Something about the place, though, was vaguely disquieting, and Wykla's sleep that night was broken and light. Several times she awakened in the darkness to find that she was on her feet, staring out towards the lake shore, but she could not guess the reason why until, near midnight, something flickered near the water like a piece of gilt cloth . . . and grew.

Then she remembered. She waved to the sentries to let them know that she had seen, then turned and woke up Manda. The maid rubbed her eyes and regarded the apparition. It soared up, lambent, shimmering. "As before," she said.

"Aye. And even Kyria had no idea what it was."

Yelps, suddenly. Howls. A sentry at the edge of the firelight screamed as he fell beneath a beast that glowed leprous yellow. "Sandyhl!" Manda cried. She grabbed her sword and ran to help, but the hound was already tearing at the lifeless guardsman, and others were bounding in behind it.

The side of the encampment closest to the lake was under attack by a large body of hounds that had come charging up out of the night before the sentries could raise an alarm. But the men on watch were armed and skilled, and they held off the worst of the attack while the sleeping members of the phalanx awakened, seized weapons, and formed up for a counterattack.

Manda led the charge, hewing through the glowing flesh, snapping out orders to her men. At her command, the phalanx circled up and bunched the hounds together, limiting the number that could actively attack. It was well that they did, for Wykla estimated that there were at least fifty of the beasts.

The warriors pressed in against the hounds, driving them together, killing those at the periphery. But phosphor flowed sluggishly and pooled on the ground, and when several Corrinians slipped and fell in it, the corrosives immediately began eating away at their flesh.

Those nearby turned to help. "We can hold the hounds," Manda shouted to them. "Take them to the lake and wash them."

The men started off, and as the beasts surged towards the thinning of the Corrinian ranks, Wykla leaped to plug the gap, spitting one hound, slashing into the throat of another. Looking up, though, she noticed that five of the beasts had managed to get past the screen of warriors and were following the men who were heading for the lake.

"Manda!"

The maid killed a hound, turned. Wykla pointed. "Aye," cried Manda, her voice nearly drowned by the shouts of men and the baying of hounds. "You and I, Wykla."

Leaving the butchery of the pack to the phalanx, they ran after the five hounds, but the beasts suddenly wheeled and turned on them. One leaped directly at Wykla, but it received a sword blade in the throat. Another tried to attack Manda, who first cut its lower jaw loose with a well-placed slash, then followed up with a thrust directly between its eyes.

The other three turned again and ran. The women followed, but they stopped suddenly when they realized that the hounds were making directly for the shimmering apparition on the shore. Milling, tumbling over one another in their haste, yipping in fear, the hounds approached the gap, hesitated, sniffed, then plunged through and vanished.

Manda and Wykla ran to the edge and peered in, but they could see nothing but faintly glowing swirls and points of light that might have been stars. Cautiously, Manda stuck her sword in, withdrew it, examined the metal. It was unmarked. Even the hounds' blood showed no change.

But there was a beating behind them suddenly, and

a presence, and they looked up into a pair of yellow eyes. Wings as large as trees blotted out the sky, and a voice thrummed about them as though the air were a struck bell.

Follow.

Wykla stared. Silbakor hovered above them, black body limned in red, eyes glaring with passionless emotion.

Follow. Quickly.

The Great Dragon was torn and rent, and it bled darkness into the dark sky. Its eyes were pained and glazed.

Follow. Quickly. Alouzon is in danger.

Wykla stared at the Dragon, then at Manda, then at the shimmering blotch. "A-Alouzon?"

Manda pulled herself out of her surprise first. She checked on the men under her command, and, satisfied that they were handling the hounds, she nodded to Wykla. "Come, then."

"O you Gods of Gryylth!" Wykla was already running for the star-filled gap, screaming. "Alouzon!"

Without hesitation, they plunged into a region where space and perspective seemed to have no meaning, where suns glowed blindingly as though a stone's throw away, where disks like moons hung in an endless night like apples in a fertile orchard. The ground under their boots was not stone, or glass, or anything they had seen before. It simply was.

They ran. Worlds and endless planes spun and tipped in the surrounding darkness, clouds swept across regions of utter nothingness, lights pulsed and flowed like water.

And then, ahead, another gap, another shimmer. Redoubling their speed, Wykla and Manda burst out of the door side-by-side and found themselves running across grass. A short distance away were trees and a small lake. The air was fetid, the sky was blank and washed out, and odd patches of light hung in the air.

But, at the water's edge, there was a splashing and

a snarling of hounds. In the glow of the lights, Wykla saw a flash of bronze hair amid the foam, and as she watched, a brown arm holding a familiar sword lifted from the frothing waves and aimed a stroke at the glowing beast that was wading in to attack.

"Gryylth!" she cried, and, with Manda, she fell on the two hounds from behind. In moments, the water was exploding in violent bursts of steam from the phosphor that gushed into it.

Kicking the writhing bodies away, the two women grabbed Alouzon and dragged her to the shore. The Dragonmaster looked dazed. "Thanks," she gasped. "Thanks both of you. I thought I was a goner. That old drunk over there got it good and—" She broke off, stared at them. "Wykla? Manda?"

Wykla nodded. "Silbakor sent us."

"You're here?"

"Aye, Dragonmaster," said Manda. She glanced about nervously. Off in the distance, a wailing started up and began to approach. "Wherever here is."

Alouzon struggled to her feet. "Silbakor? Sent you?" Abruptly, she started to laugh, a deep, sobbing merriment that was tinged with hysteria. "Into Mac-Arthur Park?" She cast her arms about the warriors, hugged them tightly. "That's the weirdest fucking thing I've ever heard!"

❖ CHAPTER 13 ❖

The war went on with dismaying pointlessness. It was indeed a war, but though Helwych called it such, he had, weeks ago, lost track of any objective beyond self-preservation, and the grandiose plans of power and rule that he had once cherished had been effectively submerged in a mire of day-to-day survival.

The Specter materialized Grayfaces, planes, and weapons in Gryylth at will, and as fast as Helwych was able to turn portions of all three to his own use and allegiance, more appeared. Like boys with bottomless sacks of toy armament, the sorcerer and the Specter fought battle after inconclusive battle, spreading the conflict from Crownhark in the south to Ridgebrake forest in the north, from the Camrann Mountains in the west to the remains of the Great Dike in the east. But whereas boys would have scrabbled shallowly in the earth and then gone home, there was no going home for Helwych, and the battles he waged with increasing desperation left the landscape deeply scarred by bomb and napalm and defoliant.

The crops, where they had not been uprooted or withered, grew unkempt and overgrown with weeds. The cities and towns were crowded with refugees, their streets congested with fragile shelters and overflowing with filth. But it was the only way. For their own protection, non-combatants had to be herded off the fields. In order for Helwych to win the war, both the land and

the people had to change from what they had once
been into something else.

But he was not sure what that something else was,
nor was he at all certain that the war could be won, or
even that the Specter wanted anything more than what
it had gotten: a prolonged and pointless conflict that
was slowly turning the countryside into a waste of
bomb craters and bare soil.

By the beginning of August, most of the fertile lands
to the north of Kingsbury had been reduced to ashes
and dead vegetation, and the women, old men, and
children who huddled in overcrowded houses or bed-
ded down at night in the open air or in the rude shelters that lined the streets of the towns were finding the
food supplies growing short.

Helwych could do nothing to stop it. "The people
should be grateful that they wake up in the morning,"
he said to Dryyim when the captain spoke of his growing concerns about the refugees. "Would they like to
go back to their steadings?"

"My lord," Dryyim said carefully, "some have said
that very thing. It is becoming difficult to persuade
them to stay."

Helwych's hands tightened on the arms of the king's
chair. "Anything outside the towns is an enemy. I want
them kept in."

"I understand your feelings, my liege, but—"

"Keep them in, Dryyim."

"But—"

Helwych pointed a finger in Dryyim's face. "If they
try to leave," he snapped, "I order you to kill them."
Did his concern stem from a desire to keep the people
safe, or a reluctance to have the damage left by his
battles known by all? He was not sure.

He realized that Dryyim was frowning. And the
other men who stood in Hall Kingsbury this afternoon
shifted restlessly. Helwych had not reassured them.

Dryyim considered his words for a moment. "You
are telling us to kill our own people, lord."

Helwych stood his ground. He had raised Dryyim up from a peevish boy to the rank of captain. The whelp would learn who gave the commands. "If they disobey me, then they deserve it. They would die out in the country in any case."

"I see." Dryyim's voice was flat.

And what was Dryyim thinking? How restless was he? Was Lytham? Was Haryn? Helwych examined their faces as they stood, watchful, and he could read their feelings: for this they had played so loosely with their loyalty to their king?

Helwych shuddered. He needed better guards. More trustworthy guards. Guards whose allegiance was indisputable.

He rose. Beyond the door of the Hall, the afternoon sunlight was hot and bright. The beginning of the month would normally have been spent in celebrating, the first of the harvest festivals, but there would be no harvest this year. There were hardly any crops left.

Starvation hovered at the edge of the country like a dark shadow. "Go," said Helwych, pointing towards the sunlight. "Search the land and bring back word of any crops that are still standing."

"We have looked already, lord." Dryyim's voice was a little too carefully controlled. "There are none."

The still air outside was stirred by a sudden breeze. Dry and hot, it seemed to promise nothing save death and dry fields. "Look again," said Helwych. "Look further. Find something."

"My lord—"

"Get out of my sight, you insolent pup!"

There was a mutter from some of the assembled guards as Dryyim stepped back, white faced, and turned away without saluting. But before the captain could reach the door, the breeze gusted to a wind, then to a sudden gale.

The sun dimmed as though clouds had covered it, and Helwych fought with panic when he realized that the random gusts had turned into a regular beating. Staff in hand, he pushed past the startled men and ran to the door.

Above the courtyard, as white as a leper's arm, was the Worm, its eyes blue-black, its mouth agape with envenomed teeth. But Helwych's gaze was caught and held by what rode on its back: the figure and image of a thin, middle-aged man in gray clothes, its eyes as violet as the Worm's, its hand gripping the counterpart of Alouzon's sword.

"Little Dremord fool," the Specter grinned. "Thought you could hole up here in Kingsbury, eh?"

Fighting with terror, his stomach clenched, Helwych grappled with his staff, tried to recall a spell that might save him. His mind, unaccountably, was empty.

The Worm hovered above the rooftops. The Specter smiled. "I'll be seeing you again, later," it said. "I'll be seeing a lot of you, and you of me. We can be friends even though we're fighting, can't we? After all . . ." It laughed, and its open mouth was a blank whiteness. "After all, you're still my boy!"

Its laughter, though, was cut short; for, from out of the glare of the sun, Silbakor blazed down at it, eyes flaming, ebony claws reaching. The Worm arose with a scream, and in a moment, the Dragon and the Worm had risen high into the air, dodging, feinting, slashing with tooth and claw. Darkness and white slime bled into the blue sky.

Helwych looked up. Dryyim stood tall above him. The sorcerer realized that he had fallen to his knees, and when he tried to get to his feet, the nausea of fear pinned him where he was. "Help me up, captain," he said.

Dryyim stood motionless.

You're still my boy! Had the captain heard that? Doubtless. And all the men, too. What would they make of it? "Help me up."

Dryyim's face was filled with contempt. He looked at Helwych for a long time. Then: "Help yourself up, little Dremord fool,'' he said, and, turning on his heel, he strode away under the bright, hot sun of a harvest that would not be.

''Dryyim!''

Dryyim continued on his way. Vision blurring, Helwych staggered to his feet, one hand clutched to his belly, the other wrapped about his staff. Fear vied with outraged pride. If Dryyim, then . . .

''Dryyim!''

The captain turned around at the gate of the palisade, arms folded. ''And who is really in charge here, Hel—''

The blast from Helwych's staff caught him in midword, and his utterance turned abruptly into a scream as his flesh whitened, then charred to black, then flaked from his bones like ashes from a burning log.

He was still screaming. And his scream seemed to continue, ringing through the air, for a long time after he had no more throat with which to scream, after he was no more than a heap of dust as black and ruined as any bombed and napalmed village of Gryylth, Vaylle, or Vietnam.

Still clutching his belly, Helwych turned to the other men. Fear stared at him from out of pale faces. ''Lytham,'' he said, ''you are now captain of my Guard.'' Guards. Yes, he needed dependable guards. Lytham and the rest would do for now, but he would have others. And there would be hounds, too. Yes. Hounds and others to make sure that he was safe and that his orders were obeyed without question.

''You heard what I ordered in the Hall,' he said. ''Go and do it.''

Lytham stared. For a moment, he seemed but a boy again, dressed up in livery and crests, a childish mockery of a warrior. And though he came to himself and saluted, Helwych still saw the boy. And fear. And distrust. ''I—immediately, lord.''

The sky was blank as Helwych stumbled back into

Hall Kingsbury, the Specter's words ringing in his head as loudly as Dryyim's final scream.

You're still my boy!

As Relys had suspected, there were no Grayfaces or battles west of the Camrann Mountains. Once she and Timbrin had crossed the pass, they found the land green and quiet. The slopes and ridges were dotted with stands of hardwood and brush, softened by fruit trees and patches of wild strawberries; and below, at the tip of the inlet, was Quay.

But out beyond the mouth of the inlet, something seemed wrong with the water: a discoloration, like a glaze of frost on an otherwise bright blade, but darker, more ominous. Relys frowned at the sight of it, and she frowned some more when she noticed that most of Quay's boats were ashore or bobbing beside docks and piers.

"What new evil is this?" she murmured.

Timbrin's eyes turned shadowed. "I remember," she said. "I remember that." She trembled. "That is what Helwych was doing when I looked in and . . . and . . ." She turned away. Relys held her and soothed her, but it was some time before she could go on.

Much of the destruction that had fallen on the town in January had been repaired. Now new thatch gleamed golden above new walls, the streets were clear of rubble, and the dark craters and burns were green with grass and the beginnings of saplings. But though, sheltered as it was by earthworks and timber fortifications, the town looked to be a safe place, Relys could not help but wonder whether she and Timbrin had simply traveled out of one snare and into another. How would they be seen here? As fugitives? Criminals? Or perhaps—since Quay was a conservative town and still held to the old ways as much as it could—unattached women fit for slavery.

For Timbrin's sake, she betrayed nothing of her anxiety, but fear was a sickness in her belly as, with Timbrin at her side, she descended the path to the road, went directly up to the town gate—no sneaking or caution here: she would meet her fate face-to-face—and confronted the earthworks and the high palisade.

Timbrin was white. Relys held her hand firmly, as a mother might that of a child. "Ho!" she cried. "People of Quay!"

The answer was polite, but cautious and suspicious. "Who comes?"

Relys looked at Timbrin, small and dark and clad as a young girl, then thought of her own appearance. Mother and child. Indeed, it had come to seem so. "Two women," she said. "Timbrin of Dearbought, and Relys of—"

She stopped. Her hand throbbed. Her groin ached. She would not utter that name and her own in the same breath.

"Timbrin and Relys," she said at last. "Lieutenant and captain of the First Wartroop. We ask refuge in the king's name."

Another voice, more familiar and less guarded, carried from the gate. "Relys? Captain Relys?"

"Hahle?" She tried to shout, but her words came out strangled as she fought with the tears that insisted upon closing her throat. "Hahle? Is that you? Do you remember me?"

"Remember you, Relys? I have prayed to the Gods for your safety since I left Kingsbury!"

The gate was swinging open, the drawbridge falling into place, but the old man did not wait. Healed of his wounds, he climbed the palisade, dropped to the earth outside the wall, and as the bridge swung down, crossed it and leaped the last few feet before it had fully settled. In a moment, he was at Relys's side.

His old eyes, already sizing up the women's condition, saw that Relys's was wrapped in bandages. Gently, he lifted it, and Relys read his question.

"I chewed part of it off," she said simply. "In order to escape."

"By the Gods . . ." He stared. "What has been done to you?"

Relys shrugged. "What is done to upstart women in Kingsbury? What does Helwych do to his enemies?"

"The queen?"

"Stricken and powerless. Her children have been bespelled. So has Timbrin. I was arrested and handed over to the Guard. For their sport."

Hahle flushed with anger. "By the Gods, Helwych will pay for this." But when he saw that Timbrin was cowering before his anger, he turned to her, bowed, and spoke softly, as one might to a timid child. "My lady Timbrin. Do not fear, I beg you."

Timbrin shrank against Relys and gave him a small, frightened nod.

The bridge had settled, and other men were coming out to meet them: large men, men with weapons. Timbrin shrank back further, and Relys put a protective arm about her. Hahle turned to those who approached. "No closer, please." The men stopped where they were. "Send for my wife and for my maid, Myylen," Hahle ordered. "And see if you can find a midwife. We need a woman's touch here."

Myylen went running. Relys stroked Timbrin's head soothingly. "Easy, my friend," she said softly. "We are . . ." She lifted her eyes, met Hahle's gaze. "Safe here?"

Hahle nodded. "As safe as you can be in any town in Gryylth."

"Helwych's soldiers?"

Hahle snorted. "They swaggered and gave orders for a time. And the way they treated the women . . . Gods!" But he smiled, and his eyes narrowed meaningfully. "We attended to them. And once the wall formed out there . . ." He swept out an arm to indicate the discoloration on the sea beyond the inlet. ". . . we all guessed what the lad was up to. But he has wartroops and magic, and we have only old men like myself, women and children, and a few youngsters like Myylen whom I kept back because of my suspicions.'' He shrugged. ''If Helwych presses matters, he will find us ready to fight to the death. But for now we can only await the return of our king.''

The men's faces—old and young both—were grim but earnest, and in their own way, kind. Relys had not seen kindness in the faces of men for a long time, and when her legs—still weak, and worn by two weeks of travel—insisted on sagging beneath her, she did not protest when Hahle reached out and supported her. ''My thanks, sir,'' she said, her voice hoarse.

There was a hint of a tear in Hahle's eye. ''Welcome to Quay, captain.'' He reached out a hand, and Timbrin, after a long hesitation, took it. ''Welcome, both of you.''

Kyria awoke in the night, opened her eyes, and stretched. Her head was pillowed on Santhe's arm, and in this quiet time of darkness, she had nothing to do save to smile at him while he snored and mumbled softly in his sleep, to press her body against his, and to think—wonderingly, with an inner shake of her head—about the life she had lived before this, the life she had left behind like a cast-off skin.

She started to kiss him, but, with the instinct of a warrior, he opened his eyes at her lips' approach. The room was dimly lit by moonlight, and she could see his soft smile. ''Make love to me,'' she whispered.

''Again?'' The twinkle in his eye was a relief after weeks of seriousness, frustration, and work. ''A hard taskmaster you are, my lady.''

''Am I really?''

The twinkle turned into a grin. ''Quite unbearable.''

She was laughing. ''Make love to me, my slave.''

''Oh? Slave?'' He turned over. ''Well then, it is high time this slave rose up in rebellion.'' And, laughing as much as she, he took her tenderly in his arms.

He had healed her, and she had healed him. There

was giving and taking in their love, and acceptance, and help. It was good, very good; and afterwards, when, full and warm and spent, they lay together, seeing nothing save one another's faces, Kyria, childless save for her indirect care of the people of an entire world, found that she was contemplating bringing forth life herself, conjuring an infant out of a magic more powerful than any that she alone could wield: a holy partnership with the man she had come to consider as one with herself.

"I could." Her voice was soft with wonder. "I am young. I could . . ."

"Beloved?" Santhe stroked her hair.

"What . . ." She, a sorceress, felt nonetheless almost impudent uttering such holy words. "What . . . would you say to a son or a daughter, councilor?"

He pursed his lips. "Grave things, children," he said. "Until now, I had not considered fatherhood."

"And what say you now?"

"For myself, I fear I would make a poor parent. But seeing as I have the finest lady in the world for my mate, I think that I might manage."

"You do not . . ." She lifted her head. "You do not think me ridiculous, do you?"

He was dumbfounded. "Ridiculous?"

"There is so much that is new to me," she said. "So much that I do not know, that I only feel." She shrugged, shook her head. "Like magic. Or love. I fear you think me foolish."

"Aye, my lady is foolish," Santhe murmured, running a hand through her hair. "And wise, and powerful, and filled with all the frightening and incredible things in the world." He put his big arms about her, his muscles taut and solid from wielding weapons. "I have no complaint, my darling."

Her heart was full, but she smiled wryly. "I see that you have been keeping company with the Vayllen harpers."

"Well," he admitted, "perhaps a little."

A soft tapping came to the door. In her mind, Kyria felt out into the hallway and caught a glimpse of a big, blond man. Karthin. She gave Santhe another quick kiss and, pulling on a robe as she went, crossed the room and lifted the latch.

Karthin looked sad. "Forgive me for disturbing you. I heard you talking, and . . ."

Kyria had guessed the reason. "Marrha?"

"Aye. A bad nightmare this time. She said that she wished to speak with you."

Alouzon's company had been together not only through the nightmare realm of Broceliande, but also through the deeper darkness of their personal and collective fear and pain. It was therefore natural that they should take care of one another, banding together even in the case of nightmares. Wykla and Manda were still out on patrol, but Marrha, sitting up in bed, showed no surprise when her husband returned with both Kyria and Santhe, and she smiled when Dindrane appeared at the door a few moments later.

"I felt it," said the priestess.

"Thank you," said Marrha. "Thank you, all of you." Eight weeks along in her pregnancy, her waist had thickened and her breasts had enlarged. Since she had returned to Lachrae, she had been eating better, and her lean body had softened into gentle curves, but now she looked haggard, and there was a furtive unease in her eyes.

Kyria knelt by the bed. "You asked for me, friend."

"I . . ." Marrha shook her blond head. Her braid waggled back and forth in the candlelight. "I have been able to deal with many of these dreams, Kyria, but this was worse, much worse. This time, Manda did not save me, and then instead of the Grayface, it was the Specter itself that was . . ."

And Kyria felt the chill of an old, half-remembered life, recalled the pain of being forced by Solomon in her own bed, night after night, for twenty years.

Marrha's hands were pressed to her face. "It hurt. And I was screaming. For the Goddess."

Karthin sat down on the bed beside his wife and folded her in his arms. Kyria shoved the thoughts of Solomon out of her mind. "The Goddess," she said with a glance at Dindrane, "is a constant presence here in Vaylle, Marrha. It is not unexpected that She would become as real to you as to the people among whom you live. There is no harm in that. It is, I think, a great good."

Marrha fought with her emotion. "I think so too," she choked. "But I knew to Whom I screamed. It was to the Goddess. It was to Alouzon."

Kyria kept her expression very carefully neutral. But Santhe spoke. "Alouzon has, perhaps, become something of a Goddess to us all," he said. "Were I in such straits, dream or no, I too would cry to her, dear friend."

"It was so real."

"Take my hands," said Kyria. "The present is terrible enough. It makes no sense for you to be tormented by the past, too."

In a moment, she had called up her power and worked her magic. She would not reach into the captain's mind and do away with the genesis of the nightmares, for that seemed to her as much of a violation as another rape, or a forced abortion. But like a nurse salving an open wound, she took the painful edge from Marrha's dream.

The captain's eyes cleared. "My thanks."

"My pleasure."

Footsteps approached in the hallway. "I called for something to drink," explained Karthin. "This is probably one of Pellam's attendants."

But though it was indeed a woman wearing the blazon of Knife and Cup, she brought news instead of drink. "My king asks that you meet him in the council chambers," she said, her face earnest, her eyes wide.

"An attack?" said Santhe.

The attendant shook her head. " 'Tis the patrol commanded by Wykla and Manda," she said. "Returned without them it has, and bearing a strange story."

Sirens. Horns. Alouzon pulled herself out of her surprise quickly enough to realize that the baying of the hounds and the screams of the dead man had not gone unheard. The police were coming. She gave Wykla and Manda a last squeeze and released them. "Look, guys," she said., "You trust me?"

Wykla looked mildly shocked at the question. "Alouzon! With our lives!"

"Then, come on. Run. Someone called the heat."

"The heat?"

"I'll explain later. Follow me."

She sheathed the Dragonsword, grabbed the beach towel, and set off towards Wilshire at a run. Her wet jeans squeaked and flapped, and Wykla and Manda pounded after her, boots thumping on the short grass. Without comment, they vaulted the low concrete wall along with her, and when she swung open the door of the VW and told them to get in, they shrugged and obeyed.

Scrunched up in the back seat, Wykla giggled nervously. "This is some kind of magic, is it not, Alouzon?"

Manda took the front passenger side. "There is nothing else to call it, beloved."

Alouzon handed her sword to Manda and fell in behind the wheel. In a moment, the VW had coughed into life, and she thanked the Grail that the black-and-whites had not yet appeared as she pulled out from the curb and squealed the car into a U-turn.

Beside her, Manda's eyes were wide, and she clutched at the strap on the door pillar. "Dragonmaster?"

"It's okay, Manda." In the rear view mirror, she could see that Wykla, her face white in the street lights, had her hands pressed to her mouth. "Just trust me, huh?"

Manda nodded, her hand tight on the strap. "We do, Dragonmaster."

"Call me Alouzon."

Alouzon reached Park View and, ignoring the light, spun the VW to the north. The police would be at the park within minutes, and she wanted to be safely out of sight on a side street, not fleeing openly down a thoroughfare as wide and brightly lit as Wilshire. At the next intersection, she turned again, and the car fishtailed for a moment, tossing Wykla back and forth in her seat and throwing Manda against the door.

The VW settled down. They were heading west on Sixth Street. Alouzon slowed to the speed limit and switched on the headlights. "That should do it. Everyone okay?"

No reply. Outside the car, Asbury Apartments flickered past, its windows a patchwork of waking and sleeping, its neon sign red against the pale night sky that was all that Los Angeles had to offer.

Manda and Wykla exchanged glances. Wykla shrugged: she had seen stranger things in the last two years. "Where are we, Alouzon?"

Her voice, though puzzled and slightly frightened, was a joyful familiarity in this alien city. "It's called Los Angeles," said Alouzon.

"Los Angeles." Wykla tried the name, and Alouzon had to fight to keep herself from stopping the car, turning around, and hugging her. Suddenly, this world was not so foreign and threatening. Suddenly she had friends with her. "A strange name."

Alouzon nodded. "It's a fairly weird place."

"Is this your world?" said Manda.

Alouzon thought for some time, and the First Congregational Church had passed before she answered. "Nah," she said with a proud tightness in her throat. "I just live here right now." She felt her smile, was sure of it. Manda and Wykla were alive and in Los

Angeles. Hope had blossomed among the asphalt, concrete, and fetid water of a metropolitan park. "If you can call this living." She laughed.

A small hand on her shoulder. "Dragonmaster," said Wykla, "we are very glad that you live."

The tightness in her throat persisted. "Were you worried?"

"Greatly."

"Me too," said Alouzon. She covered Wykla's hand with her own for a moment, then reached over and patted Manda's bare knee. "Gods, I'm glad to see you're both okay. Last I saw of you, you were in that temple in Broceliande. What happened? What's going on now?"

Staring out at the passing lights and cars, periodically shaking their heads in a kind of dazed wonder, Wykla and Manda took turns telling the tale as Alouzon navigated a circuitous route home. The rest of the company were safe. Marrha and Manda were reconciled. And Kyria—who had sloughed off her hate like an old skin—had taken Santhe for a lover, and had pledged her allegiance not only to the king of Gryylth, but to the world as a whole.

Alouzon wanted to shout, cheer, pound the steering wheel. But there were other, darker sides to her friends' story, and so her joy was, by necessity, tempered. "So Helwych had everybody fooled, huh?" she said as she turned onto the street that led to her apartment building.

"Everyone save Relys, Timbrin, and Hahle," said Wykla. "Hahle was in Quay the last we heard, but of Relys and Timbrin we know nothing. We are all afraid for them. And for all of Gryylth."

Alouzon recalled Helwych as she had last seen him: insolent, manipulating. "Fucking prick."

Manda understood her tone. She nodded. "And so we decided to help Vaylle as best we could until something happened that might give us hope of a return to Gryylth."

Alouzon's hands gripped the plastic steering wheel, but they ached for a sword. "You know, Manda, I think something just happened."

"Aye, Alouzon," said the maid. The street lights flickered over her face, gleamed in her golden hair. "I think that is so."

❖ CHAPTER 14 ❖

The night was warm, and the tall stones of the Lachrae temple stood blackly against a sky gleaming with stars. Off in the west, above the Cordillera, swung a waxing moon.

Kyria and Dindrane approached the pair of carved monoliths that marked the entrance of the temple precincts. The sun had set long before, but torchlight and moonlight were enough to show the incised figures: a young woman and an old man. The woman held a sword. The man looked sad.

Suzanne and Solomon. The Goddess and the God.

The two women bent and washed their faces and hands at the fountain, then passed into the ring of stones. Beyond the edges of the temple, the King's House and Lachrae lay soundly asleep. Sorceress and priestess were alone.

"Ignorant still I am of your plans, Kyria," said Dindrane. "You questioned me long and hard about my service to the Goddess and the God after we heard the report from the patrol commanded by Wykla and Manda, and since then you have said nothing to me."

"To anyone." Kyria tried to appear calm, tried not to look too intently at Dindrane.

She sat down on the grass, put her hands on the ground, felt the soft energies that flowed through this place. If a piece of Vaylle could embody divinity, this was it. This was Alouzon: not as she used to be, but

as she could be. Here was love and loyalty fit to make
a planet spin. Here was friendship enough to send it
whirling about a star. Here was nurture sufficient to
kindle that star into golden radiance and warm the
empty void.

And though here too was Solomon in all his uncul-
tivated potential and disappointed endeavor, here also
was that blinding moment in which he had sacrificed
himself for his people, one act of utter, selfless love
that was by these stones prolonged into something that
might in some way redeem those bleak and unremitting sins.

Had a part of her not died in the ruins of Helen's
house, Kyria would have hated him still. But with the
objectivity of death and rebirth, she looked in her heart
and found pity. It could have been so different. For
both of them.

Her eyes were damp. "Oh, Solomon," she murmured. "I am as sorry as you."

Dindrane stood behind her, arms folded. "Do you
address the God, sorceress?"

Kyria nodded. "As much of Him as I can, my
friend."

Dindrane did not move. "I have considered what
you asked me, and my answers. I think I understand
what you might want me to do. But I think you will
understand that, before I do that thing, I would
know . . ." She looked to the moon as though asking
for counsel. ". . . everything."

Kyria had expected nothing less. "It is your right."

"Who is Suzanne?" demanded the priestess. "Who
is Solomon?"

Speaking simply, Kyria told her. About Suzanne,
student from UCLA and refugee from Kent State.
About as much of her hopes and fears as the sorceress
knew. About the genesis of Vaylle.

And then Solomon. Here she knew more. Here she
knew too much. Her throat was tight by the time she
finished, her words choked with sorrow.

Dindrane had sat down on the grass well before Kyria had finished, and now her face was pressed into her hands, her sobs long and deep. "And such . . . are my Deities."

"Such," said Kyria softly. "And more. You felt the presence of your Gods when you celebrated the Great Rite. Can you say that was nothing? And such as your deities made such as Marrha and Karthin, and Pellam and Baares and yourself. People—you, me, even Alouzon—are like the surfaces of still ponds. They mirror what lies above, and they mask what lies beneath. Can you denigrate them because they are only what they must be?"

A long pause. The moon, smiling, drifted closer to the mountains. "I cannot."

"Well then."

The priestess lifted her head. " 'Tis certain the corn must be reaped for there to be bread on the table. And trees must be stripped of their fruit before apples can come to be in bowls and pears in puddings. Our brothers and sisters of four feet and of wings kill and eat one another so that they might continue to live."

"Sometimes it is necessary."

" 'Tis so. I have learned that thing." Dindrane fingered the ceremonial knife that hung from her belt. No other woman of Vaylle carried or even handled such a weapon. "So I have lost my easy confidence in my Gods, and have come instead . . . to an understanding." She let the knife fall back against her thigh. "Tell me what you propose."

Kyria did not look at the priestess. "I believe that the apparition by Lake Innael was a door, a door that leads into another world. Alouzon's world."

Dindrane was impassive.

"Alouzon is there. Wykla and Manda are there also. Tonight I intend, with your help, to find out for certain. If I am right, then there is hope for Gryylth and Vaylle."

"And what help is it that you want of me?"

Kyria's mouth tightened with the brazen audacity of what she was about to ask: the turning of sacred concerns to utilitarian necessities. "In the temple in Broceliande," she said, "you called upon the Goddess to enter into your body. She did."

Dindrane nodded. "One with Alouzon I was for a moment. I saw through her eyes."

"Had you ever done that before?"

"I had not. 'Twas the urgency of the circumstances that made me so impertinent as to request such a thing of Her."

A long pause. Kyria leaned towards Dindrane, her eyes eager. "Would you do that again?" It was not a rhetorical question. "Would you do it now?"

Dindrane took the request calmly. For a time, she considered, then, standing, she grounded her staff, and her voice rang through the night air, echoed from the massive, encircling stones:

"O, most gracious Goddess Alouzon, descend, I pray you, into the body of your priestess . . ."

The young moon had just set when Relys awoke from nightmare, her groin aching and her teeth clenched against her screams. For a moment, she was afraid that she was back in the barracks, that her hands were still shackled, that the men of the King's Guard would return . . .

She sat up, clutching her arms about herself. Her hands were free. She smelled the odors of dinner and the sea, heard the distant lap of waves. She was in Quay, in the loft of Hahle's house, as safe as she could be anywhere in Gryylth; and in the warm darkness, she waited for her heart to slow.

Beside her, Timbrin tossed and turned, a prisoner of her own frightful dreams. With a small cry, she came awake. "Relys." Small hands clutching frantically, she felt through the darkness for her friend.

"Here, child," said Relys. With her good hand, she

pulled Timbrin to her side and held her while she cried. "You are safe here. Nothing will hurt you."

Timbrin muffled her sobs in Relys's shoulder so as not to awaken Hahle and his wife, who lay downstairs near the hearth. "I . . . I . . ."

"Easy, dear lady. Did you drink that infusion the midwife brought?"

"I did not finish it."

Relys felt for the cup. "Finish it now. It will help your dreams, she said." She handed it to Timbrin. The midwife. The midwife said this. The midwife said that. Disdainful of her body and its ways, Relys had eschewed any contact with the women of that profession, but now how easily and how comfortingly that word came to her lips!

Timbrin drank, set the empty cup aside. "I am sorry, Relys."

Relys wrapped an arm about her. "There is nothing to be sorry about," she said. "You did your duty to the best of your ability, and you were wounded in so doing. Do you think the less of me because I hobble about?"

She felt Timbrin shake her head, the dark curls rustling against her bare skin. "Nay. I think well of you."

"And I of you."

Relys wanted to tell Timbrin that all the women of the First Wartroop were valiant still, that her sacrifice had been a brave one; but such talk had come to frighten Timbrin, and so Relys only rubbed her back and stroked her head until the infusion took effect.

Timbrin slept. For Relys, though, sleep had fled. For a time she listened to Timbrin's even breathing, like a mother watching over her child. Then, when she was sure that her friend's nightmares had been banished, she donned a gown, climbed silently down from the loft, opened the door to the street, and slipped out.

Not wishing to leave the door unbarred and unguarded while her friends slept, she went no farther than the bench before the front wall. Here, she sat down and, hugging her knees to her chest, watched the stars rise into the sky above the mountains.

What now? She and Timbrin were safe—for the time—but Gryylth lay like a dying thing, its bare fields parching slowly under the summer sun. In the last few days, Hahle and a few of his men, scouting across the mountain passes, had found that Helwych's forces appeared to achieve no more than a scant balance of attrition with their enemies. Nothing was ever gained, nothing was ever really lost. Hills that were occupied one day were overrun the next, retaken on the morrow; and the sorcerer and his unknown adversary used their incredible forces like rushlights on a stormy night: easily squandered, easily renewed.

Only the land suffered.

In the faint light Relys lifted her right hand and examined the bandages. "And what can such as I do?" she said. "My warrior days are over."

"And is war everything?" said a voice from the half-closed door.

Rely started and instinctively looked for a weapon, but there was none near her, and in any case she had no hand with which to grasp it. "Hahle?" she said, hating the timidity that had crept into her voice.

The councilman slipped out and shut the door behind him. "I heard you go out," he said. "Fear not: the guards at the perimeter keep out intruders, and, as for me . . ." He shrugged. "I am but an old man."

"I heard you say that once," said Relys. "Just before you beat a hound senseless with your stick."

"This old dog has a few teeth left, true," Hahle admitted. "But I speak to reassure you, for I doubt that you are comforted much by the presence of a man."

She fought down a shudder. "You are a friend, Hahle. You saved our lives."

"And you, mine," he said. He folded his arms and leaned against the wall. From the distant shore came the lap of waves. "You are a lot like Marrget," he said after a time. "Always thinking of weapons and battles. If he . . ." He mumbled at himself for his error. "If she had found herself unable to swing a sword, I do believe she would have pined away."

Relys let her hand fall into her lap. "Am I that obvious?"

Hahle's voice—factual, sad—told her his expression. "I know, Relys. I see and I know. Years have made me see a little deeper, that is all."

Relys was silent for a time. Then: "Counsel me, my friend. What shall I do with myself?"

"You are wise in your own way, Relys. You have seen much. You have led battles and slain men. And yet you care for Timbrin as though she were your daughter."

Was that it? Was Hahle telling her now that she was good for nothing save children? Should she find a man to take her—battered and abused as she was—and get babies on her?

She turned from the thought with loathing, but another suddenly struck her, one that, because of her wounds, illness, and disdain for her sex, had not surfaced before: she did not recall having bled this last month from anything save the rape.

"I myself can no longer join in the press of a battle," the councilman was saying. "But I can counsel others so that they might fight and live. I can reassure the wounded. I can comfort the dying."

Relys hardly heard. She was busy calculating, counting silently on her fingers. One week, two . . . five, six . . . eight. Eight weeks and no flow. Her disdain had never affected her womanly cycles: she had been as regular as the phases of the moon since her transformation. Now, though . . .

It could be the wounds. That and nothing else. I should ask the midwife. But, terrified as she was of what the answer might be, she knew that she would not ask.

"You also have other talents," said Hahle. "Find them. Use them. You are not helpless."

Shaking, Relys reached out with her good hand. Hahle took it in a firm grip, and she jerked her thoughts back to his last words. "I . . . will try to follow your advice, councilman," she said softly. "I fear it may be beyond me, though."

"We can only try," he said. "And with the help of friends, we may succeed. Do you have family?"

"I am from . . ." She fought with her fear, fought with the name. ". . . from Bandon."

"Oh." Hahle was silent for a time. The distant waves hissed softly. "I am sorry."

Pregnant? The very thought was a sickness. Dryyim, maybe, insolent and swaggering? Or Lytham? Or Haryn? Or one of the other men who, faceless and grinning, had taken her as she, with clenched teeth and eyes, lay motionless, unwilling to give them the satisfaction of a struggle?

O you nameless Gods . . . please . . .

"I spoke with my wife," said Hahle. "And though we agree on very little . . ." He chuckled softly. ". . . we agree on this: consider us, if you will, your family. Call us mother and father or not as you wish, but know that we will defend you, honor you, and help you and Timbrin as we would our own daughters." He squeezed her hand briefly. "Come back to bed when you will," he said. "The door will be unbarred, and there will always be a place in my house for you to sleep."

Relys hardly heard him go. She was staring at her belly . . . wondering . . .

A television sit-com, Alouzon reflected, would have made much of it: three sword-toting, fifth-century warriors holed up in a one-bedroom apartment in Los Angeles. Reality, though, was something different: a scenario rife with potentials for confusion, fear, and tragedy. There was little room for humor.

But Wykla and Manda were hardy, resourceful women. They were used to coping with hardship and battles and, more recently, inner and outer horrors that transcended mundane concerns of death or wounds; and that, coupled with the faith and confidence that they placed in their leader, made the city and its manifestations of technology less a living nightmare than a new—albeit strange—situation that they had, for the time, to accept.

Haltingly, to be sure, they accepted. Alouzon got them up to her apartment without incident; fed them a late dinner; showed them how to work the sink, shower, and toilet; and got them cleaned up and packed off to bed.

She heard them talking softly in the bedroom for a few minutes, and then they fell silent. Relieved, Alouzon assumed that they had gone to sleep; but a few minutes later, a gasp from Wykla brought her up and running. Before she got to the bedroom door, though, she realized that there was nothing wrong: the two women were simply making love, taking comfort and reassurance from the familiarity of their bodies.

Laughing softly and affectionately, Alouzon peeled out of her wet clothes, showered, and curled up on the sofa. Sleep washed over her like a wave, and when she opened her eyes, it was already well towards midmorning. Wykla was standing over her, clad in one of Suzanne's caftans.

"Hey," said Alouzon. "How's it going?"

Wykla smiled in the fuzzy manner of a woman adequately supplied with both sleep and morning sex. "A strange world, Dragonmaster. We were going to cook breakfast, and we found oats and onions and meat, but no fire. We thought about building one in the middle of your floor, but decided that you might have other ways of doing these things here."

Alouzon laughed. "You know, Wykla, I'm damned glad to see you."

Wykla's hair, unbound, had fallen into curls and

ringlets. She looked delightfully lost in the overlarge caftan. "And we you, Alouzon."

Alouzon rose and fixed breakfast, serving up double portions of oatmeal and bacon for everyone after setting milk and butter and fruit out on the table. As she spooned the cereal into bowls, she recalled distantly the last morning Suzanne had spent with Joe Epstein. It had been oatmeal then, too. And when Suzanne had returned from school—and from Gryylth—in the late afternoon, she had packed Joe's belongings into three large cardboard cartons and had told him to get out.

The change had started. Suzanne Helling, though her life had been fragmented both by the killings at Kent State and her own mismanagement, had begun to grow, to sweep away the tatters and the wreckage. True, the next months had taxed her even more, and the strain of holding to a dual personality had brought her to the edge of insanity; but there was no more duality now: there was only Alouzon. And though Suzanne had never been able to reconcile the deaths of her classmates with her own continuing life, much less devise any kind of tribute or memorial to them that might have, at last, expiated her sense of guilt, Alouzon had.

She lived, simply, so that a world might continue; and if the deaths at Kent demanded a memorial, then Alouzon would give them one. She would give them that world. She would give them Gryylth. And she would take away from that fragmentary and torn planet the last remnants of Vietnam and give its people a chance at a life that neither she herself nor America as a whole had ever had.

Eating breakfast with Wykla and Manda, Alouzon fought to keep from bursting into tears. They were so utterly, utterly beautiful. And she desperately wanted them to stay that way.

I'd do anything for them. Anything. And she knew then not only that she would have to, but that she could.

Manda finished her bowl, drained her glass of milk, and after looking curiously at the paper napkin, shrugged and wiped her mouth. "What lies ahead of us today, Dra—?" She grinned. "Alouzon."

Alouzon leaned back in her chair and thought. "What month is it, Manda? In Vaylle, I mean."

"August."

"Hmmm. Would you believe I've only been here for three days? Time goes a lot faster in Gryylth. We'll have to move quick."

She rose, opened the door, and brought in the morning paper. Manda and Wykla watched curiously as she spread it on the floor; and while she explained briefly what it was, she scanned the pages. "I don't see anything about the old man in the park," she said at last. "It probably happened too late to make the morning edition."

"Is he of particular significance?" said Wykla.

"Kinda." Alouzon tossed the paper onto the sofa, stretched out her legs, contemplated her bare toes. "He wasn't the first to be killed by hounds from Vaylle. There were a couple others two days ago. That means that the door you came through wasn't just a fluke. It was open before."

Realization dawned on Wykla. "And might open again later."

"Right."

"More hounds?"

"Well . . . maybe." Alouzon was examining her guests, estimating sizes. There was some exploring to be done today, and Manda and Wykla had to look like California girls. That was not hard: the two were as blond and shapely as homecoming queens, and the new t-shirts and jeans she had bought would disguise them completely. But though that meant that she herself would have to go back to the old clothes from Kent State, she did not mind, for now the faded cut-offs and blood-stained blouse seemed to her more of a badge of honor than even the crest of the king of Gryylth.

"Maybe hounds," she said. "But maybe something else."

They spent the rest of the day traveling about the city in the VW, as though they were three girlfriends who had decided to go sightseeing together. But though Manda and Wykla did stare at the buildings, the cars, and the people, there was more to their journey than the sights.

Alouzon, falling from Silbakor into nothingness, had landed in MacArthur Park, unhurt, and at the same point in space where she had forced a passage from the immaterial spaces between dimensions into the material and prosaic world of smog, cars, and neon signs, there was now a door connecting two locations that quite possibly did not even reside in the same universe.

There had been other forcings, though. Other passages. Might there also be other doors?

At MacArthur Park, the police had been, as usual, efficient: hardly a trace of the night's violence was left. But the three warriors easily read in the mud at the edge of the lake the signs of huge paws, frantic flight, and spilled phosphor.

"It was here, Alouzon?" said Wykla.

"Right here." Alouzon pointed. "Look: you can still see where I fell flat on my face."

Manda had straightened up and was looking around. She shook her head. "I am very glad that we arrived at night."

"How come?"

"Because, friend Alouzon, had we arrived during the day, I am sure that I must have gone mad with fright." She gestured at the traffic, the people throwing Frisbees and listening to radios, the flash of steel and glass from a far-off 747: the noise and sights and milling life of the city. There was a flicker of nervousness in her manner, as though panic were being held down only by disciplined force of will. "I am sure you can understand."

A car was passing on Alvarado, a convertible with the top down. A young man waved at them. "Oh my God," he shouted. "Look at that ass! What a goddess!"

Alouzon resisted the temptation to throw something. "Just ignore him," she told her companions.

"Aye." Wykla was bent over the tracks. She glanced at the car. The man was still waving. "Is he from Bandon?"

Alouzon shrugged. "Close enough."

But aside from a lingering sense of otherworldliness that hung in the air, there was no sign of any intrusion save the prints in the mud and the phosphor stains, and no trace of a door. The women stayed for a few more minutes, scouted the circumference of the lake, then gave up and returned to the car. Alouzon headed out Wilshire.

"Where are we going now?" asked Manda.

"I want to take a look at what's left of a house," said Alouzon. "And then I'll give you a look at a school." A sudden qualm struck her. "Is this getting to be too much for you?"

Manda and Wykla were still staring at the city. Wykla wiped sweat from her forehead. "Were you not here, friend Alouzon," she said, "we would be a sorry sight indeed. But since you are . . ." She smiled, and Manda nodded agreement.

After fighting her way through heat and traffic for most of an hour, Alouzon drove into the green shade of Bel Air and pulled up to a stop before Helen's house. The lawn—brown and withered from the heat—had been trampled, and the ruins had been roped off. Deserted now save for birds and squirrels, and surrounded by untouched trees and the quietude of the expensive neighborhood, it all looked pointless and depressing.

Alouzon got out of the VW and stood for a moment at the brick gateway. Here, all that was left of Suzanne Helling had been loaded into an ambulance. Where was her old body now? Still at the coroner's office? Or locked in some drawer in the city morgue with a tag marked *Jane Doe* attached to the toe?

She shuddered. The ruins were silent.

"Stay by the car," she said to her companions. "I'll look fast, and then we'll get out of here."

While Manda and Wykla waited, Alouzon crossed the lawn, stepped over the ropes, and approached the ruins. Desolation. The hot wind fluttered a paper and sang through the broken wood and steel. Like Bandon. Like some sections of Quay and Hanoi. Like Haiphong, and My Lai, and Quang Tri.

And, yes, there it was again: a prickling presence in the air, like the fear of a graveyard hand on one's shoulder at midnight. Something that spoke of other worlds, of strange passages, of portals and impossible doors.

Alouzon returned to the car. Quietly, thoughtfully, she drove back down towards Sunset Boulevard and UCLA. She had fallen into MacArthur Park, and there was a door there. She and Helen had been taken to Gryylth from Helen's house, and though she had no proof of a door's existence, the feeling was the same. And the university: how many times had Solomon Braithwaite set off for Gryylth from his office in Kinsey Hall?

Holes. Doors. After she and her companions had used up an hour eating hamburgers and onion rings at the cafeteria, she stopped at the archaeology office. "Is Dr. O'Hara in?" she asked the secretary.

"Um . . . I'm not sure. Let me check the roster."

He was definitely not in, and Alouzon knew that: Brian had a class this hour. Leaving Wykla and Manda standing nervously in the hall, she smiled and edged past the desk, gambling that her face was still an honest one. "Can I just go and check real quick?"

"Well . . ."

"I want to see if I brought everything he wanted."

The woman shrugged. "It can't hurt, I suppose. Last door on the—"

"On the right," said Alouzon. "I remember."

In a moment, she had darted down the inner corridor and had knocked at Brian's door. No answer. She pretended to be disappointed, but as she walked very slowly back to the desk, her senses were straining at the closed door midway up the corridor.

"I'll try again later," she said when she reached the desk.

"He's been very busy," the secretary offered. "One of our new teachers quit and left him with quite a pile of work."

"Oh. I'm . . . sorry to hear that."

She left the office without looking back. Wykla and Manda followed her down the stairs and outside. "Was it there?" asked Wykla.

Alouzon wiped her face. "Yup."

Manda was deliberating. "But no hounds. And no . . ." She shrugged. "No real door."

"Nope." Alouzon shoved her hands in her pockets and examined the campus from the landing of the outside steps. It was late afternoon. Dickson Court lay before her, green and tree-shaded, like Blanket Hill at Kent State. Perhaps it was a warrior's instinct, and perhaps her recollections of the days of protest and death had been stirred by her concerns, but she found herself half-consciously considering the best strategies for defending Kinsey Hall against an attack.

She dragged herself out of her thoughts. This was UCLA, not Gryylth. And not Kent State.

But the daylight—unremitting, blinding daylight— had triggered a thought. "I wonder if you had a point back at the park, Manda," she said. "You said it was a good thing you arrived at night."

Manda's eyes were frank. "I still say it, Alouzon."

"Yeah. And I say that maybe there was a reason you arrived at night. The same reason the hounds arrived at night." She rubbed the back of her neck. "I want to look at these same places after it gets dark. Let's head home and catch a nap. Unless I miss my guess, we're probably going to be up until dawn.''

They drove back to the apartment. Alouzon gave Manda and Wykla the use of her bedroom, and the young women, tired out by strange happenings, fell asleep instantly. But Alouzon was doubtful as she stretched out on the sofa. She had risen late, and the fatigue left by a day of wading through the mire of Los Angeles traffic was mixed with tension. She was not at all sure she could do anything more than fret about Gryylth.

But she had hardly closed her eyes when her thoughts were spun away down long corridors of darkness and void. She thrashed, but she discovered that she had no arms or legs with which to thrash. Terrified as she was, though, she felt at the same time oddly calm, as if, blindfolded and bound, she were being led along by a kind and familiar hand.

The darkness passed with an abrupt flicker, and Alouzon found herself staring straight into a pale, aquiline face framed by hair the color of night.

''Hello, Alouzon,'' said Kyria.

❖ CHAPTER 15 ❖

Alouzon wanted to rush forward and take Kyria in her arms, but she found that she was strangely immobile, her body declining for the time to obey her commands, no matter how urgent. Relief turned to fear, then abruptly to consternation. Body? A moment ago she had no body. "What the hell's going on, Kyria?" she said. "I can't move."

Kyria came forward and embraced her. "You cannot move because you are not yourself, Alouzon. You are in Dindrane's body. She invoked you as she did in Broceliande."

"Wha?"

The priestess' voice came to her from within her mind. *Hail, Dragonmaster* . . . Alouzon sensed hesitation, then: *My Goddess.*

Were Alouzon in her own skin, she would have sagged, would probably have wept. It was one thing to know what the Grail had in store for her, it was entirely another to be addressed as a deity. "Uh . . . hi, Dindrane," she said softly. "Take it easy, huh? I'm just Alouzon."

A lift of an inner eyebrow. *Just Alouzon?*

"Well, you know what I mean." Her borrowed eyes looked helplessly at Kyria. "Don't you?"

"Not really," said the sorceress. "But we have some things to discuss, and quickly. I am aware of the time differential between Earth and Gryylth. This cannot last long.''

Wykla and Manda.

''Exactly,'' said Kyria. ''Are they well?''

''Yeah,'' said Alouzon. She noticed, unnerved, that she was speaking with Dindrane's voice. ''They're fine. They're a little shook up about everything, and they keep telling me that they'd freak if I wasn't around, but they're holding out. They're damned strong women.''

''And they have a fine leader,'' said Kyria.

It was a compliment, open and without qualification, something far different from anything that would have come out of the mouth of Helen Addams. Had Alouzon been able to move, she would have shaken her head. ''Lady, you've changed.''

The door.

Kyria, blushing, bowed. ''Indeed. Thank you, Dindrane.''

Alouzon was becoming used to the fact that she could not move, and that she sounded like Dindrane, and that the priestess was inside her head. She could appreciate the unlooked-for blessing of this spiritual link. ''The door. Yeah. That's what it was, all right. And I'll tell you: we found two more things that could be doors.''

''Two more?''

Alouzon recounted the events in MacArthur Park, the appearance of Wykla and Manda, and the existence of anomalies at Helen's house and at the office at UCLA. Kyria listened, obviously fitting together her own pieces of the puzzle; but to Alouzon's surprise, Dindrane was nodding inwardly, even at the mention of Helen and Solomon and the university. Inwardly, but perhaps a little sadly.

''I have a feeling,'' Alouzon said at last, ''that when Silbakor flew between Earth and Gryylth, it left tracks . . . like places that are thinner. That's where the doors showed up. But don't ask me why they suddenly got ripped open.''

Kyria was nodding. "I can answer that. Helwych. He attempted to seal Gryylth away from the rest of the universe.''

"Why the hell would he do that?''

"To prevent the return of the army.''

It did not make sense. Alouzon attempted to wrinkle her nose, but Dindrane's body would not respond: she could speak, that was all. "But that's like killing a fly with a nuclear bomb. You don't have to wall off the whole cosmos just to keep a few ships out.''

Kyria shrugged. "For whatever reason, Alouzon, he did just that. But in so doing, he tore the fabric of space-time. At night, under proper conditions, Gryylth and Los Angeles are linked along the paths that were weakened by Silbakor's previous transits.''

"And so the hounds made it through. And then Wykla and Manda.'' Alouzon turned the facts around and around as though trying to assemble a fragmented pot. "What about your . . . I mean, Helen's house and Solomon's office?''

"The first will, I think, take you to Gryylth . . .'' But Kyria stopped, her brow furrowed. She shook her head. "But now that I think of it, maybe to oblivion.''

Helen's house? 'Tis there I fought the hag.

"Just so, Dindrane. I am sure that it muddled the passage.''

"I don't understand,'' said Alouzon.

"No time to explain,'' Kyria replied. "You can go look at the door at Helen's house, but do not try to pass through it. Your best chances lie in MacArthur Park and Sol's office.''

Again, Alouzon felt Dindrane's sadness. It resonated with her own memories, cut at her heart. She felt the chill of drying tears on the priestess' cheeks. "You . . . uh . . . know about Sol Braithwaite, Dindrane?''

The reply came slowly. *Kyria told me all, friend.*

Dindrane's sadness was deep. Alouzon wanted to hold her, soothe her, comfort her, tell her that everything was going to be all right. But rooted as she was in the priestess' form, she was as helpless as she had been when, in another life and a far place, she watched impotently as her classmates' bodies had been loaded into the ambulances. "I'm . . . I'm really sorry, Dindrane."

I understand, Alouzon. We all do the best we can.

The best, as before, seemed hopelessly inadequate. "I'm gonna make it up to you. To all of you."

Peace, my dear Goddess.

Her words fragmented suddenly, and a rising wave of darkness shimmered up from the edges of Alouzon's sight. "I'm losing you."

"These things cannot last forever. Try the gates, that is all I can say."

But as the scene faded, a thought suddenly flashed through Alouzon's mind. Sol's office: Gryylth. Mullaen: MacArthur Park. She fought against the darkness for a moment. "That's it! Dammit, that's it!" Faintly, she saw Kyria's look of surprise, and she spoke quickly. "Give everyone my love, and tell them to assemble the troops near Lake Innael. We'll see you in about a week. We're gonna try for Gryylth."

Kyria's face was lost, but Alouzon heard her voice: "A week? But . . . the barrier."

Alouzon tried to shake her head, found that she had none to shake. "It's not a problem. A week, max. Get everyone together and ready to travel. We're coming."

And then Alouzon opened her eyes. She saw her living room ceiling. She saw Wykla and Manda peering anxiously into her face.

"Dragonmaster? We heard you shout."

Dragonmaster. And if the Grail had its way with her, it would be *Goddess*. Alouzon shuddered inwardly at the thought that the affections of her friends might someday be replaced by worship: Dindrane's invocation had made the potential transformation too real, too imminent. "I've . . . been talking with Kyria and Dindrane," she said, vowing never to speak of the method by which the priestess had achieved the contact. "I think we're going to make it through to Gryylth tonight. And maybe farther than that."

Wykla and Manda stared. "To Gryylth?"

The room was shadowed. She turned her head to the windows. It had grown dark outside. "We've got just enough time to eat before we have to go," she said. "Those doors aren't gonna wait."

Lytham, the captain of the King's Guard, picked his way down the main street of Kingsbury, shooing away the hungry dogs, stepping carefully around the piles of refuse that sprawled like heaps of corpses, skirting the pools of sewage that, wet and glistening and fragrant in the hot sun, had encroached muddily into the road.

The day was hot, and tantalizing promises of evening thundershowers had been proven to be lies for the past week. Children who had cried for food were now also crying for water as their mothers, starving and thirsty themselves, attempted to soothe them with whatever might be had: a moldy piece of dried fruit, a strip of smoked meat, sometimes indeed a scant mouthful of water.

Thirst and hunger were everywhere, as were disease and fear. Helwych had ordered that the people be herded into the towns for safety, but Lytham—looking into the pinched faces of the children, the worried faces of the mothers, the dead faces of those who had succumbed to whatever epidemic was making the rounds of the towns this week—wondered whether they were really any better off here than out where the Grayfaces fought and the hounds prowled openly.

A timid voice, weak and hoarse. "Captain of the Guard . . ."

In truth, Lytham felt little like a guard, and not at

all like a captain. Helwych's guards had been replaced by the nondescript but foreign Grayfaces . . .

"Please, captain."

. . . and the title had therefore become nothing more than an accusation, for besides Helwych—and, he hoped, the queen—Lytham and the other men of the Wartroops possessed the only full bellies and unparched throats left in the land.

Reluctant, guilty, Lytham turned to the woman who had addressed him. Her face was as withered as the fields of Gryylth, as gray as the dusty lean-to from which she had tottered. He could not even say whether she was young or old, alive or near death.

"What do you want, woman?" he said, trying to maintain a sense of dignity when he felt none.

"Please, captain, my daughter, Vyyka, is ill. She needs food and water."

She was, in fact, holding a young girl whose flesh was as gray as her own. The child's eyes were closed and her breathing was labored. Behind her, about her, everywhere, the flimsy hovels that clogged the streets and commons swarmed like an epidemic themselves, and the refugees, women, all women save for a few—women with hungry children, women with dying infants, starving women, grieving women—were looking at him, as faceless and as dull-eyed as this faceless mother with her dying child.

"Please, captain . . ."

"I . . ." Lytham wanted his village, wanted fights that were no more than shouts and buffets and makings-up afterwards, wanted an end to uniforms and useless swords, wanted a sane world that possessed tables with food on them, people who smiled, and a surety that tomorrow would not find everyone dead. "I can do nothing, woman," he said. "Everyone is hungry. The enemy . . ." What was the enemy? The Specter? The hostile Grayfaces? Or maybe it was even closer than that. Maybe . . .

Dryyim's scream rang in his mind, and he pushed

the thought away as though it were a corpse come to embrace him in bed. "The enemy has burned the fields," he said. "We will have to make do without."

Without food? What was he saying? He was beginning to sound like Helwych.

The woman bowed shakily and turned away. The child she carried whimpered. She held her closer, as though solicitude could fill her belly or dampen her mouth.

About Lytham, the street was choked and stagnant with decay. Kingsbury had grown to five times its normal population, and even had there been food aplenty, the crowding alone would have bred sickness. As it was . . .

He turned and went quickly up the street, keeping his eyes very carefully averted from the sight of the huddled women and the children who did not have enough strength to play.

When he reached the palisade surrounding the Hall, he was stopped by the new guards: Grayfaces. One held him at riflepoint while the other examined and questioned him, the eyes behind the gray mask at once suspicious and blank.

"I am Lytham," he said.

The second Grayface turned to the first. "Chuck, you know this dink?"

"Yeah." The voice was strangely impassive, as though all emotion had been drained from it. "He's the captain of the Guard."

"Okay, buddy, go on in." The muzzle of the rifle dropped away from Lytham's face.

Other Grayfaces stood in the yard, lounged in the shadow of the palisade, kept watch from the platforms. Helwych, distressed by Dryyim's behavior and fearful of the Specter's forces, had taken refuge behind soldiers who did not show fear, who would follow any orders he gave them.

Lytham walked quickly across to the Hall and entered. Inside, Helwych was slumped in the king's

chair, his staff across his knees. His wounds were long
healed, but though he was young, the constant expenditure of magic demanded by the battles with the
Specter gave him the appearance of an old man.

The sorcerer did not lift his head. "Dryyim . . ."

Lytham stood near the door, conscious of the Grayfaces who stood to either side of the dais. "Dryyim is
dead, lord."

"Ah, yes. Lytham."

Helwych still had not looked up. Lytham had the
uncomfortable feeling that the sorcerer could see without actually looking. "My lord," he said, "I was in
the street just now. The people are hungry."

"Indeed."

"They need food and water."

"Indeed."

A silence. A silence that lengthened. The Grayfaces
stood as though carved out of granite. Helwych
slumped in his chair, his hands thin and white on his
staff.

Lytham mustered his courage. "Can you not—"

Helwych lifted his head. "No, hayseed," he
snapped. "I cannot."

The words and the blue-black eyes that lay behind
them carried the impact of a club, but Lytham steeled
himself and approached, for behind Helwych's eyes
lay others: gray and dull with starvation, closed in
fevered illness and imminent death. "Surely, lord,
there is something . . ."

Helwych eyed him. "What do you expect me to do,
captain? Conjure up banquets for the people? Perhaps
a few thousand skins of wine." He laughed dryly.
"They should be grateful that their own skins are
safe."

"But they are dying! They have no food!" Lytham
almost shouted the words, and the Hall was suddenly
very quiet. The captain felt cold. Dryyim had died less
than a week ago.

Helwych examined him out of those eyes. Void. They looked like void. "Come here, Lytham."

Unwillingly, Lytham came and stood before the sorcerer, mentally cursing that other time he had come, when, innocent and awkward, he had entered Helwych's room bearing a bowl of gruel.

"Let me make one thing perfectly clear," said Helwych softly. "I intend to win this war. I intend to win it thoroughly, without question, without doubt. The Gryylthan system of country life has gotten in the way, and therefore it has to be broken. When the war is over, I will devise new systems. Until then, we will just have to make do."

Lytham did not have to see the sorcerer's face to read the denial in it. The people of Gryylth, maybe the land itself, was expendable. But he tried again. "The king—"

"The king has his own battles to fight," said Helwych without raising his voice. "If he is not dead already. He cannot but appreciate our efforts in Gryylth."

"But—"

"Are you fed, captain? Have you had enough to drink?"

Lytham felt a cold loathing creep up his throat and realized that he was feeling now the way that Dryyim must have felt moments before he had been struck and killed. Very carefully, he edged away from the abyss that had opened before him. "Do you have orders for me, lord?" he said.

"Keep the people within the town. Hold them here at all costs. Should they try to leave, we must assume that they have taken sides with the Specter, and we must kill them." A flicker of blue-black eyes. "Understood?"

The abyss yawned before Lytham. He resisted the urge to plunge in. "Understood, lord." He turned and started for the door, but he stopped. "The queen, my lord," he said without turning around. "How is she?"

"She plays with her dolls, captain. Like any child should."

Lytham gritted his teeth, mustered his self-control. "Does she have enough to eat, lord?"

"All she wants, captain."

Lytham strode out of the Hall, crossed the yard, and entered the barracks. It was dim and stifling inside, and the pallet upon which Relys had been chained, though it had been shoved roughly out of the way, was still dark with her blood. Lytham looked at it and turned away quickly.

At the other side of the room was Haryn, alone. The tall, thin man was sitting over a plate of meat and bread and a full cup of wine.

"Haryn?"

Haryn was not eating, and when he lifted his eyes, Lytham saw his own expression mirrored in them. "I am not fit to be a tyrant," said Haryn.

Lytham waited.

"It is the children who are the worst," Haryn went on. "They . . . they do not even . . ."

"I know."

Haryn shoved the untouched plate away. "I cannot eat this. I cannot eat at all."

Lytham's stomach twisted. "And what of our men?" Men? Boys, rather. Foolish boys who had raped their rightful commander on that stained pallet over there.

Where was Relys, anyway? Dead, probably; dragged down by the hounds as she had staggered out of the barracks and into the rainy streets. Maybe she would have figured out an escape from the hell into which Gryylth had been plunged: a woman who would chew her own hand off in order to gain her freedom was capable of anything.

Haryn was shaking his head. "Some are fools, and they eat. Most feel as do we: they take but a morsel now and again for strength."

Lytham licked his lips. "There are others, I think,

who would appreciate what morsels we do not consume.''

Dropping his eyes, Haryn contemplated the full plate before him. "I am afraid, Lytham."

"And I also, my friend."

Haryn's lip trembled much as it had months ago when, a boy with the carelessness of a boy, he had bent over the still form of a dead puppy. Now it was the corpse of his land that he mourned. "Let us feed the people as we can," he said. "Let us begin quickly, before I turn coward."

Lytham nodded. "I will call our men. They will help."

"And Helwych?"

Lytham shook his head. "I am afraid that Helwych cares about nothing save Helwych."

Alouzon, Wykla, and Manda ate, packed sandwiches, cleaned up, and left. But as Alouzon locked the front door behind her, she knew that this was a permanent departure. She would never come here again. Like her old life and her old identity, this apartment and all the memories it contained had joined the collection of the discarded, the unneeded, the preterit.

Wykla and Manda were padding down the stairs to the street: her new life, calling her away from school, Kent State, Vietnam, everything. And beyond that was the Grail, and yet another life still.

For a moment, she stood in the warm night air, her hand on the knob. Had she wanted this? She was not sure. She was not sure that the question could even be legitimately asked.

Her lip trembled. Then: "Goodbye," she said, and she turned away.

They did not go to MacArthur Park. Instead, they drove up to Bel Air and, in the darkness that was filled with the chirping of crickets and the flutter of moth wings about street lamps, they parked in front of the ruined house and made their way across the trampled grass.

Stillness hung in the air like a dense fog. Manda and Wykla, carrying swords while still in jeans and t-shirts, looked oddly anachronistic. Alouzon, herself, in cut-offs and a peasant top ten years out of date, felt a little ridiculous with a murderous weapon like the Dragonsword in her hand.

The rubble was a black heap against the parched dichondra. The sense of unreality about it had increased with the coming of night, but Alouzon could see no trace of the flickering light that might signal the presence of an interdimensional passage.

"You guys feel it?" she whispered.

"We do," said Wykla. She bettered her grip on her sword. Though her face and form said *California girl,* her demeanor said *killer.* Half-crouched, she slipped cautiously along the perimeter of the ruins as she had once crept along the glowing peristyle of the Circle.

"Let's head around back," said Alouzon. "That's where Silbakor took Hel—" She caught herself. "That's where Silbakor took off."

The back of the house was dominated by the remains of the redwood deck that had been splintered beyond recognition. But here the oddness in the air increased, too, and now the main disturbance seemed to lie near the center of the ruins.

"I'm gonna take a closer look," said Alouzon. She stepped carefully over the rope barrier left by the police investigators and picked her way into the rubble.

The unreality grew. Alouzon stopped, cocked her head, strained her ears. Was she hearing something?

"Alouzon?"

"Shhh." She leaned forward. A faint sound, like a distant high-pitched whine. And now she was seeing light—flickering light—seething just under the fallen lath and plaster, roiling as though held down by the lid of a pot. "Yeah," she said. "There's something here, and—"

Something moved beneath the ruins. The light expanded, changed color—and suddenly the wood and concrete were thrown back as a pale head the size of an automobile reared up out of the remains of the house, its eyes glowing a no-color of violet-black, its mouth opened to reveal a cavern of blankness set about by teeth the size of butcher knives.

For a split second, Alouzon and the White Worm regarded one another in surprise. Then Alouzon noticed the figure seated astride the Worm's pale back.

"Fuck you, asshole," she screamed, and the Dragonsword leaped and struck straight between the Worm's eyes. The blade was turned by the unnatural hide, but the Worm screamed and thrashed, and then a wing heaved out of the ruins, scattering beams, raising a powder of pulverized cement and tile.

Alouzon slashed again, and again the Worm screamed, but she knew that she was fighting a losing battle. The Worm's other wing flapped up from beneath the rubble. Beams and 2x4s went flying. Manda and Wykla were wading in, but Alouzon shook her head frantically. "Run!" she shouted "Back to the car!"

They retreated only a short distance, waiting to see that Alouzon was safe. As she turned to follow, though, she saw the Specter's grin. "And where will you run, girl?" it said. "I can find you. Who's going to stop me?"

And then Silbakor struck. Without warning, without a sound, without even a flash of unblinking eyes to betray its approach, it stooped out of the washed out sky like a hawk descending upon a partridge. Its huge wings tore the air with an audible ripping as its talons slashed the Worm's face, sheared nacreous sparks from its back, and threw the Specter to the ground.

"Run," said the Dragon. "Run quickly."

Alouzon floundered out of the ruins, cutting her arms and legs on broken glass, nearly spraining her ankle on the uncertain footing. Behind her, the Worm and the Specter were struggling out of their surprise, but Silbakor had turned quickly and plunged back at them, eyes glowing, talons ready.

Manda and Wykla piled into the VW in a clatter of swords; Alouzon vaulted the hood to the driver's side. "I thought you said Los Angeles was safe," she shouted to the Dragon.

"I had not foreseen it," came the passionless reply. "I do not prophesy."

Alouzon got in and pulled away from the curb with a screech of rubber. "Run, sure," she muttered. "Dammit: run where?" Gunning the Beetle as much as its small engine would stand, Alouzon raced the length of Helen's street and picked up Beverly Glen, weaving through traffic and running red lights.

Horns honked. Drivers cursed as she cut them off.

"Sorry!" Alouzon shouted as she came within inches of a Cadillac's grille. But she could not keep up these flagrant violations for long, and in any case, what did it matter? The Specter and the Worm, in flight, were unaffected by such things as traffic, stop signs, streets, and turnings.

"We've got to get out of here," said Alouzon as she turned onto Sunset Boulevard. Quickly, she cut across the lanes and spun left onto Hilgard Avenue.

"Where?" said Manda. She was in the passenger seat again, and Wykla was in back. Both young women were white: an already frightening world had turned deadly.

"To Gryylth, I hope," Alouzon replied. UCLA lay to the west. Forcing herself to slow down, she turned onto the campus and parked next to the faculty center. Just across Dickson Court was Kinsey Hall, the archaeology office, and—maybe—a way out.

"Everyone out," she cried. "Last stop before Gryylth." Casting a glance up at the sky as though the Specter and the Worm might suddenly appear, she grabbed the bag of sandwiches and fruit, seized her sword, and ran for Kinsey Hall. Wykla and Manda followed.

They sprinted through the stands of eucalyptus trees

that occupied Dickson Court, then crossed the street and climbed the long flight of steps up to the east door of the hall. Alouzon kept an eye out for security officers as she led Manda and Wykla along the main corridor to the north stairwell, but she saw no one, not even students.

They reached the second floor without incident. Manda grunted with recognition when she saw the door to the archaeology office. "We were here this afternoon," she said.

Alouzon approached the door. "Yeah," she said softly, laying her hand on the knob. "And I'm hoping that this gate is open now."

The gate might have been open, but the door was not. Alouzon cursed herself silently for having forgotten: Los Angeles was a less trusting place than Gryylth.

For a moment, she eyed the latch and the door. The latch was metal, and the door was solid. But though in Bandon the Dragonsword had cut effortlessly through three inches of solid oak, doors were locked in Los Angeles for a reason, and there were also security guards and checks, and the occasional student or teacher who might come by. Richard Nixon's machinations had been undone by a simple piece of tape. A door that had been reduced to splinters, screws, and dangling hinges would destroy Alouzon Dragonmaster's hopes even more effectively.

But the door, if it remained closed, would dash them from the start, and so, carefully, expecting at any moment to be jarred by the scream of the Worm, Alouzon laid the tip of the Dragonsword between lock and door jamb. She was no locksmith, she had no idea how this latch was constructed, but she knew the Dragonsword's power, and she could hope for the Grail's intercession.

With pressure, the tip slid into the crack as though greased. A firm thrust, and the preternatural steel parted the wood, sheet rock, and plaster, coming to rest halfway up the blade, leaving only the smallest trace of powdered gypsum on the floor.

While Manda and Wykla stood guard, Alouzon put
her hands to the hilt, braced one foot against the wall,
and pulled. The Dragonsword, she knew, was not designed to be used as a crowbar, and straining the flat
of the blade in such a way invited breakage, but she
pulled nonetheless.

Her shoulders were aching when she at last heard a
crunch, and she jerked the sword free and pulled the
door open. ''Wykla,'' she said, her mouth dry, ''check
the office please. Fourth door on the right. You know
what we're looking for.''

As the young woman scuttled down the inner hall,
Alouzon examined the door. Not bad, but not good
either. Splintered as it was, it would withstand a casual examination, but not much more. Alouzon recalled the piece of tape at the Watergate Hotel once
again and winced.

Wykla's voice drifted back to them: ''I found it,
Dragonmaster! It fills the room!''

Alouzon wiped her forehead with the back of an
arm. They were indoors, but the Specter might well
be able to home in on her like a heat-seeking missile.
Time was running out: they had to get away from this
building, from this city . . . from this entire world.

She shrugged and sheathed her sword. Damaged as
the door was, it would have to do. She would have to
count on the Grail. *Can you help me?*

Questions again. She was still not ready, but she
took the precaution of sweeping away the gypsum dust
before she beckoned Manda into the office and closed
the door behind them.

The shimmering expanse of light filled one entire
wall of Solomon Braithwaite's old office—filled, and
even overflowed, pushing back the metal, glass, and
concrete as though in defiance of ordinary laws of
physics and perspective. Wykla stood before it, seemingly undisturbed, but Alouzon went cold. It was one
thing to be taken to Gryylth on the iron-colored back

of physical law, it was another to plod along the dimen-
sionless alleyways of the universe on one's own feet.

She swallowed. *Some God.* "Manda, Wykla: show
me how you do this."

Manda stepped up beside Wykla, but she paused.
"What about our armor, Dragonmaster?"

Alouzon shrugged. "We don't have time. We'll just
have to do without it."

Wykla nodded: she had fought without armor before. "Come Manda," she said, and, taking a deep
breath, she stepped into the shimmer. Manda followed. Stomach clenching, Alouzon entered the portal
. . . and was relieved when the door slid over her skin
like oil. More disturbing, though, was the region of
shifting shapes and colors on the other side. Void and
not-void pressed closely about her. Perspective and
distance rioted, and Alouzon recognized star clusters
and galaxies from photographs; but these were close,
very close, and they were real.

Shuddering, Alouzon plunged after her companions,
grateful that incipient Goddesses had friends. But
though the first time they had passed through the gate,
Manda and Wykla had been occupied enough by their
fears for Alouzon that they had not thought much about
what they had been seeing, now, traveling at a more
leisurely pace, they grew increasingly nervous.

"A-Alouzon?"

Wykla had stopped and was looking off to the side.
Alouzon followed her gaze. There was nothing there.
Nothing. Not even color. Cold already, she went even
colder.

But now Wykla and Manda were depending on her,
and she could not afford panics in the middle of nowhere. "It's okay," she replied, trying to sound confident. "It's just a place in the universe where there
isn't anything. Go on: it'll be fine."

"Oh," said Wykla. "All right, then." And she went
on. Alouzon hurried past the nothingness with her eyes
averted.

Alouzon's watch had stopped when she had stepped
through the door, but in what she estimated was a few
minutes, a familiar glow sprang up ahead of them: a shimmer and a flickering. The other door. Manda and Wykla
reached it, looked at one another, and stood aside.

"You are the Dragonmaster," Wykla said to Alouzon. "It is your right to enter Gryylth first."

Alouzon nodded. With a murmured thanks, she
stepped through the door. Manda and Wykla followed
immediately after.

They found themselves at the top of a hill beneath a
dark sky patched with the blackness of lowering
clouds. Below, plainly visible in the diffuse moonlight, broad plains dotted with spots and blotches that
could only have been stands of trees and forests spread
out and away.

But though Alouzon recognized this place from its
general contours—the shape of the surrounding hills,
the slope of the land, the dark lines that marked the
courses of rivers and streams—she sensed that there
was something wrong; and as her eyes adjusted to the
normal perspectives, she saw that the fields were bare
and wasted, the woods and forests shattered. Craters
pocked what had once been grassy meadows and lush
farmlands, and the odors of high explosive, napalm,
and defoliants hung in the air, metallic and rank.

"Gods . . ."

It reminded her of Broceliande, of what she had seen
when she had paused at the top of the Cordillera and
had looked out over a netherworld of shadows, fantasies, and nightmares. But this was not Broceliande:
two hours after sunset, in the heart of a warm summer
night near the beginning of August, Alouzon Dragonmaster had entered Gryylth.

❖ CHAPTER 16 ❖

The thunderstorm brought rain to Kingsbury, but though the water slaked the town's thirst, it could not cool the fevers of its epidemic, and it could not take the place of food.

Kallye trudged home through the crowded marketplace. Two months ago, this square had been occupied by stalls filled with the ample produce of a fertile, prosperous land. But now the wicker and wattle huts, dripping sullenly in the evening rain, contained only hunger and disease.

She was a midwife. And she was watching the women and children die.

She wanted to weep, but her duty decreed otherwise: where despair flowed through the streets like the rivers of filth washed along by the rainstorm, she had to be confident; where there was no hope in the women to whom she ministered, she had to be optimistic. Though she wanted to fall on her knees and scream at the Gods of Gryylth to show a shred of compassion for Their children, her labors left her with the strength to do no more than crawl into her bed at night, whisper a prayer, and sleep.

Gelyya was waiting for her when she entered the house, as was a cup of thin broth with a few bits of meat in it. "It is all we have for today," said the girl. "Praise to the men of the wartroops for their generous gift, but we must stretch it as far as we can."

Kallye nodded. "I have a wise apprentice."

But Gelyya turned away. Kallye knew her feelings.
The red-haired girl was becoming a skilled midwife,
but her heart was not in it, for since she and her companions had met Alouzon outside Bandon two years
ago, her thoughts and wishes had always taken a bent
towards swords and battle. Gelyya wanted action, she
wanted to *do* something, and this helpless waiting and
watching for death had rekindled the fire of her warlike
ambitions.

"Easy, child," said Kallye. "There is nothing we
can do."

"I want a sword."

Kallye sipped her broth, regarded her sympatheti-
cally over the rim of the cup. "Do you?"

Gelyya slumped on the stool across the table. Her
hands fidgeted with her apron. "I . . . do not know
anymore. My duty is here, among the women. But it
is hard to think in terms of duty when your duty
achieves nothing."

"I understand," said Kallye. "And if I thought that
there was a difference that you could make with a
sword, then I would send you on your way with all my
blessings."

Gelyya nodded somberly.

A knock came to the door: a soft tapping. "Someone needs us." Kallye sighed. "And I am so weary."

"Rest," said Gelyya as she went to open the door.
"I will go in your place."

Kallye bent her head and closed her eyes, her fatigue
an ache in her heart; but a sudden cry from Gelyya
brought her to her feet. The light from the lamp on
the table only just reached the open door, but it was
enough to illuminate the woman who stood there. Tall,
thoroughly wet, she was dressed outlandishly; but the
lamplight flickered in her bronze hair and gleamed on
the sword at her hip.

Alouzon Dragonmaster.

Gelyya had already thrown herself into Alouzon's

arms, and Kallye had to fight to keep herself from doing likewise. She bowed low. "Come in, Alouzon. Please, by the Gods, come in."

The Dragonmaster nodded and stepped into the room, followed by Wykla of the First Wartroop and the Corrinian named Manda. The young women were dressed just as oddly as Alouzon, but Kallye smiled through her tears: Helwych had lied. The story was untrue. But, oh what evil had been done by his lies and untruths!

The visitors accepted towels with which to dry off, but they refused food. "We ate already, and you guys don't have enough to share," said Alouzon.

"O Dragonmaster . . ." Kallye's voice broke. "You are alive. Helwych said . . ."

Alouzon nodded, but though she smiled reassuringly, her brown eyes were filled with a carefully-banked wrath. "I heard what Helwych said. I'm here to find out what he's doing now, and I'm going to try to fix it."

Gelyya dragged herself back into control, wiped her eyes on her sleeve. Alouzon gave her hand a squeeze. "I'm glad to see you, Gelyya. Hang in there. You did okay in Bandon. You can do it again." She glanced between the midwife and the apprentice. "Okay. Talk. We just got back in country, and the place is a mess. What's been happening?"

Taking turns, Kallye and Gelyya told her as much as they knew of the tale of deceit, rape, and preternatural battle that Gryylth had become. When they were done, Alouzon sighed. Her brown hands lay clenched on the table, but her voice was surprisingly controlled. "Well, that explains what happened to the Specter."

"Indeed, Alouzon," said Wykla. "It explains much."

"But the battles . . ." Alouzon shook her head. "It doesn't make sense. Why should they be fighting?"

Manda shrugged, but her eyes were cold. "Helwych

betrayed Corrin, then turned on Vaylle and Gryylth. Perhaps he has proved traitorous to the Specter, also.''

Alouzon laughed bitterly. ''The little shit's got balls, doesn't he?''

Manda turned to the midwife. ''Honored lady,'' she said, ''has there been word of Corrin?''

Kallye shook her head. ''I am sorry, maiden: there has been none. We have no news these days save what Helwych deems fit for us to know, and there is no travel in Gryylth save by Grayfaces and hounds.''

Gelyya spoke up. ''Dragonmaster, counsel us. What shall we do? The queen has not been seen in a month and a half, the people are starving, and even if the battles ended tomorrow, there would still be no food.''

Alouzon's eyes were on her hands. Kallye knew that she wanted to seize the Dragonsword and, like Gelyya, do something. Anything. The Dragonmaster's mouth worked, but she did not speak.

Kallye looked away. In her mind, she saw the hollow faces of motherless children, the still faces of dead women, the ravaged faces of starving infants. She, too, could not speak. She was certain that, had she tried to form words, she would have screamed instead.

Gelyya pressed. ''Please, Dragonmaster.''

Alouzon sighed, unclenched her fists. ''It's my fault,'' she said with an effort. ''If I hadn't been such a goddam chicken, a lot of this wouldn't have happened.''

''Shall we kill Helwych?'' said Wykla. ''We entered the town unseen. It should be a simple matter to scale the palisade and enter the Hall.''

''Aye,'' said Manda. ''The penalty for treason is death, in Corrin as well as in Gryylth, and for myself I am ashamed that a countryman has proved himself such a wretch.''

Alouzon passed a hand over her face. ''It'd sure be nice, wouldn't it?'' But she shook her head. ''Helwych is the only thing standing between the Specter and the towns. If we kill him, I guarantee that the jets will hit

Kingsbury and every other inhabited place in Gryylth within the hour.''

Manda stared. ''Do we then help the traitor?''

''No,'' said Alouzon slowly. ''I've got another idea. I'll have to deal with the Specter when the time's right. That's my job. But Cvinthil and Darham and the rest are the ones to take out Helwych. And I'm sure that Kyria is going to enjoy screwing that bastard to the floor.'' She turned to Kallye. ''Relys and Timbrin are in Quay?''

''We do not know for certain, Dragonmaster. They set out nearly a month ago. We pray daily for their safety.''

''Then that's our next stop,'' said Alouzon. ''We'll start tonight, and—''

Kallye was shaking her head. ''The guards and the Grayfaces have orders to kill anyone who tries to leave Kingsbury.''

Alouzon smiled without mirth. ''If they're running, then they're the enemy, right?''

''Well, yes . . .''

''I've heard it before.'' Alouzon shrugged. ''We'll get out the same way we got in. We'll slit throats if we have to. Given what the boys did to Relys, I don't think we'll mind much.'' She looked to her companions. ''We'll need horses.''

''I saw men and horses stationed at the base of the hill,'' said Wykla.

Alouzon nodded, but her expression softened when she rose and bowed to Kallye and Gelyya. ''Thanks for everything,'' she said. ''Thanks a million. I can't give you any advice except to hang on. In about two weeks this place is going to erupt. There's . . .'' She looked sad. ''There's going to be some fighting. I . . . can't help that. I'm sorry.''

In her face, Kallye saw deep grief, the same grief that she saw every day now in the eyes of mothers bending over the still forms of their children. She took

Alouzon's hands. "Even the Gods sometimes find Themselves helpless, dear Dragonmaster."

Alouzon nodded slowly. "Yeah," she said, "they sure do, don't they?"

She embraced the midwife, kissed Gelyya, and, in another minute, she and her companions had vanished into the rainy night.

Heedless of the rain, Gelyya stood at the open door and looked after her. "I love that woman," she said softly, and Kallye saw that the apprentice's fists, like Alouzon's, were balled in the manner of one who wished for a weapon.

Alouzon, Wykla, and Manda struck the outpost at the base of Kingsbury Hill silently, efficiently. The young men in Helwych's service did not realize that they were under attack until they were regaining consciousness several hours later, and though the Grayfaces were more alert, they had no chance to react before Alouzon emptied the magazine of an M16 into them.

The shots were loud, but no alarm was raised on the hill: either the thunder had masked the noise, or gunfire had become an accepted occurrence here in the war zone. "Come on," said Alouzon, unnerved by the lack of response. "Let's move, fast."

Mounted now on war horses, they rode as quickly as they could into the rainy night, following the Roman road that stretched north across the blasted fields. Their way was lit intermittently not only by the flashes of lightning, but also by the distant, unheard detonations of heavy artillery that turned the horizon into black cardboard silhouettes and the clouds into gray cotton; but such travel in the dark was uncertain at best, and as soon as they were well away from Kingsbury Hill and the danger of immediate pursuit, Alouzon called to her companions to slow down.

They picked their way up into the foothills of the Camrann, then, and huddled in the shelter of some blasted trees to await the dawn. It was a miserable camp—wet, fireless, with only peanut butter and jelly sandwiches to eat—and the howls of prowling hounds and the roar of high explosive sounded clearly over the miles: in Gryylth, as in Indochina, the war went on regardless of the weather.

"Get some sleep, you two," said Alouzon. "We start for Quay as soon as it's light."

Manda's face, lined with worry and mud, made her look like an old woman. There had been no word from Corrin. Anything could be happening beyond the remains of the Great Dike. "But then what? Where do we go then? To Corrin? The women's phalanxes are still there, maybe—"

"We're going to Lachrae," said Alouzon.

Manda shook her head. Wykla frowned. "But . . . the curtain wall."

"It's not a problem. Obviously, the Specter can get through it. If the Specter can get through, then Silbakor can too."

"And . . ." Wykla was nodding. "Silbakor can take us to Vaylle."

"Exactly."

Manda was still shaking her head. "But once we are in Vaylle, what then?"

"Then we get Cvinthil and Kyria and the boys, and we come home to kick some ass."

"On Silbakor?"

"Nope." Alouzon folded her arms. It was all coming together, had, in fact, fallen together when she stood in the Temple of Lachrae, an invoked Goddess manifesting in the body of Her devoted priestess. The Grail, she was sure, had seen to it.

"Helwych barred the way back," she said. "But he opened some doors, too. Remember?"

Manda and Wykla suddenly understood. Manda caught her breath. "Through Los Angeles?" she cried. "Oh, Alouzon! That is wonderful!"

Alouzon shrugged. It was a terrible risk, but the

Grail, she decided, would come through. It would have
to. She could not question it any more. She could not
afford it. "The archaeology department will probably
never be the same," she admitted. "And as for us . . ."
She thought of what could happen if the Specter found
her, recalled that—by necessity, by the need for an end
to this mazed and dialectic-ridden quest—it would have
to. "We may not be the same, either."

The sound of machine gun fire drifted across the
rooftops of Kingsbury, breaking through the stillness
with a noise like a sudden tearing of coarse cloth. Helwych's orders were being carried out with greater
ruthlessness and efficiency since the attack on the gar-
rison at the base of the hill, but day by day the people
were increasingly desperate to flee.

The rain had left a lingering humidity in the air, but
though the cisterns and wells were full again, the gra-
naries and storehouses were not. And the only inhabitants of Kingsbury who could call themselves satisfied
with the arrangement were the starvation and disease
that, stalking invisibly from house to house, left behind a death as incontrovertible as that brought by
Grayface bullets or hounds' teeth.

Seena, sheltered—imprisoned—in the chambers of
Hall Kingsbury, saw little of it, for her contacts with
the world outside the palisade had shrunken almost to
nothing. She saw no townsfolk, no midwife, no physician. Soldiers brought her food, and now and then
Helwych would come to her rooms to comfort her.

She was not comforted. In truth, she was numb.
Even had she known that Helwych had bespelled her,
it was quite possible that she would not have cared, for
her children were held in the grip of an unending sta-
sis, and she was concerned only with them.

Throughout the days, Seena tended Ayya and Vill,
catering to their needs, to the wishes and desires that
she imagined—that she wanted to imagine—they had.
Since that night of evil dreams when she had awakened

to find them unmoving, unbreathing, and yet undead, she had entered into an existence that was lapped round by an unending present, in which questions of tomorrow or yesterday had no meaning. Her children were ill, her children were in danger . . . *now*. That was all she knew.

She might have been a little girl playing with her dolls, picking up the limp bodies, bathing them, changing their clothes, putting them down for pretend sleep. Had they been simply dead, she could have mourned and eventually recovered. But with them caught forever in a state that was neither of life nor of death, neither gone nor really present, Seena could do no more than bend all of her attention and strength towards caring for them.

By day she was a devoted nurse. By night she tossed in uneasy dreams and outright nightmares, searching for her children, snatching them from peril only to find that she was too late. Fear and panic then drove her out of sleep and to their sides, but they saw nothing, heard nothing.

That evening, Helwych swept into her room in a whirl of black robes and lank hair. He bent over the children and examined them, but he straightened up with a dubious expression.

Seena hoped. A frayed, frantic hope. Maybe this time . . . "Can you—"

"I cannot." His eyes held her. "They are ensnared by powerful magic, Seena. Do you understand?"

"Have you spoken to Kallye?"

The sorcerer permitted himself a cynical smile. "A midwife, Seena? What can a midwife do?"

"I . . ." Kallye had always helped, if only by her presence. "I would like to see her."

Helwych shook his head. "Too dangerous, Seena. You have heard the guns? More of our own people have turned traitor. A grievous thing, that. Even Kallye might turn out to be a different sort of guest than we expected."

"She is my midwife!" Seena rushed to the beside,
but the only movement of her children's features was
that caused by the flickering play of firelight.

Helwych touched Seena, and she looked up. Held
by his eyes, she felt her objections dissolving. Magic
had bespelled her children. Magic would cure them.
What could Kallye do? "Play with your dolls, Seena,"
said Helwych. "Go. Play."

Obediently, Seena turned to Ayya and Vill; but after
the sorcerer had left, a lingering doubt remained in
her mind. Magic. Helwych was a sorcerer. Helwych,
as he so constantly reminded her, was saving the land
from a peril so great that even the massed might of
Gryylth and Corrin could not stand against it.

But if Helwych were so powerful, why then could
he not undo the spell that had ensnared Ayya and Vill?
If he could save a country, why could he not save two
small children?

Seena straightened suddenly. Why? And if magic
had struck the heart of Kingsbury as it had, why had
it not struck again?

Once more she bent over her children, but only long
enough to tuck the sheets about them and kiss their
cold faces. Then, turning, she left the room. The guard
at the door made as if to stop her, but her questions
had driven her to a regal glare, and at the sight of her
face he only bowed.

Helwych was sitting in the king's chair, speaking
with Lytham, the captain of the Guard. Seena entered
unobtrusively from the rear door of the main room.
No one noticed her, not even the Grayfaces who
flanked the sorcerer.

"Did the men see anything?" Helwych was asking.

"They did not," Lytham answered. "Someone
struck them from behind, and when they awoke, the
Grayfaces were dead and the horses were gone."

The Grayfaces murmured, their voices oddly distant, unfeeling.

"Is anyone missing from the town?" Helwych pressed.

Lytham was incredulous. "My lord, Kingsbury is stuffed as full as a peddler's bag with refugees. We hardly know who is here, much less who might have left."

Helwych slumped in Cvinthil's chair. Seena found that she was annoyed: by what right did Helwych presume to take her husband's seat? But the sorcerer did not look up at Lytham, nor did he see Seena. "Were there any . . . strangers seen?"

Lytham frowned, hesitated.

Even where she stood—in the shadows behind the chair—Seena could feel the crackle of power as Helwych's gaze rooted itself into the captain. "Lytham . . ." The sorcerer's voice was soft, but it all but dragged Lytham up by the front of his tunic.

"I . . . believe that there was something . . ." Lytham glanced at the Grayface guards who stood to either side of the chair, weapons in hand. They did not move.

"What?"

"One of my men on night patrol thought he saw three women making their way through the streets," said Lytham. The words came from him almost unwillingly. "He could not be sure."

"That does not matter, captain. *I* am sure. Continue."

"He thought them dressed strangely, that is all."

"Where did he see them?"

"To the north of the market square. Near the house of the midwife."

Kallye. Seena caught her breath. Helwych turned around. "My dear queen," he said softly. "Why have you forsaken your children?"

"I . . ." She swallowed. Those eyes. But she suddenly found that she had cleared a small space within her mind, a space in which she could be alone, in which she could think. "I . . . wanted to ask you . . ."

"I have told you, Seena," said Helwych, "there is nothing I can do."

Why? The question hammered at her, grappled with her recalcitrant tongue, demanded to be uttered. but Seena, thoughtful of a sudden, suppressed it. Not yet. Not now.

She turned and made her way back to her rooms, back to her children. That night, her dreams were, once again, melanges of nightmare and worry. But there was something else in them, too. Now, when she tore her children away from the mouths of the hounds, or saved them from the pits of acid or flame-hardened stakes, she lifted her eyes from their still forms and asked a question that glowed golden at the edge of thought, a question that was at once a demand, a wail of outrage, and a cry of triumph:

Why?

Alouzon, Manda, and Wykla crossed the pass in the Camrann Mountains late in the evening and made camp amid trees untouched by the defoliants that had wasted the lands to the east. As high up as they were, the night wind turned cold and cutting, and though the warriors thought it risky to kindle a fire, they did so anyway; for Alouzon, in shorts and a thin blouse, was close to hypothermia, and her companions were not much warmer.

But no hounds appeared. No helicopters. No Grayfaces. The sky on the other side of the pass flashed with distant bombs and artillery, but here, it seemed, Gryylth was as yet unscathed.

As they moved out in the morning, Alouzon was looking at the land. Her land. Separated from it, surrounded by the sterility and heat of Los Angeles, she had forgotten how lovely it was. But soft and fertile and green though it lay on this side of the mountains, it was blasted and bare on the other, a reification of all her memories of Vietnam and her bitterness over Kent.

A Goddess, though, could neutralize the defoliants that had sterilized the soil, erase the plague that raged in Kingsbury and the other refugee towns, soothe and wipe away the psychological damage that had been inflicted upon the people through year after year of war that had grown increasingly hellish from one incarnation to another. Not a Goddess who stood aloof from mortality and hid behind a cloud of impersonal transcendence, but one who stayed close to Her people, who remembered and clung to homely things like hugs, and love, and friendship.

Despite the inevitable worship, it was suddenly very tempting. To stay close. Vietnam was beyond her. Some other deity would have to attend to that one. But Gryylth, Corrin, Vaylle: these were hers. Maybe she could help. As a friend.

By afternoon the three women were well down the slopes that led to Quay. To their relief, the town showed no sign of recent attack, but the idle boats and docks and the shimmering curtain that hung a mile or two offshore were enough to make them hurry, and they ate the last of their sandwiches and fruit in the saddle and rested the horses as little as possible.

The sun was setting when they reached the main coastal road that led directly to the city gates. Alouzon rode openly, and when she signaled a halt before the raised drawbridge, she lifted her voice before she could be challenged. "I'm Alouzon Dragonmaster. Wykla of Burnwood and Manda of Dubris are with me. Is Hahle there?"

"Alouzon!" Hahle stood up from behind the parapet. "Beyond all hope!"

"Let us in, Hahle," she said. "I don't have much time. We're all going to have to move fast." The drawbridge ground down. "Is everyone all right? Did Relys and Timbrin make it?"

"Aye," said the councilman. "We are well. And Relys and Timbrin are here." His face turned sad for a moment. "They are as well as they can be, I guess."

Alouzon and her companions rode in and dismounted. Faces surrounded them, and hands reached out to clasp theirs, but for the most part the faces were all above middle age and the hands were gnarled with years. With few exceptions, all the young men were overseas with Cvinthil and Darham.

Alouzon shook hands and made greetings. She was going to change all that, she said, but she had come to Quay essentially to find Relys and Timbrin.

"They are at my house, Dragonmaster," said Hahle. "But will you not even stay the night?"

"Can't," she said. "I don't think I brought any jets with me this time, but I don't want to take the chance. I'm going to check on Relys and Timbrin, and then we're off."

"Off?"

"On Silbakor."

By the time they reached the councilman's house, a large number of men had gathered around the three women. Hahle waved them back as, accompanied only by Wykla and Manda, Alouzon went to the door and opened it.

They entered quietly. Two women were sitting before the fire, their backs to the door. One, small and slight, was being held by a taller companion, whose right hand—chewed and mangled and livid with still-unhealed wounds—was wrapped protectively about her shoulders.

Even from a distance, even without seeing their faces, Alouzon could sense their inner wounds. Could she do something about that too? She had resolved to try. "Relys, Timbrin," she said softly, "you have friends to see you."

The two whirled, startled, and Relys's damaged hand went to her side as though for a weapon. But she had no weapon, and no armor: she was clad in a simple gown. Shaking, her eyes downcast, she stood up. "Alouzon."

Rape, the loss of a hand, fever, hardship: though

Relys remained unbroken, she had been bent and splintered. Alouzon went to her and Timbrin, arms outstretched, but Relys drew back. "Come on, Relys," said Alouzon. "I've come all the way from another planet to see you."

Relys looked as though she wanted to run. "A-Alouzon."

"Come on." Alouzon wrapped her arms about them both, felt Timbrin shake, felt Relys on the verge of hated tears. "I'm back. It's gonna be all right . . ." She lifted her eyes, wishing she could see the Grail, addressing it nonetheless directly. *You hear me? I'm telling them it's gonna be all right. Cut me some slack, please. Not for me. For them.*

"Dragonmaster . . ."

"Really, Relys. We'll get Kyria to fix up that hand of yours. She's changed a lot. You'll like her. But she fixed Manda's arm, and she can fix your hand. Give her a chance. And Timbrin . . ."

The small woman lifted dark eyes. Alouzon might have been staring down twin wells. The lieutenant had been shaken, shocked into a loss of her very identity, and as Alouzon held her tightly, she willed strength and recovery into her. *Not for me. For them.*

". . . you're going to get better," she said. "I swear."

You hear me?

Timbrin shut her eyes, laid her head against Alouzon's blouse. "I believe you, Dragonmaster. I . . . believe you."

"What of Marrget and the others?" said Relys, and her tone—stronger now—said that she too was starting to believe.

"Parl and Birk bought it. Everyone else is all right. Vaylle's on our side."

Timbrin wept with relief. Relys's eyes were open, black, hard . . . dry. "Where have you been, Dragonmaster? In Vaylle?"

"Farther away than that, Relys. I didn't have much choice."

A touch of renewed shame. "You . . . know . . . about. . . ?"

Alouzon nodded slowly. "Yeah, Relys. I know. We'll settle that score, too."

Hope kindled in the cold darkness of Relys's eyes. "I wish that very much, Dragonmaster . . . but . . ." She looked away for a moment as though the shame were again attempting to break loose, but then she mastered herself and pushed free of Alouzon's arms. "But what lies ahead of us?" Her voice was cool, professional. "Helwych has warriors, but he also has Grayfaces and what he calls jets and guns and napalm. What shall we do?" She noticed Wykla and Manda then, and she saluted them formally. "I am very glad to see you both."

Relys had taken what she had needed, and then had moved away. That was all right: Alouzon, the Goddess, was not here to force Her children into growth or recovery. In fact, she could not but respect Relys and admire her strength.

Holding Timbrin still, Alouzon called in Hahle and a few of his advisors and told them of her plans regarding the troops in Vaylle. "It'll be crazy getting everyone here," she said. "I'm not even sure when we'll arrive. But whoever wants to meet us is welcome."

Hahle was cautious. "But what about the Grayfaces and their weapons? And the hounds . . ."

"Kyria can take care of the Grayfaces and the jets. She's getting pretty used to it by now, I think. And she can magic up the swords and pikes so they'll take out the hounds."

Hahle nodded, bowed. "Clubs and burning sticks have served us well," he said, "but if Kyria can give us back the use of swords and spears, then I am well satisfied. I, for one, will be there." A chorus of ayes erupted from the men in the room and those who had gathered outside the door.

"If Kyria will attend to my hand," said Relys. "Then I also. I would settle my own scores."

"She'll do it," said Alouzon. "But it's still going to be rough. Helwych is pretty well entrenched in the town."

Manda spoke up. "Has there been any word from Corrin?"

"We have heard nothing from Corrin," said Hahle.

"In Corrin are at least eight or nine phalanxes of warriors," said the maid. "You have but to send for them."

Hahle blinked. "So many? I thought Darham took all his men with him."

Manda could not suppress her smile. "He did indeed. All his men. But Tylha and her women were left behind, and they have been spoiling for battle for the last five years . . ." A murmur from the Gryylthans made her stop. "I mean . . ." She colored.

A moment of uneasy silence. But then Hahle spoke with the air of a man dismissing trivialities. "Those battles are long done," he said. "We have common enemies now, and if the women of Corrin will help the barbarous men of Gryylth . . ." He grinned, reached a hand to Manda. The maid clasped it. ". . . why, then, we will thank them heartily." But amid the shouts of affirmation from the men, he turned thoughtful. "But how shall we send to them? The land between the mountains and the Dike is patched with wastelands now, and the villages are all destroyed. Burnwood, the closest to Corrin, was in fact the first to be struck by the bombs."

Wykla, who had been sitting quietly and smiling her agreement, started. "Burnwood?"

"Aye," said Hahle. "So Relys said."

"It is true," said Relys. Though uncertainty lurked still in her eyes, and though the determined set to her face might well have been a mask covering oceans of shame and bitterness, she stood straight and spoke evenly. "Yvas of Burnwood brought the word and then died of his wounds. The news became well known in Kingsbury despite Helwych's best efforts to suppress it."

Wykla looked worse. "Yvas . . ."

"But as for sending to Corrin," Relys continued, "I myself will go. I cannot wield a sword save with my left hand, but swords are useless against the Grayfaces and their—" She caught herself suddenly, considered, turned to Wykla. "I am sorry, my friend," she said kindly. "You are from Burnwood, are you not?"

"I am indeed." Wykla's voice was faint. "Yvas was my father."

Relys stood for a moment, struck. Then, as if Wykla's need enabled her to put aside her own shame and uncertainty, she bowed and said softly: "I grieve with you, Wykla. The Gods will hear his name."

Alouzon's feelings were mixed. Yvas had rejected his one-time son, now daughter, and had done so cruelly. Wykla still suffered from the rebuff. But Wykla had never denied her father, and she was obviously shaken by his death.

"I'm sorry, too, Wykla," said Alouzon.

"I . . ." Wykla lost her words, shook her head. "Pray continue, Relys."

Relys shrugged. "I will go to Corrin."

And, unexpectedly, Timbrin lifted her head. "And I also." Her voice shook a little, and she was still trembling, but she met Alouzon's eyes. "I can do it, Dragonmaster. And if swords are useless out in that land, then a warrior who is afraid to pick one up will fare no worse than anyone else."

Alouzon hugged her. Maybe she could indeed be a Goddess. "Go for it, lady," she said. "With my blessings." She turned back to the others. "That's it, then.

We'll assemble on the north side of that jagged spur of mountains northwest of Kingsbury.''

The men and women murmured agreement. Wykla nodded absently. Manda put her arms about her.

''Then let's go.''

Alouzon pushed through the knot of men at the door and made for the town square. What she was about to do was risky, but if the Grail could stake the existence of a world on the faded idealism of an old hippie, then Alouzon Dragonmaster could hope that the Great Dragon could return to Gryylth undetected by the Specter and the Worm.

Planting herself in the middle of the square, lifting the Dragonsword above her head, she cried her summons into the gathering darkness:

''Silbakor, I call you!''

❖ CHAPTER 17 ❖

The sun had slid behind the Camrann Mountains, the light was just beginning to fail, and Kallye was returning home after another long day of watching women and children die. The men of the wartroops had donated their food to the people, but the act could only prolong the inevitable and agonizing end for a few weeks, unless . . .

Unless Alouzon . . .

She could not but hope. The Dragonmaster herself had said that Helwych would fall. The matter, therefore, was settled. It was only a question of how long Kingsbury and the other refugee towns could hold out against starvation and disease. Would Alouzon and the rightful king arrive first, or. . . ?

"Midwife."

She turned. Lytham stepped out of the shadows of an alleyway. "What do you want, captain?" she said tiredly. After Lytham's order that the wartroops' food be shared, she had difficulty hating him in spite of his part in Relys's fate. At times, in fact, she could not help but see him as yet another one of Helwych's victims, a boy who was not so much grown up as damaged by the years.

And true, Lytham, thin now from shared malnutrition, looked like an old man. Glancing over his shoulder as though fearful of being seen, he took Kallye's arm and walked her quickly around the corner.

"Helwych is suspicious of you," he said.

"Indeed?" She was too tired to care.

"I had to . . ." He stopped, debated. "It was reported to him that some strangers were seen the night of the attack on the outpost. They were seen in the vicinity of your house."

Kallye shrugged. Behind Lytham were shelters and hovels. To either side were shelters and hovels. All around were shelters and hovels . . . and death. But there was hope now too, and only with difficulty did she keep from betraying it with her tone, her eyes, a stray gesture. "My house is one among many."

"He seems most fixated upon you."

She pulled her arm free. "Maybe he should be," she said. "Maybe he should be fixated upon everyone. Maybe he should take a good look at the swollen bellies of the children, or drag himself out of Hall Kingsbury to see the corpses that the Grayfaces burn every afternoon. Alouzon—" She caught herself.

Lytham leaned forward. "What about Alouzon?"

"Nothing."

"What about her? Was she one of the strangers?"

Kallye was silent for some time. Then: "What do you expect me to tell you, Captain of the Guard? The truth?"

His face fell. She might have slapped him. For a moment, he looked at the hovels as though contemplating his own end. "Beware," he said at last. "That is all I can tell you. The Grayfaces are in charge now, and I cannot help."

"My thanks, captain." Kallye turned away and went off through the darkening streets. Someone was sobbing dryly in the distance. Nearby, someone was gasping. Still nearer—and worse—was silence.

We are dying. All of us. Sweet Alouzon, if Gryylth has a God, then that God is you. Dear Lady, save us!

Still in the midst of what she could only call a prayer, Kallye opened the door to her house. Gelyya was away—tending to other deaths—and so Kallye was surprised when she sensed a presence in the room.

She closed the door behind her. ''Hello?'' she said. More than likely a woman, hungry or ill or grieving, had come to her for aid. ''Have you a need? I will help if I can.''

There was no reply, but a movement in the rear of the room caught her attention. Something there was glowing yellow, and eyes like blue lamps suddenly flicked open. Silently, quickly, the hound came at her . . .

Even in the dusk, Silbakor's arrival darkened the sky over Quay as though sudden clouds had gathered. Torn, bleeding, its iron-dark hide split and rent in a thousand places, it plummeted like a black meteor straight into the square, touched down, and furled its great wings.

For a moment, Alouzon stared, shocked. Black blood spilled from the Dragon's wounds, glistened in the torchlight, splashed on the hard-packed earth. Gashes in its iron hide opened into darkness, like windows into the spaces between worlds. Its eyes were dimmed, but their dispassionate gaze held nonetheless a note of defiance.

''Oh, Silbakor . . .''

''My lady, I beg you: mount. Command me. I have little time.''

The people of Quay had fallen silent at the appearance of the Dragon, and the only sounds were those of the distant sea, the wind through the thatched roofs, and the steady drip of Silbakor's blood. With difficulty, Alouzon thrust aside her shock and dismay, and the sight of the Dragon's eyes—pleading for merciful haste—made her mount without further comment or protest. She scooted forward to make room for Wykla and Manda, smearing her bare legs and arms with blood the color of midnight, and when they all were settled, she leaned forward to the Dragon's ear. ''To Lachrae, Silbakor.''

''I understand, my lady.''

"And no Los Angeles bullshit this time. You know what's running about there now. I'm not safe anywhere. I just have to get through this."

In reply, the huge wings spread, and Alouzon had barely enough time to wave farewell to Quay before the town fell away below, turning from houses to toys in an instant. Silbakor circled out towards the ocean and the curtain wall, and the dark barrier grew, black against the last shreds of sunset, stretching up for miles.

As though disdainful of such a paltry obstacle, Silbakor made straight for it. The blunt nose of the Dragon struck the barrier with no discernible sense of impact save that the dark sea and the darkening sky vanished, to be replaced by gleaming nebulae and star fields. For an instant, Silbakor and its passengers traveled in void and darkness . . .

. . . and then below—far below—lay the city of Lachrae, gleaming with lamplight and torchlight, its radiating avenues and streets wheeling slowly as the Dragon circled.

Alouzon glanced back. Wykla was obviously still in shock from the news of her father. Behind her, Manda looked concerned, but there was a satisfaction lurking about the corners of her mouth that someone who had hurt her lover so badly was no more.

Silbakor dropped, and the main plaza of the city came up fast: the Dragon had little strength left for gentle approaches. With a thud that shook its passengers and sent Alouzon clawing for a handhold on the ragged edges of a wound, the Dragon struck the pavement and folded its wings.

The yellow eyes followed Alouzon as she dismounted and helped her companions down. "May I be of further service, Dragonmaster?"

Alouzon reached up. Silbakor's jaw was the size of a piano lid, but she stroked it gently, as if it were made of nothing more than mist and spiderwebs. So huge. So powerful. So vulnerable to her unconscious nightmares. Here was something else for which she had to take responsibility. "No, Silbakor," she said. "I can handle it from here." Its wounds still dripped: splashes of night on the white marble pavement. "Can I . . . can I do anything for you?"

She read the answer in the yellow eyes. No: there was nothing. Silbakor was Silbakor, and the Worm was the Worm. The battle would continue—forever, if need be.

"Go on, then," she said. "Beat it. Do what you have to. Thanks for coming."

"I had to come," said the deep voice. There was no blame in its tone.

There did not have to be. "I know." Alouzon's voice caught. Silbakor, though traitorous in its own way, was a friend. "And I had to call."

The great wings opened and Alouzon waved Manda and Wykla away as the Dragon rose into the air. The stars were blotted out by its passage, and then the sky cleared: Silbakor was gone, searching once again for its antithesis.

But in the silence left behind by its departure, Alouzon could hear the murmur of voices, the tread of boots and sandals. From the direction of the houses and shops came the Vayllens: quietly, almost fearfully. But from the other direction—from the King's House— men and women were running, waving, shouting to her. They were not afraid, and their voices and gestures were free and open as they rushed forward to welcome her.

The people of Gryylth and Corrin.

She hung her head. In a moment, she feared, she was going to have to be Alouzon Dragonmaster: confident, competent. Los Angeles had been a respite in a way, a chance to eat, sleep, and plan; but it had also served to remind her of all the little perquisites of anonymity that she had given up.

The crowd was very close: footsteps crisp on the marble, shouts ringing in the clear air. Manda and

Wykla had already run to meet them. Alouzon heard Marrget—no, Marrha now—crying her gladness at the safety of her lieutenant.

And then Marrha was before her, and Kyria and Dindrane, and Karthin and Santhe. Cvinthil, tall and slender, was offering his hand, and Darham, the Corrinian king, had wrapped Manda and Wykla in his large arms. From the Gryylthans and Corrinians there came shouting and welcome, and even the Vayllens were mustering tentative smiles and greetings. For the moment, Alouzon realized, she did not have to be a God or a hero. She had only to be Alouzon, a friend, and the only struggle she faced was how to widen her arms far enough to embrace so many loved ones.

And she would do her best to keep it that way.

Marrha hugged her last and longest. "Alouzon . . ."

"You made it," said Alouzon. *"Damn* but I'm glad to see that."

"I made it in many ways, Dragonmaster," said Marrha. Her face had lost the old leanness; and though the steely glint in her eyes told Alouzon that the old, hard captain was still there, still as indomitable as ever, the woman he had become smiled with a warmth that the man had never known. "But Relys, Timbrin," she said. "What of them?"

Manda shook her head and could not look at Marrha. Rape had joined them in many ways, and now it had intruded again.

"They're alive, Marrha," said Alouzon. "But it's bad. Real bad."

Marrha's eyes took on a chill that Alouzon had seen before, and when, in the King's House a few minutes later, Alouzon explained just how bad it was—for Gryylth as well as for Relys and Timbrin—their chill deepened into an arctic cold of mingled anger and sorrow.

Mouth working, the captain turned to Manda. "Relys now . . ."

Manda was nodding. "That score will be settled, Marrha."

"I . . ." Marrha turned away, fought for composure. Manda went to her, and, arms about one another, heads pressed together, the two women shared for a moment both their griefs and their strengths.

Darham and Pellam had listened quietly, but it was Cvinthil who surprised Alouzon. In sharp contrast to the rages and quick decisions that had characterized him during the councils preceding her initial departure for Vaylle, he had turned thoughtful, careful.

"And what of Relys and Timbrin now?" he said.

"They're going to Corrin to raise the women's phalanxes," said Alouzon. "They'll meet us north of Kingsbury."

"Good," he said slowly. "For Gryylth has a reckoning to make with Helwych."

Darham lifted his head. "Do not forget Corrin, my brother. Helwych is one of ours, and therefore is he a double traitor, for he has betrayed both Corrin and Corrin's friends."

Cvinthil allowed himself a brief nod of agreement, then turned back to Alouzon. "*Us* you say, Dragonmaster. You have a plan, I assume, for bringing the wartroops and phalanxes home."

"Yeah," she said, "I do. It'll be risky, and it's a little crazy, but I think it'll work." Alouzon looked to Kyria. "You know more about these things than I do. Let me know if I've gone nuts."

At the news of Gryylth, Kyria's black eyes had kindled with a smoldering anger. But she banked her wrath, and, that done, forced a smile. "I believe I have already guessed what you have in mind, Alouzon. It is a rather brazen act, but I believe it is the only way."

With the three kings, her friends, and representatives of the wartroops and phalanxes listening intently, Alouzon explained. The door beside Lake Innael and the ruins of Mallaen led to MacArthur Park. The door in the archaeology offices at UCLA led to the hills near Kingsbury. The distance from the park to the offices was a little over ten miles, all of it on city streets, and a forced march from one to the other could be made in a single night . . . with luck.

Alouzon finished. Silence.

Kyria laughed suddenly. "Alouzon, I believe we may hardly be noticed at all. Wilshire Boulevard can be a very strange place."

"I don't want to use Wilshire. I'm going to use . . . like Sixth Street or something. Less traffic."

Pellam was suppressing a smile. Cvinthil and Darham were conferring. Cvinthil finally spoke. "Alouzon, into what kind of a place are you taking us?"

While Alouzon dithered over how to explain, Wykla spoke up. "Very strange, my king. There are . . ." She waved her hands, groping for words. "Metal wagons that travel of their own at great speeds, and tall buildings made of stone that was poured like thick cream. And lights without smoke that burn all night . . ."

Cvinthil, doubtful, looked to Darham. Darham chewed on his beard.

"But as we were with Alouzon," Wykla continued, "Manda and I were not afraid. Truly, it is a strange place, and often frightening, but we lived to return to Gryylth."

"Can you handle it, Kyria?" said Alouzon.

"I can," said the sorceress. "I can cloak the army in darkness. No one will see us." She smiled. "Or at least no one will remember us."

"And if they call the cops, no one's going to believe them anyway, huh?"

Kyria's smile broadened. "That is quite possible."

Alouzon grinned, then turned to the kings. "Are the wartroops and phalanxes ready to travel?"

No one replied for a moment. Alouzon could understand. Her plan held all the accents of insanity. Pellam, though, with a glance at Cvinthil and Darham, lifted his white head. " 'Tis not for me to speak of war and battle," he said. "But I will tell you, Dragonmaster, that most of the troops have been sent ahead to Lake Innael . . . in accordance with your instructions. There are but fifty warriors left in Lachrae.''

"Okay, good.''

Cvinthil was speaking softly with Darham. The Corrinian shrugged. Cvinthil shrugged back. Silence. At last, though, the Gryylthan king sat back, his lips pursed. He glanced at Darham. Darham nodded reluctantly.

"We accept your plan, Dragonmaster,'' said Cvinthil. "Let us thank the Gods we have such a . . .'' His eyes searched her face, awed, almost frightened. ''. . . a hero as you to guide us.''

"We're pushing time, Cvinthil,'' said Alouzon. "How long before we start?''

"We can depart with the sunrise.''

"Then let's do it.''

Pellam stood. "You have hard times ahead of you: a fearful journey, a worse destination. There is food and rest provided, and I implore you all to take both. I regret only that we of Vaylle cannot be of more help.''

Boyish and silent, Dindrane had said nothing until now, and when she spoke, it was with a suddenness that startled everyone. "But we can,'' she said. "I have spoken with the harpers and healers of the city and have sent word to those along the road to Mullaen. Three score will be accompanying us. Though they will not fight, they can cure; and I cannot but think that skill invaluable against such weapons as await us in Gryylth.''

Pellam's voice was warm. "I am proud of you, daughter.''

Dindrane bowed. "My thanks, my king.''

Pellam gestured to his attendants, and the liveried men and women took those present off to dinner. Alouzon, though, stayed behind. She wanted some time alone with Kyria and Dindrane, and when the hall was silent and empty, she put her arms up and hugged the sorceress. "I said it before, lady, but I'll say it again. You've changed."

Kyria returned to embrace. "And you also, Alouzon. You are not the frightened woman who left the temple in Broceliande."

"I'm not?"

Kyria shook her head. "The Grail continues to work."

"Well . . ." Alouzon released her, shoved her hands into her pockets, shrugged. "I'm here. I guess that counts for something."

"Indeed."

"You . . . uh . . . happy with Santhe?"

Kyria smiled broadly. "Very," she said. "As happy as Wykla is with Manda, or Marrha with Karthin, though I confess I did not think that possible."

"I was up at your house. Did you know we're both dead?"

Kyria's dark eyes flickered. "I suspected that. I cannot say that I mind. Gryylth, Vaylle . . . this entire world is my home now. And it is a goodly place."

"What about Los Angeles? Can you handle going back?"

"I can," said the sorceress. "And the magic will be no great matter, though it would be best if I had help." She took Dindrane's hand. "What say you, sister?"

"I . . ." Dindrane regarded Alouzon with a sense of worship. " 'Tis a healer I am," she said. "Or rather, that I was. I know not what I am now. But I can help. And I will."

"I am very grateful," said Kyria.

"Surely. But . . ." Dindrane's eyes turned sad. "There is another matter." Gently, she went down on one knee before Alouzon. "Great Lady," she said formally, "would it please you to forgive me the harsh judgments and unkind words that I made and uttered in the past?"

Alouzon stared, and her stomach wrenched.

Someone was kneeling to her. *No . . . not that . . .*
"Please, Dindrane . . ."

"Goddess?" Dindrane's tone was not that of fanat-
icism or idealistic devotion. She knew Alouzon. She
knew her faults and her virtues both, and yet she wor-
shipped.

Mortified, Alouzon pulled the priestess to her feet.
"I . . . I don't know how things are supposed to be
done," she said. "But I know how I want them done.
Yeah, the Grail's real close, but I want you and everyone else to know that when I find it I'm not going to
be this big time Jehovah figure off in the distance. I've
always just wanted to be friends with everyone. That's
all. And that's not gonna change. Just call me Alouzon. Your friend."

Dindrane's eyes were brimming. "I could not ask
for a better Goddess, Alouzon. My people and I are
indeed privileged."

"It's just something I've got to get through," said
Alouzon. "I . . ." Dismayed, she felt the distance between herself and those she loved widening. Even
Kyria seemed farther away. It was only a matter of
time.

She hugged Dindrane, relishing the feel of mortality. But it could not last. "I guess it had better happen
soon," she said. "It's not really good to have Gods
wandering around in the flesh. It just gets too messy
that way."

Gelyya found Kallye late that night. In the light of
her lamp, the heap of bones and glistening flesh was
no more than an abstraction of ochers, yellows, and
dull reds, and she was mildly surprised that she felt
so little in response. But there was only so much grief
that could be spent in a lifetime, and Gelyya had over-
drawn the account.

The night was dark, and a distant baying blended
with the dull roar of far-off battles. Death in the towns;

death in the country. It no longer mattered. Midwifery no longer mattered. Healing no longer mattered.

And, like Alouzon, she wanted to do something. Anything.

Silently, she doffed the apron she wore and covered up the stripped skull that was all that was left of Kallye's face. And then she turned around and left.

The hovels that cluttered the streets were silent, some with sleep, others with death. Gelyya made her way among them. Once, she had played in the streets of Bandon, dreaming of freedom and independence. But she and her companions had grown older, marriages had been arranged, and life had closed in on them. And though Alouzon's coming had briefly rekindled her hopes, the fantasies had finally guttered into darkness amid the bombs and napalm of an aerial attack.

But it was not dreams that lured Gelyya through the streets and toward the wall that surrounded the town. Her dreams were gone, burned clean in the white-hot fire of experience, and what was left was necessity. Gelyya could do no more for the women and children of Kingsbury. Perhaps she could do something for Gryylth. Or, that failing, perhaps for Gelyya of Bandon.

As a girl she had practiced moving silently—like a warrior stalking an enemy—and now, tying up her skirts and belting her scrip close to her waist, she recalled those childish exercises and made them her own once again. Her soft woman's shoes noiseless among the clutter of the street, she slipped from shadow to shadow, drawing ever closer to the wall.

Others had died attempting escape. But theirs had been a desperate and frantic climb over the walls and a heedless run down the road. Not so Gelyya of Bandon. Where others had broken through the gate, she picked her place and climbed carefully, inching through the shadows, waiting—heart pounding, holding her breath, her cheek pressed against the rough wood—for a guard or a Grayface to pass by. Where others had sprinted along open ground, she slid to the ground outside the walls, crept along the ditches, and took cover beneath bushes and hedges, using the darkness of night and moon-shadow for concealment.

By midnight, she had passed the earthworks and was halfway down Kingsbury hill. Far off, lights flickered, and dull thunders testified to the continuing bombardment of the land. There was little hope for her out there, but there was none at all within the walls of the town, and so she continued—silently, steadily—down the slope.

But where the hill gave way to the flat fields, the way seemed blocked. Floodlights lit the ground brilliantly. Barbed wire lay in spiral tangles. Trenches and walls of sandbags lay in zigzagged rows.

She crept to the edge of the concealing darkness. There was a way out. There had to be a way out.

She had to do something.

In another hour she had worked her way around the base of the hill and had found the place where the wire and the trenches were thinnest. Here to the south, neither Helwych nor the Grayfaces expected much of a land attack, but a profusion of rocket launchers and machine guns indicated that they were taking no chances.

Gelyya eyed the guns. Gleaming metallically in the moonlight and the spill of the floods, they stood on their posts within sandbagged emplacements, the bullets in their cartridge belts gleaming like so many copper-jacketed teeth. She had seen them in operation many times, and maybe she could . . .

Movement. Behind her. She started to turn, but her arms were suddenly pinned, and a hand covered her mouth. Struggling, striking futility, she was dragged back into the bushes.

''Be quiet, girl.''

The words were spoken in a whisper, as though her

assailant had no more wish to be discovered than she. But Gelyya struggled.

The whisper turned fierce. "Damn you, Gelyya, shut up!"

The voice was familiar, and when she paused, puzzling over it, her mouth was uncovered and she was abruptly spun around to be confronted by a face hardly older than her own.

Lytham.

"What are you doing here?" he said. The ensign of the King's Guard sparkled in the moonlight. "Nay, I can guess."

She glared at him, wanting nothing so much as to spit in his face. "I found Kallye. I found the scraps the hounds left."

He looked away. "I had nothing to do with that."

"Helwych did."

"How do you know?"

She wanted to scream at him: *Alouzon told me, you fool! Your master is a lie, and the Dragonmaster will return and put him to death like the vile worm he is!* But she bit back the words, looked for others. "I know."

"Kallye, too, refused to answer my questions."

"And she is dead now. So kill me, Captain of the Guard. Kill me and have done with it, or I shall surely try to kill you."

"I do not want to kill you."

"Then let me go."

"I said that I do not want to kill you. If I let you go, you will die. Whether the Grayfaces kill you here or the hounds kill you within a league, it will be all the same."

"I am leaving, Lytham. I might survive. I am willing to accept the chance that I might die."

He hung his head. "I did not want Kallye to be killed."

Gellya was defiant. "Little enough good that did."

"Aye . . ." He looked up. "If you escape, what will you do?"

She shrugged. "I will try to reach Quay. I have hopes that there are men and women there who have been spared this destruction."

"And if there are not?" ·

"Do not play with me, Lytham. You are no longer a child. You showed that when you raped Relys."

The words stung him. "How did—?" He stopped, stared guiltily, then, as though he had no wish to know how she had found out about Relys, spoke carefully. "I will help you."

She hardly believed him. "Why?"

Lytham's words were a whispered torrent of denial. "Because I no longer believe in Helwych. I no longer believe in anything. What difference does it make whether the refugees die within Kingsbury or without? Men and women should be able at least to choose whatever kind of death suits them. Therefore, if this is what you want, I will help you."

Gelyya was stunned. "What . . . what are you going to do?"

"Wait here," he said abruptly. "There is a section of wire directly ahead of you that can be opened. When the shooting starts on the far side of the hill, run to it, open it, and escape. I will do my best to make sure that you are not seen."

"But—"

Lytham stopped her question with a look. "The Grayfaces have powerful weapons," he said. "But though they kill without conscience, their nerves are as frayed as ours. They will shoot at anything, real or imaginary."

And with that he turned and disappeared into the shadows.

The sudden rush of fear and the equally sudden relief was making Gelyya shake almost uncontrollably. She wondered whether Lytham had noticed, and whether as a result her threats had seemed absurd and childish to him. But she put aside those thoughts. Alouzon would not worry about such things: she would wait for a chance to act. And so would Gelyya of Bandon.

Crouching in the cover of a hedge, she listened, watched. Ahead was the thin point in the wire, and, straining her eyes, she picked out the fastenings of a gate.

A faint whistling in the air grew suddenly into a sound as of the ripping of canvas, then into a roar. A shell burst on the far side of the hill and sent a rush of hot wind across the fields. Shrapnel hissed through the air, and then a detonation from one of the gun emplacements at the foot of the hill and the whine of spun-off retaining bands sent her hands to her ears.

This was no diversion. This was an attack.

More shells. The pop and crack of small arms. The thump of departing mortar rounds. She had heard them all before, knew all of their names and something of their use. All were common sights and sounds in Kingsbury these days, and the Grayfaces had not hesitated to direct them at refugees and enemies alike.

She ran for the wire. Tracers reached out of the darkness and licked the base of the gate as she fumbled for the fastenings, and a spray of gravel peppered her arms and legs as she swung it open.

She sprinted across the flood-lit ground, leaped the trenches one by one, and threw herself beyond the reach of the lights. But where she expected darkness and open ground, she found instead a troop of attacking Grayfaces running towards her out of the shadows.

Unable to stop, she plowed straight into the man at the head of the troop. He went down, his weapon flying from his hands, and Gelyya, rolling to the side, fighting to escape the clutching hands and the aim of the rifle barrels, came up against something long and hard and metallic. Her hands recognized the shape of the dropped rifle.

She seized it, and her untrained fingers were already

settling on the trigger as she brought it up. Before the rest of the Grayfaces could react, she had sprayed them with high velocity bullets. Gas masks, uniforms, equipment, flesh—all disintegrated before her, and in a moment, she was alone in the company of corpses.

Staring, she almost dropped the rifle. The deaths she had seen in Kingsbury were at least comprehensible in terms of cause, and in any case she herself had never killed. But now she had taken life, and she had taken it grandly: not singly and precisely with well-placed sword strokes, but broadly and indiscriminately by means of a weapon she did not at all understand.

On the other side of the hill, the attack went on; and now the detonations of mortar rounds were walking slowly and steadily around the perimeter of the slope, making straight for her position. Swallowing the sudden nausea that welled up at the sight of so much blood and so many torn bodies, clutching the rifle, Gelyya filled her scrip with ammunition clips and ran for the deeper darkness that lay beyond the battle.

❖ CHAPTER 18 ❖

As the sun rose, shining fitfully through the blackness of the distant curtain wall, the wartroops and phalanxes assembled in the square before the King's House, their military efficiency and discipline quaintly complimented by the gracious disorder of the small band of Vayllen harpers and healers that gathered off to the side.

The horses that Kyria had, months ago, sent away from Kent had found their way back to Lachrae, and so Alouzon was astride Jia again this morning, grateful that, even in the face of imminent godhood, the beast had recognized her and cheerfully taken her on his back.

Now Jia turned his head and looked at her out of brown eyes. Alouzon leaned forward, scratched him between the ears. "Did you miss me, guy?"

"I assume that he did," said Marrha, who had cantered up beside her. Her braid gleamed in the morning light. "We all missed you."

Alouzon nodded. "It wasn't my idea."

"We suspected that," said the captain. "But our joy was great when Kyria announced that she and Dindrane had spoken with you."

"Uh . . . yeah." Alouzon wondered how much Dindrane and Kyria had said about their methods. But Marrha's manner was as straightforward as ever, and if there was a trace of awe in her eyes, it was the awe

of a woman who had seen a dear friend return from
far distances and great danger.

A friend. But would that friendship hold when. . . ?

"Listen, Marrha," said Alouzon. "You'll . . . uh . . .
take care of Jia if anything happens to me, won't you?"

Marrha frowned. "I will see to it, Dragonmaster.
But I have always felt it unwise to speak in such a
fashion before a battle."

"I'm not talking about dying," Alouzon blurted,
trying both to hint at and to skirt the issue. "I'm just
. . . well . . . you know . . ."

Marrha's eyes were shrewd. "In truth, my friend, I
do not. But do not fear."

"Yeah . . . good . . ." Confused, unsure of what
she had been trying to say, Alouzon trotted to the head
of the columns. There, Kyria nodded to her, and Cvinthil and Darham took her hand briefly. Alouzon
scanned along the columns of mounted warriors—the
pikemen and infantry had been sent ahead—and the
square fell silent, waiting for her command.

"Pellam's not coming?" she said suddenly.

Kyria answered. "He is a priest, Alouzon. He knows
nothing of war. His people will need him here."

At the head of the harpers and healers, Dindrane's
cropped hair was a blond gleam. Alouzon could not
make out her face. "But Dindrane . . ."

The sorceress shook her head softly. "Dindrane
knows too much of war now," she said softly.

"Yeah . . . that's true."

The streets were full of people, come to see the
departure. But though there were still smiles among
the citizens of Lachrae, they were wistful smiles, and
the sadness behind them had deepened. They also
knew too much of war now.

And Alouzon, desperately hoping that she could
make that knowledge obsolete, had nonetheless to
confront the reality of what she faced. Helwych was a
problem, true, but the real problem was the Specter.

And she still had no idea how to deal with that reification of her own unconscious fears and hates.

If she attacked it, she attacked herself. If she killed it—or if it killed her—she killed herself and her world. But regardless of her quandary, somewhere at the end of this march that would lead along the west road of Vaylle, the streets of Los Angeles, the corridors of UCLA, and the paths of Gryylth, it was waiting for her: powerful, lethal, undying save by her own death.

Some God.

She lifted her hand to give the signal to start, wondering as she did how much of Gryylth, of the whole world, would be left after she confronted the Specter.

They traveled throughout the day, and by sunset they were halfway to Lake Innael. Given the time differential between Los Angeles and Gryylth, the trip from MacArthur Park to UCLA would take over a week by the Gryylthan calendar, and conditions in the refugee cities were such that even that obligatory delay might prove fatal. Reluctantly, therefore, Alouzon ordered a stop for the night, and the men and women made camp, the efforts of the day evident in their manner and speech.

Wykla, too, was tired, but when she sat down with her food, a slump to her shoulders and a set to her face said that there was more to her weariness than simple physical exhaustion. Alouzon knew the cause, though: Wykla, rejected though she had been by her father, had just lost her own family.

Alouzon filled her bowl and cup, then wandered over to the young woman. "Can I join you?"

Wykla's food lay untouched beside her, but she mustered a smile. "Aye Dragonmaster. Of course."

Alouzon settled down, crossed her legs. Coming from someone like Wykla, the title disturbed her. "Are we back to Dragonmaster now?"

Wykla's eyes turned questioning. "But . . ."

"But nothing. Yeah, there's some hellacious stuff

going on, but let's stay friends. I just want to be friends. That okay?''

Wykla nodded. ''It is well, Alouzon.''

''Good.'' Alouzon tore off a piece of bread, dipped it in the stew in her bowl. ''Where's Manda?''

''She is seeing that the Vayllens are provided for.'' Wykla picked up her own food. ''They are frightened of us, and Manda has a good smile and a way with words.''

''She's a fine woman. I'm glad you two found one another.''

Wykla blushed. Still wearing her t-shirt and jeans, she still looked like a coed. Young, pretty . . . sad.

''I'm . . . uh . . .'' Alouzon swirled the wine in her cup. ''I'm sorry about your father.''

Wykla fingered her bowl. ''I . . . do not know what to say, Alouzon. He, I am sure, no longer considered himself my father. I suppose I showed myself foolish when I insisted upon claiming him as such.''

''I can understand why you did, though. We only get one father.''

''Well . . .'' Wykla lifted her head as though searching. Off near the fire stood Darham, his beard sparkling in the light. He was speaking with Cvinthil, but he seemed to become aware of Wykla, and he smiled at her and bowed.

Wykla dropped her eyes quickly. ''It seems that I have been provided with two,'' she said. ''Darham offered to adopt me when I was in Benardis.''

''He's one hell of a guy.''

''I wounded him at the Circle.''

''Just goes to show, doesn't it?''

Wykla set down her bowl, covered her face with her hands. ''What shall I do, Dragonmaster?'' she whispered. ''What shall I do? I cannot unmake the past. I cannot deny what has been. And yet Darham . . .'' She sobbed for a moment. ''When he put his hand on my head and called me daughter, my heart filled near to bursting. I . . . I think I loved him from that moment. But . . .''

She stopped, swallowed her tears, wiped her eyes.

"Advise me, Alouzon," she said.

"You love him?"

"I do. He is a fine and noble man."

Alouzon looked up at the stars, considering. Wykla had been rejected. Back in 1970, a whole generation had been rejected, and some had been killed. But here was a chance for renewal, a chance, despite Wykla's words, to unmake the past. "We grow up," she said. "Sometimes we have to leave things behind. Sometimes we have to take on others."

Distantly, she sensed a smile. The Grail.

"You . . ." Wykla sniffled. "You think that I should accept?"

Flustered by the divine approval, Alouzon fumbled for words. "I think that you've got to follow your heart. You can't do something like this for profit, or for nobility, or any of that crap. You just have to do it because it's the right thing to do."

Again the smile.

"But . . . my father . . . Yyvas."

"He's dead, Wykla. Sometimes . . ." Alouzon looked up at the stars again. "Sometimes you have to take family where you can find it." Or, she thought as the smile widened, a world. "But don't rush it. Take your time. Anything or anybody who loves you that much will wait for you." She picked up Wykla's bowl—yet another manifestation of that all-nourishing Cup—and put it into her hands. "Eat now. You need it. It's gonna get hairy in L.A., and you and Manda will have to show everyone the ropes."

Wykla's eyes had turned thoughtful. "Thank you, Alouzon."

"I hope I helped."

The young woman hugged her.

But late that night, Alouzon sat by the fire, keeping a lonely personal vigil amid the sleeping camp. Wyk-

la's love and trust were unquestioning, unconditional.
And so, for that matter, were everyone else's. And she
was going to be leading them all off through a wormhole in space that should not exist, into an incomprehensible city, and then back through another wormhole
and into the hellish devastation and demonic attack of
a world that might not even continue to exist after she
met the Specter for the last time. "It's too much responsibility," she murmured to the Grail. "I'm still
not sure I can handle it. No matter what you say, I'm
not a God . . ."

"Not yet," said Kyria from behind her.

Alouzon looked up. "I'm going to be leaning on you
a lot in Los Angeles. And then there's Gryylth . . .
There's no way I can do this by myself."

"I think you devalue yourself, Alouzon, for I think
you can indeed do it by yourself." Kyria smiled en-
couragingly. "Indeed, you will more than likely have
to."

"Oh, great. You just signed the death warrant for
this whole goddam planet."

A howl drifted through the night.

Alouzon was on her feet instantly, her sword in her
hand. "Sentries."

"Hounds in the distance, my lady, but no attack
yet," came the reply.

The howl, repeated, was joined by others. The camp
started to stir: men and women struggling out of sleep,
reaching for weapons, tightening armor.

Kyria spoke. "Hold, please." She hardly raised her
voice, but her words cut through the night with a razor
edge.

The camp fell silent. With Alouzon following, the
sorceress went towards the edge of camp closest to
the disturbance. The moon was full and bright, and the
Vayllen fields gleamed like polished glass. Off in the
distance, yellow shapes were milling, yelping, gathering into a pack.

Kyria's face was a mask of moonlight and night-shadow as she lifted her right hand. The moon appeared to flare, and the rain of its silver light turned the color of steel. The hounds' yelps and howls suddenly changed pitch, became a frantic whining, vanished. The fields were empty. The hounds were gone.

"That's . . ." Alouzon was staring. Kyria stood proud and unfatigued. Her powers now came to her effortlessly. Maybe the army would indeed make it through Los Angeles. "That's pretty good."

"Such is the power with which Helwych will be comfronted," said Kyria softly. "I am not the hag, nor am I Helen, but I share some of the sympathies of both. And one who allows women and children to perish will himself die." She turned to Alouzon. "Fear not, Goddess. Your people will triumph."

Alouzon paled. "I'm not a—" she started, but there was black fire in Kyria's eyes, fire of a strength and passion that stilled the protests even of a frightened and incipient diety.

Slumped in his chair in Hall Kingsbury, surrounded by the expressionless forms of the Grayfaces, Helwych did not have to lift his head to see the wattle and daub walls about him, to examine the thatched roof above his head, to scrutinize the flagstones on the floor or the gray plastic gas-masks of the beings who guarded him. It was all there in his mind, all one with the magic that he had wrested from the Specter.

And also within his mind were the battles: the virulent conflicts that crawled across the land like so many poisonous slugs. He saw Grayface pitted against Grayface. He saw the swarming packs of hounds. He saw the Skyhawks and the F-16s spraying bullets and dropping napalm.

And he saw more coming all the while, materializing in an instant, armed and ready and looking for something to kill, forcing him to reach out, to turn their loyalties to himself, to turn them against their fellows, keep the battles raging, the defoliants falling, the bombs bursting.

He could never turn them all. At the most, expending all his strength, driving himself into a red-eyed and fevered exhaustion, he could turn half of them. He could achieve parity, he could prolong the deadly attrition.

His mind was only half on the report that Lytham was giving, for he was searching the land, feeling out its soil and its rivers, looking for something that might live, that might promise some kind of hope for the future. The coastal plains were still untouched, and Corrin appeared to have been spared; but he did not doubt that, given time, the battles would spread, would overtop the Camrann, would pass the Great Dike. And then all would be gone.

I do not want this. I never wanted this.

"My lord?"

Helwych opened his eyes. "What do you want, Captain?"

"I . . . ah . . . was making my report."

"Indeed you were . . ." Helwych was about to close his eyes again, but he detected a trace of dissemblance in Lytham's manner. "Was there something else, captain?"

Lytham squared his shoulders. A boy, Helwych thought, a boy in the armor of a man. Perhaps they were all little boys, then. Little boys dressing up as men, playing at power and rape and domination until the real adults returned and—

"Kingsbury itself was unhurt by the bombardment," said Lytham. "Most of the shells fell short and struck the Grayface positions at the base of the hill."

"Most?"

The report was a formality only, something to keep Lytham busy. Helwych already knew the extent of the damage, where the shells had fallen, how many Grayfaces had been dismembered in the detonation of high explosive and spray of shrapnel. But the sense of dissemblance still clung about Lytham, and Helwych began to probe beneath the surface of his words, examining his fleeting thoughts. Mutiny was always a possibility. Betrayal was a constant threat. Relys had been only the first. Dryyim had come then, and then Kallye.

Those strangers in the town. And, before that, Relys's strange disappearance from the men's barracks. And Timbrin had never been found either . . .

Lytham swallowed nervously. Helwych watched him intently. "Those that did not fall short," said the captain, "detonated in the air. There were a few scrapes and cuts among the refugees, no more."

"The refugees," Helwych said, "who continue to drop like summer flies in the first frost." He leaned forward, gripping the captain in his glance. "Tell me, Lytham. What do you think of that?"

"I . . ." There was fear in Lytham's eyes. "I think it is . . . unfortunate."

"Unfortunate, indeed. Do you have any criticisms of my actions in this matter?"

"I . . ."

"Be careful, Lytham."

"I . . ."

And then Helwych saw it: Gelyya. She was crouched in the shadows at the base of the hill, silhouetted by the floodlights of the Grayface defenses.

Interesting.

"What about Kallye?"

Lytham blinked. "She was killed by a hound."

"Indeed. What of her apprentice? Where is Gelyya?"

"I . . ."

"She escaped, did she not, Lytham? She escaped with your help?" Useless, all of them. He would have been better off with Grayfaces from the beginning, and he was now sorry that he had not sent these little scrubbed boys to share the fate of Cvinthil and Darham and their warriors.

"There was an attack that night, lord. She . . . might well have made her way into the countryside in the confusion."

"All by herself, too, I imagine. And perhaps someone took the trouble to show her the location of a gate." Helwych sat back. Dryyim. And now Lytham. "I want you to go and find her."

"Find her?"

Helwych grounded his staff, and the flagstone cracked beneath it. "Find her. Take ten of your men . . ." Men! He almost laughed. ". . . and go after her."

Lytham was plainly frightened. "But, lord, the land is—"

"Infested with Grayfaces and hounds, yes," said Helwych. "It is almost certain death to enter it. Quite correct, captain. You should have thought of that when you helped the girl escape. Now go: you leave within the hour."

"But—"

"*Go!*"

Weeping with fright, Lytham stumbled away and out the door. Helwych slumped back down in his chair. Had he allowed himself, he also might have wept, for as surely as Lytham faced death out in the open countryside, Helwych was beginning to believe that he himself would never leave Hall Kingsbury alive.

A boy. A little boy dressed up in the robes of a sorcerer . . .

With the dawn, Alouzon led the columns along the west road. The last time she had been this way, spring had lain several weeks in the future, and the land had been tricked out in pastels and gray. But while she had been in Broceliande and Los Angeles, summer had come, and as though to spite the Worm and the Specter and the blight across the Cordillera, Vaylle had rip-

ened. Barley was bearded. Wheat stood tall and kingly.
Oats fluttered and laughed. Wildflowers had unrolled
in a variegated carpet, and pastures glowed so green
that they hurt the eye with pleasure.

Alouzon rode out from the road. About her was a
fantasyland of innocence and fertility set with fairytale
cities and villages as a crown might be set with jewels.
Struck with the beauty, she stared openly, unabashed.

Dindrane had followed her. " 'Tis good work you
do, my lady.''

"Me?''

Boyish and girlish both, the priestess spoke as
though uttering common fact: "You made it, did you
not?''

"Yeah . . .'' Alouzon agreed, and she suddenly
wondered how she could be so reluctant to claim such
a place as her own.

Maybe it was the power. She had said it herself: *I
don't want power. Power kills.* Or maybe it was the
sense of hubris that clung to such a claim. But power
did not inevitably have to kill. Power could make.
Power could heal a wound, or soothe a spirit, or keep
an entire planet up and running. And even the question of hubris was rendered meaningless in the end,
for what she faced in the Grail was not in any way
based upon pride or vainglory, but—again the simple
fact—upon the absolute humility of passionate and
gentle sacrifice.

Dindrane was watching her as though witnessing a
mystery as deep as that which, once, she had celebrated with Baares, conjoining cup and knife in a symbol of quintessential union. "From love can come only
creation,'' she said.

Alouzon was still reeling. "Thanks, Dindrane. I'll
remember that. I think that'll be one of those things
that keeps me going until . . .'' She groped for words,
shrugged.

Dindrane bowed slightly in acknowledgement.

They reached Lake Innael in the late afternoon. The

kings' instructions had been that the assembled troops should be ready to move at a moment's notice, and they were indeed prepared. Wagons were loaded, horses fed, saddles and bridles at hand. Supplies and weapons were at the peak of condition.

Alouzon, aware of the transience of the doors and unwilling to delay even a minute, ordered an immediate departure. By the time darkness was settling firmly over the plains about the lake and the first glimmerings of the door were flicking into existence, over five hundred warriors had formed into orderly columns and were waiting for the word to move out.

Of all those assembled on the shore save Kyria and Alouzon, the harpers and healers of Vaylle—steeped as they were in magic and the spiritual realms—were perhaps the best equipped to deal with the sights and images that lay between the Worlds. Dindrane had taken the precaution of scattering her people throughout the ranks of the warriors so that they could soothe any fears that might arise; and at her word, the harpers struck up a gentle strain that lifted even Alouzon's spirits.

But Alouzon called for the march and rode towards the gleaming door with a sense of dread. It was starting. Her plans—the product not of years of training and combat, but rather of a liberal arts education and anti-war protests—would now be shown to be successful or disastrous. For a moment, she paused before the shimmer.

Kyria was at her side. "Shall we?" she said.

"I'd say *after you,* but it's my job," replied Alouzon. She looked behind. Cvinthil's brown eyes were thoughtful, calculating. Marrha rode proudly beside her beloved Karthin. Santhe, at the head of the Second Wartroop, grinned and saluted Alouzon and the woman he loved.

Darham, though, was regarding the gate dubiously, and Alouzon could read his thoughts. Tarwach had acted hastily and with bad counsel: perhaps his mistake was about to be repeated. Then too, the sight of the gate, reaching from earth to sky in an elongated gothic arch of liminal nothingness, was a daunting one in spite of the Vayllens' music and magic.

But, silently, Wykla rode up beside him. Shaking, she hesitated, and then, with a sense of resolve, she extended her hand to the Corrinian king. For a moment, Darham looked at her in wonder, but finally, as though his action were fraught with meaning—for himself, for Wykla, for his people—he reached. The scar on his forearm flashed whitely as their hands clasped, gripped.

When the king turned back to Alouzon, he gave a short nod. With the assurance of his daughter, his doubts were gone.

Right on. Alouzon bent over Jia's head. "Can you do this, guy?" she said.

In response, Jia started forward. Without flinching, he passed through the gateway, and he balked only in the slightest when faced with the whirling planets, shifting planes, and rayed colors that lay on the other side.

Kyria followed, chanting softly to herself: a subtle spell to quiet the horses. Two abreast, the army entered after her. Supply wagons creaked. Horses' hooves made even clopping sounds. The harpers' music rang out hollowly. The healers' staves were bright.

Alouzon checked her watch. Paradoxically and stubbornly, it had once again stopped. But to her recollection, it had taken but a few subjective minutes to make the crossing from UCLA to Gryylth. Manda and Wykla had reported that it had taken no longer to reach Mac-Arthur Park. A few minutes. A few kiloparsecs. That was all.

The army wound on. Alouzon looked over her shoulder and was presented with the unsettling sight of fifth-century warriors and wagons progressing in double columns over what seemed a bottomless abyss. And, indeed, the way from one gate to another could well be as narrow as the blade of a sword: a single step in the wrong direction could—

Kyria came out of her chant enough to murmur: "Keep at it, Alouzon. We are safe."

"Safe? You call this safe?"

The sorceress broke off for a moment more. "We are with you. The Grail wants you. Therefore . . ."

Jia shied, and Kyria resumed her chant quickly.

The reactions of the warriors were mixed. But with the help of the Vayllens, the crossing was quiet and smooth, and the MacArthur Park gate appeared ahead at about the time that Alouzon expected it.

Again, Kyria broke off her chant. "Dindrane?"

"Here."

"Can you take over with the animals? I have to go through first and make sure that we are not seen." Kyria trotted her horse forward. "Alouzon, please hold everyone."

Alouzon lifted her arm, and her gesture was relayed to the rear. The columns halted.

Kyria nodded her thanks. "The police are, I daresay, concerned about so many strange happenings in the park," she explained. "Better one sorceress and a quick spell than many search lights and a few SWAT teams."

Alouzon nodded. "Uh . . . yeah. I'm glad you thought of that."

" 'Tis what I am here for," said Kyria. With a quick smile, she dismounted and slipped through the gate.

The army waited. Horses stamped impatiently. Men and women murmured to one another. Bravely, the harpers kept up their music, and Dindrane's chant blended with the sweet chime of bronze strings.

After a minute, Kyria's head appeared through the sheet of mist and shimmer. "Done," she said.

Alouzon gave the signal, the columns started up again, and Jia carried her through the door and into a world of grass and artificial lights, of cars and airplanes, of air that smelled of exhaust and sulfates. It was what she had once called reality, what she had once called home, but she could no longer consider it either. It was too sterile, too common, too infused with the mundane to have anything to do with the world that had chosen her just as she had chosen it.

Encircling the region directly about the gate, though, was something familiar, something magical: a shining circle of blue light. Almost unbelieving, Alouzon trotted Jia northward under cover of Kyria's protective spell as the evening traffic moved slowly down Alvarado and sped along Wilshire, the cars passing, stopping at red lights, flashing turn signals, the drivers and pedestrians unaware of the growing company of Romano-British warriors forming up on the lawns and asphalt walkways of MacArthur Park.

❖ CHAPTER 19 ❖

Traveling by night, resting in ditches and in the splintered concealment of shattered forests, a rifle in her hand and her belly empty, Gelyya made her way northward.

She had only a vague idea of where she was going. The women of Gryylth had never been expected to find their way across open countryside, and so she had no detailed knowledge of the roads or the passes. All she knew was that Quay lay somewhere to the north and across the Camrann mountains, that there was nothing left behind her, that she could only go on. And even if she died by hounds or by Grayface weapons, she would at least have tried to accomplish something, and she would therefore be able to stand before whatever Gods ruled Gryylth, look Them in the face, and be unashamed.

And, yes, there were hounds: great, shaggy beasts that glowed even in daylight; plump, eager things that roamed in packs of twenty-five and fifty. Near the end of the second day, Gelyya came suddenly upon a group of them as they feasted on the shot-up remains of a troop of Grayfaces. They sensed her presence and, seemingly glad of something living that they could rend, they came at her.

A thirty-round clip emptied into their grinning faces at close range dropped most of them, and part of a second dealt with the rest. Gelyya no more understood the workings of the weapon she carried than she understood magic, but she could use it, and she did. In less than a minute, the hounds were dead.

Among the half-eaten Grayfaces, she found rations, canteens of water, and more ammunition; and after filling a pilfered knapsack with what she could carry, she put some distance between herself and the carnage, ate and drank, and then moved on.

The countryside, already wasted and cratered, became more so as she made her way north, skirting the foothills. Evidence of artillery and bombs gave way to listless and withered tracts of brown vegetation, and more than once she was confronted with the sight of league upon league of once fertile crop land that had been turned suddenly dead and lifeless: a still, brown sea stretching off to the horizon.

But she was lost. After several days, the mountains all looked the same, and the broken remains of the roads had entirely disappeared. She guessed that she was to the north of Bandon, but since she had no map, she had no idea where.

Alone, exhausted, she sat down in the shelter of a dusty ravine and ate ham and lima beans and a can of peaches that she had salvaged from the Grayfaces. She considered her position. Once she crossed the mountains, finding a town the size of Quay on the narrow strip of coastal plain would be fairly easy. The problem, though, lay in the crossing.

There was a pass to the north and west of Bandon. That she knew, for her father had been a tradesman and had used and spoken of it often. But she would have to backtrack for at least a day, locate the ruins of her native town, and then spend several more days puzzling over and perhaps trying the paths and trails before she found the right one.

There was nothing else to do. After discarding the empty cans and drinking a little water, she picked up her rifle and headed south.

* * *

Kyria's magic circle widened and lengthened to contain the troops as they materialized in MacArthur Park, and the columns of men and women snaked up along Alvarado Street and wound through the graffitied underpass beneath Wilshire Boulevard.

Kyria was masking sound as well as sight, but Alouzon, unwilling to tax her any more than necessary, turned around, caught Dindrane's eye, and held a finger up to her lips. At a murmured word from the priestess, the harpers damped their strings, and it was a somber and quiet company that entered the northern half of the park, passed by the fire-fighters' training center and the amphitheater, and at last drew up at the northwest corner and faced the length of Sixth Street.

Streetlights shone bluely on the asphalt and the tall buildings to either side, and from the Park Plaza Building, sword-bearing angels gazed down at the company with stony, sightless eyes, as though offering tacit approval or guardianship.

A jogger approached, thumping along the north edge of the park. Veering suddenly to his left, he made straight for the columns.

"Just let him through," Kyria called. "He cannot see us."

The columns separated a little at his approach, and the lanky, puffing Los Angelino passed within inches of Wykla's horse, the sweat gleaming on his forehead. He slowed for an instant as though wondering why he sensed the anomalous presence of so many people and animals, then shrugged and jogged on.

"Good deal," said Alouzon. She cantered back along the columns. "Okay, everyone," she said. "We're going to stay on the sidewalk as much as possible—that's the pale stone to our left—but it'll probably peter out now and then and we'll have to hit the street. If anyone comes along on foot or in those . . . uh . . . boxes you see with the lights on them, just get out of the way and let the magic do its stuff. Pass it on." She lifted her head. "Dindrane? The horses?"

The priestess gave a terse nod. "I will attend to the good beasts, Dragonmaster. They will not fear."

"Manda, Wykla, you've been here before. Will you take charge of the rear and keep an eye on everyone?"

With a nod, the two women faded back along the length of the line. Darham watched Wykla go, his eyes moist. He lifted the hand that had been holding hers, examined it, kissed it, and settled himself in his saddle. Whatever this night might hold for him, he was satisfied.

The columns crossed Park View, moving against the flow of traffic. Oncoming cars betrayed their presence with their headlights well in advance, and Kyria simply countered with a subtle fluctuation in the magic. Drivers closest to the curb found themselves changing into the left lane for no apparent reason—if they were even conscious of their action—and the way was left clear for Alouzon's people.

Alouzon, Cvinthil, and Darham ordered a quick march, but the speed of the traffic made the columns appear to crawl along the street, and although Alouzon had calculated that the army could make the crossing from the park to the campus in a little over nine hours—a reasonable time, considering the lengthening darkness of these autumn nights—she wondered whether the troops could really keep to that schedule. If they did not, dawn would witness the stranding of the entire company in Los Angeles.

"We'll just have to do it," she said to herself.

Cvinthil was riding at her side. "We can," he said. "The warriors of Gryylth have been force-marched for greater distances than this. And I am sure, Dragonmaster, that you remember the drive for the Circle."

Yes, Alouzon remembered. But Roman roads in Gryylth were very different from streets in Los Angeles: tonight's journey stretched through a broad band of urbanization that could not but exact a psychological toll on veteran and novice alike. She hoped that Dindrane could help, but the priestess herself was unfamiliar with the metropolitan nightmare in which the troops moved.

Lafayette Park was dark and shadowed as they passed by a few minutes later, the palms and the maple trees an impenetrable canopy that blocked out the sight of the too-bright Los Angeles sky. Ahead, the First Congregational Church was a tall, illuminated, gothic presence.

Sixth Street curved to the left, then straightened out. It would take the army a good distance, but Alouzon knew that, just beyond San Vicente Boulevard, she would have to lead her people away from it, picking a way north through the residential sections of Beverly Hills and even traversing part of westbound Sunset Boulevard at its widest and most luxurious.

One thing at a time, she told herself. For now, it was Sixth Street and its battered office buildings. That was enough.

A stop light ahead changed, and there was a lull in traffic. Alouzon turned around. ''Everyone keep together,'' she called. ''Come on, people, close it up. Don't wear out your sorceress.''

Westmoreland, then Vermont. Alouzon checked her watch and wondered how much time had passed in Gryylth, how many more had died.

Lytham stood over the remains of the Grayfaces and hounds. The days had been hot, and the unnatural flesh was fragrant with decay. He had to turn upwind and catch a breath of fresh air before he could speak. ''Hounds,'' he said at last, ''might feed, but they do not shoot one another.''

Haryn, still in his saddle, nodded without reply. He was busy scanning the horizon, looking for signs of movement. This far from Kingsbury, away from friends and support, movement could mean only attack and death.

Helwych had told Lytham to take ten men to search for Gelyya; but, unwilling to order anyone into the wastes and the battlefields, the captain had only been able to find but four who would accompany him voluntarily. All were glad to be away from the helplessness and despair of Kingsbury, and small difference it made in any case to be in open country rather than behind earthworks and wooden defenses that would do little against napalm or bombs.

The land was silent save for the whining of the wind in the withered bracken. The hot sun glared down as though pasted in the sky. Lytham considered the remains. Gelyya, resourceful and brave, had obviously learned the use of Grayface weapons. He would have to remember that.

"Which way do you think she went?" said Haryn.

"North, I would say," Lytham replied. "She was making for Quay."

"Then she should have angled towards the mountains long ago."

"She is a girl," said Lytham. A few months ago, swaggering, gloating, he would have uttered the statement in a tone of derision. Now it was only simple fact. "She knows the streets of Bandon and of Kingsbury, but little else. Quay is but a name to her."

"Then she could be anywhere."

"True." Anywhere. And with an M16 in her hand. "But I will wager she continued north."

Haryn slumped on his horse. "And do you expect that any of us will collect any bets, my friend?"

Were it not for the fact that constant death had taken the tears from their eyes as much as the dry wind that swept across the desiccated plains, they all would have wept. Somewhere out there was Gelyya, but Lytham was no longer sure that he wanted to find her. She had become a reason to continue the search, a reason not to return to Kingsbury, a reason to keep living for another hour, another day. And if, by some chance, she was actually found, Lytham knew that he would be hard pressed to decide what to do with her.

Back to Kingsbury? Where else was there to go?

Quay would only last a few more months. Winter would see it bombed and napalmed. And even Corrin—even assuming for a moment that that woman-dominated land would take them in—would be as Gryylth by spring.

Perhaps, Lytham considered slowly, the girl would buy their re-entry into Kingsbury, and maybe their survival. For a little while. That was something.

One of the men straightened in his saddle and peered off across the plain, shading his eyes from the glare. "There is something to the south," he said. "Gray-faces, I think."

"Movement by air?"

"Nay. None."

"If there are Grayfaces," said Haryn, "then jets cannot be far off." He looked at Lytham. "To the north?"

There was nothing to the north. Nor in any other direction. Lytham shrugged. "To the north."

Two weeks of rest in Quay and a meeting with Alouzon had done much for Timbrin. Astride a good horse and clad in the breeches and tunic of a boy, she was sitting straighter, and though she seemed to regard even the small knife at her belt with a sense of unease, the old, frightened timidity that had clung to her since her encounter with Helwych's magic had perhaps cracked a little.

Relys hoped so. Grievous as her concerns were about herself and what might be growing within her womb, the transformation of her comrade from competent warrior into frightened girl had exacerbated them, and the prospect that Timbrin might be recovering was a bright flicker of hope.

They left Quay in the early morning and crossed over the pass in the Camrann. On fresh horses and with rations enough to see them through to Corrin, they made good time; but once they reached the wastes of craterized and defoliated fields, they had to travel more slowly, for here there was little cover, and the Grayfaces and the hounds prowled at will.

On the second day, they saw both. With cracks and explosions and shrieks of warplanes, the land towards the south erupted into a battle that spread with the passage of a few hours to encompass miles of territory. Each minute brought more jets, and as phosphorus bombs detonated in bursts of blinding white and napalm billowed up in red and black clouds, ground-to-air missiles streaked up to turn the warplanes into shattered metal.

Relys judged times, distances. "I believe we can make it past if we circle far to the north," she said.

The sight and sound of gunfire and bombs had brought the fear back to Timbrin's eyes, but she was fighting it. "Aye," she said. "But I am afraid that I will be glad to do that."

Relys patted her shoulder. There were many things in the world to fear. Timbrin was afraid to be afraid, afraid of even the small knife at her hip. Relys herself was afraid of her own body, afraid that the lot of womankind was falling upon her like a winter avalanche.

Another two weeks, and still no flow. There were a hundred reasons for it, but there was only one that was likely.

They detoured northward, crossing rivers and streams choked with dust and dead branches. A day later, they entered the Cotswood Hills. Here the land was rolling, and in places it still showed green grass and stands of trees.

"Is this not where Mernyl kept his house?" Timbrin said towards noon.

"A little further on, I think," said Relys. "But—"

The sharp crack of a rifle interrupted her. In a moment she and Timbrin had dismounted and led the horses into the cover of a dry stream bed. Timbrin was trembling. "I am sorry, Relys," she said. "I strive to master this, but I fail."

"Peace, my friend. That you can so strive shows that you are healing."

Timbrin nodded with wide eyes and attempted to compose herself. Relys reached to her right hip and loosened her sword. The First Wartroop had always trained in the left-handed use of weapons, but her skill could at best be described as merely adequate. She was, she knew, no match for an unmaimed warrior, and it was absurd even to think of facing Grayface weapons.

Another shot. A muffled curse, then a call: "Give it up, girl."

Relys and Timbrin exchanged glances.

They tethered the horses. Relys started cautiously towards the source of the sounds. Timbrin hesitated, then followed. Together, they inched their way up to the lip of the stream bed, then crawled up the hillside above. Gaining the top, they were just in time to see a young, red-haired woman streak across the valley. Shots and tracers pursued her, but she dodged nimbly and dived at last into the shelter of a ruined stone cottage.

"O you nameless Gods," said Relys. "It is Gelya."

"What is she doing here?"

"Nay, I know not. But—"

And then came the Grayfaces. There were perhaps ten of them, running in single file. when they came in sight of the cottage, their leader motioned to his men, and they spread out along the tree line.

"Come on, girl," he called. "We've got you now."

Two of the Grayfaces detached themselves and circled to the far side of the ruins. The rest stayed in front.

"Why do they not just kill her?" whispered Timbrin. "They have bombs."

"They wish to take her alive," Relys said tonelessly.

"But why?"

Relys's mangled hand throbbed. "For reasons that I know well."

Timbrin flared, a spark of her hot temper taking sudden fire. "Those dogs! We cannot let them—"

Relys held up her good hand. The Grayfaces were moving. Having obviously decided that a single, unarmed girl could be captured without caution, they stepped out of the trees and closed in on Mernyl's old cottage. If Gelyya stayed where she was, she would be caught. If she ran, she would be caught.

But Gelyya suddenly opened up with a burst of machine gun fire that scythed them down as though they were ripe wheat. In a moment, the two men who had circled to the rear were the only members of the troop left.

"Timbrin," said Relys, "quickly."

Timbrin followed her around to the back of the house. Silently, they circled wide and approached the remaining Grayfaces from behind. Relys heard the men conferring, peered through a screen of ferns and saw them reaching to their belts for grenades.

Relys deliberated quickly. Shouting to Gelyya would merely turn the grenades and bullets on her and Timbrin, and Gelyya would be killed eventually in any case; but doing nothing was not an acceptable alternative.

Relys mouthed a silent question. *Can you help?* Timbrin shrugged, shook her head helplessly: her shackles had loosened a little, but they still bound her. Relys nodded. It was up to her alone.

She drew her sword and slipped towards the Grayfaces as they prepared to throw their explosives. A single grenade would do, but they were taking no chances. "You put yours on the right," one was saying in the distant, passionless voice that characterized them. "I'll take care of the left."

"You got it."

The bloodlessness of their tone made Relys shudder. The Grayfaces moved like men asleep, like dream walkers who were playing out a role of which they knew nothing, their movements as unconscious as those of infants.

The pins came out of the grenades. Relys's sword swept in. Her left arm was weak, but its strength was sufficient to sever the arm of the first soldier, and it cut deeply into the wrist of the second. Primed, lethal, seconds away from detonation, the grenades fell at the feet of the wounded men.

"Timbrin!" Relys cried. "Down!" She pivoted and ran, expecting at any moment to feel a hot blast of wind on her back, the jagged peppering of steel slivers.

Behind her, the Grayfaces were crying out and fumbling for the grenades. Ahead was a dip in the ground, and Relys rolled into it just as the two grenades went off and knocked the wind out of her even where she lay. Shrapnel sang through the air like a flock of deadly birds, and then silence returned.

Relys opened her eyes. On the dry brush a few feet away was hanging a scrap of what could only have been a face. She gagged. She had seen worse in her days of battle, but it was the thought of the weapon that had produced such a thing that made her retch, not the thing itself.

She struggled to her feet, her maimed hand throbbing. "Timbrin!" she called. "Are you well?"

"Aye."

"Gelyya?"

"Who is that?" The girl's voice sounded thin and weak.

"Relys of Ba—" No. Not that name. Another. Hahle had made a generous offer, and now Relys accepted it. She took a deep breath. "Relys and Timbrin," she said. "Of Quay."

Gelyya's head appeared at the sagging door of the cottage. Her malnourished face was dirty, and her red hair was matted with leaves and dust. "Relys? Timbrin?"

"Aye, we are here." Relys detoured around what

was left of the Grayfaces and stepped into the cottage's overgrown garden. Dropping her rifle, Gelyya ran to her.

"I thought that surely I would die in there," said the girl, embracing her. "I knew they had bombs, but there was nothing I could do against them."

"It is well, Gelyya," said Relys. "You did what you could with the weapon you had. In you Gryylth can claim a resourceful warrior."

"I? A warrior?"

Relys allowed herself a thin smile, gave Gelyya's shoulders a squeeze. "I would call you that."

Gelyya's eyes were bright. "My thanks, Relys."

"It is no more than you deserve." Relys looked up. Timbrin was not in sight. Where was she? "But . . . what are you doing out here?"

Gelyya's face turned bleak. "Kallye—" she started, but her words suddenly froze on her tongue and she stared away to the left. Relys followed her eyes and saw a man standing at the edge of the trees. He was dressed in the armor of the King's Guard. His face was one that she would never forget.

Lytham.

Relys swallowed her sudden nausea and bettered her grip on her sword. "It would be unwise for you to approach, man," she said.

But Lytham's swaggers and arrogance had deserted him. Sword in hand, he stood at the edge of the Mernyl's overgrown and withered garden, his face as gray as the piece of flesh that had confronted Relys from the bushes a minute before. "I am not here for you, Relys," he said. "I am here to take Gelyya back to Kingsbury."

"By whose authority?"

"Helwych's."

Relys spat. "If I had been more clever, I would have spitted him on my sword months ago."

Lytham was guarded. "But you were not, and now

he has sent me for Gelyya. I have tracked her the length
of Gryylth, and now she must come with me.''

Gelyya moved suddenly, sprinting for the cottage in
a flurry of skirts and flying hair. In a moment, she had
reached the M16 and aimed it at Lytham. Her finger
found the trigger, squeezed . . .

But nothing happened. The gun had jammed, or
perhaps the clip was empty.

Lytham approached cautiously. ''I will leave you
alone, Relys, if you allow me to take the girl.''

''You settled any question of leaving me alone some
weeks ago, Lytham. If you approach, I will smite
you.''

''With your left hand?''

''With my teeth if need be.''

Lytham paused, licked his lips. ''Come now. This
does neither of us any good.''

''Stay where you are,'' said Relys. ''You are but one
man, and I am armed.''

''I am but one man, indeed,'' said Lytham. ''But I
have others. More than enough to deal with you.''

Relys stood her ground. ''Then they will have to
deal with me. And this time I will not be chained and
helpless. Let them come.''

His face pale, Lytham turned back to the trees.
''Haryn. All of you. Come help me.''

Several seconds went by. No reply. No movement.

Lytham licked his lips. ''Haryn! Come forward.
Bring the others.''

The bushes rustled, but what appeared was not a
group of armed warriors, but rather the small and
slight form of a dark-haired woman. Timbrin. A
bloody knife was in her hands, and a hot fire burned
in her eyes. Her shackles had at last given way: the
quick-tempered warrior was back. ''Your men are
dead, Lytham,'' she said. ''They are all dead.''

Relys was already in motion. ''As you soon shall
be, dog.''

Stunned, Lytham turned, struggled to raise his

sword. But the heart, seemingly, had gone out of him, and with only the strength of her left arm, Relys knocked the weapon from his hand.

For a moment, Lytham seemed to be struggling with words, his beardless cheeks shuddering with emotion. But boyish and impotent though he was, he had played the part of a man once on a dark evening in Kingsbury; and Relys cut back with her blade, striking not just at this single individual who had so violated her, but at all the memories of rape and torment that tortured her by day, haunted her dreams by night, and now lent strength to the blow that severed Lytham's head and sent it rolling across the weedy ground, its boyish features still contorted with an odd mixture of sorrow and fear.

❖ CHAPTER 20 ❖

Beyond Saint Andrew's Place and Gramercy Drive, Sixth Street turned wider, more residential. Apartment buildings and lawns replaced the office buildings, and the constricted concrete canyons of urban life .were supplanted—at least for the time—by open spaces and broad sidewalks.

But though Alouzon saw the change as an improvement, she knew that such subtleties were lost on the majority of her people. For them, Los Angeles had in the first few minutes gone well beyond any qualities that could be adequately expressed by terms like *foreign* or *alien,* and the milieu it offered was uncompromising and relentless. Automobiles swept along the street with a roar and a blare of radios, the tall buildings were lit with the unflickering glow of mercury vapor and fluorescent lamps, and the pale night sky was filled with lights of its own: the steady, blinking progress of jetliners, the strobing and noisy abruptness of police and news helicopters.

Near Windsor, where the street was lined with fine, old mansions and carefully tended landscaping, the steady, dull roar of the living city was broken by a siren. Shrill and sudden, it exploded into life somewhere ahead and drew closer. Flashing lights came into view.

"I cannot block him," cried Kyria. "He is too single-minded."

Alouzon wheeled. "Everyone out of the way, quick!" She glanced to her left. The house on the corner, a blend of the characteristic Spanish and 1940s architecture of the city, was dark and set away from the street. Like its fellows in this neighborhood, it had a broad lawn. "Up on the grass!"

As the police cruiser, still shrieking, rushed towards them, the men and women in the vanguard scrambled out of the street. Pressing up against the house, beside rose bushes, behind hedges, they clustered thickly on the front lawn of the house; but farther behind, the foot soldiers milled uncertainly.

"Santhe!" came Marrha's cry. "Clear the byway!"

Santhe took charge of the middle of the line with quick commands, and the men of the Second Wartroop wheeled as one and herded the infantry off the cross street. At the rear, Wykla and Manda shouted to those about them, and with a clatter of boots and weapons, the pikemen stumbled out of the way in a tightly packed mass. The few wagons that had strayed into the street creaked and rumbled to the curb.

"Get those wagons out of there!" Alouzon yelled. "He's in the near lane!"

The Corrinian soldiers threw down their pikes and ran to the wagons. With the headlights on the approaching police cruiser gleaming on the bronze bosses of their armor, they put their shoulders to the recalcitrant carts and heaved them up onto the grass.

The cruiser's headlights cast long shadows along the street, and its flashing lights lit the trees in staccato bursts. Alouzon made one last check to see that the way was clear . . . and swore aloud when she noticed that a lone soldier—a pikeman—was standing in the middle of Sixth Street, watching, transfixed, as the whirl of lights and noise swept towards him.

She was in full gallop in a moment. Swinging down while still in motion, she hauled the pikeman to the side just as the police car roared by, siren shrieking.

The soldier was sobbing in her arms. "I do not understand," he choked, his pike hanging limply in his hand. "This is a terrible place." Wiping his streaming eyes, he saw that Darham was hurrying up on foot. "My king," he said, "I am sorry."

Darham stood over the pikeman, his arms folded. "There is no place for cowards here, sir," he said slowly.

"Just a damned minute—" started Alouzon.

Darham shook his head. "But I cannot blame you. I brought you to Vaylle to fight a battle, and you came willingly enough for that. But we both find strange weeds in our fields."

The soldier swallowed his tears. "Thank you, lord." He looked up, realizing who had dragged him out of the street. "Dragonmaster! I—" Shame clouded his features again.

Alouzon shook her head. "It's okay, guy. Hang in there. There were a few times at rush hour that I felt the same way."

Darham offered a big hand to his soldier and pulled him to his feet. "Form up," Alouzon called. "Let's go." She noticed that lights were flicking on in the house. "Kyria?"

"Done," said the sorceress with a lifted hand; and though bleary-eyed faces were suddenly pressed against the windows, it was obvious that they saw only horse droppings, foot prints, and wagon ruts—and nothing whatsoever of the animals, men, women, and carts that had put them there.

Alouzon got everyone started off, and when she was sure that Kyria's magic circle was once again firmly in place, she cantered to Darham's side. "Thanks," she said warmly.

"For what?" said the Corrinian. "For showing compassion?" He shook his head. "I but attempt to correct a deficiency, Dragonmaster. Had there been more compassion in the lands of Gryylth and Corrin, I believe that none of this would have occurred in the first place."

Alouzon was staring off into the heat-shimmered night. And had there been more compassion among the rice paddies and jungles of Vietnam, none of that would have happened. And had there been more compassion at Kent State . . .

Darham was right. But where, save in the depths of the Grail, was there sufficient compassion to sweep away the last vestiges of the past—without regret, without sorrow—and so end forever the existence of the Specter?

She caught her breath. The last she had seen of it, the Specter had been in Beverly Hills. Given the slippery time factors involved, that was only about two Los Angeles hours ago. The Specter, then, was doubtless still looking for her, and the closer the army came to UCLA, the closer it would come to the Specter's widening search.

And so, inevitably, the Specter would not only find her, but also the massed armies of Gryylth and Corrin. Suddenly, her concerns about the damaged door at the archaeology office and even the potential stranding of the troops in Los Angeles seemed paltry things indeed.

O Gods . . .

She realized that she could only be addressing herself, but she shook herself out of the thought. "Come on," she called to the troops. "Hurry. The sun rises at about seven, and it gets light before that."

She nodded to Darham once again, and then she was off, riding towards the head of the columns that, step by step, were nearing their goal. And the Specter.

Why?

Seena tended her inert children, going through the motions of living within the confines of a glorified prison. But though Hall Kingsbury was large enough to contain her and her griefs, it had become insufficient to pen her suspicions and her certainties.

Why?

She knew why. Helwych was why. Far from being
the heroic defender of her children and her people, the
sorcerer was instead the cause of their afflictions.
Seena no longer doubted that the story he had told of
the Vayllens' treachery was a lie designed to send
Cvinthil and the men of Gryylth overseas—so that he
could take control of the country. And Ayya and Vill
were but further stones in the path that the Corrinian
sorcerer was building, stones designed to bear down
upon her back so that she would be too occupied and
stricken to object to his assuming full command of the
country.

The days passed. Seena tended to Ayya and Vill,
but her mind was racing, battling through her immediate concerns, and winning its way through to broader
issues that, far from eclipsing the plight of her children, only added weight and urgency to it.

Helwych. Her children. The whole country.

She began asking questions of the soldiers—slowly,
so as not to attract attention—and realized that matters
were being kept from her. She knew nothing of what
was happening outside the palisade, and no one would
tell her. Her guards, true, were still nominally loyal
to her husband and herself, but it quickly became obvious that their fears were centered about Helwych.
Regardless of their loyalties, simple self-preservation
dictated that they remain silent.

But the preservation of her children dictated that
Seena find out more; and one night, muffling herself
in a rough cloak, she slipped along the corridors of
Hall Kingsbury and made her way to a small gate at
the rear of the palisade. Here there were no Grayfaces.
Here was only a single soldier of the Guard.

"Who comes?" he challenged.

She approached, threw back her hood. "The Queen
of Gryylth."

"My lady, I—"

She fixed him with a glance. Her children were all
but dead, Gryylth might be dying, and a man who

seemed made of equal parts madness and foolishness was sitting in her husband's chair. "You will be silent, sir," she said. "You will open this gate, and you will let me out. And when I return, you will open it again, let me in, and say nothing of it."

"My queen—"

"The penalty for treason, sir, is death."

He stared at her. The moon—a few days past full— shone straight down upon her, and she knew her eyes were defiant and commanding.

He let her out.

For an hour, Seena wandered the streets of Kingsbury, alone, undetected. She peered at the hovels, listened to the gasping breaths of the dying, smelled the odors of rot, corruption, and plague. Wanting to scream, wanting nothing so much as to run back to the Hall and rend the sorcerer with her hands, Seena forced herself to walk carefully, unobtrusively. She was a Gryylthan woman: she knew how not to be noticed.

But when she re-entered Hall Kingsbury, she went not to her chambers, but to the main room. This late, it was empty, and she wanted to think.

What would Cvinthil do? Vorya? Alouzon? Seena was but one woman, alone and unarmed—her very upbringing, in fact, had conditioned her to eschew anything more deadly than an eating knife—surrounded by men and weapons and magic. What could she do?

Very little, it seemed. But she had seen enough of Kingsbury and had inferred enough about Gryylth to know that doing nothing would be far worse.

Still wrapped in her cloak, she sagged against the wall, sat down on the floor, buried her face in her knees. "O Gods," she said. "Help me. Help my people. Help my children."

There was no answer. But when, discouraged, despairing, she dropped her hands, her fingers touched something cold and hard that lay in the shadows and rushes against the wall. Curious, trembling, she groped at the thing, learned its shape; and at last she took it up and lifted it.

It was a sword. Not a man's sword, though. Slender and light, it seemed meant for the hand of a woman.

But only the First Wartroop carries weapons like this.

Whose was it? What had happened? With a sudden dizziness, Seena recalled that Relys and Timbrin had stayed behind when the troops had left for Vaylle. She had seen neither of them for months. Where were they now? And how had one of them willingly allowed her sword to be tossed so carelessly away?

Footsteps. Seena recognized the heavy, even tread of Grayfaces, and she rose and hurried off down the corridor: back to her rooms, back to her children. But she took the sword with her.

At Highland, elaborate landscaping and topiary gave way to neatly trimmed lawns. Here was archetypal Los Angeles: small bungalows of imitation Spanish design—white walls and red tile roofs—the depression-era housing projects of what had been a modest, Southern California city serviced by the Red Car lines until the automobile had declared its ascendancy amid the growing urban sprawl.

Kyria's shields were holding admirably, and the sorceress had made herself a constant, cheerful presence among the troops. Somehow, she kept up her spells while trotting along the columns, chatting with the warriors, asking questions of the harpers and healers. It was a long hard march—the heat wave had not abated in the slightest, and asphalt and concrete were unfriendly and unyielding surfaces for feet and hooves both—but Kyria kept everyone's spirits up; and her pale face, lit by an open smile, cheered even Alouzon, who was still wondering what would happen if the Specter suddenly appeared.

Kyria, I hope you've got something up your sleeve, because I sure as hell don't.

Past La Brea, the street was flanked by undistinguished apartment buildings, and the traffic and noise increased. There was little danger of odd sounds attracting attention here, and Kyria asked for a tune from the harpers.

"Give us something joyful," she called. A convertible raced by, leaving behind a trail of blaring rock and roll. Kyria winced, sighed, shoved a tendril of sweat-dampened hair out of her face. "Surely," she said, "we can do better than *that*."

The harpers conferred among themselves for a moment, then struck up what turned out to be a hymn to the Goddess.

> *Though I am a harper and a singer*
> *I know not how to praise you, O Great Lady.*
> *Therefore, direct me, that I might bring*
> *To my music a power mightier than my own.*

Kyria smiled. Dindrane nodded. Alouzon felt herself growing warmer than could be accounted for by the heat wave alone.

By midnight, they were approaching San Vicente Boulevard, which terminated many of the smaller east-west streets, Sixth among them. Here, Sixth was dark and quiet, and the harpers had fallen once again into silence.

Alouzon deliberated. "Kyria?"

The sorceress rode up. "Is something amiss?"

"We have to turn north here somewhere to get up to Sunset. Sweetzer looks okay, but I'm not sure, and we don't have time to get lost. Do you remember?"

"Some days, Alouzon, I am not sure I can remember where the San Diego Freeway goes. But I think I can recall a few things. I seem to remember riding a bicycle in this area for a long time. Solomon . . ." Kyria's eyes clouded, but she shook off the pain: it belonged to another life, to another person. "Solomon kept the car by the terms of the divorce, and the settlement money was slow in coming. So Helen had to make do with two wheels for a time." She eyed the

surrounding buildings—little chateau-styled apartments with gingerbread and turrets—and folded her
arms. "You did not bring a map?"

"Nah. I had one in the car, but the Specter was on
our tail. We didn't even have time to bring our armor."

"Indeed."

"By the way, do you have any idea what you're going to do if the Sp—?"

But Kyria had turned thoughtful, necessity forcing
her to reach into an old discarded life just as Alouzon
had been compelled to carry a driver's license with
another woman's name on it. "I think we would do
best to cut north along Sweetzer, then cross San Vicente at Drexel."

"Traffic."

"Well, yes . . ." Kyria frowned.

"Never mind," Alouzon said. "We can cross in
small groups. Go on."

Kyria's brow furrowed with the strain. "I think that
Elevado would be best to take to the west, once we
have traveled northward enough on . . . say . . . Al-
mont or Lapeer . . ." She shook her head with what
appeared to be an almost physical pain, but forced
herself onward. "We can take Crescent or Rexford to
the north. We will reach Sunset near Will Rogers
Park."

"And then," said Alouzon, "it's a pretty straight
shot down Sunset."

"And then into the campus?"

"I figured we'd go down Hilgard and cut in just
south of MacGowan Hall."

Following Kyria's route, the columns reached Will
Rogers Park at about three in the morning. Sunset was
broad, the grass on the center divider lush, and though
the automatic sprinklers came on and soaked the warriors, the heat was such that no one seemed to mind
save the harpers, who yelped in alarm and scrambled
to cover their precious instruments.

Off to the right, the Beverly Hills Hotel was set back behind tall pines and palms, floodlights bathing its pink stucco in a daylight glow.

"Is that a king's house, Alouzon?" asked Cvinthil.

"Well . . . some rich people live there. It's actually more of an inn."

The king's eyebrows lifted. "How do they sleep with all these lights?"

"Dunno . . . I prefer Kingsbury."

"As do I, Dragonmaster." Cvinthil squinted at the sky, but in the constant false dawn maintained by the city lights, the stars were invisible. "How much further have we to travel?"

"A few miles. We're making pretty good time."

Traffic on Sunset, as Alouzon had expected, was light, but heavier than on the side streets. Fortunately, there was plenty of room on the center divider, and by breaking the columns into short lengths, she managed to keep them on the move with little interference from red lights and cross traffic.

Now the city was hidden by trees and high hedges, and aside from the cars and the washed-out sky, the way might have been taking them along a forested section of Gryylth. The troops relaxed. But at Whittier Drive the center divider ended, and the columns bunched up once again on the sidewalk and in the left lane.

Kyria looked worried. "I am just glad that there are two lanes in each direction," she said. "It is hard enough to divert these drivers." A Porsche whined by close enough that even the sorceress jumped. The car passed, and she mopped her forehead, thoroughly wilted.

"And they're all smoking dope, too, right?" said Alouzon.

"Aye. And that makes it far worse."

No sidewalk now, but broad lawns. The way wound on past Beverly Glen, where a tall gate announced the entrance to Bel Air estates.

Kyria stopped before the gate, and as the columns passed her by, Alouzon saw the soft shake of her head. Helen was dead. The hag was gone. Bel Air lay far in the past, but the sorceress still had a few memories left of her old home, and at least some of them were good.

Kyria bent her head quickly as though to hide tears. How many times had she driven up Beverly Glen, proud of her success and her triumphs, and spun her car into the circular driveway in front of her house? Hundreds, maybe thousands. Alouzon could not guess. But she understood Kyria's feelings, for she herself had felt something similar when, closing the door of Suzanne's apartment for the last time, she had allowed Manda and Wykla to go on ahead so that she could bid, in private, a last farewell to a lifetime.

Kyria stayed at the corner of Sunset and Beverly Glen for a long time. Alouzon was about to turn around and go to her, but with a quick clatter of hooves, Santhe appeared, and after a moment, Kyria lifted her eyes, smiled at the man she had chosen, reached out. Santhe took her hand and kissed it. Together, they rode off into the darkness that lay to the west.

When she had ridden into MacArthur Park, Alouzon had determined to pace herself and to take things calmly, but she was shaking with strain by the time the army reached Hilgard, and the sight of the large sign on the corner made her want to cry. Even at night, the letters, carved in stone, stood out in deep relief.

UCLA

A turn to the south. "Keep to the right now," she ordered, trying to suppress the tremor in her voice. "The entrance I want to use is just past Comstock . . . I mean . . . uh . . ." Curious glances from the men and women. "Never mind. Just keep right. I'll tell you where to cut in."

There was not much farther to go, and a good thing that was, because even now the sky to the east was beginning to lighten. Silent once again save for the clop of hooves and the creak of wagon wheels, the columns entered the campus. The grass of the Sculpture Garden cushioned foot fall and hoof fall, and the trickle of the fountains was a welcome relief after the dinning noise of traffic and aircraft.

Bunche Hall. The concrete underpass resounded with the movement of warriors, healers, and harpers; and more than one looked up at the pile of glass and concrete above them as though afraid that the slender supports would not prove adequate to the load.

Haines Hall appeared on the right as the columns tramped along the street that bordered Dickson Court. The flagpole at the center of the old campus held the Stars and Stripes aloft in the glare of floodlights, and beyond the glare, swimming up out of the darkness, was Kinsey Hall.

"Keep them moving, Kyria," said Alouzon, and she dropped to the ground, handed Jia's reins to one of Cvithil's guards, and ran for the north door of the hall.

She crossed the lawn, bounded up the steps. The door was locked.

"Shit!"

Kyria appeared a moment later and laid her hands on the lock. With an audible snap, the latch opened. She bowed. "Forgive me for not following orders, Alouzon. I suspected this might be the case."

Alouzon shook her head. "I can't keep track of everything, Kyria. I can't even remember that doors in L.A. get locked. How the hell am I supposed to handle being a God?"

Kyria shrugged softly. "And how was Marrha supposed to handle being a woman, or pregnant? And Wykla? What did you tell them in those days after their transformation?"

"I told them that they couldn't fight it, so they just had to go with it."

Kyria nodded. "Exactly."

"Yeah . . ." Alouzon looked back across the lawn. She saw nothing. No horses, no columns of marching pikemen, no harpers and healers in bright Vayllen livery. Nothing. "You're right . . . but . . ."

But Kyria had turned back to the invisible army, and Alouzon, recalling the imminence of sunrise, took the stairs to the second floor two at a time and burst out of the north stairwell hoping that no professors had decided to get an early start on their work this morning. But the office was deserted. The door was as she had left it hours—days—before.

With a murmured thank-you to the Grail, Alouzon entered, darted down the inner corridor and swung the door open. The gate was still there, shimmering with the glow of plexed dimensions, but the clock on one of the solid walls said 6:00.

She ran back downstairs. The lawn, while still appearing vacant at first, filled with men and women and horses and wagons as she crossed towards Haines Hall. The columns had broken up into smaller teams that were separating the supplies into easily carried bundles; and the wagons, designed to break down for travel by ship, were quickly disassembled into sections that could pass through the doors and stairwells of the hall.

The first group entered the passage between the worlds at 6:15. More followed quickly. Men and women, already worn out with the night's exertions, puffed up the stairs carrying wheels and boards and supplies. Under the care of the priestesses of Vaylle, horses climbed docilely in threes and fours and threaded single file through the inner corridor of the archaeology office.

Marrha and Karthin stood at the north door, directing the steady stream up to Wykla, who took over at the foot of the stairs to the second floor. Manda had stationed herself in the corridor outside the office, Dindrane at the mouth of the gate. Kyria was everywhere, reinforcing the shields when the campus security trucks drove by, quickening the steps of the fatigued warriors with encouraging words, darting in and out of the gate to see that the lines were moving steadily along the interdimensional passage.

By 6:40, the lawn was almost empty. Santhe and the Second Wartroop, acting as a rear guard, were just assembling their horses in preparation for the passage, and the First Wartroop was climbing the stairs. Alouzon ran a hand back through her sweat-soaked hair. Almost finished. And sunrise was a good twenty minutes away. There was plenty of time for—

A howl like the blast of a klaxon suddenly rang across the lawn, answered immediately by chorus of eager yelps. Glowing eyes flashed out of the bushes and paths of Dickson Court, and milling shapes appeared in the dark passage between Royce and Haines Halls: leprous yellow bodies, mouths that glowed as with the phosphor of rotten corpses.

❖ CHAPTER 21 ❖

Alouzon was already running down the stairs. With most of the army either in transit or already in Gryylth, the hounds could not have appeared at a worse time. But what added a weight of sickness to her worry was the thought that, with this many hounds suddenly materializing, the Specter could not be far away.

The beasts milled briefly and then, in spite of Kyria's shields, charged directly at the warriors left on the lawn between the halls. Alouzon estimated their number at well over fifty, and they were massive creatures: a few were actually the same size as the Gryylthan war horses.

Santhe was barking orders to his men. "Mount! Defensive line!"

Marrha, with Karthin at her side, descended the steps two at a time. "Fighting retreat, Santhe," she shouted as they reached their horses. "We have no time for a battle!"

Santhe's blond curls bounced as he looked up. "Aye," he said. "Ever the wiser in a fight." He brandished his sword. "Fighting retreat," he called, "as the captain orders."

Alouzon summoned Jia with a whistle and rode to help. The wartroops dropped many of the first wave of hounds instantly, but these beasts were large and determined, and by sheer weight of numbers they broke through the line. Most wheeled immediately and set upon the warriors from behind, thereby blocking the planned retreat, but several bolted for Kinsey Hall.

Alouzon severed the spine of a hound that was gathering itself for a spring onto Marrha's back, then helped her deal with the three that were snapping at her from the front. She caught a glimpse of a determined smile from the captain and heard a quick "Hail, Dragonmaster," but she was already turning Jia back towards the hall to intercept the hounds heading for the door.

She need not have bothered. When the hounds were halfway up the stairs, they were met by a brilliant burst of violet light, and what was left of them smoked and cartwheeled down the brick steps, leaving nothing more behind than a thin smear of black ash.

Kyria had appeared at the north door, and the cluster of stars at her shoulder scintillated in the light of the approaching dawn as she gathered double handfuls of the night, held them to her breast until they glowed with violet intensity, and flung them at the hounds. Flat-trajectoried and quick, the bolts drove straight into the massed clusters of the beasts, and where the energy did not incinerate them on the spot, it tumbled them over the lawn like bowling pins.

But though Kyria could help, she dared not intervene magically when the hounds closed in on the members of the wartroops. Backing steadily towards the steps of the building, the warriors had to do most of their own fighting.

Alouzon plunged into the thick of the pack, feeling a sense of angry release as she hacked glowing flesh and smashed the Dragonsword's pommel into ranks of needle teeth. These hounds, she knew well, were but symbols of the war she had protested, emblems of all wars and all suffering. At other times, in other conflicts, they stayed out of sight, dragging down the wounded and the innocent invisibly. But in creating

Vaylle and Broceliande, she had made them real, visible, physical.

The Hounds of War. The Hounds of Hell. The craven, bestial things that made battles and killing what they were. Alouzon slew them without qualm.

If I'm gonna be some kind of God, this kind of shit is gonna end. You hear that?

Jia took a vicious bite in his left shoulder that, placed a few inches farther back, would have severed Alouzon's leg. She felled the hound, but Jia was left limping in pain: the phosphor, saturating the wound, burned its way in slowly.

"Easy boy," she said as she battered away another beast. "We'll get you out of here in one piece."

Time was growing short. Moment by moment, the sun was nearing the horizon, and in another few minutes the passageway into Gryylth would dissolve. Under the direction of Santhe and Marrha, the wartroops were keeping the hounds at bay while backing towards the hall, but the glowing beasts were numerous and strong, and there was a good chance that they would follow the warriors into the gate and so continue the battle in the darkness and void between the Worlds.

A flash of incandescent light. Alouzon looked up to see a campus security truck pull down the street that bordered Dickson Court. It stopped, its tires clawing at the asphalt, and a searchlight stabbed out at the carnage on the lawn.

Faced with battle, Kyria had allowed the shields to dissipate, and Alouzon knew what the officers in the truck were seeing: writhing, dying beasts that looked like nightmares come to life, and, locked in battle with them, sword-wielding warriors and a sorceress who dispensed seething globes of magic like so many water balloons.

The truck spun a quick U-turn and vanished into the darkness. Alouzon could image what the radio operator at the security office was hearing, what, in fact, the Los Angeles Police Department would hear in another minute.

Cursing, she hacked more furiously, leaning down from her saddle to scythe a hound's legs out from under it as it ran at Jia's wounded shoulder. Up at the top of the steps, Kyria was placing her bolts with care. The ranks of the hounds were thinning, but not fast enough.

With the hounds still snapping and biting at them, the First and Second Wartroops had reached the base of the stairs. Here was the worst prospect: a fighting retreat up a long flight of brick and stone steps, with a door at the top that would allow the passage of only one warrior at a time. And by Alouzon's watch, barely ten minutes remained before the gate would disappear.

Alouzon galloped onto the carcass-strewn lawn that lay behind the hounds, slashing at hindquarters so as to distract the beasts. Kyria continued with her bolts.

A whinny, and Karthin was unhorsed. He fell heavily on the steps, and the hounds closed in. Marrha cried out and plunged straight for him through the thick of the beasts; but the big man rose, eyed his attackers, and calmly, methodically, cut one to pieces while his huge fist smashed the face of another into a ruin of phosphor and brains.

His hand smoked as the flesh began to dissolve. He examined it, shrugged, and dealt similarly with another hound.

But above the clatter of hooves and the demented chorus of the hounds, Alouzon heard a steady, rhythmic beating, felt a turgid pulsation in the air. At first, she thought it was a police helicopter—and indeed, looking up, she saw approaching strobe and search lights—but as the beating and pulsation increased, she recognized them for what they really were: the flap of immense wings.

With a scream, a huge white head suddenly reared up above Haines Hall, and pallid wings lofted the White Worm over the rooftops. Astride it, carrying a parody Dragonsword in its hand like the severed head of a defeated enemy, was the Specter.

The hounds broke off their attack and retreated. Whining, frightened, they rolled on their backs and pawed at the air submissively as their master approached; and when a quick hand signal from Marrha regrouped the First and Second Wartroops and sent them cantering towards the steps of the hall, Kyria saw her chance. While the hounds lay open and exposed, she blanketed the lawn with a wave of incandescence that turned them to cinders in a heartbeat.

The Worm screamed at the sight, its talons clawing at the roof of Haines Hall. Marrha reached the landing halfway up the steps, and Alouzon grabbed her hand. "This is going to be tight," she said. "Get everyone up the stairs and through the passage. You'll have to make it all the way to Gryylth before the sun rises here, and you've only got a few minutes."

Marrha sent the men and women ahead, and Santhe took over the command, leading the warriors and horses through the door of the hall. At a touch from Kyria, the phosphor vanished from Karthin's hand and arm. He bowed to her, grabbed the bridle of his horse, and led it away. But he stopped at the top of the steps, waiting. He would not desert his wife.

Marrha had stayed at Alouzon's side. For a moment, she glared defiantly at the Specter, then turned to Alouzon. "And what about you, my friend?"

"I've . . ." This was it. She could not escape this final confrontation. "I've got things to do here. You'll have to go on without me."

Marrha's voice shook. Alouzon heard anger and fear both. "My friend Alouzon . . ." said the captain. "I . . ."

"Go on."

The Worm had spread its wings and gained altitude, and now it stooped towards the figures on the steps. A bolt from Kyria smashed it back into the air, and its wings flailed as it fought for balance.

Alouzon leaned out from Jia's back, opened her arms, and hugged the captain. "Marrha," she choked, "this is goodbye."

"I will stay and fight with you, Alouzon. Karthin too."

The Worm righted itself and hung, hovering. The Specter lifted its sword, and a distant howling drifted over the campus, mingling with the wail of approaching police sirens. The helicopters circled, searchlights stabbing down at the field. The dawn was brightening, the sun nearing the rim of the world.

"You can't do anything," said Alouzon. "I have to do this myself." She was shaking with terror, but she hugged Marrha all the tighter and hoped that the captain would not notice. "I'll get the Specter out of here. You get everyone through, and you tell Wykla I love her and that she made the right choice. But I have to go now. I might live through this, and if I do, I'll be around. I'll always be around. But you probably still won't see me again."

Understanding suddenly dawned on Marrha, and she stared into Alouzon's face.

"It's true, Marrha." Alouzon choked out the words. "I'm Her."

"My Goddess!"

Alouzon kissed her. "I love you, Marrha. Now go on. Take off."

Marrha gave Alouzon a last hug, backed her horse, and lifted her sword in salute. "Do what you must, my friend," she said, her face radiant. "And never forget that Your children love You." And with that she turned her horse and galloped up the steps. Karthin swung into the saddle at her approach, and he followed her into the building, dipping his head slightly to clear the top of the door. Alouzon heard the clatter of hooves on the inner stairs.

The howls continued. A surging luminescence appeared in the darkness of Dickson Court.

Kyria spoke suddenly, dropping her arm. "Solomon." Her tone was calm, almost loving.

The Specter's head snapped up, its empty glare swinging about like the helicopter searchlights. The luminescence faded, as did the howls. "You again," it said. "You'll never learn. But you can't stop me now. You haven't got the balls."

But Kyria spoke again, and the love in her voice increased. "Come," she said softly. "It is time to give this up. You have to. It is killing you."

The Specter blinked at her tone. Even in this cynical reification of everything that Suzanne had despised in Solomon, her government, and the Vietnam War, something was obviously responding to the voice of a once-loved woman out of a quiet New England past. "Who are you?" it said warily.

Kyria held herself tall. "I am your wife."

Alouzon stared. Kyria was trying to undo a lifetime of horror with simple affection and love. It was as if the sorceress had reached an existence in which she could pity even the Specter.

Darham had said it, too: compassion.

Was that what the Grail demanded? Alouzon shuddered at the thought. She was not sure she was capable of it.

But the thing on the back of the Worm jerked its gaze away from Kyria, the void in its eyes suddenly uncertain, troubled. "Leave me alone," it said petulantly. "You want to feed me those pills again?"

Kyria lifted her hands. "I can learn, you can learn. Come."

With a cry, though, the Worm flapped up and reached out with an adamantine claw. Kyria had left herself open, defenseless, gambling on the hope that, through her reconciliation with what Solomon had been, the Specter might be tamed. But the Specter was not her creation: it belonged to Alouzon, and to a certain extent to Solomon himself. It could play out a part in a dialog, but it would remain unaffected by her love.

The Worm reached. The Specter lifted its sword.

But both were struck by something that exploded from the doors of Kinsey Hall like a sunrise, and a vast, golden light dazzled the eyes of void that were closing on the sorceress. Dindrane had returned, and now she stood at the top of the stairs, the healing energies of a Vayllen priestess coursing through her staff.

Dazed, the Specter fell back only to be struck again, for now Silbakor, black as iron, darted in from the south and slashed talons across its face.

The Specter flailed. Alouzon slid to the ground and handed Jia's reins to Kyria. "Beat it."

Kyria nodded. "I will. I can do no more here, and my king will need me in the battles that lie ahead." She smiled graciously at Alouzon for an instant, curtsied deeply, and then, leading Jia, entered the building.

Alouzon did not wait for the Specter to re-orient itself, for she knew that, together with the Worm, it would be able to counter Silbakor's defense and follow her wherever she went. But that, for now, was what she wanted. The army would be safe, Helwych would be in trouble, and the Specter would be pursuing bait considerably more attractive than five hundred warriors, harpers, and healers.

Still, she had no idea what she herself was going to do, and since she needed as much of a head start as she could get, she sheathed her sword and took off across the campus at a run. Clad as she was only in shorts and a light blouse, her steps were light, and the rubber soles of her sneakers clapped rhythmically on cement walkways and patches of grass as she made for her car.

But another set of footsteps—light, sandaled—was following, gaining on her. Alouzon suddenly discovered that Dindrane was at her side.

"What the hell are you doing here?"

"Assisting my Goddess," came the reply. "Where are we going?"

"To my car, but the gate—"

Dindrane shook her head and pointed at the long shadows that were streaking the campus. The sun had risen: the passage into Gryylth was no more.

Accompanied by the priestess, pursued by the Specter and by the rising sounds of sirens and police helicopters, Alouzon sprinted across Dickson Court and rounded the corner of Murphy Hall. There, waiting in the parking lot, was her Volkswagen. She shoved Dindrane into the passenger seat and scrambled behind the wheel, afraid that, at any moment, she might feel a blast of hot breath on her back—as deadly as a claymore mine—followed by the crunch of opalescent teeth.

The sky was turning to the gray of smog and haze as she pulled out of the lot. The VW squealed down Circle Drive East and out onto Hilgard just as the black-and-whites were pulling onto the campus, the officers in them more concerned with frantic reports of hounds, Dragons, and armed warriors than with what were obviously two student types heading home after an all-night study session.

But once on Hilgard, Alouzon poured on the gas, and the VW, protesting, sped down the street. Eventually, she knew, her speed and her erratic driving—not to mention the inevitable attacks from the Specter—were going to attract attention, and the police would close in. But for now she was concerned only with putting as much distance as she could between herself and the hellish vision of war and slaughter that was beginning to search for her.

Dindrane watched owlishly as Alouzon sped up the ramp of the northbound San Diego Freeway. The priestess' hands, slick with nervous sweat, were tight on her staff, but her expression was trusting.

Alouzon swung immediately into the fast lane, urged the VW up to top speed. She glanced at Dindrane. "Sorry about this."

The priestess nodded. "My Lady," she said formally, "whatever comes is acceptable."

The unconditional trust shook Alouzon, but she kept her right foot pressed to the floor. "I love you, Dindrane."

"And I you, Great Lady."

This early, the freeway was mercifully clear, and Alouzon had no difficulty keeping her speed up by switching lanes and passing slower vehicles. But while she drove, she was calculating. A ten-gallon tank of gas, freshly filled, and twenty-five miles to the gallon. Two hundred fifty miles then, at least. Far enough to make, say, San Luis Obispo, or maybe even Monterey. But what then? The Specter did not have to worry about gas, or about eating, or, in fact, about anything save killing a certain Alouzon Dragonmaster and bringing to a final, hopeless conclusion the tale of blood and destruction that had started with hound attacks on Vaylle and the bombing of Bandon.

A crash. The VW careened to the side. Alouzon fought with the wheel and barely succeeded in pulling out of a fatal skid. Sweeping ahead and out to the right, gaining altitude after its attack, the Worm was beating great wings and swinging around for another pass in spite of Silbakor's efforts to intercept it.

Dindrane struggled to turn around. "How can I get to the rear of this . . . automobile?"

Speeding, passing cars, braced for another clanging impact from the Worm's talons, Alouzon explained how to recline the seat. Dindrane nodded, flopped it back, and clambered into the rear. Darting a quick look upward, Alouzon noticed that the Worm's claws had left dents and holes in the roof.

Another crash, but not from the Worm: Dindrane had smashed the rear window with her staff. A pause, and then the sudden sense of warmth and health that infused the car told Alouzon that the priestess was drawing energy into the consecrated wood.

"Steady, Goddess . . ."

With a soundless concussion that was so ephemeral that Alouzon sensed it with her mind more than her body, Dindrane's staff flared and sent a bolt of healing straight at the white face and eyes of void sweeping in from behind. A scream from the Worm told of a direct hit.

" 'Tis backing up," said the priestess proudly.

The VW strained up the slope of the pass, its speed, maddeningly, decreasing. Alouzon dropped to a lower gear, and the automobile responded with a lunge. "Thanks."

" 'Tis my duty, Goddess."

"Well, thanks anyway."

The Worm and the Specter were undeterred. Mounting abruptly into the sky, they struggled once again with Silbakor, and the Great Dragon's belly was sliced open by the Specter's sword. Blood welled out, and pieces of Dragon were shredded into the air, pinwheeling against the dawn like chunks of night.

The Worm plummeted down on the VW. Alouzon swerved across three lanes, but the talons found her hood, lifted, and threw the VW onto its back. The car skidded madly up onto the shoulder of the road and bounced off the guard rails, then, with a shriek of metal on asphalt, it lost speed and finally dumped itself off the pavement and onto the bare dirt, righting itself with a final lurch.

Alouzon's vision was swimming. She blinked stupidly at the mountains and the sky.

And from somewhere close by came a voice:

". . . weather service indicates no let up in the heat wave before the weekend. High today is expected to be a sizzling one hundred and five, with a low tonight in the mid-eighties . . ."

She blinked again, shook her head, found herself staring at the dashboard radio. The voice and a trickle of blood winding its way down the side of her nose told her that she must have struck the on/off switch with her forehead.

". . . KHJ News Radio time is seven-thirty . . ."

Her hands were not working, and she lay as one anesthetized. Memories and thoughts drifted through her mind, random and incoherent. She saw bits and pieces of Gryylth, of an army of healers and warriors forming up and assaulting the slopes of Kingsbury Hill. She saw the grinning faces of hounds and the impassive, vacant eyes of the Grayfaces. And—lastly and most strangely—she saw the rotting features of Solomon Braithwaite, still and dead in his coffin.

The professor's eyes opened suddenly and fixed her with their glazed stare. Alouzon cried out and struggled towards consciousness, but the withered corpse-hands grabbed her and held her. "I told you I'd help you, girl," said the dead man in a voice like the rustle of rotting leaves. "Take advantage of it."

"H-how?"

The glassy eyes bored into her. "I'm here, dammit. Use your pathetically over-educated head."

". . . and, turning to local news headlines: the body of the unknown woman found in the wreckage of the house of noted feminist author and lecturer Helen Addams has been identified as that of Suzanne Leah Helling, a graduate student at UCLA."

The vision faded. The VW came back. Dindrane was sprawled beside her, and the sound of far-off screaming was paradoxically loud. Forcing her hands to grab the steering wheel, Alouzon hauled herself up and stared through the windshield. Thirty feet away, Silbakor was grappling with the Worm, and the Specter was cutting into the Great Dragon with its sword.

"Police say they know of no connection between the two women, and the cause of the destruction of the house is still unknown."

Bruised and cut, Dindrane was struggling back to her senses. "A-Alouzon?"

"Right here."

"That voice . . ."

Alouzon switched off the radio, reached for the ignition key. The engine coughed into life. "Don't worry about it."

"O Goddess—"

Pain and fright had shortened Alouzon's temper, and she was tired of Dindrane's insistent formalities. "Call me Alouzon, dammit. Now hang on: this is gonna be rough."

Dindrane scrambled into her seat. After revving the engine for a moment, Alouzon popped the clutch, and the VW suddenly surged forward in a cloud of dust. The Worm, about to deliver a killing stroke to the struggling Dragon, jerked its head up at the sudden motion; but before it could move, Alouzon smashed the car straight into it.

The Worm was thrown off balance; and not only did it dump the Specter on the ground, but—wings flailing, head reared back—it left itself open for a lunge from Silbakor, and the Dragon's black teeth tore a gaping rent in the pale throat. Ichor and mucus spilled out onto the bare ground, smoking where they touched. Crippled, screaming, the Worm floundered.

Satisfied that she had given Silbakor a fighting chance, Alouzon guided the VW back onto the freeway. The car was damaged, but it was still mobile, and, lurching and coughing, it picked up speed.

She looked up through the windshield. Police helicopters were circling. Ground forces would be on their way.

I'm dead, Solomon had said once. *I'm supposed to know a few things.*

Alouzon drove on. "Didn't you say once that the God dies and is reborn, Dindrane?"

"Indeed. Surely. But Solomon . . ." The priestess passed a hand over her face, struggling with her griefs. "But Solomon was a man, and not a very good one at that."

I'm supposed to know a few things.

"Maybe so," said Alouzon, "but I think he had more to him than we gave him credit for." The front alignment of the VW had been thrown completely off, and the car shuddered down the asphalt as though shaken by a terrier; but Alouzon forced herself to accelerate. ''I think he's still got some things to do. You might find that your devotion wasn't so misplaced after all.''

She prayed that her words—and her suspicions— were right. For now she was following Solomon's advice and his offer of help. She was heading for the cemetery where he was buried.

❖ CHAPTER 22 ❖

Heartbeats before the sun rose over the eastern plains of Gryylth and severed all connection with Los Angeles, Kyria and Jia ran out of the gate in the Camrann Mountains. Panting, her robes soaked with sweat of her magical and physical exertions, the sorceress collapsed into the arms of Santhe and Marrha.

"I was afraid we had lost you, beloved," said Santhe. His strong arms upheld her, and his smile, though strained, was as much a tonic as the cup of water he held to her lips.

She drank. "No," she said between breaths. "Almost, but not quite."

"What of Alouzon and Dindrane?"

"They stayed behind to draw the Specter away from us."

Santhe looked grave. "They are truly heroes."

"Dindrane, perhaps, is a hero," said Marrha. "But Alouzon is a Goddess."

Her words, blunt and incontrovertible, hung in the cool dawn air. Someone had finally said aloud what everyone had been thinking, and no one objected or protested. It was simple fact.

Cvinthil, though, was staring out across the plains, his arms folded. "Our friend Alouzon has her battles," he said softly. "And we have ours."

He fell silent. Kyria looked up from Santhe's arms, followed the king's gaze, and gasped.

Alouzon had tried to convey something of the destruction that had been wrought on the land, but as the sun rose higher and lit the rolling downs and meadows with the warm light of late August, it showed her words inadequate. Destruction, waste, devastation: all these were paltry descriptions when applied to fields that lay burnt to a uniform grayness as though by acid. Forests—Kyria had to guess that they were forests—were no more than heaped and tumbled ruins crisscrossed by the tracks of napalm and bomb strikes, and even the rivers and streams appeared to have dried up where they were not clogged with dust and eroded topsoil.

The men and women of the army stared in shock and dismay, and the Vayllens huddled together like frightened children. They had thought that they knew what lay ahead. But their thoughts had never grappled with such absolute, terrible negation of life.

"Speak to us, sorceress," said Cvinthil. "Do you have anything to say that might help the kings of Corrin and of Gryylth?"

"It is . . ." The sun lifted into the sky over blank plains. Kyria felt her powers overshadowed by the magnitude of what she was seeing. "It is what are called defoliants, mostly," she said. "Things that . . . that kill the plant life."

"Will it go away in time?"

Kyria stared. She knew the answer. She was unwilling to say it.

Cvinthil turned to her. His eyes were sad. "Please, sorceress. Advise me."

"It will take years, I fear."

Darham was frowning. His big arms were folded, and his eyes were fixed on the horizon as though trying to peer across the distances. If this was Gryylth, then what of Corrin? "Can you make it fertile again?"

Kyria felt herself sag. Could she make it fertile again? With mighty powers she could blast B-52s out of the air. With more subtle energies she could heal.

But turning a desert the size of England into a garden was something else.

Cvinthil was waiting. Kyria shook her head, overwhelmed. "I . . . will try."

Her uncertainty was obvious, and therefore her words gave no comfort. Cvinthil passed his hands over his face. "It has been a very long and a very hot night," he said in a whisper. "We should rest. I am . . ." His voice broke, then firmed. "I am sure that it is not safe to travel by day in this place. We will start at twilight." He lifted his head. "Harpers and healers of Vaylle?"

A senior priestess dismounted and came forward. She was a solid, matronly woman, and her blond hair, though shot with gray, was bright in the dawn. "What do you wish, King Cvinthil?"

The king spoke with courtesy. "Dindrane has stayed behind with Alouzon. I have no authority over you or your harpers. May I ask you if you are willing to stay with us and obey our commands?"

The priestess considered. Loyal and trusting, the Vayllens had followed Dindrane into the company of warriors and through Los Angeles, but in Gryylth they faced not only the horrors of war but also the obscenity of a defoliated and wasted land. And now Dindrane was gone.

But the priestess nodded at last. " 'Tis certain I could say, lord, that we have very little choice. But our trust for our High Priestess goes beyond her presence or absence, and since she thought it fitting that we aid you, then surely we will. We ask only that you do not look to us for fighting or killing, for sworn against such things we are."

Cvinthil bowed to her. "Our deepest thanks, priestess."

Together, Cvinthil and Darham gave orders for a camp to be set up, and for the wagons to be assembled in preparation for an evening march. "And what of Hahle?" said Darham. "Is he not to meet us here?"

"He will be here soon," said Cvinthil. "I wish now that I had listened to the man more, but I know him well enough to say that."

But Cvinthil fell abruptly silent and turned again to the gray and blackened plains. Kyria read his thoughts. He was responsible. He had ignored Hahle, he had trusted Helwych, he had forsaken his land.

"Lord," she said softly, "you could have done no more than Helwych against the Specter."

"I know," he said after a time. "And perhaps I and all my people went to Vaylle in order to bring back a sorceress who can defeat such weapons."

Kyria felt herself grow warm. As Cvinthil and the others had once looked to Alouzon, so they now looked to her. "My king," she said with a faltering curtsy, "I will in all ways strive to do what is best for our land."

Cvinthil's face was deeply troubled. "Gryylth," he said softly, "has been destroyed. It will take the hand of a God to restore it."

Kyria was afraid that his words were true.

Something was wrong.

It was not that the prying, omniscient eyes had suddenly disappeared from Helwych's inner sight, though that, in fact, was disturbing enough. Nor was it that the Grayfaces and hounds in the land were suddenly shifting their loyalties to him almost without effort on his part, though that was indeed raising his suspicions. No, it was rather that his perception of the land, the subtle sensation he carried with him as he carried his own name and identity, had abruptly shifted.

He swept his disembodied vision over the face of Gryylth and, impossibly, caught sight of troops and wagons, of men and women in armor, of bright Vayllen garments and vestments, of shining harps and harpstrings, of swords and consecrated staves of healing.

And there was something else, too. Robed in deep

blue, a cluster of silver stars at her shoulder, a woman rode at the head of the army, and her brooch bore the arms of the king of Gryylth. She carried no staff, for her hands and her mind and her will were enough; and when she appeared suddenly to become aware of his scrutiny, black eyes that had nothing to do with the void of the Specter or the Worm met his, and Helwych sensed power and determination. Her pale hands went up then, and his sight was suddenly clouded.

The vision vanished, and though he tried to will it back, it would not return. Alarmed, he summoned energies to himself, and the Grayfaces and hounds across the land lifted their heads and turned instantly to do his bidding. At an inward command from the young sorcerer, they set out for Kingsbury.

A day, and they would begin to arrive. Another day beyond that, and the army and its pale sorceress would find themselves pitted against both magic and enormous reserves of weaponry.

He opened his eyes. About him in the Hall were his personal Grayface guards and the one or two soldiers that he still permitted to attend him. The young man who now wore the ensign of the captain of the King's Guard noticed his movement and saluted. The sorcerer could not remember his name, but that was unimportant. He asked only that his orders be obeyed.

"Send to the troops in the other refugee towns, captain," said Helwych. "Send with all possible speed. Tell them to make for Kingsbury immediately."

"But lord," said the lad, "the Specter. The battles. What if—"

Helwych was on his feet instantly, raging. "Do not tell me about battles, sir. The only battles in the land will be the ones that I will fight to save your miserable skin. And I will save Kingsbury if I have to raze it to the ground. Go! Fetch your men and tell them they are to hold the city against—"

He caught himself. Against whom? Against the rightful king? He could not say that.

"Against whatever comes," he finished lamely, and, with an impatient gesture, he sat down. The young man ran to follow his orders.

Kingsbury Hill could be defended against conventional forces with a handful of men. And magic, bullets, and bombs would settle the sorceress. It was only a matter of time and effort.

He sat back, annoyed to discover that he was shaking. He hid his trembling hands in the sleeves of his robe, and when he looked up, Seena was standing in the shadows close to the wall.

"What do you want?" he snapped.

Seena only regarded him levelly.

"Go attend to your children, Seena."

The queen of Gryylth turned away. "Yes," she said. "I will attend to them."

Something about her tone made Helwych uneasy.

As Cvinthil had expected, Hahle arrived as the camp was being broken in the early twilight, bringing with him a score of men from Quay. With the exception of a few youngsters like Myylen, they were almost all older fishers who had some skill with a club or an axe. But though they had traveled much of the day, they fell in with the assembled columns without comment, for their king needed them, and a night without sleep was a small thing compared to a usurper on the throne of Gryylth and a dead land.

But what took even Kyria by surprise was the appearance, an hour after the army had started off into the falling shadows, of four riders silhouetted against the indigo sky. Side by side, a hint of threat in their manner, they blocked the road where it climbed a low rise.

Cvinthil signaled a halt. "Who comes?" he said, his voice even, his hand hovering near the pommel of his sword.

"We seek Cvinthil, king of Gryylth, and Darham, king of Corrin," came the reply. "I am Relys of the

First Wartroop, and with me are Timbrin and Gelyya.
Tylha of Benardis, commander of the women's phalanxes of Corrin, is also here.''

Cvinthil was already riding forward. "Relys! Timbrin!'' But where before he might have leaped to the
ground and rushed to them with hasty enthusiasm, now
he trotted up and saluted them in the manner of a king:
warmly, heartily, but with dignity. "I am very glad to
see you, my dear friends. Alouzon told me of your
trials. Your names rank among the honored of
Gryylth.''

Relys smiled thinly, equally reserved. "Our thanks,
lord.''

But Cvinthil had been followed closely by Darham,
and at the latter's approach, Tylha dismounted, drew
her sword, and dropped to one knee. "My king,'' she
said, offering the weapon to him, "Relys arrived with
the news of your coming, and I thought it best to meet
you.''

Even in the failing light, it was easy to see Darham's
joy. Leaning down from the saddle, he touched the hilt
of Tylha's sword. "Well met, commander. What word
comes from Corrin?''

"Good and bad both, my king. The hounds attack
nightly, but torches and clubs hold them off tolerably
well. And as yet the Grayfaces and what Gelyya calls
jets have not intruded.''

Darham looked relieved. "I thank the Gods . . .''
He paused. Alouzon was a sudden presence. "I thank
the Goddess that you were there, Tylha. But what now?
Have you come alone?''

Tylha stood up, grinning broadly. "Trust me not to
arrive at the banquet without a gift of wine,'' she said.
"The doughty housewives of Corrin defend their
homes for the time being, for behind this ridge are ten
phalanxes spoiling for a fight, eager to help our Gryylthan brethren overthrow a countryman who has proven
himself a traitor to all.''

Darham laughed with delight, and Cvinthil reached

down and took Tylha's hand. "Welcome, commander," he said. "I would I could show you a feast and a soft bed in Hall Kingsbury, but . . ."

Tylha saluted him. "That, my lord, will come later, I am sure."

But Marrha had gone quietly to Relys and Timbrin. "Dear friends," she said. "I grieved at the tale of your afflictions."

Relys's right hand was a misshapen mess of swelling and scars, and so she reached out and gripped Marrha's in her left. "I am glad to see you, my captain. I hope you are well."

The tears on Marrha's face glistened in the twilight. "I am indeed well. Thank you, Relys."

"Your . . ." Relys stared, then spoke as though frightened. "Your hair is braided, my captain."

Marrha smiled with quiet pride. "I am married, Relys. I have taken Karthin for a husband."

Relys's face went slack. "Oh."

"I bear our child."

A long pause. Finally: "May . . . may your time be easy, my captain."

Kyria, her senses augmented by magic and her emotions still raw from the unrelieved wasteland about her, picked up the torment that gripped Relys as though she had been struck with a lance. Relys was terrified, and yet determined not to show it.

Terrified? Of what? Of Marrha?

But with an almost visible effort, Relys steeled herself, nodded, and brought Gelyya forward with a gesture. "My king, my captain," she said formally, "I present to you Gelyya of Bandon. She bears strange weapons, but she has shown herself as brave a warrior as any man or woman of Gryylth. I commend her to you for training and admission to the ranks of the First Wartroop."

Gelyya's skirts and aprons were gone: she was clad in the clothing of a boy of Corrin. But though she did not look like a boy, neither did she resemble in any

way the girl who had once ministered to the women
and children of Kingsbury. In her hand was an M16,
and from a web belt about her waist hung ammunition
clips and several grenades. The look in her eyes said
that experience had taught her their use. "Gods
bless," she said.

"Gelyya learned much of the Grayface ways during
our journey to Corrin," Relys explained. "There were
many corpses with weapons intact, and she had ample
time to examine them. She knows their use and their
limitations. But for her we would not have survived."

Marrha nodded contemplatively. "A new warrior,"
she said softly, almost to herself. "And a woman
among women." But then she lifted her head. "However, it is not for us to accept or reject her. That is
your decision, Captain Relys."

"Marrget! I am your lieutenant!"

"Nay," said Marrha. "You are the captain of the
First Wartroop. And I am Marrha now: a warrior, true,
but a wife and a mother also." Her gray eyes were as
uncompromising as ever: she spoke as a soldier who
had been given new duties. "After this last battle, I
will have other tasks ahead of me for a time, and therefore I give the First Wartroop into your hands." She
turned to Cvinthil. "With your permission, my king."

Marrha's sentiments surprised no one who had
known her during the last months. "It is well," said
Cvinthil. "But I do not release you from my service,
Marrha of Crownhark. I name you councilor of
Gryylth, and I look forward to hearing your advice in
Hall Kingsbury." Marrha gave a nod of acceptance.

The columns started off once again through the
wasted hills, their numbers augmented by the women's
phalanxes, and, come dawn, with Kingsbury in sight,
the men and women camped behind a fold of the
mountains. Kyria redoubled her cloaking magic, casting the invisibility across the mundane spectrum as
well as the magical, but the rising light showed plainly
the fortifications that now encircled the capital. The

earthworks at the edge of the plateau had been strengthened and expanded, and barbed wire and sandbagged strong points ringed the foot of the hill. Floodlights were only now being shut down for the day, and Kyria recognized the uplifted barrels of heavy artillery.

As the morning progressed, the kings and their advisors discussed strategies for the battle that lay ahead, slowly assembling a combination of feint, direct assault, and infiltration that might survive an encounter with artillery and air strikes. They did not comprehend the technology that was arrayed against them, but they did not have to: it was enough for Kyria to explain the striking power of the weapons.

But inwardly, Kyria's worries and doubts were increasing. Though she knew that the powers she commanded were almost inexhaustible, she had, in the uncompromising reality of the wounded land, been confronted with their limitations. And now she was faced with the complicated problem of using such destructive energies not only in the middle of a conventional battle, but also in the proximity of women and children.

Women and children. Starving. Dying. And more children climbing the slopes of their hill beneath a barrage of magic and bullets. She had said it herself, once, in a different life, but her sentiments had not changed: *Why is it always the goddam kids?*

Kingsbury and its defenses stood clear and distinct in the sunlight, challenging the ingenuity of the kings and their warriors, defying Kyria and her powers. She brooded on the sight.

"Sorceress?"

She lifted her head, almost startled by Darham's deep voice. "I cannot guarantee . . ." she paused, swallowed, found herself unable to continue.

Darham examined her with wise eyes. "There are no guarantees in war," he said, "nor do we ask for them. We have lost some to the hounds. We have lost some to . . ." He looked off at the hill. "To traitors. We will doubtless lose some to Grayfaces and to swords." He shook his head. "It is the lot of a warrior."

Kyria faced him, hands clenched. "It is not the lot of women and children," she said.

Cvinthil bowed his head, looked away. His wife, his son, and his daughter were in Kingsbury.

The council ended, but as Kyria turned for her blankets and for Santhe's arms, Relys detained her. "Mistress sorceress," she said, "may I speak with you?"

Again, Kyria sensed the fear in the captain, but she hid her knowledge and smiled gently. "Of course you may speak with me, captain."

Obviously unused to asking favors, Relys hung her head. "Mistress sorceress," she said at last, "tomorrow will be a great battle, and I would not enter into it maimed." She lifted the scarred mess that was her right hand. "Alouzon said that you might be willing . . . to heal me."

Again, the flash of tormented fear. Kyria knew how Relys had lost her hand, but she could not understand how a reasonable request for healing could be the cause of such distress. "I would be happy to heal your hand, Captain Relys. After so much talk of warfare and death, I would find healing to be a great pleasure."

And, taking Relys's damaged hand in her own, Kyria called up the energies that would recreate the lost flesh and restore what was damaged. But as Relys's hand turned incandescent, as the missing fingers coalesced out of living light and took on the properties of solid flesh, Kyria, by necessity deeply engrossed in Relys's being, suddenly understood the cause of her fear.

She was pregnant.

Relys herself was not sure, but she suspected, and that was quite enough. Continuing with the healing almost absently, Kyria looked a little further into Relys's mind and emotions and saw there the stark fear and horror that seethed as poisonously as the phosphor in the maw of a hound.

Confirmation of the pregnancy would bring to fruition all the shame, abuse, torment, and pain that Relys had suffered, would put a capstone of permanency on the arch of degradation and violation that Helwych had so casually constructed. If it did not kill her outright and physically, then it would slowly and inwardly, eating away at the proud soul until it faltered and was no more.

Helwych, you fiend.

Sickened by the obviousness and the inevitability of her response, Kyria prepared herself, altered the energies; and when Relys's hand had healed without a blemish, when the muscles and bones and tendons were as healthy as they had ever been, Kyria continued but a moment longer with her magic, turning it briefly to another end.

A moment. Only a moment. And then she was done.

Why is it always the goddam kids?

Forcing a smile, Kyria released Relys's hand, and as the captain examined it, eyes wide, Kyria saw the brief upwelling—immediately suppressed—of tears of gratitude. "My . . . thanks, mistress sorceress."

"It was . . ." Kyria's smile had turned brittle, tragic, but she cloaked her emotions. "It was nothing. Is there . . . anything else I can do for you, captain?"

Relys hesitated. She wanted to know. She had to know. She was afraid to ask.

Kyria nodded. In order to heal in heart as well as in body, Relys had to know. "Ask, my friend. What passes between us will stay between us."

Relys's shame was a breaking wave, her voice almost inaudible. "Kyria . . . I am afraid that . . . that I might be . . . with . . ."

"With child?" said Kyria softly.

"Aye." The captain choked. "That."

Kyria shook her head. "Fear not, captain. You are not pregnant. I am a sorceress. I know."

And, indeed, she did know. Relys stared with relief, her tears breaking free at last.

"Be easy," said Kyria. "Go now and rest."

And when Relys thanked her again and, weeping, turned away, Kyria sought out her beloved Santhe and curled up at his side. Sleepily, the councilor kissed her and folded his arms about her, but Kyria knew that she herself would not sleep. Nor were Santhe's arms such a comforting refuge anymore.

The kids. Why is it always the kids?

The Volkswagen shuddered and rattled along the Ventura Freeway, but Alouzon could maintain a speed of no more than forty-five miles an hour. Even so, the car was in the process of shaking itself apart, and she fought with the wheel, willing the vehicle to stay together long enough to reach the cemetery. *Just a little farther, dammit, just a little farther.*

In the back seat, Dindrane, bleeding and bruised, was holding off the Specter and the wounded Worm with blasts of healing; and Silbakor swooped and attacked from the air, keeping the police helicopters at bay, intercepting the Worm's descents and smashing it away from the Beetle with slaps of its huge wings. The Great Dragon was wounded, true, but now so was the Worm. Alouzon, in interfering with a confrontation that would surely have been fatal to Silbakor, had succeeded in her objective: she had evened the odds.

But only for Silbakor. She still had an impending confrontation with the Specter; and as she neared the cemetery, she wondered what Solomon's corpse, dead now these nine months, could accomplish.

No matter. She was willing to grasp at straws now, however flimsy they appeared. While Dindrane abruptly shifted her powers to the police cars that were closing in—confusing the officers to the extent that they missed the exit completely and, in fact, became unsure of what had happened to the Volkswagen altogether—Alouzon bowled down the Pass Avenue off ramp,

shuddered and skidded around the turn, and headed
south.

"We're almost there, Dindrane."

The priestess did not have the time or the strength
to reply, but Alouzon, deciphering the blurred images
in the vibrating rear view mirror, saw a nod as Dindrane sent another wave of golden light out toward the
approaching Worm.

A turn onto a broad avenue that skirted the mountains, then, and in a minute, the gates of the cemetery
came into view. Tall, sturdy, made of thick, wrought
iron that lent a sense of peaceful gentility to the orderly graves within, they were at this early hour closed
and padlocked.

Alouzon did not stop. Despite ethical questions of
trespassing and sacrilege, she had to get into the cemetery. Shouting for Dindrane to brace herself, she
floored the accelerator, aimed the shuddering wheels
straight at the gates, and rammed them.

The wrought iron buckled, the chain stretched. But
they held. Alouzon and Dindrane scrambled out of the
wrecked car to find that their way into the cemetery
was still blocked, and the police sirens, guided by the
circling helicopters, were approaching once more.

The iron fence was over ten feet tall, the sharpened
tips of the uprights bent outward. There was no time
to climb, and though the Dragonsword had shown itself capable of splitting solid oak, Alouzon did not
want to risk an attempt to cut her way through.

"Silbakor! Get your ass down here!"

The Dragon responded, batting the bleeding Worm
away with a quick slash of its talons and roaring down
at the cemetery gates, its wounds scattering chunks of
darkness through the air. Just before it reached the
women, it leveled out, flared its wings, and extended
its claws.

With a leap, Alouzon and Dindrane seized Silbakor's feet and were lofted over the fence and across
the even rows of gravestones and memorial markers.

Alouzon peered down, deciphered the meandering avenues below, called directions to the Dragon. At her command, it descended and slowed once again.

They dropped to the grass, tumbling their momentum away. Dindrane had caught her arm on one of the razor-sharp talons and was bleeding freely from the crook of her right elbow, but Alouzon dragged her to her feet, thrust her staff into her hands, and set off up a grassy slope. At the top, surrounded by birch trees, was Solomon's grave.

But the Specter was already there, standing between her and the grave, waiting for her with drawn sword.

❖ **Chapter 23** ❖

Why is it always the kids?

Kyria's initial salvo, unleashed just at moonrise, tore into the Grayface emplacements at the base of Kingsbury Hill like a tidal wave of violet passion. Melting barbed wire, leveling sandbagged strong points as though they were made of cardboard boxes, flinging mortars and 155-millimeter artillery to the ground with such force that the weapons were bent and crumpled beyond use, the bolt drove on and on. It charred the ground halfway up the slope, uprooting and incinerating bushes and even tall trees as it surged forward; and only when it reached the earthwork defenses at the lip of the plateau was its incandescent fury finally spent.

Why is it always the goddam kids?

Within a few moments, the potencies had cleared the hill of Grayface defenses, and the Gryylthan and Corrinian infantry that had readied itself under cover of darkness and magic now attacked up the slope.

While they moved—running quickly, occupying the ruined Grayface positions, spreading out so as to offer less of a target to mortars and air strikes—Kyria, standing on a small rise to the north of the hill, struck the tears from her face, shoved back her sleeves, and prepared for the inevitable reprisal. Helwych, she knew, would counterstrike, and not only with magic: he had more weapons and more Grayfaces stationed

within the perimeter of the town—sheltered from her
blasts by the presence of women and children.

Women and children. And why, she wondered bitterly, should that stop her anymore?

In a moment, dull thuds from the top of the hill
announced the firing of mortars, and the occupied positions were raked by machine gun fire. Tracers were
an orange rain in the darkness. Mortar rounds detonated in brief kindlings, puffs of smoke, and spreading
pressure waves that made the stars shimmer with their
passage.

The kids . . .

Kids in the town. Kids on the hill. Kids in other
parts of the country. With her own words—foreign,
angry—ringing in her mind, Kyria countered, smashing her energies against the earthworks in a wave of
lethal silver as the foot soldiers who had taken the base
of the hill dug in, throwing up barricades of sandbags,
refuse, and even Grayface bodies to shield themselves
from the automatic fire that ravaged their positions.

A minute later, the scream of jet engines announced
an imminent air strike.

Grimly, the infantry stayed put, hugging the earth,
pressing themselves against soil that at any moment
might erupt beneath them in a concussion of high explosive and a hail of razor-edged shrapnel. They were
counting on Kyria to turn the weapons and the magic
away.

Impelled by mixed sorrow and rage, the flow of
power from the sorceress was a geyser of white heat
that soared up from her lifted hands and flung itself at
the fortifications. The machine gun emplacements exploded in violet flames and a rattle of detonating ammunition.

And how many did I kill that time?

There were a hundred possibilities that she tried to
keep from her thoughts. Helwych was quite capable of
herding the refugees into the trenches and the barricades, there to be slaughtered by the very magic de-

signed to set them free. And perhaps there were
infants—newborns, toddlers—strapped alongside the
M60s and the mortars, screaming themselves black
with each concussion, dying in the fire of magic that
lapped about the plateau like a sea of magma.

And Relys's child . . . but Relys would never know.
Never.

The infantry struggled a few yards forward and dug
in again, cheering as Cvinthil and Santhe led a picked
troop of cavalry up the slope, leaping craters and
dodging the scattering of fire that attempted to track
them. The Skyhawks were lining up for a bombing
run, though, and Kyria shifted spells, altered potencies, and battered the warplanes away. Tumbling to the
ground in long arcs of burning fuel, they exploded in
fireballs that lit the hill like torches. Smoke mush-
roomed into the air and obscured the faint moonlight.

Cvinthil and his troop climbed further towards the
fortifications, and for a moment, aside from the crackle
and snap of burning jet fuel and melting aluminum,
there was silence about Kingsbury Hill. But the lull
was abruptly shattered by a deep groaning, a rumbling
and a tumult that struggled up from the earth and
stone, gathered itself into a roiling cloud of unlight,
and, with a sound as of shouting voices and a flash of
blue-black void, launched itself through the air.

Helwych had turned to direct magic, the magic of
the Specter, of pure, heedless destruction. Had his
spell been aimed to follow the contour of the hill, it
would have instantly scoured it clean, stripped it even
of topsoil and left it a gleaming, fused monolith of
naked bedrock, a vitreous waste more permanent and
barren than that which now constituted most of
Gryylth. But it was not directed at the army. Helwych
was, instead, striking for Kyria, unleashing powers
against which he was sure she had no defense.

Had he acted a day before, he might have been right,
but despite all her worry and doubt and grief at what
she had done and what she could not do—and, maybe,

she admitted, *because* of them—Kyria, the real Kyria, now had full access to all her powers, glorious and tragic both.

Lifting her arms, she called up the memory of her dead children, the hopelessness of her former life, the utter despair of the dirty warehouse and the blood-stained table, and, eschewing rage, rejecting even the faintest shred of anger, she forced herself to find in those symbols of death and powerlessness the promise of something better.

It could be otherwise. It *would* be otherwise.

She felt something give within her, a snapping as of corroded heartstrings, perhaps; and as Cvinthil and his cavalry continued their charge straight up to the edge of the earthworks, defying the darkness that towered above them like an angry fist, the rise upon which she stood was suddenly enveloped in light the color of a hand held up to the sun, and—shining, throbbing like a live thing—it rose up, seized the cloud of unlight, and squeezed it into nothingness.

Kyria sagged, weeping, as Cvinthil's voice rang out, calling upon the Gryylthan soldiers within the walls of the town to renew their allegiance to him and join the fight against the usurper. There was no answer, but a burst of fire from an M16 cut his horse out from under him, and he had just enough time to drop behind the carcass before the dead flesh was shredded into a bloody froth.

Mouth set, Kyria stilled the gun with a flicker of white heat. Santhe dragged Cvinthil up behind him and, with a shout, led the cavalry back down the slope, leaving Helwych's wartroops to their realization, their horror, and their treason. In the brief lull, the infantry advanced a little further up the slope and dug in again.

Now came the sound of helicopters and jets. Braced for another blow from Helwych, Kyria prepared her spells as, out on the dark hillside, points of golden light and the incongruous sound of chiming harpstrings testified that the healers and harpers of Vaylle were caring for the wounded.

The first jets streaked in, low and fast, and dropped their napalm. Kyria quelled the fire. Missiles streaked at the infantry. She knocked them aside. Helicopters dropped to the ground and disgorged gray, gas-masked figures; and as Kyria worked her magic against them, another bolt from Kingsbury soared through the air, threatening to incinerate her.

She looked within, confronted once again the despair, turned the bolt aside. And the battle continued.

"Give it up, girl. You can't take me."

The Specter, lean and swaggering in a three-piece suit, stood before Solomon's grave, daring Alouzon to approach. Its words were nothing new to her. *You can't take me.* You can't beat the system. You can't escape ·the draft. The war in Vietnam is impossible to win, but losing is unthinkable.

And here it was again. Futility. If Alouzon won, she lost. If the Specter won, she lost. And about Kingsbury, a battle that had perhaps become a moot contest over the ownership of a desert was raging. As in Vietnam, no one could win.

But unlike Vietnam, the issue here was not the saving of face or the victory of one political system over another. It was, rather, the fundamental existence of a world and a people. There was nothing for Alouzon to do but attack, and so she did. If it were humanly or divinely possible, she would extirpate this thing of reified destruction and slaughter from her inner self . . . and therefore from her world.

Caught off guard by her sudden rush, the Specter took a step back. Its polished oxfords made hollow sounds on Solomon's marker, crunching and sliding on the remnants of the flowers that, days ago, Suzanne Helling had placed on the grave along with a drop of blood and an adjuration to the dead man to awake and live again.

But as police sirens drew closer and Silbakor locked the White Worm in titanic combat above the treetops, the Specter drove back in, smashed Alouzon's guard down with a heavy blade, then turned and ripped back towards her throat. She fell back and ducked, and before her opponent could react, sprang forward again and aimed a vicious cut at its head.

But the blue-black eyes were laughing. The Specter knew as well as she the results of a killing blow. As though amused by the joke, it parried her blow and kicked her down the hillside.

"What are you going to tell the police, Allie?" it sneered. "What did you tell the National Guard?"

She struggled to her feet. "We told them they were murderers."

"And you know all about murder now, don't you?"

The Specter planted its feet and grew into a colossus the size of the trees that flanked Solomon's grave. Alouzon backed off, wondering how she was going to fight such a thing, but a golden wave of warmth and healing suddenly arose from behind her and drenched the Specter with a shimmer the color of warm honey.

The colossus vanished. The Specter was again man-sized.

Dindrane dismissed the energies and lowered her staff. The gash in the fold of her elbow was running with crimson, and the blood streaked her white skin as she pointed at the Specter. "If there has been murder," she said, " 'twas you who taught us of it."

The Specter's eyes narrowed. "Are you a boy," it mocked, "or a girl?"

Dindrane sneered back. "I am something you do not understand. Something you can never understand." She lifted her staff again.

The Specter flinched. "That arm of yours will never clot," it said. "You will bleed to death."

And, in accordance with its words, the blood welling from Dindrane's wound began to quicken. The priestess examined it, shrugged. "Then I will die knowing that I helped my Goddess."

"Helped her to what? To die?"

Dindrane replied with a raised staff, but the Specter batted the healing away and threw itself on Alouzon.

Swords met, clashed, parried, withdrew, clashed again. In the back of her mind, Alouzon knew that police cruisers were gathering in the parking lot while the cemetery attendants opened the gates, but she also knew that there could be no mundane resolution to this conflict. What could guns do against a being that was, in fact, all guns and all weapons and all destruction?

An unexpected kick from the Specter sent her reeling back across Solomon's grave, and she lost her grip on her sword as she fell heavily to the grass. Dindrane attempted another healing spell, but the Specter whipped around with a fist and sent her to the ground. As the priestess floundered, it turned back to Alouzon. "This is it, girl. You should have taken my offer in the temple. Now everyone's going to die."

Alouzon tensed for a quick lunge for her sword and a roll that might allow her to regain her feet. "Don't try to pin it on me, guy. You had this planned all along. You were going to make sure everyone died anyway."

The Specter bent over her, eyes boring into hers. "Maybe. But you'll never know now, will you?"

Could it ever have been otherwise? The Specter was as it was, so locked into its need for destruction that it could not exist otherwise. And so single-minded and obsessed was it that it could not even comprehend that, in killing Alouzon, it too would cease to exist.

Alouzon shook her head. "Just like Nam," she whispered, and the uselessness and the sorrow of it brought the tears to her eyes. "And you don't even know it. You know, dammit, I kinda feel sorry for you, you dumb schmuck."

Dindrane was staggering to her feet, groping for her staff. But her attention was not really on the staff, nor, in fact, on the Specter. Rather, she was staring at the ground directly behind it, staring at Solomon's grave.

The stone was moving.

As in Suzanne's vision at the cemetery, the ground was buckling as though thrust up from below. Soundlessly, the marker rose, wavered, then tipped back and fell, upside down, onto the thick grass. Dull, fevered light streamed into the morning sky.

As the Specter bent over Alouzon, hands appeared at the edge of the hole. They were withered hands, their flesh slimy with the action of anaerobic bacteria and the inevitable dissolution that followed death: the hands of a corpse.

And then with a stiff lurch, Solomon Braithwaite stood up in his grave, his face glowing with a focused rage, his eyes—glazed and yellow and dead—fixed on the Specter.

By dawn, the forces of Gryylth and Corrin had managed to take most of the slopes of the hill despite constant air strikes, automatic weapons fire from the defenses at the lip of the plateau, and a brutal deluge of 155-millimeter shells from Grayface artillery emplacements miles away from Kingsbury. But an impasse had been reached. Because the town was inhabited by refugees—diseased, starving, but nonetheless alive—Kyria would not bring greater force to bear on it, and Helwych's weapons, falling in a constant rain of death, precluded any further advance by the infantry and cavalry.

The sun rose, but the battleground remained shrouded in darkness: a prolongation of night arranged by Kyria for the benefit of the men and women still holding the slopes. But though the jets were thereby restricted to infra-red scanners, flares, and navigation points radioed by the besieged Grayfaces at the top of the hill, they continued to arrive laden with napalm and bombs, and the artillery shells continued to fall.

A few, inevitably, reached their targets.

After nearly five solid hours of work, the healers and harpers of Vaylle were nearing an exhaustion that was both physical and psychological. Priestesses sworn to peace found themselves confronted with shrapnel wounds, amputated limbs, and dismembered bodies; and harpers who had once made music by the quiet bedsides of the sick now plucked their bronze strings with blistered and bloody fingers, playing as loudly as they could in order to be heard over the shriek of jets, the coarse ripping of M60s, and the mingled screams of falling shells and the mortally wounded.

Kyria worked on, blasting the jets, quelling the outbreaks of fire from the defenses, incinerating the helicopters before they could touch down and release their platoons of Grayfaces. But she too was wearing down, and she knew it. The stalemate had to be broken.

Near noon, Helwych's attacks—mundane and magical—broke off, doubtless, Kyria thought, because the sorcerer was as tired as she. The infantry on the hill held its positions, ready for any chance to rush and breach the wall, but Kyria, still deep in her magic, detected riders approaching her. After a startled moment she realized that they were friends: Cvinthil and Darham, their councilors, and a few captains of the phalanxes and wartroops.

The men and women who dismounted were tired, dirty, and their eyes were full of the death and blood they had seen. But in the slump of their shoulders there was also a sense of futility: Helwych was holding against the might of three nations, and he showed no sign of any weakening.

Tersely, their voices heavy with fatigue, the allies exchanged reports. A Vayllen priestess told of the exhaustion of her people, and Kyria explained what she knew of Helwych's position.

"He continues, eh?" said Marrha.

"Indeed," said Kyria. "He is controlled by the same forces that formed the Specter, and he draws his

strength from them. And more Grayfaces will be arriving from the east by morning.''

Darham was frowning. ''It cannot go on this way.
The numbers of the wounded have already outstripped
the Vayllens' ability to heal. Men and women are dying out in the open, and often the fire is so heavy that
their comrades cannot reach them.''

Marrha turned to Kyria. ''It appears that, once
again, we need a another way. And this time we cannot wait.''

Relys was calculating, her eyes hard. ''I think I understand such things now.''

Kyria stared at her for an instant, then turned away
as though to reconnoiter the hill.

Wykla, standing at Darham's elbow as a princess of
Corrin, spoke up. ''Alouzon, Manda, and I entered
Kingsbury unseen and made our way to the house of
Kallye the midwife.'' She paused, lips pressed together, jaw clenched. Everyone knew about Kallye.
Everyone from Kingsbury had loved her. ''The Gods
will hear her name,'' she said softly. ''But could not
some of us, with the help of darkness and magic, make
our way into the town once again and—?''

''And crush the adder's head?'' said Relys. ''I would
like that indeed.''

Kyria still kept her eyes away from Relys for fear
the captain would read the truth there. She would never
tell. Never. But her eyes might betray her, and right
now Relys's gaze, hot and bright as the new sword in
her hand, might be able to see beneath her gracious
veneer into . . .

No. Never.

''Entering a town under siege is a difficult matter,''
said Darham. ''I do not wish to send anyone to certain
death.''

''It is certain death to allow matters to remain as
they are,'' said Wykla. ''But Gelyya has skill with
Grayface weapons, and I am sure that she will go with
us willingly.''

Darham blinked. "Us?"

Relys and Timbrin spoke almost together, their voices eager, angry. "Us."

"Us," said Wykla. She offered her hand to Manda. The maid took it.

Relys bowed formally to Wykla. "Will you allow me to command you, princess?"

Wykla was obviously uncomfortable with the title: she almost grimaced. "In war, Relys," she said, "you will always command me."

Relys turned to Cvinthil and Darham. "For too long has a snake inhabited Hall Kingsbury," she said. "With your permission, lords, we will go and dispatch him."

"You have my permission, captain," said Cvinthil.

Darham nodded his assent almost reluctantly. "I pray you, cloak them well, sorceress. I do not wish to lose a daughter so soon after finding her."

"I shall," said Kyria. "As well as I would . . ." She caught herself looking into Relys's eyes, turned away hurriedly. "As well as I would cloak myself."

The Specter straightened and, slowly, as though to relish the terror and defeat it expected to see in Alouzon's eyes, lifted its blade. But Alouzon was paying no attention. Instead, she was held by the impossible sight of Solomon Braithwaite rising up out of his grave, shoving aside dirt and sod, climbing out onto the grass with determined jerks of his decaying body.

Staggering and lurching in the brightening morning, he stood up, and though the Specter suddenly became aware of his presence, it did not even have a chance to turn around before Solomon lifted his putrefying arms, clenched his fists together, and struck.

The Specter toppled to the side, nearly losing its grip on its sword. Before it could right itself, another blow from the corpse knocked it nearly senseless.

Alouzon, still stunned by what she was seeing, felt a dull surprise. Though the Specter was under attack, she felt no pain. A part of her own mind was being beaten by a reanimated corpse, and she sensed nothing.

But fascinated though she was by the scene before her—the Specter, gray and formal, picking itself up off the ground to face the shabby decay of a middle-aged man nine months dead—she felt at the same time detached. The Specter was hers, to be sure, but it was more than that. It had grown beyond her. Or maybe she had grown beyond it. She was not sure anymore.

I could have been the same way, I guess.

The Specter fumbled its way to its feet. Solomon's corpse fixed Alouzon with the same stare with which, at one time, Suzanne Helling had been rooted in her chair during arguments about Romano-British civilization. "I told you I'd help," he said hoarsely. "Now get on with it."

She blinked, pulled out of her thoughts. "Get on?"

Dindrane was suddenly shouting, but Alouzon, confounded, did not understand, and the Specter was giving Solomon no time to explain. Seizing its fallen sword, it lifted the blade and struck the corpse, carving a slab of dead meat from Solomon's side.

Solomon stood his ground, turned his lifeless gaze on the parody of himself. "You damned fool," he snapped. "You can't hurt me. Nothing can. I'm already dead."

The Specter was lifting its sword again, but Solomon moved quickly. With a leap, he launched himself, wrapped his arms about it, pulled it down. Clawing, fighting, struggling to be free, the Specter could not break loose from the embrace of the dead, and Solomon dragged it slowly towards the open grave.

"Alouzon!" cried Dindrane. "Alouzon! Look!"

Alouzon was transfixed by the struggle. With its sword proving useless at such short range, the Specter resorted to gnawing ferociously at the dead face inches from its own. Solomon, his features bared to the skull, inched towards the grave, and finally, with the gnashing of preternatural teeth and the harsh, shrill cries of frustrated desolation, Suzanne's dead professor and Alouzon's undead antithesis tumbled into the pit.

Light erupted, pouring into the air like a torrent of blood. The earth shook. Solomon's voice rang out, hollow, echoing, reverberating like a struck gong— *"Go!"*—and then was lost in a roar of shattering stone.

Dindrane was screaming, pulling on Alouzon's blouse, shaking her, spattering her with blood from her wounded arm. "Alouzon! Alouzon!"

Alouzon finally lifted her eyes. Dindrane was pointing towards the Santa Monica Mountains that rose up immediately behind the cemetery. There, on the upper slopes, something was shining with a golden light, and Alouzon had to squint at it for several moments before she realized that she was looking at a tall white tower, its marble sides as smooth as molded glass.

The Tower of the Grail.

❖ CHAPTER 24 ❖

Cloaked as they were in magic so powerful that the moon and stars were distorted into shimmering wisps, the machine gun fire was dulled into a heavy but incessant thudding, and the shriek of jets sounded as though it came from out of an empty well, Relys and her four companions, undetected, made their way up the dry, brittle slopes of Kingsbury Hill.

Once, Relys might have eschewed such protection with the claim that it was unmanly; and she still remembered her prejudices against Mernyl, prejudices that now struck her as both valiant and foolish. If Mernyl was unmanly, how much more so was this woman named Relys, who had finally come to bend her head to her sex and its strengths and weaknesses.

Yes, she would accept magic, would in fact, accept anything that might lead her to a situation in which she might confront Helwych with a sword in her hand. But children, never. Marriage, never. She had been bent, but she would not be broken. Marrha, perhaps, had allowed herself to dwindle into a wife and a mother, but not Relys of Quay. Her womb, barren, would remain so, and her arms would embrace only armor and sword.

It had to be. It had to be. She could not live otherwise.

A bare ten yards from the edge of the plateau, she lifted her hand. They were close enough to the wall of earth and timber to hear the detached murmur of Grayface voices and the stammering quaver of a few boys from Helwych's wartroops. The latter sounded absurdly young, close to tears in fact, and Relys wondered if the sorcerer had been drafting children out of the refugee families in order to fill the ranks.

Children. The thought was a pang. She stifled it.

The party was in the open, but Kyria's magic was holding. Relys beckoned to Gelyya. The girl, carrying her rifle, slid noiselessly to her side.

Relys put her head to Gelyya's and whispered: a movement more of lips than of air. "Can you kill them?"

In between shell detonations from the far side of the hill, Gelyya whispered her answer. "Noise, captain. I doubt that Kyria's spell would hold against a grenade, and more Grayfaces would come."

Relys nodded in the faint moonlight. "Then it shall be Timbrin and myself."

The party crept to the wall. Relys sheathed her sword and stuck a knife between her teeth. Timbrin did likewise and dropped a coil of rope over her shoulder. With Gelyya covering them from below, the two women put their hands to the wall at a shadowed place and began to climb.

Cautiously, they scaled the rough-hewn timbers, fingers digging into cracks and ledges, arms wrapped about an occasional outthrust beam, toes feeling for support; and when they gained the top, they were but a few feet from those who guarded this section of the wall. Three Grayfaces were there, their features invisible beneath the goggling masks they wore, and there were two men of Helwych's Guard.

Men? One was barely old enough to have a beard, though Relys recognized him from her time in the barracks and knew that he possessed more than a beard. The other was much younger—the straps of his armor had required several new holes to fit him properly.

She looked to Timbrin. The lieutenant nodded. Together, the two women dropped to the ground, their knives in their hands.

Timbrin had developed a deft and effective way of slipping a dagger beneath a gas mask, and two of the Grayfaces were down before the third was even aware of it. Given the cloaking magic, Relys had no idea what he was seeing as he tried to get his rifle up, but she knew that he would see very little more as Timbrin's blade found his throat in turn.

The two guards were another matter. Too terrified even to scream, the younger huddled into the shadows, his hands over his head; but the youth who had raped Relys tried to put on a brave face as he reached for his sword.

He did not appear to recognize the woman he had violated, but he was dead before his sword was entirely drawn, and Relys stood for a moment longer than was necessary, her blade in his chest, feeling his heart fluttering into stillness. *And your master shall be next, youngling.*

When she turned around, the boy in the shadows was staring up at the moon, his features slack, his throat open. Relys said nothing. Children. And only by luck had she—

"Captain?" Timbrin's voice was a whisper. She wiped a bloody dagger.

Relys shook her head. "It is nothing." She took the rope from Timbrin, made it fast to one of the rough beams, and dropped it over the parapet.

In a minute, Wykla, Manda, and Gelyya stood beside their comrades; and silently, still cloaked, the party slipped across the fields behind the earthworks. When they reached the palisade that surrounded the town, Relys nodded to Timbrin: they would climb once more. Her knife was ripe with the metallic taste of blood as she stuck it between her teeth, and she wondered suddenly if in some way she were not now defiled as much by her rapist's blood as she had been by his semen.

No matter: he was dead. And Helwych, the author of the atrocity, soon would be.

But as she and Timbrin examined the uprights of the palisade, there was sudden movement on the other side, and a rifle bolt slammed home. As a sudden roar of artillery and mortar fire drowned out the shout of warning, Gelyya kicked Relys and Timbrin brutally aside, dropped back, and fired her rifle straight through the intervening logs.

Gelyya lowered her weapon. The far side of the palisade was silent. The roar of artillery had covered the shots. "My apologies, my captain," she said. "Forgive me for striking you."

Relys sheathed her knife. "You did well, warrior."

They pried the damaged logs apart and squeezed their way into the town. The faint moonlight and the distortion from the magic turned everything into abstractions, but there was nothing abstract about the stench that flowed from the refugee hovels like a polluted river: a compounding of the odors of death, decay, and disease.

Hall Kingsbury. There was utter silence among the company now. Despite the cloaking magic, a single word could betray their presence. With hand gestures, Wykla and Manda volunteered to go over the outer wall. Relys nodded. Gelyya covered.

The lovers climbed, and, after a moment, Wykla opened a small gate from the inside. Her sword was dripping, but Relys found upon entering that only one Grayface had been guarding the gate. Helwych had obviously sent most of his troops to the outer defenses.

All the better for us. All the worse for him.

A jet streaked overhead, but a fireball from Kyria turned it into melted steel and aluminum. It left an afterimage of brightness as it plunged down toward the ground.

And then Kyria, as though aware that Relys and her company would now need additional cover, intensified her magical attacks. To the north, the night sky suddenly burned with hues that shaded from violet into invisibility, and long arcs of energy sped away into the distance, seeking the artillery batteries that had been shelling the allied positions since late afternoon.

Helwych replied, and the air above the town turned bloody with energy as the company slipped across the courtyard.

Another door. Relys paused, listening. From within came voices:

". . . lord, please. I implore you to surrender." The voice young and frightened, was again familiar to Relys. Was this not the one that had giggled like a child as he had attempted to penetrate her, the excitement overcoming him and making him spill his seed all over her raw thighs? "That is our king out on the slopes," he was saying now, his laughter gone. "How can you order us to attack our king?"

"The enemy you face is very subtle, captain," came the reply. "Very subtle indeed. You saw what happened to Seena's children, and Captain Relys herself was ensnared in evil spells . . . for which she paid."

Relys' brain was on fire with the nearness of the sorcerer. Her lips moved soundlessly. *Helwych.*

The first voice was close to tears. "Lord—"

"Shut up."

"Please."

"Guard."

There was a crack of a rifle butt striking home. The young man cried out.

But a sudden assault would do nothing. Patience. Endurance.

She drew the new sword that Tylha had given her— "This will fit a woman's hand better," the commander had said, as though she understood Relys's motivations—beckoned to Gelyya, entered the Hall. Wykla and Manda followed. Timbrin positioned herself at the door.

Helwych was a bent, shrunken figure in a chair at the end of the room. To either side stood a half dozen

Grayfaces, fully armed, their weapons at ready, and one was stepping away from a young man, hardly fifteen by the look of him, who was picking himself up off the floor, holding his jaw. Blood was seeping out between his fingers.

Helwych had not even looked up. "You and your men," he said, "will fight whomever and whatever I tell you to fight. You are ignorant, all of you. You would be dead by now but for me."

The boy was weeping. "Please . . ."

But Relys was suddenly distracted, for, silently, from a door behind the dais, Seena entered the room. Small and slender, her dark hair plaited in a single braid down her back, she was as Relys remembered her, and with quiet, unobtrusive steps, she made her way towards the sorcerer.

Gelyya looked at Relys, eyes questioning. Relys shook her head.

Still silent, still unnoticed, Seena approached Helwych from behind . . .

"Get out," said Helwych to the boy.

. . . and drew nearer. Her face was pale and haggard, and the light of one whose patience had run out, whose endurance had been pushed far beyond its limits, was in her eyes. Her gaze fixed on Helwych, she took something from beneath the folds of her cloak. It flashed in the torch light.

A sword. Relys's sword.

At the sight of her old weapon, Relys caught her breath, and at the sound Helwych's head snapped up. "Guards!" He struck his staff on the ground. Kyria's cloak began to dissolve.

But as the Grayfaces swung their weapons towards the door, Seena struck. Unpracticed, ignorant of swordwork, she might have been chopping wood as she lifted the weapon over her head and brought it down at the juncture of Helwych's neck and shoulder.

The sorcerer screamed, toppled. The Grayfaces turned back to Seena.

Relys screamed. "Seena! Down!"

Seena wavered for a moment, then, more in a faint than in accordance with Relys's orders, fell to the ground as Gelyya opened up with her M16. The slugs struck the Grayfaces and the captain of the Guard with a high-velocity tumble that ripped them open in a spray of blood and bone and punched straight through to leave exit wounds the size of a man's fist.

Helwych, bleeding, breathing in harsh, bubbling gasps, was dragging himself towards Seena. His wound was immense, a dark rift in his robes and his body that seemed to pulse from within as though something were trying to escape from the dying flesh.

Methodically, her face set, Gelyya was changing ammunition clips, but Relys was already running for Seena. Vaulting over the heaped form of the struggling sorcerer, she clasped her arms about the queen and dragged her away from the dark vision that, dying and yet undead, was closing in on her.

Helwych's eyes were enormous. Wide with shock and surprise, black with void, blue with the radiance of invisible flame, they filled Relys's sight, expanding to encompass the room, the city, the world. *Well, little girl, what do you think of motherhood?*

In her haste to aid her queen, Relys had dropped her sword, but even had she had it in her hand, she would have been unable to fight off the eyes or the words that formed a booming, echoing, godlike pronouncement of all that she had feared.

And is it a boy or a girl that grows in your belly?

Wykla and Manda approached the wounded sorcerer, but were smashed back by a surge of dark power. They tumbled to the earth. Relys, dragging Seena away, suddenly found her way blocked by the back wall.

The eyes came closer. *Well, little mother?*

Helwych—or whatever he had become—was still tormenting her, attempting to prolong her agony beyond the hours she had spent shackled to a barracks bed, unreeling it like thread from a full spindle to enmesh the future.

It would not work. She carried no child, had never carried one. Kyria had said so.

Gently, she lowered Seena to the ground. One sword was out of her reach, but the other—the sword Helwych had taken from her—lay beneath the roiling pool of darkness that was the sorcerer, its hilt projecting just enough to be seized by a determined hand.

Endurance, Kallye had said.

Well?

Relys moved, diving for the sword, grabbing the hilt, turning the blade edgewise and jerking it up and away so as to split the sorcerer through the groin. Helwych screamed again, and the darkness was suddenly falling on Relys, but she bent once again and struck expertly, economically.

A spurt of severed arteries, a gurgle of vocal chords that had lost all connection with the lungs that had given them voice, and Helwych's head dropped to the floor. The eyes closed. The darkness evaporated.

Seena was curled up on the floor, fetal, sobbing, her hands pressed tightly to her head. "My children . . . my children . . ."

The captain fell to her knees beside her. "My queen, Alouzon told us what Helwych did. We shall do everything we can. Kyria is a powerful sorceress, and I am sure that—"

But her reassurances were cut short by the detonation of a shell in the street outside the Hall, and the wall nearest the blast buckled inward, showering the interior with thatch and filling the air with the dust of pulverized mud and plaster. Another blast followed quickly after. Splinters and stone fragments spattered down like rain.

Seena writhed free of Relys's arms, picked herself up, and stumbled towards the door that led to the inner corridor. "Ayya! Vill!"

Beslimed with the sorcerer's blood, Relys struggled

to her feet. ''Wykla, Manda: protect the queen,'' she
shouted, and then she ran for the door of the hall with
Gelyya and Timbrin following.

Shells were falling on Kingsbury, powdering the
wood and mud of the refugee hovels. Between the detonations, Relys heard the sounds of grenades and machine guns, saw, inexplicably, tracers directed *into* the
town.

A group of Grayfaces suddenly rounded the corner,
gleaming shadows slipping through the darkness. They
saw Relys and her companions and leveled their weapons, but when Gelyya let off five rounds in a chattering
burst, they ducked for cover.

Calmly, Gelyya slung her rifle, slipped a fragmen-
tation grenade from her belt, pulled the pin. The
strength of her arm was no match for that of a man,
but she gave the bomb plenty of loft. It plummeted to
the ground just behind the soldiers, and as she and her
comrades dropped flat, it mingled its detonation with
that of a mortar round.

In the darkness, the town was bright with explosions
and fire. Mortars were pounding their way along the
street, sending houses and shops tumbling to the
ground, burying whatever inhabitants—alive or dead—
remained within them. A burst from an M60 chain-
sawed its way through the wood of the palisade, and
now the hounds were coming too, pouring over the
street like a river of slime.

And now more Grayfaces. And planes. And artillery. From out of the distance came the sound of the
detonation of five hundred and thousand pound bombs
as the B52s began a pass. The earth shuddered. The
Grayfaces and hounds closed on the Hall.

But a violet lance darted suddenly up from somewhere just inside the city walls and filled the night sky
with the glowing fragments of bombers, and the approaching Grayfaces found themselves being ridden
down by the First and Second Wartroops. Marrha's
blond braid was as bright as Santhe's curls as, side by

side, they led their men and women straight into the gas-masked soldiers, who, taken off guard, had no chance to lift their weapons before the horses' hooves crushed them and the riders' swords found their marks.

Relys was staring at Marrha. Wife and mother she was: she could have stayed away from the battle. But instead, she was here, in the middle of a town that was swiftly being destroyed by explosives and bullets.

Her eyes teared. Marrha. A woman. Maybe—

Another wave of bombs began to track in along the distant fields, making its way straight for the hill.

Baying. Howls. Now Kyria was galloping along the street, heading for the Hall, pursued by a pack of hounds. Eyes the color of a gas flame were barely ten yards from her, eager and hungry; but she pulled her horse up short, wheeled, and pointed. The sea of white light that flowed from her hand submerged the hounds and left nothing behind.

The B52s were still coming, the hill shaking with the advancing detonations as though it would split.

"We have taken the walls of the city," the sorceress gasped. "But everything has gone mad!"

Marrha turned her gaze on Relys. "Captain?"

Still dazzled by her former commander, Relys could not, for a moment, find words. "Helwych is dead," she said at last, and she remembered to spit after uttering the name.

Kyria sagged at the news. "Then the Specter is in control now. And the Grayfaces will do as they please. And Alouzon . . ."

The bombs were approaching, sweeping towards the town like a wrecking ball. Kyria dismounted and lifted her arms, but Relys sensed that it was going to be useless. This battle would go on and on, increasing in ferocity and bloodshed until there was nothing left.

But, abruptly, there was silence.

The bombs and the bombers vanished. The gunshots faded. The mortars ceased. The Grayfaces and hounds evaporated. In a moment, the only sound was that of the wind blowing through the splintered ruins. The town, the world, the heavens . . . all seemed hushed, as though poised between two futures, two fates. Even the screams of the wounded were no more. But there was no sense of death: only of waiting.

Waiting . . .

Kyria, shaking, slowly bent her knee and bowed her head. "O most Sacred Cup," she said softly, "accept that through the blood of many has the soul of one been purified."

Dindrane was still losing blood by the dishful, but she pulled Alouzon in the direction of the Tower. "Come, Goddess. Please . . ."

Tearing her eyes away from the sight of the grave that was glowing as if filled to the brim with white hot magma, Alouzon followed her priestess, at first blindly and in shock, then, as her awareness of what was happening increased, willingly. Finally, she ran, leading Dindrane, dragging her along until they reached the far side of the cemetery.

A wrought iron fence again barred the way, but Alouzon did not hesitate, and the Dragonsword cut through the iron bars effortlessly. And although she heard police sirens screaming up the normally tranquil avenues of the cemetery—racing to cut her off—she knew that the Grail would allow no mundane forces to interfere with what lay ahead. If there was to be a final test, it would be through the choice and methods of the Sacred Cup itself.

She clambered through the fence and drew Dindrane after her. The priestess' skin was as white as alabaster from blood loss, but she followed; and together the two women began to struggle up the slope towards the vision of golden radiance that had appeared above them.

Alouzon climbed, breaking a path for Dindrane, but the scrub oak and sage of the California mountains were gone, replaced now by twining thorns that dug into her clothes and flesh, ripping with points as sharp as sorrow, methodically stripping her of everything save the Dragonsword. But she struggled on, and when, naked, bleeding, exhausted, she felt that surely no more could be taken from her, the thorns dug even deeper: into her thoughts, into her memory.

Here was a thicket that took away Joe Epstein. Here a knot that rooted out the other faceless and nameless men who had shared her bed and had gone away with small pieces of her heart and soul. Here was a ravine—steep-sided and wide—filled with twisted branches and long, eager spikes: it grappled with her abortion, her despair, and the empty apartment that had been waiting for her on a rainy afternoon in Dallas.

It had hurt then. It hurt now. But she kept climbing, leaving past pain and old memory hanging in shreds on the reddened thorns.

In spite of her torment, she was mildly surprised that the thorns were not reaching for Kent. But after a time, after the anger had been taken, after the last shreds of resentment had been spitted like a shrike's victim, she realized that those memories of death were, in their own way, empowering her, strengthening her. And so, paradoxically, she struggled to the top of the thorn-studded slope and stood at last at the edge of the wide lawn surrounding the Tower, buoyed and fired by a belief and an urge for creation and re-creation that took for its roots the utter despair and sorrow that was Kent State.

There had been hope once. There would be hope again. She could not resurrect her classmates or undo the grief, but she could make a world live.

The Tower rose up: white, unblemished. Alouzon's skin was a tapestry of deep red wounds, and her hair was matted with blood and dust. Dindrane, who had been allowed to pass through the thorns unscathed, stepped up beside her, as pale as the Tower. "I can heal you, Goddess," she said softly.

"Nah . . ." Alouzon shook her head. "We don't

have the time. Besides . . .'' She tipped her head back,
gazed at the single window of the Tower. ''. . . it's
gonna have to take me as I am. None of this shit about
white samite robes.''

And, with Dindrane, she stepped onto the lawn.

The sirens and the sounds of the helicopters cut off
as though a switch had been thrown. The Dragon and
the Worm, still locked in battle that could only lead to
mutual negation, vanished. Los Angeles disappeared.
The Tower stood on a sunlit hilltop surrounded by
mist.

Dindrane was murmuring. ''A time that is not a
time, and a place that is not a place . . .''

The door to the tower was unfigured. There was
nothing left for it to depict. Only a single carved word
appeared in the middle of the expanse of dark wood:
Listinoise.

Alouzon stared at it for a moment, traced it with her
finger. What would this door say for the next Grail-
seeker? *Los Angeles?* Probably.

Without a word, she turned the latch and pushed
into the white marble room beyond. The air was filled
with a golden glow like a mist, but the floor was
stained with blood and with the passage of muddy feet;
and when she had climbed to the top of the stairs, she
found the landing strewn with splintered wood and
broken glass.

And from the door . . .

Light. Light so bright, so radiant that it had long
since passed from the visible to the invisible, a flow
of quintessential luminescence that, ephemeral though
it was, formed nonetheless a harrowing torrent that
flowed through Alouzon and blurred her vision with
the pain of imminent fulfillment.

She stood at the threshold. She did not look. It was
not time to look yet.

She took off her sword and put it into Dindrane's
hands. ''Take it,'' she said. ''I'm not going to need it
anymore. Take it. It . . . it might help you.''

"I shall guard it well, Goddess."

"I . . ." The Grail was within sight. All she had to do was look, enter, take. But she had responsibilities to those who loved her, to whose whom she, in turn, loved. This was the first. There were many others. And she would fulfill them all. "I don't know what's gonna happen when I go in there," she said. "I don't know what'll happen to you. I . . ."

The door. And then the Grail. And after that her knowledge ended. All knowledge ended. She wanted to say something reassuring, could think of nothing. She did not know. She could not lie.

"I'll try to make sure you get home, Dindrane."

The priestess—pale, her arm still streaming—was nodding. " 'Tis without regret I will be in any case, Great Lady. I am your priestess. I have performed my duty. I am satisfied."

"Yeah . . ." The radiance was stripping away even more than the thorns. Alouzon was no longer sure of her own name, no longer certain of her past; but, holding to the redeeming memory of murders a decade old, she stooped and kissed Dindrane on the forehead. "Love you, kiddo."

And then she turned, groped her way to the door, stepped through.

The light dimmed so that she could see, but the torrent remained. Ahead of her, floating just above the surface of a simple stone altar, beating like a live thing, was a Cup the color of a hand held up to the sun. Its bowl as broad as the welcoming arms of a young child, it was brimming with water, overflowing with water, streaming with water.

Alouzon approached. She might have knelt, but the action would have been superfluous. She might have prayed, but she had no one to whom to address a supplication. She was, and the Grail was, and that was all.

But she remembered that there were words that she

had to speak, and, standing before the Cup, she spoke them.

"I know who You are," she said. "I know Whom You serve. You called Me. I'm here."

Take.

She was not even trembling as she bent, reached, gathered the Grail into her arms as one might lift a sleeping infant, cuddling the smooth baby-flesh soothingly so as not to disturb a gentle sleep more sacred than shouts, cries, gurgles . . .

The water flowed over her arms, over her body. The wounds from the thorns vanished at its touch. She felt warm.

Drink.

"Yeah," she murmured. "Yeah, that's it."

The bowl was filled with stars, suns, worlds—all shimmering in liquescent motion. There were continents, lovers' wondering eyes, blessings, hope, expiation . . .

. . . redemption . . .

"Yeah . . ."

And she lifted the Grail and let the waters cascade into her mouth, into her heart, into her soul. They swept through her and widened her, stretched her affections and her powers out to contain the universe, then folded them back inward to swaddle the world she had guarded and guided, the world she had chosen, the world that had chosen her. And when the flood was done, there was no one left who could call herself Alouzon or Suzanne, no Kent or Vietnam, no Dragon, no Worm, no Specter—nothing, in fact, save quiet divinity and omnipotent, unconditional love.

❖ CHAPTER 25 ❖

Kingsbury was silent. The stars were bright. In the east, the thin crescent of a waning moon cast half-hearted shadows on the tumbled remains of the hovels, the bombed-out earthworks and palisades, the cratered streets, the burned and empty buildings.

And beyond the town, Kyria knew, was a pocked and half vitrified hill. And beyond that was a rolling, lifeless waste that went on and on. And beyond that . . .

She sat down on a pile of rubble and covered her face. It was not just the town. It was not the fires and the wounded and the peaked faces of the refugees whose last meal had been a crumb of bread three days before. It was the fact that the destruction and famine and death continued for miles and leagues, spreading like a metastasized cancer throughout the body of Gryylth.

The hooves of Cvinthil's horse made hollow clopping sounds as he rode towards Hall Kingsbury, and Darham rode at his side, shaking his head dejectedly while he attempted to wrap a strip of bandage about a particularly grievous wound. Like the Corrinian, Cvinthil was wounded, bloody, his bare arms and legs scored and smoking from hounds' teeth, his skin spattered by flying shrapnel. But even had he been unscathed, the look in his eyes and the set of his shoulders were such that what refugees were left alive

and willing to stand up would have stared at him with
no more recognition on their faces than there was now.

But Helwych's men knew him and, disarmed and
under the impassive eyes of the First and Second Wartroops, they shrank back at his approach. Cvinthil
paused before them, regarded them evenly, handed his
cloak to an attendant. There was no haste in his manner. There was no anger. Both had been burned out
of him as though one of the white phosphorus bombs
that had scarred his land had found a mark in his own
heart. Quietly, almost politely, he asked the prisoners
if they would surrender to his mercy, and when they
had said yes in scattered whispers, he told the wartroops to keep them under guard until he was prepared
to pass judgment.

Darham spoke. "Treason is a deadly crime,
brother."

Cvinthil nodded slowly. "Aye," he said. "And so
is stupidity, of which I myself am guilty." A gust of
wind blew smoke into his eyes, and he paused and
wiped them. "There is too much death in this land. I
will not add to it now."

Kyria stood up, paced slowly to him, bowed. She
was a sorceress and a councilor of Gryylth. She had
to say something. "What do you command, my king?"

He stared, unseeing, as if the thought of uttering a
command in such a place was obscene. Like death,
there had been too many commands in Gryylth.
"Bring the supply wagons into the city," he said at
last. "Feed the hungry. Heal the sick and injured. Care
for everyone as best you can, whether friend or one-
time enemy." He looked at Kyria at last. "Where is
my wife?"

"In the Hall, my king," she said. "She is alive."

"My children . . . are they. . . ?"

She shook her head, trying not to show the sick
helplessness with which she had confronted the hid-
eous web of sorcery that had ensnared Ayya and Vill.
Helwych—schooled by the Specter, fired by his warped

ambition—had done his work well. "Given time, lord, I might . . ." She shook her head again. "But not now."

And beyond Ayya and Vill, even supposing she could unweave Helwych's magic without killing them, there was more. There was the land itself. What could she do for the land?

Cvinthil nodded, his eyes empty. "I will go to them," he said simply, and he rode into the courtyard of the Hall, alone.

Relys was leaning on a sword that still dripped with Helwych's blood. "Sorceress," she said softly, "you can do nothing for the children?"

Kyria turned away. Among the ruined hovels, beneath the shattered buildings, there were people who needed healing, food, rest, and some assurance that the nightmare was over. The first three she could provide. The last, though . . .

"I cannot do many things." She felt empty, drained, the flow of magic that had sustained her throughout the battle now replaced by a cold knowledge of inflicted death and a boneweariness that made her want to curl up in a small dark place—away from Santhe, away from friends, away from everything—and cry herself to sleep. She, too, needed some assurance that the nightmare was over.

The men and women of the army were already probing the ruins for survivors, fanning out through the town to tend the wounded. The Vayllens were arriving also: the priestesses with determined steps, the harpers with a song that blended with and soothed the cries of the helpless.

Kyria paused at the nearest building. Of stone and wood, it had caved in beneath a mortar round. A child was crying from somewhere within the wreckage, and, at her side, Relys's womb was an aching void. *Why is it always the goddam kids?*

One of the women of the First Wartroop was calling

out from the tumbled stone: "I have found her. Someone give me a bit of rope."

Relys took the coil from Timbrin and went to help. A young girl was dragged from the ruined house. Kyria bent over her, her hands moved with gestures of power, and in a moment, Relys was helping the child to her feet. "Come, Vyyka," said the warrior with uncharacteristic gentleness, "there is food. Come with me."

"Mother . . ." Vyyka wept. "They all . . ."

"Come." And Relys led the girl off.

Gryylth, as a world, was complete. Alouzon was a Goddess. Silbakor's reason for existence was gone, and so the Great Dragon had faded back into the obscure abstractions of physical law out of which it had sprung. But as Kyria worked among the refugees and warriors—making wounded flesh whole, curing disease, banishing death—she felt the terrible loneliness. Divine Will was a dispassionate and objective thing, and, in effect, Gryylth, Corrin, and Vaylle were on their own now, left to make what they could of a ruined land, a decimated people, and grieving hearts.

The digging, healing, and harping went on. The dawn brightened. Pink and crimson splashed the eastern sky. And as Kyria finished with a final healing—closing a wound, mending shattered bones—Alouzon's words came back to her softly, like the whisper of a lover: *I've always just wanted to be friends with everyone. That's not gonna change.*

Kyria lifted a dirty sleeve, wiped at her face. "I would like that," she murmured. "I would like that very much."

The woman she had healed was puzzled. "My lady?"

Kyria shook her head, patted her arm. "Nothing. A hope, that is all."

The rising sun glittered on the eastern horizon as Kyria made her way back to the Hall. She wanted to sleep, but she knew that before bed would come councils, and plans, and suggestions, and desperate strategies, and wild hopes. But nothing, not even magic, could change the fact that Gryylth had no food and no hope of growing any for years.

But when she reached what was left of the palisade, she noticed that the shadows were fleeing eastwards, back towards the dawn; and, turning, she saw that there was brightness in the west, a white radiance above the mountains that made even the tarnished and dusty bosses of the warriors' armor glitter as though freshly polished.

Puzzled, wondering, Kyria shaded her eyes against the light, and from the Hall behind her, she heard a child's voice: bright, sudden. "Mama! Mama!"

An infant began to cry.

"It is Ayya and Vill," she whispered. "They have come back."

A sign. It had to be a sign. Something to ease the memories, to stem the guilt left behind by that small thing shuddering into stillness within Relys's belly, to say that the nightmare was at an end. Something.

But now Dindrane was walking up the main avenue of the town, treading firmly and evenly among the ruins. Her boy's clothes shone as though new-made, a gold torque was about her neck, and the sparkle of the staff in her left hand was matched by the gleam of the Dragonsword in her right. As she approached the Hall, the brightness in the west faded, and the sun—as though stilled for a moment in mid-dawn—resumed its climb into the sky, illuminating her glowing face, gleaming in her bright eyes.

Kyria ran to meet her. "Dindrane!"

Simply, unaffectedly, the priestess bowed. " 'Tis I. I have come home."

"But who . . . what . . . how. . . ?"

"Alouzon," said Dindrane, as if that single name explained everything. " 'Tis Her love She sends for a greeting. And She sends a sign, too." She smiled as though her meaning was obvious.

Kyria stared blankly. "I do not understand."

Dindrane's smile grew broader, and she gestured with a sweep of her arm that included all the world. "Go and look."

"Mama!" Ayya was shouting in the Hall. And though Vill was screaming with all the strength of his infant lungs, Cvinthil's glad laughter and Seena's joyful tears were even louder.

Robes fluttering, hair streaming behind her, Kyria ran for the edge of the plateau. Shouting for anyone who would witness a miracle to follow her, she forced her way through the rubble, streaked across the cratered fields, clambered over the earthworks, and looked out to the west.

The sun was still low, but though the rolling hills left some valleys in shadow, the light showed plainly the verdant wave of fertility that overtopped the Camrann Mountains, crashed down the eastern slopes, and rushed in, surging, to fill the plains. The waste was greening. Crops were springing up out of withered fields: growing up, flowering, and fruiting in the space of a few minutes. Dry stream beds and empty rivers suddenly gushed with water that sparkled in the new light. Meadows and fields took on the hues of spring, then of summer, and finally of a ripe autumn.

Just call me Alouzon. Your friend.

Refugees came to watch, the grass growing up thick and springy under their feet even as they stumbled from the town to the outer walls. The wave of life went on and on, crossing the plains, cresting the hills, frothing in a riot of wildflowers, rushing away into the east. Clouds puffed up from the south, white and gray: there would be rain that afternoon. Not too much. Just enough.

And the wind turned round, softening, carrying the scent of herbs and greenery as, in the distance, the dark shadows of thick forests spread out to replace the thin, shattered lines of the burned-out woods.

Now the people of the town were crowding the earthworks. Cvinthil was there, his daughter sitting astraddle his neck and his son wriggling safely in Seena's arms. Darham and Wykla and Manda were embracing. Marrha˘ stood nobly beside her husband, her hand on her belly and her face aglow with pride. Even the cold face of Relys had been touched with light and warmth.

And Kyria noticed that the hunger and starvation were being taken from the emaciated faces of the refugees. They stood straighter, and their voices and spirits took on strength along with their arms and legs. There was suddenly laughter and cheers, and the air was filled with a sense of holiday.

Santhe stood behind Kyria and wrapped her in a close embrace. She looked up at him, her eyes dazzled by the light. A new day. A sign. And more . . .

Greening, growing, living. Within an hour, the land had turned into a ripe garden ready for harvest. And though among the men and women of the three lands there was sorrow and grief still for all the death and bereavement that had gone before, there was also, once again, hope. The nightmare was over. The world was, once again, alive.

Kyria's eyes were streaming. "It was the right thing," she murmured. "I know it. And there . . ." Santhe's eyes held a question that she banished with a smile. "There will be other children."

"Aye," he said. And he kissed her.

Just call me Alouzon . . .

There was hope. There was holiday. There was homecoming—in Gryylth, in her heart, in many hearts—and Kyria turned and held Santhe in her arms as though in token of the larger Arms that now held all the world.

Just call me . . .

"Alouzon. Yes," she said. "Our friend."

About the Author

Gael Baudino grew up in Los Angeles and managed to escape with her life. She now lives in Denver . . . and likes it a lot.

She is a minister of Dianic Wicca; and in her alter ego of harper, she performs, teaches, and records in the Denver area.

She lives with her lover, Mirya.

Her previous books include *Strands of Starlight, Gossamer Axe, Dragonsword,* and *Duel of Dragons. The Wire Strung Primer,* a method she wrote for the wire-strung harp, is now in its second printing, and a cassette of her performances on Gothic and Flemish harps has been released by Raging Celt Productions.